I0608049

# ALL OF THE ABOVE

# ALL OF THE ABOVE

TIMOTHY SCOTT BENNETT

BLUE HAG BOOKS • EASTPORT, MAINE

This is a work of fiction. All of the characters, organiza-
tions, and events portrayed in this novel are either products of the author's imagination or are used fictitiously.

ALL OF THE ABOVE

Copyright © 2011 Timothy Scott Bennett

All rights reserved. No part of this book may be repro-
duced, stored in a database or other retrieval system, or
transmitted in any form, by any mean now existing or later
discovered, including without limitation mechanical, electronic, photographic or otherwise, without the express
prior written permission of the publisher.

Published by:
Blue Hag Books
3 South Street
Eastport, Maine 04631

http://bluehagbooks.com/
https://www.facebook.com/alloftheabovebook

Cover design by Timothy Scott Bennett, Sarah Erickson,
and Sally Erickson

Library of Congress Control Number: 2011912092

ISBN-13: 978-1936879007

First Edition: August 2011

Printed in the United States of America

To Sally, my *sine qua non*.

# Acknowledgements

My deepest thanks go to Hannah Bennett, Rocco Anderson, and Sally Erickson, who tag-teamed each other in the editing process, pushing and pulling me toward the finish line. Hannah, now studying publishing at Pace University in New York, has a keen eye for copy edits and clichés, and made sure that Linda Travis pushed back against Obie when he most needed it. Rocco is a wizard at syntax and a ceaseless demand for clarity and compassion. His skilled critiquing style left me laughing out loud more times than I'd have imagined possible in what proved to be a sometimes grueling process. Sally added what felt like a "director's touch" to the process, helping me step more fully into the emotional, psychological, and spiritual lives of my characters. Without these three, the book would not be what it now is.

Thanks to Andy Erickson for his ongoing partnership in the process of publication, distribution, and marketing. Thanks to Sarah Erickson for her last-minute cover makeover. Thanks also to Rick Gottesman, Jeff Jones, Mary Bennett, and Nancy Bennett, early readers of my first draft, whose words of encouragement and feedback were greatly needed at that point in the process. And thanks to Keith Farnish, without whom the phrase "hoiking his clavicles" would never have made it to print.

This story did not spring solely from my own mind and soul. The Blue Lady was the one who sat me down and requested, firmly, that I put fingers to keyboard in a process that felt, at times, more like taking dictation than mere "writing." And there are many others whose presence I can feel in the pages herein. Some taught me to write. Others taught me to think. Most taught me to question the beliefs, assumptions, and stories I'd been programmed with by the culture in which I was raised. A representative list, though woefully incomplete, includes David Abram, Douglas Adams, Isaac Asimov, Richard Bach, Itzhak Bentov, Thomas Berry, Octavia Butler, Orson Scott Card, William Catton, Richard Dolan, Stephen Donaldson, David Edwards, Raymond Fowler, Chellis Glendinning, Graham Hancock, Richard Heinberg, Frank Herbert, Richard Hoagland, Russell Hoban, Derrick Jensen, John Keel, W. P. Kinsella, Joanna Macy, Terence McKenna, Robert Monroe, Daniel Quinn, Tom Robbins, Carl Sagan, Jonathan Schell, Starhawk, Whitley Strieber, Michael Talbot, Jacques Vallee, and Kurt Vonnegut. Thanks to you all, and to the many more whom I have not mentioned here.

And thank you, finally, to a certain rabbit, who often strays from my thoughts, but never from my heart. You know who you are.

Timothy Scott Bennett
Eastport, Maine
August, 2011

*Those who cannot remember the past
are condemned to repeat it.*
GEORGE SANTAYANA

*There are none so blind as those who will not see.*
JOHN HEYWOOD

*Out beyond ideas of wrongdoing and rightdoing,
there is a field. I'll meet you there.*

*When the soul lies down in that grass,
the world is too full to talk about.
Ideas, language, even the phrase each other
doesn't make any sense.*

JELALUDDIN RUMI
(translated by Coleman Barks)

# Chapter ⊘ One

## 1.1

"She's gone, Bob." Mary spoke into the darkened room, her voice clogged with disbelief.

"What happened?" Bob rubbed at her eyes with the heel of her palm.

"Slipped away somehow. At the farm." Mary's voice hardened. "We fucking lost her."

Bob ran her fingers through her hair, dislodging an elastic ponytail holder. She squinted at the opened door. "She should never have been told." Bob untangled the rubber band and placed it on her bedside table.

"It wasn't our decision. You know that. Spud insisted. Despite what the General said."

Mary reached over to flip the light switch, stopped when Bob shook her head.

"It doesn't matter." Bob laid her head back down on her rumpled pillow and closed her eyes. "We've got to stop her."

Mary nodded. "Yeah. I'll work the public side. Manhunt, cover story, the works. We'll find her."

"I'm not so sure. She's not like the rest of them."

"So what will you do?"

"Guess I'll go back to sleep," said Bob with a smile.

"Sweet dreams." Mary left, closing the door quietly behind her.

## 1.2

Cole Thomas frowned at the stop sign before him. He scrunched his nose. How long had he been sitting here? He couldn't say. His head felt strange, unclear, as though spattered with thick mud, and he shook it, trying to dislodge the heavy gobs now clinging to the inside of his skull. A gust of cool air buffeted him through his open window and he shivered. The woods to his left were strangely silent, stripped of the usual cackling laughter of waking thrushes and jays. The street sign said he was at the corner of Boston Spoke Road and Gray Mountain, but he had no recollection of the past couple of miles.

A flash to the right caught his eye, a movement through the wall of white pines lining the ditch, back-lit by the rising sun. Darkness eclipsed him for a moment, then passed, as though a huge bird had just glided by. He knew, without even knowing it, that that bird was not a bird. He looked at the clock on the dash: eight-ten. It had taken him twenty-five minutes to drive the three miles from the kids' school. It didn't make any sense.

Cole glanced up Gray Mountain Road. Nothing. Of course that didn't mean much. The rise to the right blocked any reasonable view of an oncoming car. Bad design, thought Cole, the same thought he had every morning at this particular spot. Someday he was going to ask the selectmen to put up a sign, or one of those huge convex mirrors. Not that the tiny Vermont town of Hindrance had the money for such things. But for today, nothing to do but take your chances and hope that if somebody is coming they know enough to slow down. There was never much traffic on this road anyway.

Gravel from Boston Spoke flew off into the ditch as Cole gunned the engine of his dusty, white Subaru, turning left onto Gray Mountain. The morning air fluttered his dark, thinning hair as Cole reached out to turn on the radio. He glanced up into his rear-view mirror. "Shit!"

The car behind him leapt over the hill, huge and dark, a striking shark. It gave no sign of slowing. Cole floored the accelerator, jerked the steering wheel to the right, and punched his horn, all without conscious thought. The car behind honked in return and swerved into the other lane, grazing his Forester's left rear corner as it sped past. Its horn blared on, shouting high then low as the car skidded counterclockwise and plunged over the hill on the road's opposite side, punching deep into a shuddering tangle of pine saplings, sumac and honeysuckle. Cole hit his brakes and pulled over onto the grass-choked shoulder. "Shit!" he spat again.

Late September's morning sun peeked through the treetops, reaching across the front passenger seat with its offer of comfort and warmth as he sat, stunned. His breaths came in ragged gasps, each fighting the others for attention. Slowly he raised his shaking hands to his face, rubbed his eyes with his fingertips. He reached down and shut off his engine and sat. The silence cooled his pounding heart. A full minute passed.

"Hey!" A voice came from far away, ragged, angry. Who was yelling at him? Cole couldn't remember, didn't care. He wanted only to close his eyes and rest.

"Hey! Is there anybody there?" The voice again. Cole remembered.

Pushing the door open, fumbling his seatbelt, Cole clambered out, steadying himself with a hand on the luggage rack. His lanky legs were numb and heavy, still drunk with the toxins of fear. He pocketed his keys, glanced up and down the road. Not a car in sight. Dust settled slowly onto the pavement, flickering as it fell through the tiny spotlights that filtered through the trees. Hidden in the branches above, a mourning dove sang a timely lament. Latching the car door, Cole walked stiffly forward, brushing at his jeans with scarecrow flourishes. He knew that he had to help, but he didn't want to go. There might be blood. Shards of memory hit Cole like shrapnel: a severed arm with three fingers missing. He crumpled that old photo in his mind and tossed it away. Cole did not like blood.

The other car had almost disappeared down the ditch's deep bottom, leaving only the right rear corner to protrude from the vast curtain of honeysuckle and sumac, the skeletons of wild chervil and the fading blossoms of Japanese knotweed. Faint tire tracks led back up through the wet grass to the road. A passing motorist would likely notice nothing. Cole picked his way down the hill.

"Hello?" he said, choking on the word. "I'm coming!" Near the bottom he slipped, lurched forward to catch his balance, stumbled right into the back of the car, banging his shin on the rusted bumper. Cole bent to rub his leg. "Hello?"

The car was old, a dark green Oldsmobile Cutlass with a shredded vinyl top that had once been white. The lock had been ripped out of the trunk long before. A piece of wire looped through the rusty hole to hold it down. Cole moved around to the left, running one hand along the car's top as he pushed back knotweed with the other. The smell of gasoline assaulted his nose and set his eyes twitching. Once through the wall of foliage he could see the rest of the car. The front end had crumpled into an awful smile, the Cutlass having been finally stopped by a thick white pine. Fluids leaked out in hissing drips.

There was a woman in the car, shoulder-length blonde hair spattered with blood, leaning to the right from the driver's side. Her left hand flopped erratically on the steering wheel. Cole moved forward. "Hello?"

At the sound of Cole's voice the woman's head jerked up and around. Cole froze. He knew that face. Everyone knew that face. From the covers of magazines. From the net. From the evening news. It was bloodied now from a cut on the forehead, and the eyes were crumpled and worn and wild with fear, but there was no mistaking that face. This was Linda Travis. The President of the United States.

"So, are you gonna help me or what?" said the President.

1.3

"Oh, God," Cole mumbled, looking around for help. This couldn't be the President. Not here. It didn't make any sense. Up on the road a car slowed and passed by, a prattle of rubber on gravel and it was gone. They must be wondering about his car parked on the roadside. Cole turned back to the woman in the car, lurched forward on wobbly knees to paw at the door. "Let me get you out of there. I, uh—" He pulled at the handle.

Pinched by the crumpled fender, the door would not move. Cole jerked on the handle. Again. He put a foot up for leverage. With a snap and a moan the door swung open, sending Cole backwards into the tangle. He landed on his backside with a crunch and a yip, laughed nervously and rose to his feet. "Are you—?"

The woman in the car glared back. "We'll deal with that later. Right now I'd like to get the hell out of this car in case it's thinking of catching fire."

Cole nodded frantically. "Sure." But Cole wasn't so sure. With the door now open he could better see the situation. This woman's legs, presidential or not, were pinned beneath a broken dash and steering wheel. Sticky blood seeped through her khaki slacks where part of the dashboard, a jagged dagger of green plastic, had plunged into her right thigh. The blood's rich, rusty scent crept into Cole's nose and sat there, poking and teasing and sneering at him. Cole wasn't sure he could pull the woman out. "Perhaps we'd better call for some help."

The woman in the car shook her head fiercely, her eyes wide. "No! You can do this. Pull the knob and slide back the seat and help me out." She fumbled with the seatbelt latch, yanked it open and pulled on the belt to free herself. "Just try the knob."

Cole squatted to find the black plastic handle under the seat, thankful for the instructions. "Slowly," said the woman, pointing at the wound in her thigh, her face a stern mask. She closed her eyes. Cole nodded. He was sure now. This had to be the President. The face, the voice: there was no mistaking her.

Cole glanced back over the length of the Cutlass. "The car's pointing downhill a bit," he said, trying to wrap his mind around the situation. "You'll need to push against gravity. Against the steering wheel. And the floor."

The President opened her eyes, grasped the wheel with both hands, and nodded. Cole put one hand on the plastic dagger to hold it in place and with his other hand pulled the adjustment knob. The seat started to move forward and the President gasped in agony as the plastic dagger pushed deeper into her leg. With an angry cry she pushed against the floor. The seat slid back and Cole released the knob, locking it into place. The President bit down hard against the pain.

With the seat back, Cole could better see both legs. The right leg, in addition to the gash, had a noticeable bend in the wrong place, just below the knee. Cole's stomach sprang forward, searched frantically for escape and, finding none, fell back into place with a frustrated splash. "We've got to get some help!" Cole rose to go.

The President shouted "No!" and lunged forward to open the glove box. The door swung down from the broken dash at an awkward angle and something black and heavy dropped into the President's hand. Cole drew back. Too late. The President brought her arm up, pointed a gun at Cole's heaving chest. "Sorry," she said. "I hate this, but you have to listen to me right now. No help. You're gonna have to get me out of here yourself." She nodded back toward the road. "Let's get going."

### 1.4

Linda Travis had moved into the White House only eight months earlier. Because she was an independent, with no real money and little political experience, not to mention the fact that she was a woman, the pundits had been certain that it could never happen. Yet Linda Travis, just forty-four years of age, had taken forty-eight states.

Her political career had begun just eight years earlier when her husband, Earl Travis, a Michigan State Senator, had up and died on her two days before her thirty-sixth birthday. He'd been away for the weekend, fishing with some friends, when, inexplicably, he drove his bass boat straight into a concrete pier, killing them all.

Because he would have wanted her to, Linda Travis, who had spent the previous two years running the family farm while Earl had served, ran as a Democrat for her husband's vacant Senate seat in the special election that followed. She won. Most said that her victory was due to her husband's glowing reputation. Others declared that she would never have won had not her opponent, a Republican lawyer named Richard Sims, checked himself into rehab shortly before the election.

In any event, it soon became apparent that none of that mattered. Linda Travis deserved to serve in the Senate if anyone did. Her strong and certain manner, and her blunt honesty, made her popular with both press and public, though many of her colleagues – "shoeshines," the new Senator called them – regarded her with scorn. To them she was nothing more than a farmer's wife now pretending to be one of them, floating along on a wave of sympathy.

But a senior Senator, Ed Billings, an old farming man himself, impressed with her courage and intelligence, took Linda Travis under his wing. They became good friends and political allies. Two years later Billings ran for Governor, bringing Travis on board as his candidate for Lieutenant Governor. They won easily.

Billings died three months into his term. A massive heart attack. Close chapter.

Linda Travis, now the Governor of the State of Michigan, eulogized her friend and mentor with grace and humility. She would do her best to carry on, she said, and she vowed to always tell the truth. This she did. As the U.S. economy continued its long, slow death spiral following the disruptions of '07 and '08, as the housing bubble deflated and the market collapsed in on itself like a planned demolition, as the bankers splashed about in their quickly-draining betting pool of liquidity and solvency, jumping into their lifeboat bonuses and shouting for bailouts, Governor Travis was quicker than most of her peers to see that the situation was far more systemic, and far more serious, than they were willing to admit, and she warned the people of Michigan that the road through this would be long and hard. As budget deficits piled up, even in the face of drastic cuts, and as jobs in the hundreds of thousands disappeared overnight in a puff of smoke and mirrors, she hammered at the state political apparatus, demanding and getting the cuts and concessions she asked for, to delete the waste and keep online the essential services people would need if they were to avoid falling through the cracks. At the same time, she used her bully pulpit to call people together as communities of first responders, helping them organize themselves as much as possible into the interwoven and resilient safety nets she knew they could become. She said straight out that things would be changing dramatically in the coming years. Many, at the very least, appreciated the straight talk.

As surprised by her current situation as anyone, Linda Travis plunged into the job. She was a quick study. While there were those who pointed out that Ms. Travis was now governor as the result of two tragic deaths and one mental meltdown, most of her colleagues grew to respect and admire her for her own abilities.

There was no doubt that she could touch the public. When asked, at a news conference, why she and her husband had never had any children, her response was quick, charming and to the point. "Oh, I'm sorry," she said, looking about the room in mock confusion. "I thought we were talking about state government."

When the reporter persisted, asking the governor whether or not she agreed that the people had a right to know who it was who governed them, Linda Travis put down her notes, took off her glasses, and smiled.

"Have you ever flown on an airplane?" she asked the young man sweetly.

"Of course."

"When you got on the plane, did it matter to you whether the pilot was married, or had kids?"

"Uh ... no."

"Did it matter to you what the pilot had for dinner?  Or

whether he enjoyed the opera?" She arched an eyebrow. "Or whether *she* wore boxers or briefs?"

The reporter just stared.

"What did matter?" asked the governor.

"Just ... whether he ..." the young man flushed, "or she ... knew how to fly the plane."

Linda Travis nodded smartly and looked out over the press-room. "Any other questions?"

The people of Michigan loved it. And they loved her. The rest of the country met her in the wake of the Bellevue Chemtrail disaster and the ensuing scandal that shook the executive branch to its very core, sinking the incumbent's hopes for re-election. At the Democratic National Convention in Toledo, in what later came to be known as the "Weevil Speech," Governor Travis offered her views on Senator James Russell, one of the "new faces" that had shaken out of the woodwork during the scandal, and the Democrats' panic-inspired nominee for President. Before a crowd of Russell's adoring fans, and ignoring the speech she had given convention organizers to run on the prompter, Travis presented an unflinchingly honest assessment of the Senator's political career, balancing praise for his fiscal acuity and legislative prowess with scorn for his environmental voting record, his own brushes with scandal, and his questionable relationships with lobbyists. Reflecting on her early years on the farm, Travis related how her father was once faced with two different crop weevils at the same time, but had the resources to deal with only one. He made the common sense choice and dealt with the more destructive pest. "And now folks," she went on, "we're faced with the same dilemma my Daddy faced. Two major party candidates, both major pests, and we gotta choose. I say we vote for Senator Russell, the lesser of two weevils."

She was booed and shooed out of the convention hall, but she was applauded and cheered in living rooms across the country. And though she was quickly disowned by the Democratic leadership, polls showed that her speech actually helped Senator Russell, who went on to defeat, by a narrow margin, his Republican challenger. It was as if the public, just knowing that there were people like Linda Travis in the government, were heartened enough to vote. Hearing what sounded like the truth from the mouth of a politician, voters were able to forgive the shortcomings and mistakes of a man who now seemed a bit more like them.

Governor Travis returned to Michigan a hero and enjoyed her own re-election two years later. A year after that, declaring herself tired of the politics of party, and seeing how severely the Chinese "Rare Earth Crisis" and the Miami Nuke had wounded both the Russell administration and the Democrats in general, she left the Democratic fold and launched her own independent campaign for the Presidency of the United States.

Her announcement was unusual. She stood before the assembled reporters and supporters dressed in a Michigan State hoodie and khaki slacks which, though decidedly casual given the occasion, worked wonderfully, setting the tone for her entire campaign: no pretense. Her friendly, pretty face, tanned and natural, was relaxed, her eyes full of secret jokes. Her ginger blonde hair, newly bobbed to shoulder length, gave her an air of healthy readiness and intelligence. "I'm Linda Travis, Governor of the State of Michigan," she began. "It is my goal to be elected President of the United States next November. I will serve one term only, and I will always tell you the truth. And I promise you this: when I have finished my term of office, the government of this great nation will work more efficiently, more sensibly, and more humanely than it has in a good long while. I am an alcoholic but have not had a drink in almost twenty years. I had a miscarriage in my senior year of high school, before I met Earl. I will speak no more of that. I play a mean game of online poker. I've been known to cuss. And I've shoveled a great deal of manure in my day, which should suit me perfectly for the job. Any other dirt you'll just have to make up for yourselves. Thank you."

Contributions from the grassroots flooded in. Travis would accept no corporate or interest group money. It didn't matter. Her campaign was fueled by "people power." She was one of them, a real person running for President. Volunteers lined up at the door. The press adored her laughing face and her blunt retorts, providing her with coverage and exposure she could never buy. When a reporter asked her about the "extra challenges" that faced her bid to become the first woman President, she just laughed. "If you think this will be the first time there've been two boobs in the Oval Office, young man," she said, "then you have not been paying attention." Her face was everywhere after that.

In a live interview on ACN News two days after "throwing her bonnet into the ring," celebrity anchor Stendahl Banks pressed Linda Travis on her announcement, accusing her of trying to rewrite the rules of modern politics.

Travis nodded. "Of course I am, Sten," she replied. "The rules in place are absurd and corrupt."

"But don't you think the American public has a right to know about your alcoholism, or your pre-marital affairs?" Banks smiled.

"If the American public decides it can't handle having an alcoholic in high office, we're going to see a great many empty executive suites in Washington. As for my sex life and my miscarriage, that's between myself and forces way larger than you or anyone else who may feel entitled to have some say in the matter. I've said all I'm going to say. The people of this country will have to choose."

Banks sat back, a look of disbelief on his face. "Are you saying you won't answer the question, Ms. Travis?"

Travis smiled. "I'm saying, Mr. Banks, that this is one of those times when you're just going to have to go fuck yourself."

Her handlers cringed, leaping into emergency damage control mode, but the public and press ate it up, quickly pushing those thirty-nine seconds of video to the top of YouTube's "most viewed" category. Against all expectations, Travis's exchange with Stendahl Banks actually helped her with evangelicals; confession, honesty and personal power apparently trumping foul language and "past mistakes."

One morning, two weeks before Election Day, Linda Travis's southern-Michigan farmhouse burned to the ground, for reasons the fire chief was never quite able to determine. Back home for a weekend's rest, she managed to escape the fire unharmed. But her old beagle, Marlin, was not so lucky. Some said that the Democrats were behind it. Others pointed at the Republicans. A few thought Travis had lit the match herself in a ploy for sympathy. Travis refused to comment on the speculation. "Houses burn down all the time, folks," she said, "I'm just grateful to be alive." Whatever the "real" story, the incident could only help Travis. Sympathies and suspicions could weigh heavily in the minds of many voters. And voters seemed determined, at times, to thwart the polls. Though the consensus had Linda Travis still trailing by fourteen points the day before the election, the individual surveys were all over the place. One even had Travis in the lead. So she and her campaign staff stayed on message: it was still anybody's race.

For most of Election Day, it looked as though Linda Travis would go back to Michigan empty-handed. Early results showed the incumbent, Russell, the clear winner, to the point where ACN News as much as declared him so. But a last-minute blizzard of lopsided returns pulled the red carpet out from under Russell's celebration party and put Linda Travis squarely on top, giving her the popular vote, the Electoral College and the White House. It looked like just the sort of electronic fraud people had been complaining about for years, but as it worked against the party establishment this time, nobody could imagine that the results had really been tampered with. Surely the independents and the regular folk could never have pulled off such a coup. And none of the inevitable post-election examinations and challenges proffered any proof. It was just one of those things, a statistical fluke, a five-hundred-year-flood of votes that had to happen sometime.

Linda Travis had pulled off a miracle.

So what the hell was she doing here, bloodied and battered in a rusty Oldsmobile in the Vermont mountains? Cole stepped back from her gun. He had no idea.

## 1.5

The President stood now, balancing on her good leg, steadying her weight between Cole's shoulder and the open door. Pulling the President from the car had proven easier than Cole had imagined. The shard of dashboard had cut wide but not deep and the bleeding had already slowed. Thankfully, the President's resolve seemed to override her pain; either her tolerance was high in the first place or the shock of the accident was keeping the hurt from really sinking in. Cole had heard of this latter possibility, and had reasons of his own to hope it was true.

Together he and the President looked up the hill, through the hole the car had punched in the knotweed. A spray of sumac, now bright red with autumn, reached across the field of view like a party decoration. The sun, rolling higher, brought a laundered brightness to the grassy slope before them. Drops of flickering air splashed into the shadows where the two rested, hinting at the warmth of the day to come. Cole scrunched his nose.

"I can't carry you up," he said, noting the President's clenched face. She looked as if she was determined to contain her pain and fear within a thick outer layer of commander-in-chief. "It's too steep and the grass is still wet."

Travis scanned the woods around her nervously, her eyes dark and wet. Nodding her head, she pushed the gun into her belt. She looked up through the treetops to the sky above, then back at Cole. "What's your name?"

"Cole. Thomas."

"You live around here?"

Cole shrugged his bony shoulders. "A couple of miles away. I was headed home when..." He motioned toward the crumpled car.

"Got it. So, Cole Thomas, help me get out from behind these damned bushes so I can see. Then we'll find a way to get me out of here." Linda grabbed Cole's farther shoulder, pulled herself to him to lean against his weight. Cole put his arm around her back to help steady her. With the President hopping and Cole holding back the vegetation, they moved slowly along the car and out into the tall grasses that ran along the embankment's bottom.

Travis stopped. She searched the pale morning sky for a long time, motioning Cole to silence, listening. Cole scanned the sky as well, trying to see what the President was looking for. Nothing but unblemished blue, one of those cool, clear mornings that promised a beautiful fall day. Cole had a fleeting fantasy of dropping her and running, but he knew his feet would not obey. There was no hiding now. He'd given his name. He'd be found and tried and stuck in prison. Or something. He stood quietly and held firm as the President watched the sky. He was afraid to speak.

Travis, apparently satisfied at last, dropped her gaze to the terrain around her. She looked along the ditch in both directions. To the right, back toward Boston Spoke Road, the hill grew steeper, with trees and brush pushing up toward the road, reaching the shoulder not ten yards away. To the left, the grassy embankment continued, falling gently at first as the bottom fell away, then rising in the distance as the slope eased off. The line of trees and undergrowth bent back from the road, leaving an open view. Travis could just make out the end of a drainage pipe.

"What's that?" asked the President with a wave of her hand.

Cole peered up the road. "Looks like a driveway."

"Okay. Good. Let's go there."

It took at least ten minutes, hopping and resting, the President relying more and more on Cole to carry her weight. She insisted that they stay out of sight in case a car approached, hugging the embankment where it was high, venturing near the undergrowth as the slope fell off. No cars passed by. They came to a gravel driveway that led off to the left, into the woods. They could see no house from where they stood. Using Cole for support, Travis eased herself to the ground with a quiet grunt.

"This is crazy," said Cole.

The President wiped the sweat from her forehead with the sleeve of her flannel shirt. "Yeah."

Cole knelt down, noticing how colorless was the President's face. "You okay?"

Travis rolled her eyes. "My leg hurts."

"Why can't we call for help? What are you doing here anyway?" Cole looked out over the road, then crouched further into the concealing shadows of the overgrown ditch. Something strange was going on, that much he knew. It seemed best to hide. "You are Linda Travis, right? You know? The President?"

Travis looked him in the eyes as if searching for something. After a moment she gave him a thin, fleeting smile.

"Okay. So where is everybody? Secret Service, CIA, guys like that?"

"It's a long story, Mr. Thomas. Not sure it would do you any good to hear it. I don't—" The President stopped at the sound of an approaching car. Quickly she lay down, hiding in the tall grass at the driveway's edge. Cole sank back into the brush. The car sped past.

Cole scrambled back out on hands and knees. Travis was sitting up again, her gun drawn and aimed at the sky. The President's eyes were moist and ruined and her hands shook like a starving dog. Cole's attention bounced between her face and the gun, as if uncertain where to make his appeal. "I'm sorry about the gun," said the President. "I don't much care to use this thing. But we've got to get out of here. And we must not be found." She motioned back down the road with the pistol. "Go get your car. It's time to go."

## 1.6

Cole thought about running again. His car was a ways up the road now. Maybe he could ditch her. Make it up to the next house. Call the police. They could handle this better than he could. He was just *not* up to having guns pulled on him. This was not how his morning was supposed to go. He struggled to his feet and stepped cautiously to the edge of the pavement, squinting in the sun. "I'll be back in a minute."

Travis turned to face the road, pulled up her good knee to use as a rest, and sighted the car with her pistol. "I'm a good shot, Mr. Thomas. Earl and I spent a lot of Saturdays at the firing range. You just keep cool and bring the car back here."

Cole whirled back on wobbly legs. "Listen. I don't know what—" He fumbled for his words. "I got kids, you know? Whatever's going on—" Cole's shoulders slumped.

The President lowered her gun a bit and smiled weakly. "Listen to me. I'm sure this is all very confusing. But you're doing fine. Lots of people would have fallen apart by now, what with the President showing up in the middle of nowhere and pointing a gun at them. But the truth is that I need you, Mr. Thomas. Cole. It's more important than you can imagine. I can't do what I need to do without your help."

Cole bowed his head, rubbed his eyes with the palms of his hands. Had he been ten seconds later at the stop sign none of this would have happened. The President would have gone speeding by with Cole none the wiser. Cole had moved to the country to get away from crazy shit like this. He just wanted to play on the farm, grow something, raise the kids, do a bit of writing. This was the last thing he needed. But this was the President. And she was hurt. And no matter how scared he was, Cole knew that he couldn't just walk away. He looked at Linda Travis, still seated in the grass. Without the business attire and the Presidential Seal, dressed in khakis and a flannel shirt, she was just another human soul, frail and afraid. "Okay. I'll help you. Just don't shoot me."

The President nodded. "Got it. But you need to know one thing."

"Yeah?"

"There's something I have to do. I can't afford to fail. I'll use this gun if I have to."

Cole stared at the pistol, now hanging loosely in the President's hand. "What is it you have to do?"

The President shook her head and waved him away. "Just get me out of here," she said, glancing again at the sky. "The rest will have to wait."

1.7

"Watch your leg." Cole pushed the car door closed, then circled around front and climbed in. At six-foot-four, with long legs and a growing paunch, Cole found the Forester a good fit. He started the engine. "We should get you to a hospital."

The President shot a glance at Cole, a look of both amusement and frustration. "You don't give up, do you? I think it's best if you take me to your house."

"But—"

"Cole, listen to me." The President's eyes were dark and tight. "They're out there. Right now. Looking for me. If they find me..." She ran a hand along her fractured leg. "We'll handle this. There's no other choice. You have to hide me." Her face softened. "Please."

Cole nodded. "Okay." Checking his rear-view mirror, he pulled out onto Gray Mountain Road, the gravel grumbling beneath his tires. "Mrs. President, I—"

"Call me Linda. Please."

Cole paused. He didn't know if he'd be able to do that. "Alright. Are you ever gonna tell me what's going on?"

Linda reached out, punched on the radio. She raised a hand. "Listen."

"... but as of now there has been no word from the White House. Vice-President Singer has flown back from Brazil and is now meeting with congressional and military leaders and law enforcement officials. A press conference has been scheduled for 9:30 this morning. Once again, President Travis was kidnapped last night from her vacation retreat in West Virginia. No group has yet come forward to claim responsibility."

The President reached out, clicked the radio off. "They wish."

"What?"

Linda motioned toward the radio with a sardonic huff. "Kidnapped, my butt." She looked at Cole with a guilty smile and a defiant lift of the chin. "I escaped."

Cole smiled feebly in return. There was too much he didn't know. In silence he drove on, turning off Gray Mountain onto Bent Hollow, the gravel road that would take them to the farm.

The land rolled dramatically here, the fields cut and baled, thick clots of trees now stained with the first colors of fall. Cole had seen it all so many times: the land, the trees, the farms and homes and fields. This was his home. And today none of it looked real.

The President spat a soft curse and pounded the car door with her fist.

"What's the matter?" asked Cole.

"My sleeping pills! Fuck!"

"What about 'em?"

"I need them, Cole. We have to go back."

Cole glanced into the rear-view mirror. No one was following. "I've got things that'll help you sleep, ma'am. It's no big deal."

The President put a hand on Cole's shoulder. "It is a big deal, Cole. I need my pills."

"But I thought you were in a hurry to hide."

"Just do it, Cole. Please. Trust me. Turn the car around and drive back and find my pills. They should be in a green shoulder bag in the back seat."

Cole opened his mouth to protest yet again. But a glance at the President stopped him. Linda's face was hard and tense, her cheeks streaked with tears. Her hand, resting now on the gun she cradled in her lap, trembled slightly. The President was terrified.

Cole pulled into the next driveway and turned around.

# Chapter ⌀ Two

## 2.1

"Report," said the General.

Mary flinched. The boss was never this abrupt. She drew a deep breath and took a seat before his expansive cherry desk. "Little news, General," she said. "The word is out. We'll find her." Carefully she smoothed her jacket.

"The media?"

"They've got the story. Surprise attack last night at dusk. Helicopters, explosives, a small-scale war, the whole nine yards. As far as the public knows, a bunch of terrorists from God-knows-where invaded the President's family home, overpowered and murdered a dozen or so agents and security people, kidnapped the President, and slipped away into the night. Throw in some stock footage of helicopters, a couple of interviews with some of the People posing as agents who saw the whole thing, before you know it, the story has a life of its own."

"The people who were there—?"

"— have all been taken care of, General. We were lucky to have had our People present in the numbers that we did. We could clamp down tight before some meat-for-brains had a chance to call the dogs."

"The search?"

"Just as you predicted, Boss. Every yahoo with a badge from here to Seattle has been mobilized. Of course they all think they're looking for heavily armed lunatics in helicopters, but with a posse this large, any clues Ma Kettle leaves behind ought to turn up quite quickly. We'll let the badges do the grunt work for us and move in when the search starts to narrow."

The General nodded, his eyes closed. "And Bob?"

"Bob spent the night in flight. Took a couple of trips this morning, too. Nothing conclusive. Bob could see a car. Something big and old, she said. Long stretches of secondary road. Travis was listening to the news. She must have driven all night, but her defenses never faltered. Oh, and Bob saw knotweed this morning. That was all."

"Knotweed?"

"Japanese knotweed, General. *Polygonum cuspidatum.* It's an invasive."

"*Polygoni*—. Don't tell me. The plants told you."

Mary smiled. "Bob's good with plants, sir."

## 2.2

Cole slowed the car, switched on his blinker, and turned onto the narrow gravel road that led through the community and back to his house. A large wooden sign, carved and painted with brightly colored flowers, greeted them as they passed.

"Harmony: A Cooperative Farming and Residential Community," the President read aloud. Her tense, tired face melted momentarily into a smile. "You a farmer?"

Cole smiled and nodded. "Well, sort of. Among other things."

"Good for you. So what's the story with this place?" She indicated the land around her with a wave of her hands. To the right of the road was a hayfield, recently cut, dropping off and rolling away to a thin row of maples that lined a creek. Past the creek, the mountains to the East rose abruptly. The September sun, just now cresting those mountains, gave it all a golden, burnished look, like a painting by Bruegel.

Cole hesitated, unsure of how much to say, as if it were still possible to not get involved. "Bunch of friends," he said finally. "They bought this old farm about ten years ago. Built this road, carved out some home-sites, built houses and moved out here and started working the fields together. Mostly small-scale stuff. A few animals, lots of gardens, an orchard. That sort of thing. Ruth and I were living in town but knew one of the couples that lived out here. And then a house opened up. We've—" Cole sighed and looked out the window. "I've been here almost five years now."

Linda pointed back over her shoulder with her thumb. "That sign makes you sound like some sort of a commune or something."

Cole scrunched his face in distaste. "Yeah, well, we get that response quite often. We're not a commune. At least not by any definition of the word I know. We don't all live in the same house and share food and all that. We were just all looking for some place where we could live amongst folks we knew and loved and wanted to be with. We've all got our own houses, and plenty of privacy, but we do work together on projects, and we eat a good many meals together. We take care of each other."

Cole looked over at the President. Linda had her head against the window, scanning the sky as if she were afraid of being followed by an airplane. Her head bumped lightly against the glass.

"So... not married anymore?" she asked, still looking to the sky.

"I, uh, no. It's just me and the kids now." Cole noted how the sunlight made the President's hair look like freshly varnished pine. He cleared his throat. "What are you looking for?"

The President ignored the question.

Cole drove slowly down the slender country road. They passed an old farmhouse, now partially restored, with shiny new tin on the roof and new lap siding still unpainted. A newly built barn stood behind the house, with a pair of miniature donkeys in the overgrown pasture. Cole gestured toward the orchard, just starting to produce this year and fenced with tall posts and electrified wire, and pointed out the solar cell that brought the thin strands to jittery life. Across the fields, somebody drove a tractor with a bush-hog. Cole started to wave, then thought better of it. Linda crouched low in her seat.

They followed the road, turning hard to the left and heading down a steep hill that plunged back into more woods. At the bottom they crossed a long timber bridge, the creek bed underneath nearly dry from the summer drought. The road rose up again into the light of another open field, this a pasture with a horse, a number of black-faced sheep, and a pair of tall, brown, Nubian goats, all standing nose-to-nose near a weathered gray barn, as if plotting the overthrow of the government. Behind the field, against the wall of trees, sat a long, one-story building lined with windows. Farther on, past the field, stood more woods, glowing with the fall. Cole pulled up the driveway that hugged those woods and parked the car in a short spur set into the trees. He turned off the engine. Its rumble faded quickly, leaving only the sounds of the breeze and the shallow breathing of the President sitting next to him.

He was home. And he was pretty sure he'd brought trouble home with him.

## 2.3

Cole Thomas was born and raised in rural Minnesota by hard-working parents, surrounded by an extended family of grandparents, great aunts and uncles, and cousins. They lived side-by-side in neat, clapboard farmhouses on Thomas Road, rooted to their little corner of the world by generations of habit, held together by shared work, shared stories, chromosomes, and potlucks. Cole's had been a relatively happy and normal childhood, whatever that meant. Gangly and lean, highly sensitized to the world around him, nervous of tapping foot and facial ticks, he'd never quite learned how to inhabit his body, as if he'd grabbed it off the rack on his way in without checking the label. There was about him a peculiarity of both movement and focus that followed him through life, a presence that caught the shameless stares of children and the confused smiles of passersby, as if they'd just seen a jester, a king, a dancing bear, or a tourist from some distant star. But the web of love, safety and continuity that held him as he grew left him surprisingly hale of heart and whole of mind, as odd as he might sometimes appear. His quick wit and talented intellect had been nurtured and encouraged, not only by his elders and teachers, but by the last full fading flush of American exuberance. Post-modern ennui and existential despair took their own sweet time settling onto the rural play-fields of his youth. He grew up believing the script he'd been handed; he could do and be anything he wanted.

But what *did* he want? That was the question that plagued him. Cole's father, Ben, had broken free from the family model and had gone, not into farming, but banking, a move that echoed the social patterns of his time. So, although he grew up sur-rounded by a farming family, Cole could dimly sense that he was not a part of it, as though his father's break from the agricultural life had bastardized his children, making of them pretenders and outcasts. The roots had been severed. The old answers no longer served. All four of Ben's boys were raised with the expectation that they would do well for themselves in the outside world, find-ing there a destiny far grander than their parents had even dreamt possible. Doing well looked like having a career, making money, and using your brains and talents to accomplish something big. Doing well meant moving away from the land and never looking back, taking one's place in the new scheme of things.

Cole shrugged along, taking the script he was handed and running with it. He went where his teachers pointed him, passed easily through high school and into college, and acquired the skills and knowledge he would need to be successful. He tried astrophysics at the University of Minnesota, switched over to anthropology, ended up in religious studies, tolerating the courses the college said he needed and thriving in the courses that interested him. He always did well. But he never really had a vision of what he would do with his education. He could never see where he was headed. He just trusted that his parents and teachers knew what they were talking about. One day, his place in the new scheme would become clear.

He met Ruth Weston during his freshman year and courted her with intention, even though she couldn't stand him, even though he'd never had a clue how to talk to a woman, even though he had little idea what he'd do with her if he got her. Ruth *did* seem to know where she was headed, and that was powerful magic to Cole. His persistence paid off: they were married the summer before his senior year.

Cole graduated *summa cum laude*, worked a year selling shoes, then went on to a Master's program at a small seminary on the campus of Northwestern University, following in the footsteps of a former roommate. He did well there and looked forward, for a while, to a university teaching career. But at some point he realized he didn't really care about his course of studies. So he left. And for the first time in his life, he faced a blank page in the script. It hadn't occurred to him that such a thing was possible.

With nothing better at hand, he worked short stints in a series of low-paying jobs in retail and food service and security. A part of him felt feeble, diminished, and lost, a disappointment to his potential and a failure as a husband. But a part of him was relieved to stop pretending that he knew where he was going. Iain was born. Then Emily. Day-care was depressing, and none of the individual baby-sitters they tried worked out. So Cole quit working altogether and stayed home with the kids. They could afford for him to stop. Ruth's career in pharmaceutical research was on the rise.

The culture shock was excruciating. In the course of two years he had gone from grad-student with a promising career, to stay-at-home dad with not much on the horizon. Where was the success he was destined for? Was this it, folding towels and changing diapers? He tried to go back to school part-time, but the needs of his children were too great. It seemed, indeed, as though this was it. Sometimes a brittle resentment would settle into his bones like a cold draft, driving him to brief outbursts of anger or vague protests of pain that even he could not understand. This was not how it was supposed to go.

It was not that the work had no value. When he was able to think clearly about the subject, he was forced to admit that the raising of his children was the most important and valuable thing he could be doing. But he was embedded in a society that did not seem to agree. Homemaking was what people did when they couldn't make it in the real world. It was boring, menial, unfulfilling, stultifying. And it was a woman's work. Those were the stories that colored the culture in which he'd been raised, and he was certain he was being judged according to them. And what could he expect? He was a product of that same culture. He judged himself.

Yet their arrangement made perfect sense. Ruth had a wonderful job, a successful career with a salary that allowed them to live comfortably, even luxuriously. What better solution than to have Cole run things at home? In addition to raising the kids, and avoiding the bleaker aspects of day-care, it would give him time to write, something he had always thought he might want to do.

Eventually Cole began to wake from his upper-middle-class dream. He came to see how profoundly his thinking had been shaped by the world in which he had been raised. By the time Grace was born, he had distanced himself from the expectations of his parents and forged his own definition of success. He crafted an identity apart from careers and money, one more connected to how he lived and loved and laughed. He began to write. And paint. He took care of the house and the kids. Somewhere in there they moved to Vermont, when Ruth made a career leap to Laird. Life moved on. Ruth was driving. Cole could just watch the scenery.

The opportunity arose to join the intentional community at Harmony and they grabbed it. Ruth, a "city girl" if ever there was one, and the product of a bent home, if not a broken one, had longed for the sort of close, land-based interdependence Harmony promised. She was ecstatic. What surprised Cole was that he was happy as well. He suddenly found himself more at peace than he'd been for some time: working the land, raising the kids, writing when the baby slept. There was something almost mystical about his return to the farm, living and working within the loving arms of a real community, raising his children in the same sort of extended family he had known as a kid. It was as if he was doing what he had been born to do, carrying on the work his grandparents and aunts and uncles had done before him, picking up the ancient tune that still sounded in his soul, singing the song his father had tried to refuse. It was as though he had been anointed, appointed, fated, remembered. His was a simple life, a peaceful life, a meaningful life. The question of what he would be when he grew up had been answered; he would recapture his place in the Thomas family of his youth. He was back on script.

But new demons came to call, taunting him in the dark of night when sleep refused him. There was an urgency in these voices, as they whispered over the background murmur of global populations rising and forests dying and climates changing and resources dwindling. "Just look at you," they would sneer, "thirty-something years old and what do you have to show for it? No resume! No money! No success! Don't you have some great work to do in the world? Should not you be putting your brains and talent to some real use?" The voices buzzed around the steel frame of his skull like daredevils on motorcycles, chuckling and sighing and hissing soft misgivings, stirring up the pain and resentment he thought he'd assuaged. And one truly terrifying voice joined the fray, asking Cole if he really knew what love meant, and challenging him to consider whether even his marriage needed to be questioned.

Had Cole truly found his calling, or was he hiding from his own grand destiny? Had his father stumbled upon a truth he could ignore only at his peril? Was this right where he'd been meant to be all along? Or was he just a lazy Wendell Berry wannabe living off the good graces of a complacent wife he didn't really love? He did not know. He wondered why, and for how long, Ruth would put up with his unknowing, his inexplicit, distant anger, and his failed commitment.

As it turned out, Ruth hadn't had to put up with it for much longer.

2.4

Cole helped the President out of the car and along the short, graveled walk that led through the woods toward his house, bending to give Linda a shoulder on which to lean while she hopped along on her good leg. The house rose before them, two stories of simple contemporary design with large, tall porches on the north and south sides. Unstained, rough-cut pine siding gave the place a rustic look that fit in well with the surrounding woods. The double-shed tin roof glinted in the sun above. Here and there were the signs of children: a bicycle, a sandbox littered with toys, and, buried in the fallen leaves, a cracked and sun-bleached squirt gun. Cole and the President paused at the bottom of the stone steps that led into the house. Linda reached out to steady herself on the handrail and let go of Cole's shoulder.

"How many kids?" she asked, motioning with her head at the sandbox.

Cole climbed the steps and pushed open the door. "Three," he said after a pause. He felt exposed, his life opened up to forces too great for him to fathom. An alien world of politics and intrigue had stuck its heavy boot in the entryway to his private life. Instinctively he pushed back. If the door opened further his whole world might spill out onto the ground.

Because he could think of no alternative, Cole stepped back down to help the President inside.

"Did you see them?" asked Linda from her spot on the brown leather sofa. She picked at the bloody stain on her slacks, pulling it away from where it stuck to her skin. Already the blood was beginning to stiffen and dry.

Cole stood next to the sofa, unwilling to sit down yet, as though sitting would confirm the long-term nature of the situation. "Who?"

"The police. Local boys, from what I could tell. Two of 'em. Between where I ran off the road and here."

Cole sighed and nodded. "Yeah, I saw them." He remembered the tickly shudder that had passed through his body when the patrol cars had passed. Police cars made him nervous even on normal days.

The President shifted in her seat. "A bit unusual, don't you think? For way up here, I mean."

Cole rubbed an eye with the heel of his hand. "I suppose. I see them down on 100 quite often. But not up here in the hollow. Why? You think they're looking for you?"

"Of course."

Cole's knees went weak. "You mean they know you're around here?" Cole took a seat next to the wood stove and put a hand over his churning stomach.

Linda smiled. "I doubt it. There hasn't been enough time. But I would suppose it's like this all over the country: police and sheriffs on the lookout. Their President is missing, Cole. I would guess most people take that pretty seriously."

Cole flushed in anger at the President's tone. "Yeah. So what's next? When do we get your leg fixed and when do you tell me what the hell's going on and when does my life get back to normal again?"

Linda let her body go slack on the sofa cushion behind her and closed her eyes. A great sigh escaped from her body, like a cloud of bats leaving a cave. "As for what's going on, Cole," she said at last, "I'm in trouble and I need your help. As for what's next, I have no idea at the moment. The leg we fix ourselves as best we can." She raised her head to look at Cole, her sharp, sad eyes glaring out through prison bars of desperation. "I don't even know what normal is anymore."

Cole started to speak, then clamped his jaw shut tight and sighed through his teeth. "I'm sorry."

Linda waved a hand. "Forget about it." She straightened back up. "Now, I need to see some news. Where's your TV?"

"In the rec room."

"Which is...?"

Cole stood and pointed out the kitchen window. "It's a whole other building. You could see it if the leaves were gone."

"Got it. Could you go get the TV and bring it here?"

Cole nodded.

"And is that today's paper?" Linda motioned across the room.

Cole retrieved the paper from the dining room table, still wrapped in its blue plastic cover, and handed it to the President. He started to leave.

"Cole?"

"Yeah?" answered Cole, turning back.

"I could use some Tylenol or something. My leg hurts. But get the TV first."

Embarrassed by his negligence, Cole flushed. It was unlike him, to miss something so obvious. He opened his mouth to apologize but Linda raised a hand, stopping him with a gentle look of acceptance and understanding. Cole sighed and left to get the television.

Alone, Linda drooped forward and slammed herself repeatedly in the forehead with the heel of her hand.

## 2.5

Cole ran down the stone steps and along the wooded path, past the Forester and out into the driveway. A single, lenticular wisp of cloud hung overhead like a pull in the fabric of the sky. The rec room, a long timber-frame structure that housed the Thomas family's play room, TV room, work and storage areas, and a swimming pool, sat kitty-corner across the field, hugging the woods. Cole ran the cobbled path that wound through the garden's raised beds and led directly to the rec room door. He hurried inside, slammed the door behind him, then stood for a moment, breathing in the familiar scent of the room, a combination of pool and pine and pizza rolls. On the wall across the TV room an antique clock, his great-grandfather's clock, stepped quietly and evenly through the seconds.

Cole wanted desperately to call his father. He would know what to do. He always knew what to do. Ben Thomas was smart and Ben Thomas was strong and Ben Thomas held up under pressure and Cole needed all of that right now. But calling his father was ... complicated. It would come at a cost. And Cole was not sure he was ready to pay the price.

Perhaps it was almost over. Perhaps the President's people were on their way to the house right now. Perhaps they were only testing him. Perhaps the President was already gone. Perhaps she had never even been there. Cole looked back towards the house through a small window in the door. There lay the garden before him, the root crops awaiting the frost, the kale still going strong, the chard remains. There was the line of trees that hid the house. It all looked so normal.

But Cole knew that back in his house sat President Travis with a broken leg, clutching a terrible secret at her core. With a flush of shame at his weakness, Cole walked to the phone hanging on the wall over the pool table and dialed his father's home number. The phone rang. Again. A buzz and a click sounded in his ear. The answering machine. *Hello*, came Ben's abrupt answer, then a long pause, meant to fool the caller into thinking he'd actually answered, and then the beep. Cole hung up without a word and went to unplug the small television sitting on a wooden cart in the corner.

Walking back to the house, Cole's heart began to sputter frantically, as though it were choking on a chicken bone. He stopped, hands shaking, and placed the television on the path, afraid he would drop it. The sky to the north lit up brightly, once, then again, then a third time, as if God Himself was trying out the flash on His new camera. The trembling passed and Cole continued on.

## 2.6

Linda Travis aimed the remote and switched off the set. She looked hard at Cole, sitting across from her in a small wicker rocking chair. "So, *that* tell you anything?"

Cole scratched his nose, folded the newspaper spread wide on his lap and clutched it to his stomach. "It tells me that they're lying," Cole said. He brought his eyes up to meet those of the President. "Or you are."

Linda laughed. "Me? You heard them, Cole! You read the story! According to the government and the media, I am now in the hands of a group of skilled and fanatic terrorists. Are you suggesting that these terrorists dropped me off in the boonies and gave me an Oldsmobile?"

Cole looked down at his feet. "But the Vice President ... he—"

"Albert Singer only knows what he's been told, Cole! He was in Brazil, for chrissake. How the hell would he know anything?"

"So it's all a cover story? How could they do that?"

Linda took a deep breath and let it out slowly. Her eyes grew dark, then closed. "Things aren't much like they seem, Cole. Just believe me; they can do it."

"Who?"

Linda looked up at Cole for just a moment, then hung her head and closed her eyes again. She became very still.

Cole put the paper on the floor. "So you escaped," he said, gently. "Why? From whom? Why does the President of the United States need to escape from anybody?"

Linda raised her head to look out of the window behind her. The house was surrounded by trees, a loose weave of dark fall greens and yellows and reds, with fragments of blue sky behind it. She scanned those splotches of morning sky with methodical intent, then turned back, hunching forward, pulling in on herself as though she were cold. "I don't know what I can tell you," she began at last. "I don't know what will help. I don't..." Her voice trailed away to silence. After a few moments, inhaling and straightening her back as though sloughing off a heavy burden, she looked into Cole's eyes. "There are people ... groups, about which the public, and that includes most of what you would call the government, knows nothing. Some of those groups are involved in highly questionable activities. A few months ago they brought me in. And I have decided not to play their game." She picked again at the drying blood on her slacks. "They're like cockroaches, Cole. They only prosper when nobody knows they're there." She turned to scan the sky again. "I intend to flush the fuckers out," she added, her voice stained with anger.

Cole rose and went to the kitchen, filled a kettle with water and placed it on the stovetop. He returned to his chair. Linda, on the leather sofa that Ruth had recovered, sat in silence, her head to one side as though lost in thought. Her face was ashen, her eyes red. Nodding stiffly as though she had come to some internal decision, she faced Cole. "I've put it off long enough. My leg hurts like hell. It's time to straighten it out and get a splint on it."

Cole's stomach dropped to the floor.

"You got any whiskey around here?" asked the President, smiling weakly.

## 2.7

"Oh God! Oh God! Fuck! Fuck! Fuck!" panted the President as Cole pulled on her leg. She clutched her bare, swollen knee with both hands, trying to keep it from splitting apart. The agony in her knee joint was far more fierce than at the break itself, where the grinding of bone on bone had so overwhelmed her senses that she hardly even noticed it anymore, as if her brain had shut down a breaker before the circuit could blow. The hydrocodone left over from Cole's root canal wasn't even beginning to touch the pain.

Cole went down on one knee, shifted his hands to get a better hold. Linda's leg, stretched out over the glass-topped coffee table and supported with a neck pillow, slumped just a bit in Cole's unsteady grip and she gasped again. "Pull, goddammit!" she screamed, throwing back her head, exposing her pale, juddering neck to the sky as if even execution would be better than this.

Flushing with guilt and confusion, even anger, Cole yanked harder. What the fuck did he know about setting bones? Nothing you couldn't learn from old westerns, which effectively meant nothing at all. How the hell could he have known he'd have to pull her leg *all the fucking way off* in order to fix it? He should have run while he had the chance.

He grunted and dug his fingers into Linda's calf, trying to peer through her flesh to the bones underneath. He could feel her tibia sliding and grating beneath her trembling skin. Linda moaned like an approaching ambulance, a plaintive, keening, warbling cry that begged for God's mercy. Cole sucked in a breath and pulled even harder, so hard that he was sure he would tear the President in half. He felt something click softly into place, like the balance knob on an old stereo. Linda's moans dopplered down as if the ambulance had turned a corner and was now speeding away. She started to sob.

Sensing that something had fallen into place, Cole allowed Linda's leg to settle gently onto the pillow. The President drew a deep, calming breath at the movement but did not scream. Cole swiped at the globs of sweat pouring from his forehead and shifted to his other knee to relieve the cramping in his joints. "Did it—?" he asked, unwilling to put the process into words, as if afraid he could jinx it.

Linda nodded through her tears, closed her eyes.

Cole sat back on his haunches and studied the President's leg. It looked straight enough, much straighter than when he'd begun, though some bruising was starting to show. He glanced up to see Linda breathing a bit more easily. That was probably a good sign. Cole scrunched his nose. It would have to do. All that remained was to wrap it all up.

"You did well," said the President, her voice a raspy whisper, her eyes still closed. She'd sunk into the sofa as though Mother Earth herself had turned up the gravity to keep Linda still. Driblets of cooling perspiration gathered in eager mobs on her forehead and rappelled down her temples.

Cole smiled briefly with relief. Hands still shaking, he rose to retrieve the supplies from the dining table, then returned to the sofa. Slowly, taking care not to disturb the gauze-and-tape bandage he'd fashioned for the puncture wound in her thigh, he wrapped her bare right leg with a pair of elastic bindings he'd found in his son's dresser drawer, threading the fabric through the space between her leg and the glass tabletop, then winding it up and over and around and through again and again. He hoped he'd gauged the bandage's tension well enough to give the bones some support without cutting off her circulation. He reached for the old leg-brace, left over from Ruth's knee surgery years ago, and began to work it under Linda's leg, inadvertently displacing the neck pillow as he did so. Linda barely seemed to notice. When the brace was in place he locked the hinges, pulled the straps and fastened the Velcro tabs as firmly as he could. He tested the hinges with a gentle pull. They seemed to be holding.

Embarrassed by such intimacy, Cole kept his gaze tightly controlled to the work at hand. "It doesn't look like much, Mrs. ... Linda, but it should work," he said, his voice low. "That leg isn't going anywhere. I'll get you some sweat pants." He risked a glance up.

Linda Travis was not going to respond. She'd fallen asleep.

Quietly, Cole stood and began to clean up. There were drops of blood on the hardwood floor under the sofa and on the edge of one of the cushions, a job for some old rags and a bucket of warm, soapy water. He gathered in one arm the pieces of bloody khaki slacks he'd had to cut away from her leg, and stooped to pick up the scissors from the floor. His shaking hands fumbled the heavy shears. They fell with a clatter on the coffee table glass and bounced to the floor.

The President jerked up to a sitting position, screaming like a lost soul, her eyes a dark forest of wild terrors. She saw Cole and snapped her jaws shut, slicing the scream in half. The sound of it echoed in the memory of the room. She buried her face in her hands. "Oh, Jesus!"

Cole knelt at the President's feet, placed a hesitant hand on her knee. "I'm so sorry, Mrs. President. I didn't mean to wake you. Are you okay?"

"How long was I asleep?" Linda's voice was broken shards.

Cole shook his head. "Not long. Just a minute. I—"

Linda grabbed Cole by the wrist, her grip fierce. "Where are my sleeping pills?" she snarled.

Cole pointed to the green athletic bag by the door. "Aren't they in your bag?" He rose to get it, hoping that in doing so the President would release his arm. Linda let go, looking with puzzlement at the hand that had held Cole. "You want 'em?" Cole asked.

Linda nodded. Cole knelt beside the bag, opened it to search for the pills. Inside was the President's gun, small and black and heavy, with the words *Sig Sauer* stamped on the barrel. For a moment Cole had a crazy, cowboy fantasy of taking charge, using the gun to back the President to the wall while he called the sheriff to come and clean up this mess. But he knew immediately that he would do no such thing. He was already too caught up in the situation. He had given his word. And he had no idea how to handle a gun. He found the container: a prescription bottle with a childproof cap, filled with tiny red discs the size of ladybugs. He pulled the pills from the bag and rose to take them to Linda.

Linda twisted the top and shook two of the tablets out onto her palm. She smiled grimly. "Not this time, Bob," she said, tossing the pills into her mouth.

## 2.8

"So, it's just you and the kids, you said. You divorced?" The President smoothed the old gray sweatpants that covered her leg brace.

"No. She, uh ... Ruth died a couple of years ago."

"Oh?" The President looked off into the distance, her eyes losing focus, as if she were lost in a daydream. When she spoke again, her voice was soft and moist. "I'm sorry," she said. "That's rough."

Cole nodded warily, unsure of how much to say. There was too much he did not understand. The door into his privacy was opening even wider. He sat poised on the arm of the loveseat across from the sofa, ready to run. His fingers stretched and squirmed in his lap, as if he were trying to calm a wild bird with his touch.

"How?" asked the President.

"She was on NewAir 413." Cole sighed.

"Jesus. I remember that one. That must have been horrible."

"Yeah. It was."

Linda adjusted the sofa pillows for a second, then laid back. She pointed at the windows above her. "Can you get these blinds?"

Cole stood to work the pulls. The room darkened a bit.

"Thanks. The pills will take a few minutes." Linda shifted onto her side. "And your kids? How many?"

Cole started to freeze up, then caught himself. It was just small talk. The President was just chatting to fill the space. To figure out her situation. And it wasn't like he was giving away family secrets here. Cole smiled at his own paranoia, hoping to put the President at ease. "There's Iain, he's ten. And Emily, eight. And Grace. She's five."

The President closed her eyes and smiled in return. "Grace. I like that. A very gentle name." Linda waved a hand, indicating the quiet house. "They all at school?"

"Yeah. I was on my way back from dropping them off when you … when the accident happened."

"So, will you have to go pick them up?"

"No. They get a ride from a neighbor in the afternoons. We've got a network here, to get the kids to school and back. The buses stopped running years ago. Why?"

"I need to sleep for a bit, Cole. But I'm thinking it would be best if I was gone before they got home."

Cole looked at the floor. "Yeah. You're probably right."

Linda smiled as Cole lifted his eyes to hers. "Gimme an hour or two and then wake me. We'll figure out my next step then. Okay?"

"Okay."

Linda touched her forehead lightly, ran a finger along the adhesive bandage that covered the cut above her left eye. She yawned. "So what do you do?" she asked. A shaft of late-morning sun caromed off an end table and found the President's face, highlighting her tired smile. Her ginger blonde hair, the blood from which had been mostly cleaned away with a damp towel, glowed like candlelight.

"I work the farm here, take care of the garden and the animals, make cider and cheese, run the kids around to their various activities, stuff like that. In the mornings I usually write."

Linda opened an eye. "What do you write?"

Cole wrinkled his nose. "Oh, lots of stuff. A couple of half-finished novels. Some stories for kids. Essays on my blog. Nothing published yet."

Linda yawned again, raising a hand to cover it. "Sorry. Long night."

Cole sipped at his tea and made a sour face. It had grown cold. He sat the cup on the wood stove to warm it. "You were up all night?"

"You got it," Linda mumbled with a sigh, settling back in.

"Driving?"

"Yep."

"From where?"

Linda opened her eyes and rolled onto her elbow, looking at Cole. "You trying to figure this out?"

Cole smiled. "Yeah."

The President lay back down, closing her eyes. "I guess you got the right."

Cole tried again. "Where did you escape from?"

"West Virginia. Up in the north. Near Mount Olive."

Cole had heard of Mount Olive. The President had a vacation place around there somewhere, some old family farm. Ground Zero Ranch, the press called it. "So that part of the story is true, eh? You were at your retreat. But there must have been Secret Service there. How did you get away?"

Linda sat silent for a full minute. Cole watched as her eyes moved beneath their lids, as if she were dreaming. At last she frowned and opened her eyes. "It's weird, Cole," she said. "I don't really remember. I was walking the trail to the falls. Regular security, three agents. It was getting dark. And then ... I was running through the forest. And it was fully dark at that point. And I came out behind this house, and there in the drive was that old Cutlass. The keys in the ignition. And that gun," she indicated the pistol in her bag with a nod of her head, "was on the front seat. Inside that green bag."

"Lucky you," said Cole.

Linda flashed him a puzzled smile. "I hadn't even planned it, you know? It's like ... the opportunity arose." Linda closed her eyes again, as if hoping to access a clear memory. "I guess I just lost my security detail in the dark woods and ran for it."

Cole nodded. "And you drove all night to get here. And that's what, like, thirteen, fourteen hours? You made pretty good time."

The President frowned. "I don't know. I guess. I took a lot of back roads. And I got lost once. Had to backtrack." She raised a hand to cover a cough. "I don't know how I got here so quickly."

Cole shook his head, as if he didn't know either. "So you stole that car?" he asked.

Linda did not respond, as if she hadn't heard.

"So how come nobody saw you?" Cole asked. "Didn't you have to stop for gas or a bathroom or anything?"

Linda stifled another yawn. For a long time she said nothing.

Cole wondered if she was asleep. "Didn't—"

Linda raised her hand to cut Cole off. "I stopped for gas and a pee just like anybody else. Had a hat on and wore my jacket collar up. That was enough. Nobody expects to see the President driving alone in the middle of the night on the back roads of Pennsylvania. I was invisible." She stopped to adjust the small sofa pillow under her neck. "I can feel the pills," she said.

Cole rose to place the quilt he'd grabbed from the closet over the President's legs and stomach, then returned to his seat. "So you can sleep now, with the pills?"

"Strong pills, Cole."

Cole didn't answer.

"Make my head all cloudy. Nobody can find me."

Cole watched the President fall gently toward sleep. Linda's face had regained some of its color and her eyes, in rest, seemed peaceful at last. The gray sweatpants and blue t-shirt and hoodie she now wore, found in a box of winter clothes Ruth had left stored in the barn loft, gave the President a cozy look, and Cole was struck by how young she seemed. The fingers of her right hand fluttered lightly on her stomach. Cole sat in silence and watched.

"Cole?" The President's voice was low and shallow.

"Yes, ma'am?" Cole rose and walked around the coffee table, knelt beside the sofa again.

The President's breathing was soft, easy. "I need your help, Cole," she whispered.

Cole patted the President's knee lightly. "Okay," he said.

After a while, Cole retrieved his tea.

# Chapter Three

## 3.1

"Spud says of course they know where she is." Mary closed the door and walked into Bob's room, taking a seat on the edge of her bed.

Bob was leaning against her headboard, three fluffy pillows wedged behind her back. She put aside her knitting and hugged her knees to her chin. "Will he tell us?"

"No. He says that's not his job."

"Fucker. How about Mork?"

Mary absently smoothed the blankets that were bunched at Bob's feet. "Mork won't say a thing. She hardly ever does anymore."

Bob hunched her shoulders and pulled the covers up over her knees. "I don't know why they can't keep it any warmer down here," she said. She shivered.

Mary reached out and took Bob's hand. "Yeah, I know."

"She's using some kind of sedative, Mary," Bob said. "Feels like benzodiazepine, but it's hard to tell from the outside. All I get is garbled bits and fuzz, wobbly images of a house and some tall guy. Trees all around. She seems to be in a fair amount of physical pain, like she's broken something. But I can't get inside."

Mary rose and adjusted the thermostat on the wall near the door, then found another blanket in the closet. She spread it out over Bob's bed, then turned to look through the simwindow.

"How for fuck's sake did she get benzos?" asked Bob, her voice sharp with anger.

Mary flinched but did not turn around.

Bob pulled all of her covers up to her chin. "This is a Grade-A clusterfuck, Mare. Ma Kettle's gonna talk if we don't stop her." She reached out and touched Mary's hand, demanding her attention.

Mary turned back to look down on her colleague. "Yeah," she said.

"Don't they care?" Bob gestured toward the sky with a roll of her eyes.

Mary tried to rub the fatigue from her face. "Who knows what they think?"

Bob slid down into the bed, rolling to her side in a fetal position, pulling the covers up over her head. "You should if anyone should," she said.

A dark cloud passed over Mary's face. With a long slow inhale, she softened her features, refusing to fight. She sat back down on the edge of the bed and placed a gentle hand on Bob's shoulder. "What's the worst that could happen?"

Bob spoke from under the blanket. "They could leave."

Mary bowed her head. "Will you try again?" she asked.

"In a while."

Mary rose to leave. "I'll talk to Spud again. They must have tagged her. That may be why she ran." She closed the door softly behind her.

Bob hid under the covers, as she had so often as a child. After a while she fell asleep.

3.2

"Is she dead?" whispered Grace, wiggling down from her father's lap. She moved around the coffee table and squatted to peer more closely into the President's face, then stood and stepped back, absently sucking on the collar of her flowered blouse.

Cole pulled her gently into his embrace. "She's just asleep, hon," he spoke softly into her ear. "She's not going to die." Cole wondered at the truth of his own words. Were the people chasing the President out to kill her? His eyes blinked repeatedly at the thought of it. He knew in that instant that his words to his daughter were not a prediction, but an oath.

"She looks funny," Grace said. "Like those wax people."

"You mean at Madame Toussaud's?"

"Yeah. That." Grace broke away from her father's hold and ran off, heading up the stairs to her room.

Iain and Emily stepped in from the kitchen with their after-school snacks and wedged themselves in on either side of their father, overfilling the blue and white-checkered loveseat that sat kitty-corner from the sofa. They sat in silence and watched as the President slept, the small blue quilt pulled up to her chin. Iain stared down at his fidgeting feet. "This is creepy," he whispered. He stuffed some cheese balls into his mouth.

Grace ran back down the stairs. "Here!" she called. In her arms was cradled a tattered Minnie Mouse doll, the black paint peeling from its head, pink plastic exposed underneath. She walked quickly across the room and placed the doll gently on the President's chest.

Linda Travis opened her eyes and Grace jumped back with a yelp.

The President looked around the room; saw Grace huddled in her father's arms. A wide smile washed over her face as she withdrew her hands from under the quilt to pick up the doll. She held it out to look at it. "Minnie Mouse!" she said with a laugh, "my old friend!" She leaned up on an elbow, scanned the room with exaggerated motions. "Who brought Minnie here?"

Grace beamed and raised her hand. Tentatively she stepped away from her father. Linda looked at Grace with joyful surprise. "You did?"

Grace nodded.

Linda hugged the doll to her chest. "Thank you. She's wonderful. Do you want her back or can I hug her for a while?"

Grace pulled her shoulders up toward her ears and canted her head. "You can keep her. Until I say and then you have to give her back."

Linda nodded gravely. "Of course. Thank you." She threw off the quilt and swung her broken leg out with a sharp inhale, letting it slide slowly from the sofa to the coffee table so that she could sit up. "You must be Grace."

Grace walked up to the President's leg and ran her tiny fingers along the knee-brace. It was quite noticeable beneath the sweats. She looked up at Linda. "Dennis pulled your pants out of the garbage. They got blood on the floor, but Daddy cleaned it up." She hopped up onto the sofa and sat next to the President. "But you can make messes 'cause you're the President, right?"

Linda's face flushed with embarrassment. "Well, I'll try not to do it again." She looked around the room. "Who's Dennis?"

Grace slid off the sofa and started to dig in the pocket of her jeans. "Just the dog. He's not here right now because he's afraid of strangers."

"I'd like to meet him sometime."

"Okay. I got some mermaid Band-Aids Dr. Jim gave me." With a grunt, Grace pulled a handful of crinkled bandage strips from her pocket.

"I might need one."

Grace raised a finger. "Only one."

Linda looked around the room at the rest of the family. Her eyes stopped at Cole. "Hello, Cole. It seems I slept longer than we had planned. You doing okay?"

Cole's wrinkling nose betrayed his nervousness. His fingers repeatedly flexed and extended, moving beneath his conscious notice as if his subconscious were signing an SOS to some secret observer. "I'm fine, Mrs. President," he said. "I was ... you were sleeping so peacefully. I couldn't—" Cole could not explain it. How could he rationalize what he did not himself understand? The moment was too complex. He pointed at Linda's leg. "How about you?" Already he could see that the President's color was better, and her mood had certainly improved. Perhaps the worst was over.

"Good enough. Are you going to introduce me to the rest of your family?"

"Okay, well, Grace you've met." Linda winced as Grace crawled onto her lap, taking back her Minnie Mouse and dropping it to the floor. "Grace!" Cole was certain his youngest would manage somehow to kick the President's broken bones.

"It's okay." Linda raised a hand. "She's fine." She stroked Grace's short dark-brown hair. "And these two?" she asked, nodding toward the other children on the loveseat.

Cole stood, dragging his two older children to their feet beside him. "This is Iain," he said, hugging his slouching son to his side. "And this is Emily." Emily shook off her father's hand and stepped to the side, watching the proceedings like a lawyer. She was dressed in her favorite wool slacks and silk blouse. Iain smiled and flopped a wave. "Hi, uh, Mrs. President. Ma'am."

Linda extended a hand to Iain. "It's nice to meet you, young man," she said. Iain, in slouching jeans and a baggy UVM T-shirt, stepped around the coffee table and shook her hand. "Yeah."

"And Emily," Linda continued, shifting her gaze, "I'm pleased to meet you, too." The President offered her hand again, but Emily stared at the floor and pretended not to notice. "Yeah," she mumbled.

"Emily," said Cole slowly, as if calling a preoccupied student to attention.

Linda raised her hand to stop Cole. "It's okay, Cole. I understand. I'm not supposed to be here." She turned to the eight-year-old girl. "Am I, Emily?"

Emily glared at the President and shook her head, a move of nascent elegance and soft power that barely ruffled the long brown hair that hung limp and straight around her beautiful face. She turned to her father. "Can I go?"

Cole nodded sternly and Emily rushed out the front door. Cole sighed heavily. "I'm sorry, Mrs. President."

"Linda."

"Okay. Right. Linda." He ran his hand through his thinning hair. "She's not usually like that."

Linda smiled and shrugged. "I understand," she said. She hugged Grace's hair to her face. "And she's right; I *don't* belong here."

Cole sat back down, draping a hand over Iain's knee. His face relaxed. His fingers fell still. There was a sweetness in Linda's interactions with his children that touched him deeply. She was right there with them. And for no reason he could understand, that give him a tremendous sense of relief.

## 3.3

"Watch out for the President's leg!" scolded Cole from the kitchen as Iain strode to his seat. Iain swerved like a quarterback avoiding a tackle and fell into his chair next to the President, as if that had been his plan all along. He shot his dad a "gotcha!" grin.

The President patted him on the shoulder and smiled. "Don't worry about it," she said, motioning toward her splinted leg, which stuck out from the table and blocked the path around the round oak dining room table. A zippered bag of ice cubes balanced on her knee and shin. She reached out and grabbed the chair upon which her foot rested, slid it carefully toward the wall to make a bit more room. "I'll try to keep my big feet out of the way." Linda winked and Iain smiled.

Cole stepped in from the kitchen carrying a large stoneware tray piled high with hamburgers and hot dogs from the grill. "Here we go." He placed the tray on the table and took his seat. The earthy smell of charcoal smoke filled the room. "Sorry it's just burgers and dogs," he said.

"I'm just some lady from Michigan, Cole, not the Queen of France." Linda laughed.

Cole blushed, busying himself with his napkin and silverware. Linda watched, noting how his long, cantilevered arms seemed confused as to where to go, how his slender fingers stretched and danced, how his face revealed an interior discussion that was both passionate and unending. There was a bewilderment in his eyes, an innocence, as if this soul had just arrived on Earth the day before and had yet to find its bearings. Feeling her gaze, Cole looked up, brushing an unruly shock of dark hair out of his eyes. He smiled, and Linda could see that beneath his odd confusion were deeper layers: calm certainty, a profound intellect, even a quiet splendor. Inside this goofy, sometimes awkward, lost-child body lived a good, kind man and loving father, doing his best in a crazy situation.

The phone rang. Emily excused herself and went to the kitchen to answer it.

Linda leaned over to whisper to Grace, who sat wiggling impatiently at her right side. "So which do you like best, Grace? Burgers or dogs?"

"Dogs!" shouted Grace with a laugh.

Linda nodded decisively, as if this were serious business. "Me too! I'm a dog lady from way back." She pulled two buns from their plastic bag and stabbed two hot dogs with her fork. "Mustard? No? Ketchup?" Grace shook her head. "Nothing?" Grace nodded.

Linda laughed again. "Nothing it is then, little lady." She placed the hot dog on Grace's plate. Grace grabbed a handful of potato chips from the bowl to her right and stuffed one into her mouth with a grin.

From the kitchen came the sound of Emily's markedly mature voice. "Who is this?" Both Cole and Linda looked up to see Emily pull the phone from her head and stare intently at the earpiece. She clicked off the phone with a shudder and tossed it onto the counter as if it were a rattlesnake, then stepped back and watched it closely.

"Emily?" asked Cole. "Something wrong?"

Emily's brow wrinkled and she inhaled deeply, as if finally remembering to breathe. "That was weird." She looked at her father. "It was like ... there was this voice. It was strange, like it had been slowed down or something. And it said 'pook' or 'pooch,' or something like that. Then there were all these beeps and clicks, like an answering machine or something."

"Oops!" Grace had dropped her hot dog on the floor. She slid down to retrieve it from under the table, stuffing it under her arm as she climbed back onto her chair. She examined it carefully, then took another bite.

"Was there anything else?" Linda's voice had a hard edge.

Emily threw the President a sidelong glance, then looked at her father. "I asked who it was and there was like ... somebody coughed. Then it went dead."

"Probably nothing," said Cole. "Just some kids or something."

Linda felt a nudge at her side. She leaned over so that Grace could whisper in her ear.

"Can I have a different hot dog?" asked Grace.

## 3.4

"That was great, Cole. Thank you." Linda pushed her plate back and stretched her arms and shoulders, then ran her fingers through her hair, pulling at the tangles. She motioned toward the table. "You attend enough State Dinners, you start praying for a hot dog."

"So why are you here?" Emily broke in, eyeing the President coldly.

Cole started to protest but Linda waved him off. She smiled at the girl and nodded her agreement. "That's a good question, Emily. I wondered why you weren't speaking much during dinner. Now I know why. You've been saving the most important questions for last."

Emily's gaze dropped down to her plate, then back to Linda. She nodded briefly and allowed a slight smile to cross her face, as if to accept the President's recognition of her as a smart and respected ally.

"I can't tell you much," answered Linda after a moment's thought. "It's ... classified. And I don't want to get you in trouble. But I'll tell your father more tonight, after you go to bed." Linda cleared her throat anxiously, as though fearful to drop even a crumb of the awful truth into this dear family. "There are some very bad people in the world. And ... others. And I've found out about some of the things they have been doing."

"Is this like the mafia?" asked Iain, his face alive with nervous excitement.

"Sort of. Yeah. And they don't want me to tell anyone what I know. They're trying to stop me. So I had to run away. I was headed—" She stopped for a moment, and stared off toward the window. Her eyes took on a daydream focus. After a moment she shook herself out of it. "Well, this is where I ended up. Quite by accident." She flashed Cole a look of shared secrets, then returned to Emily.

"Why did you have to run away?" Emily asked. "You're the President, aren't you?" She rolled her eyes at the self-evident nature of her statement.

Linda turned to stare out the glass doors that led to the porch. The woods beyond were softly lit by the setting sun, giving the tree trunks a furtive quality, like spies watching the house from the shadows, signaling each other with the voices of whippoor-wills. "There are people and things even more powerful than the President of the United States," she said absently, her voice low and distant. She turned back to Emily. "I'm not running away. But I couldn't stop them where I was. I had to get help. And I didn't know whom I could trust."

Linda gazed around the table as Cole's family watched, wait-ing for more of her story. She glanced down as Grace took her hand and turned her wedding band around and around. Should she tell them more, when knowing more might endanger them further? The People would not hesitate to kill them all if they deemed it necessary. Jesus! What was she doing hiding amongst these children?

Linda slapped the table. Over her dead body. "Enough of that. Don't you worry, Emily. It'll all work out. Because I say so. In the meantime, I'll feel a lot better if you keep asking me tough questions." She smiled grimly and Emily nodded, as if to accept the assignment gladly.

A tugging at her sleeve told Linda that Grace had yet another secret. She lowered her ear to hear. "My Daddy likes you but my Grandpa doesn't," Grace said, loud enough to make her father squirm in his chair.

"Is that right?" A look of mock horror filled the President's face, then she grinned at Cole with delight.

Grace wiped her hands on her blouse. "Yep. Grandpa said you couldn't find your own butt with both hands."

Iain choked on his milk and Cole buried his face in his palms.

Linda winked at Iain, then put her hand to her mouth and whispered conspiratorially to Grace. "I think your Grandpa may be right."

## 3.5

*"The Prince held the frog close to his face. 'You said the witch had a special?'*

*'Two for one,' the frog said with a nod.*

*The Prince glanced up at the castle, then back at the frog.*

*'Your appointment's at 10 o'clock,' the frog said. 'It's already paid for.'*

*The Prince, with his tiny, green wife in his hands, walked out into the forest to find a certain witch."*

Linda closed the handmade book with a flourish and looked down at Grace, who sat beside her at the head of the bed. Dennis, a white and brindle Whippet, having made his reluctant peace with the stranger in the house, slept between Grace's legs, his head propped on her knee.

"Did you like it?" asked Grace.

"I did!" said Linda with a laugh. "Did your father really write that?"

Emily, lying in the bed across from Grace's, raised herself up on her elbow. "Yeah. But he told it to us first. He found this frog in the woods and brought it in and pretended that the frog was talking. Iain laughed so hard milk came out of his nose."

Grace laughed at the memory of it and Dennis, eyes still closed, thumped his tail in concurrence.

Linda let out a long, slow breath, sank back into the pillow, and let her shoulders relax. "It's funny. When I was a girl my Daddy would tell me stories about a boy named Jumping Jack. Jack was half human and half frog and he'd get in all sorts of trouble, jumping around and breaking things and hitting his head. He was really good at basketball, and rescuing kites from trees. But he was sad, because the girls were afraid of him."

Grace scrambled around to her knees and put her face right into Linda's. "Would you want to be a frog's wife?" she asked theatrically, her voice deep and round, her face a mask of seriousness that burst into hilarity.

Linda hugged the laughing child to her chest. Grace buried her face in her mother's old sweatshirt and sighed. "I would have married Jumping Jack," she said wistfully.

"Can we read another one?" asked Emily, springing out of bed and heading toward the bookshelf, the answer self-evident to her.

Linda glanced around the room and out the window. It was fully dark now, with only a spittle of moon. The farm girl from Michigan wanted nothing more than to sit here forever, reading to these smart, open, lovely girls, soaking up the wonderful normalcy of it all. But the President of the United States knew that she had to get moving, that there were things she needed to do, or there would be no more normalcy for anyone. For now, for just a while longer, she would let the farm girl decide. Linda watched as Emily headed toward her, book in hand, thankful that the girl had decided to set aside her mistrust, at least for the time being. "I guess," she said. "If it's okay with your father. You girls do have bedtimes, right?"

Grace glanced over at the clock on her bedside table. "It's only eight-four-one. We don't have to be in bed until nine-zero-zero. And Iain gets to stay up until nine-three-zero, but he only plays on his stupid computer."

"Okay." Linda agreed. Emily handed her a book: *The Little Prince*. "Do you want me to sit on your bed for this book, Emily?"

Emily thought for a moment, looking at Linda's pillow-cushioned leg, as if remembering how long it took to get her upstairs. "That's okay. You can stay there."

"All right. I can do that." The President leaned back against the headboard of Grace's bed and opened the book. Grace nestled more deeply into her embrace and closed her eyes. "I don't think I've ever read this one," said Linda, reading the cover.

"It's about a boy who comes from another planet," said Grace. Her voice was low and soft, the gentling breeze of summer dusk. She was not far from sleep.

"Really?" The President looked up, glancing around the room, listening for unseen dangers. From the kitchen below came the ringing of the phone.

"Uh huh," explained Grace, rousing slightly. "And he has to get some water for his flower so he comes to Earth and—"

"Grace!" chided Emily from her bed, "just let her read it!"

Cole walked into the room, his face pale. Linda looked up from the book. Her heart began pounding. "What is it, Cole?" she asked, her voice suddenly sharp with fear.

Cole motioned absently back down the stairs. "The phone. Weird."

Linda closed the book and placed it on the bedside table. "Who was it, Cole?"

"More beeps and clicks at first," he answered, taking a seat on the end of Emily's bed across from the President. "And then a voice. Like Emily said, all very strange sounding. Slowed down. Warbled. Sort of like Darth Vader."

"What did the voice say?" asked the President. She was sitting up straight now.

"It asked 'Is Linda there?' That was all. Then ... more beeping. And then there was music. You know, that President song." Cole hummed a few notes.

"Old MacDonald," said Grace, almost asleep.

"Hail to the Chief," murmured Linda.

## 3.6

"Please just let it ring," snapped Linda.

Cole sat back down in the loveseat opposite the President. "This is about the tenth time. It's driving me crazy." Behind him the window revealed the darkness of the night woods.

"Will it wake the kids?" Linda reclined on the sofa, her broken leg supported on the coffee table with small pillows and an afghan.

Cole rose. "I'll unplug it."

"Good idea."

Cole pulled the line from the wall-jack. The phone continued to ring. Exasperated, he lifted the receiver. "Who the hell is this?" He listened for a moment then hung up. Immediately the phone began to ring again. Cole picked it up, walked to the front door, and pitched the phone out into the bushes and the darkness of the night. Silence for a moment, then ringing again, but fainter. Cole closed the door roughly and walked back to the living room. "Who is that, Linda? And how in the hell can they do that?"

There was defeat in Linda's voice. "It's a long story, Cole."

"Well suppose you tell it to me," Cole replied harshly. He sighed, regretting his anger immediately. He softened his voice and continued. "I mean, you've been telling me all day that you're in terrible trouble and that you need my help. And I've agreed to help you in any way that I can. I think I deserve to know what's going on." The edge returned to his voice. "I need to know if my kids are in danger."

Linda recoiled. "It wasn't supposed to work out this way," she answered defensively. "I told you to wake me."

"Like you've got a back-up plan here, Linda? Your leg's broken and the fucking mafia is chasing you. Were you thinking you'd call a cab?" Cole could hear old voices in his head - his dead wife Ruth calling him on his acerbic tone, his mother warning him to watch his smart mouth - but he didn't stop. He knew he'd regret it later, but his heart was pumping adrenalin. These were his *kids*!

Linda closed her eyes and took a few slow, deep breaths, as if letting Cole's words sink in. She tucked the afghan more tightly around her legs, then looked up at Cole and nodded, her eyes moist and red. "I almost believed it," she said at last, her defensiveness shed, her voice little more than a whisper. She lowered her gaze to her lap. "Almost. Almost believed that everything was normal, that the world was really like I'd always thought. All day, spending it here with your lovely family, just sitting and talking, eating, enjoying each other's company. I wanted so much to forget." She looked up at Cole. "I wanted this to last forever." The President swatted at a tear. "Whatever happens, I want you to know how precious these last few hours have been for me."

Cole nodded but said nothing, dumbfounded by how gracefully Linda had dropped her defenses, and how easily that had disarmed his own.

Linda sighed. "I got caught hoping, Cole. I'm sorry. You have every right to want as much information as you can get. You need to protect your children, and my showing up at your doorstep in terrible need has put you in an awful position." She reached out to reposition the cushion beneath her knee, then cleared a strand of hair from her face with a shake of her head. "I've been alone with this for so long ... I haven't known whom to trust." She glanced up at the ceiling, then came back to hold Cole's gaze. "I don't think there's any immediate danger here, but I do need to keep moving. I'm sorry that you and your children got dragged into this. But I think – Jesus, I can't believe I'm saying this – I think we're at war, Cole. Whether anybody knows about it or not. A war that could change the whole world. And I'm afraid we're all going to be dragged into this before it's over."

Linda held her chin high, a gesture of steely defiance and utter surrender. Her eyes looked like rainy days. Cole rose, stepped carefully around the President's leg, and took a seat next to her on the sofa. Tentatively he reached out to comfort her, his hand a cautious, curious chipmunk at the base of a tree, advancing step by step across the cushion. "It's going to be okay," he said, wanting desperately for his saying to make it so. Linda's hand took his and held it tightly.

From outside came the faint ring of the telephone from the bushes. The dome of the sky flashed white like a photographer's lighting umbrella, illuminating the entire room. Then the darkness crashed back over them like a tsunami. "I can't get away from them!" hissed Linda, scrunching her eyes tight.

"Who are they?" Cole asked quietly.

Linda let go of Cole's hand and hugged herself against the cooling evening. "Okay," she muttered absently, as if Cole had made a demand she did not know if she could meet. "Okay." She rubbed at her temples with the heels of her hands. "In a second, okay?" Linda looked at Cole. "I need to see what's happening out there first. Can you turn on the TV? CNN or something?"

Cole grabbed the remote and flicked on the television, flipped through the channels and found some news.

"... *are briefing the Vice President. Senior officials report that they are following every lead and expect to have a statement soon. The White House also confirms that the President's mother, Ellen Warren, has been taken to St. Theodore's Hospital after collapsing this afternoon in her home in Falls Church. There have been no reports yet regarding her condition. Vice-Pres—*"

"Turn it off," sputtered Linda. Cole hit the power button. The whole room went silent, save for the faint sound of snoring from the girls' room upstairs.

Linda sat back and kneaded her eyes with her fingertips. "They've got Mom."

"Who does?" asked Cole. "It just said she was in the hospital."

Linda exhaled her exhaustion. "There is no St. Theodore's Hospital in the D.C. area, Cole. It's a message. For me."

Cole squeezed her hand. "Tell me, Linda. Okay? Tell me why I shouldn't just go out to those bushes and call the police and be done with all of this."

Linda glanced sidelong at Cole, about to speak, but something outside caught her attention. She gaped through the sliding glass doors at the south porch, and the trees beyond. Cole swung his head around to follow her gaze. The lights in the house flickered and went dark.

Down by the curve in the creek a light danced, a small blue globe that sparkled like diamonds at its center as it bobbled over the dry stones. Soon another light joined it, this one a brilliant white beam that shone down from above the treetops, scanning the black woods like a spotlight. The blue globe weaved between the trees and the spotlight followed, both working their way slowly up the slope toward the house. The globe seemed to blink out and back on as it passed behind the trunks of trees. Another spotlight, also bright white, joined the first, following in lockstep, sliding across the ground-cedar that carpeted the forest floor. The spotlights closed in on the house, following the blue globe as it looped and wove.

Cole rose from his seat on the sofa, stepped away from the window behind him. Absently he took a few steps across the room, reached out to flick the switch that would turn the lights back on. Try as he did, he couldn't seem to reach it, though his arms felt longer than ever. The switch was always too far away.

He sat back down on the sofa. The blue globe came closer, passing by the edge of the south porch, blowing shadows through the pickets like leaves in the wind. There were many white spotlights now, six, seven, eight, ten, weaving through the trees, scanning the grounds like a prison break; and darting in and out amongst the tree trunks, approaching the house like schoolchildren on a field trip, a cluster of tiny stick-people, a swarm of locusts, an army of robots, and yet nothing more than fog and shadows in the swirling light.

The blue globe swept past the window behind the loveseat, zipped around the corner of the house and hovered, for a moment, right behind them, just inches away from the plate glass above the sofa. Linda and Cole turned like automata, staring in silence, their faces theatrical in the rich, blue glow. The globe pulsed and the room filled with an electric blue radiance so intense that neither of them could see. A deep rumble filled their minds and hearts, as if angels and earthquakes were two aspects of the same phenomenon, as if the sun's splendid demise had come billions of years early.

With a clap, all of the strange lights went out. The globe was gone. The spotlights and the stick-people had faded away. The rumbling drained off and the woods hushed. At the window before them was a pair of orange-red eyes the size of angry fists, glowing like dying coals. The eyes blinked. Cole gasped. The eyes rose up and were soon lost from view.

Cole shook his head as if shooing a fly, then stood and looked around the dark, starlit room, blinking. Was that lightning he'd seen? There were no storms in the forecast. Why had the power gone out? He walked to the kitchen and poured a glass of water and drank, swirling the liquid around in his mouth before spitting it back into the sink. He poured another glass and swirled and spat some more, then glanced up through the window. Angrily he stepped to the front door, reaching out to grasp the knob, then pulling away with a shudder. The anger flaked away like dried mud and fell to dust. The house lights flickered back to life.

Cole turned at the sound of snoring. The President was asleep on the sofa, her face peaceful and relaxed.

## 3.7

Linda threw off the little blue quilt with a grimace, as if it were full of bedbugs. She blinked herself fully awake. "What happened?"

Cole took a seat across from the President. "There must be a storm coming or something. Lightning flashed and the lights went out, so I got up to check the box. But then the lights came back on and I saw you'd fallen asleep and I thought ... you know..." Cole shrugged. "The pills and all. Maybe I should wake you up. It couldn't have been more than a minute."

With a grunt, Linda pulled herself into a sitting position. She brushed at her clothes with trembling hands, then looked at Cole with tangled, bewildered eyes. "Were there bugs in here? Moths or June bugs or something? Did you see them?"

Cole shook his head slowly. "I don't think so," he said, looking around the room.

"And an owl?" she continued as if Cole hadn't answered, twisting to look over her shoulder. "Did we see an owl outside?" She pointed at the window just behind the sofa. "Right there. An owl. We saw an owl."

Cole leaned forward on the loveseat. "I don't remember an owl," he said. "The lights went out and you fell asleep. I saw lighting flashing in the treetops." He smiled gently, as if hoping not to insult her. "Maybe you were dreaming."

Linda frowned and crossed her arms in front of her chest and face, hugging herself as if to protect against a blow. Cole stood, picked up the crocheted blanket from the back of the loveseat, and laid it over Linda's injured leg. The President's face had paled. "Can I get something to drink?" she asked, looking up, forcing a slight smile onto a pained face. "Some tea, maybe?"

Cole nodded and headed to the kitchen, apparently eager for the opportunity to help ease their confusion. "You want caffeine?" he called. He glanced out the window.

"God, yes!"

Linda, huddled under the blanket, watched thoughtfully as Cole filled the kettle. Her wariness softened and her breathing eased and she relaxed her arms, letting them fall into her lap. She smiled at the strange elegance of Cole's movements. He was really an attractive man, when you got used to him. Not that he couldn't use a little tweaking around the edges. A new haircut, maybe. A different shirt. And the way he kept twitching his face. But the raw materials were certainly there. Cole turned to her and smiled, as though he could hear her thoughts. Linda blushed, brought a hand to her heart. What the *hell* was she thinking?

Cole put the kettle on the stovetop and leaned over the sink to look out again into the night. Linda spun quickly to follow Cole's gaze, her mind suddenly filled with the image of a huge, furious owl, its talons outstretched to seize her, swooping down from a lightning bolt and battering its beak against the windowpane behind her head. Her heart hammered and she raised an arm to protect herself. But there was no owl. All she saw was her own reflection and the black trunks of trees. And the small shards of sky she could see beyond the trees were clear and full of stars: not the sort of sky that would bring lightning.

She took a deep breath and turned back around. The owl soared from her thoughts as quickly as it had attacked. Her heart caught a snag as she looked at Cole; God, he was beautiful. She could feel his arms around her and— But Jesus! Her thoughts! She cleared her throat, shifted her bottom on the sofa, hoping that physical movement would ground her in reality. "It feels different from a dream," she offered, needing to hear her own voice resound in the real world, needing to feel at least that much control.

Cole walked back to the living room and sat in the loveseat. He took a long breath and closed his eyes, ran his fingers through his thinning, black hair, as if plowing for memories. He looked at Linda. "I don't know. All I remember is that the lights went out and the lightning flashed and I got up and got some water. But the lightning was ... strange." His face clouded with dismay. "What just happened, Linda?" he asked. "Did something just happen?"

Cole's simple question called Linda to attention like an inspired teacher finally reaching a distracted student. Yes. Of course. Something *had* just happened. And she could dimly imagine what it was. Linda pulled the blanket up over her arms and considered Cole with eyes full of cheerless secrets. She could feel the explanations he needed piling up in her throat, straining against her fear, demanding to be heard. They'd been talking of her mother, and who had her, and why. Linda knew that those questions would not just go away. Still she hesitated, as if, by refusing to speak her nightmare, she could keep it from entering the world. Over the past few months, this dreadful knowledge had devastated her own sense of who she was and what she was doing. Only now was she beginning to truly accept that the reality of their collective situation was not as it seemed. How could she bring that to Cole and his kids? How could she bring that to her people? It was as if she'd been given Pandora's ancient box as an inauguration gift. If she opened the lid, its contents might destroy the whole world.

And yet she knew she would speak. She saw little choice. In the end, it's why she'd fled. Cole had earned the right to know, and she saw no way she could continue on her own. She swallowed her fear like a mouthful of gravel. The words began to flow. "So, I'm not sure where to start."

Cole puffed a mocking snicker. "You could start by telling me why you think we just saw an owl at the window." He winced, as though immediately regretting the reckless sarcasm in his voice. "Sorry." He reached out to the President as if to retrieve his words. "I just ... I need to know what's going on."

The kettle sang and Cole rose at once to get the tea. In a moment he was back with a steaming cup of Black Dragon.

Linda took the cup and smiled. "I want to tell you about a dream I *did* have."

"Not a dream about bugs and owls?"

"No. A different dream. I had it this afternoon, lying here on your sofa, though how I can manage to remember a dream with those pills in my system I'll never know."

"So what was the dream?" Cole sat next to the President on the sofa.

"I've had it before. Lots of times, especially in the past few months. And it's always the same." She paused, took a sip of her tea. "I'm walking. Just walking. All around. Through a city, lots of people, tall buildings. At first I'm not sure where I am, but eventually I realize I'm in D.C. I walk around the Mall, through the government buildings. And everywhere I go there are a few people who start to follow. Pretty soon I've got a fairly big crowd tailing after me. And I keep walking, through more cities, across the countryside, over farms and bridges, through mountains and woods. More people join up, following me. And all the time I'm headed somewhere, looking for someone. I never know who, though I know they're dear friends of mine, people that I love. I'm going to be with them. There's an excitement in my heart, a joy so strong it hurts. And the people following me, they all share this with me. We're going someplace together, though I'm the leader. I'm the one who knows how to get there. Or supposed to anyway. But we never get there. I always wake up." Linda pulled absently at the teabag in her cup. "Except for today."

"What happened today?" asked Cole.

Linda glanced at Cole, then back down at her tea. "Today I turned the corner."

"Corner?"

"I always come to this street corner. I'm back in a big city with lots of traffic, and the sidewalks are just packed with people following me. And I know that what I'm looking for is right around that corner. If I can just keep walking I'll see it. But always before, just when I got to the corner, I woke up. Today I walked around the corner."

"What did you see?"

Linda opened her mouth to speak, then stopped. She frowned and moved her head slowly from side to side, unsure, confused, as if trying to adjust an antenna that could better access her memory. She started again, dropped her shoulders in resignation, closed her eyes. "I don't ... nothing ...," she said with a deep out-breath. "As soon as I think I have it, it's gone. I thought I knew. I know I turned that corner." She looked at Cole and slumped again into the sofa. "Apparently I'm not allowed to remember."

# Chapter Four

## 4.1

"I had her! Shit, I had her!" Bob punched her pillow, then threw it across the room, knocking her current knitting project, an Andean-style hat in rainbow colors, from the tiny white table that stood between her two armchairs.

Mary took Bob's hand and stroked it gently. "It's okay, hon," she cooed, "It's okay." A soldier passed by in the hallway, muttering curses under his breath as he hurried. Mary slid over and quietly shut the door, then picked up the pillow and returned to the end of Bob's bed. "They've got a lead on a car."

Bob stared at the wall.

"A green Cutlass. 1983. It was stolen from some guy's driveway. About a mile from Ground Zero. The guy says he noticed it this morning when he went out to feed his dog."

Bob gave no sign that she had heard a word.

Mary rose and went to the window, adjusting the blind so that she could look out into the night sky. It was only a simulation, but it was disturbingly real. "Spud won't say whether they tagged her or not. And Mork just smiles, if you can call that a smile. I think they did. That's probably why she ran. I think they want her to run."

Mary returned to sit on the end of the bed. Bob looked her in the eye for the first time since she'd entered.

"So what happened?" asked Mary.

Bob closed her eyes to remember. "I had her. I was right inside and she was pretty clear. But he woke her up really quickly, that motherfucker." She opened her eyes to look at Mary. "That tall guy she's with."

"Anything else?" Mary knew to ask. There were always more details, but sometimes it took a bit of work to pry them out.

"They're there. Following her."

"You mean the Life?"

"Yeah. Half a dozen woks, maybe. And I think I saw an Angel."

"Fuck."

Bob shuddered. "Yeah."

"So did you learn anything from Ma Kettle?"

Bob shook her head. "I didn't have time to read her. She was right in my face the whole time, cussing me out something fierce. Like that's gonna help."

Mary rubbed her eyes. "I talked to the General again."

"Yeah? What'd he say?"

"He said 'kill the bitch'."

Bob's eyes went wide. "When?"

"As soon as she screws up and goes to sleep again without her pills. As soon as you can get in."

"Ellen is protecting her. I had to fight her to get past."

Mary rose and walked to the door, stopping to wick a tear from her eye before she opened it. "That won't be a problem next time," she said. She closed the door quietly behind her.


4.2


"Do you remember this last summer? It was the 4th of June. I was supposed to give the commencement address at my old high school in Pierpoint." Linda was stretched out on the sofa, her eyes closed and shielded by her left arm.

Cole nodded, coming back from the kitchen with another cup of tea. "Yeah. I remember reading about it in the paper. You showed up late and spoke for, what, ten minutes or something? And it didn't seem to make much sense. You took off without a word. Everybody was upset." Cole slid the loveseat closer to the sofa and sat softly, setting his cup on the glass-topped table between them.

"And Weiner, my Press Secretary, came out the next day and apologized and explained how sudden crises in the Middle East had distracted me and almost kept me from showing up at all."

"Oh, yeah," Cole answered. "He said something about you defusing some new hostage situation."

Linda scoffed. "It was all bullshit." She glanced up through the window. It hung black above the sofa like a door to another world. Cole followed her gaze. The trees were barely discernible in the darkness. Above them, through the canopy of leaves and needles, he could just make out the moon, a thin fang of ash and bone. Linda leaned forward and fluffed the pillows that propped up her back, sank back into them, and then pulled herself into a sitting position with a frown. Wincing, she moved her leg. A puzzled expression passed over her face, as if something was not right. She looked over at Cole, one eyebrow raised in bewilderment. "All bullshit," she said again.

"So why *did* you screw up that speech?" Cole asked, his face tense and tight, caught between the rock of ignorance and the hard place of knowledge, angry to be stuck anywhere at all. From outside came the dim ringing of the phone.

"I'm ... I'm afraid you'll think I'm crazy," said the President.

Cole clapped his hands and began to laugh. "Gods, Linda, I already think you're crazy! I think *I'm* crazy! There's a phone outside that keeps ringing even though it's not plugged in. And twenty minutes ago the house was surrounded by helicopters or who knows what the fuck and ... and those eyes... I think I can take a little more craziness!"

"Shh!" Linda cautioned. She pointed toward the kids' rooms upstairs.

Cole caught himself and nodded. "Okay," he whispered. "But keep going." His voice was heavy with warning.

The President stared at Cole, the dense and pointed gaze of a wounded animal, pain and need flavored with a touch of dread. Cole stared back, unwilling to give ground, sitting tightly at the edge of breath. This woman, President or no, had invaded *his* home, and the secrets she carried and hesitated to divulge could threaten *his* children. And himself. The eyes at the window had ignited a cold fear deep within him. His heart pounded. His hands could find no rest, skittering across his lap, clenching and unclenching like the pulse of his distress. He raised his eyebrows high, as if he could stretch his face to make it fit his anguish, then inhaled deeply, forcing a slight smile through his frustration. He needed her to trust him. He needed her to know that he was on her side. "You have to tell me," Cole said softly.

With a long inhale, Linda closed her eyes. "Okay. On June 2nd, at nine in the morning, I attended what I thought would be my daily briefing, down in what they call "the classroom." For some unexplained reason it'd been moved from the Oval Office and Bickle, my Chief of Staff, had not shown up for our usual session beforehand. When I walked in to that meeting, I found something I would never have expected."

## 4.3

The President strode down the hall to the "classroom," noting Bickle's absence at the door. She'd hoped to find him waiting for her, and to have at least a moment with him alone before the briefing. But the door was closed and the hallway was empty. Something was off, but she felt too hurried to say exactly what. She opened the door and stepped in, expecting to see her staff seated at the long, leather-clad mahogany conference table that nearly filled the low-ceilinged, windowless room usually reserved for roundtable security discussions. At the table's end nearest her sat four men, only one of whom she knew: Frank Edmonton, a junior member of the Secret Service detail assigned to her personal protection. Edmonton, young and redheaded and handsome, like a leading man from the golden age of cinema, smiled and rose and walked to the doorway to shake the President's hand.

"Mrs. President," he said.

"Mr. Edmonton?" answered the President. She sniffed the air in the room. There was a faint odor she could not quite place. Oil? Perfume? "Am I in the wrong place? Where's Bickle?"

Edmonton smiled even wider, showing bright, even teeth. He laughed. "You're in the right place, ma'am. Bickle ... um ... Please, sit down. Let me explain." He motioned toward the empty leather chair at the head of the table.

Linda eyed the agent suspiciously. "Not quite yet, Mr. Edmonton. I think I'll stand right here until you tell me what's going on. Where's Bickle? Where's Weiner? Where's the meeting I thought I was walking into?" She motioned toward Edmonton with a wave of the hand, an angry teacher waiting for the truth from an unruly student. This was way outside the bounds of protocol. "Well?"

Edmonton's eyes went dark and bitter, the smile pushed to the sides by a look of undisguised contempt. He glanced over Linda's shoulder and nodded. Linda turned to see a fifth person in the hallway behind her, a small, pale, and strikingly beautiful woman holding a small pistol at her hip.

"What the fuck is going on here?" Linda blurted. The woman advanced and pushed the gun into the President's stomach.

Edmonton, behind her, put his hand on Linda's shoulder. "Please, Mrs. President, sit down. Let me explain."

Linda backed away from the gun, slid into the chair that Edmonton held for her. Her mind was blank, save for an image that crowded into view: her dead husband with a look of shock on his face. Edmonton took his own seat across from the door.

Linda looked at the men around her, then at Edmonton. How could men she'd never seen before get into this room? "What do you want?"

Edmonton was back to his smile. "You're probably thinking about calling for help, Mrs. President. Or that somebody will come looking for you any minute now for one thing or another. You're wondering where everybody is, the folks who were supposed to be here. Please believe me when I say that all of this has been taken care of. You will not be missed, you will not be heard, and you will not be found. And as long as you don't do anything stupid, you will not be harmed. Do you understand me?"

Linda could only stare. Edmonton had the smart-ass attitude of many young men with power. Power but no perspective. Washington was full of such types, but she had worked hard to rid her staff of them, or so she had thought. They insulted her at some visceral level, and she wanted nothing so much right now as to put a knee to this young man's groin. Her lower lip trembled with rage.

Edmonton smiled and slapped the President's shoulder. "I think you do understand," he said cheerily. "Good for you." He nodded toward the woman. "I guess that'll be all for now, Bob. You can go. But don't go far." The woman slipped her gun into a black leather sling under her suit jacket, nodded quickly at the men at the table, and left.

Edmonton winked, nudging Linda with his elbow. "I just love a powerful woman, don't you?"

Linda stared, waiting until Edmonton's smile faded away. "What do you want?"

Edmonton wore a look of shock. "Why, to brief you ma'am! That's why we're here, isn't it gentlemen?" The others nodded. One, in military dress, highly decorated, wiggled his nose like a ferret.

"Cut the bullshit, Edmonton," said the President, her voice tired. "Just get on with it."

Edmonton looked wounded, but not for long. His smile, grounded in the confidence of real power, bounced right back. "Okay!" he chirped. He looked at the others. "She's the boss, right?" More nods, some laughter.

Linda pounded the table with open palms. "Mr. Edmonton! What the fuck do you want?"

Edmonton laughed, a loud, high-pitched chuckle that stumbled drunkenly up the stairs, then passed out on the landing. His face went slack. "First of all, Mrs. President," he said, "my name's not Edmonton. It's Rice. Theodore Rice. And I am, indeed, here to brief you."

Linda glanced around the table. Rice caught her question. "To my left is Antonin Gellow. It's pronounced like the dessert, but spelled with a G and a W." Gellow, a huge man with curly, dark hair and a full beard, nodded respectfully. "Across the table sits General Lowell." The General was a small man, thin, no more than five foot six, his gray hair cut short and stubbly. His uniform looked too large, and sagged under the weight of more medals and ribbons than good taste would normally allow. The General nodded.

Rice went on. "And to your right, Colonel Phelps." Linda would not have guessed him for a military man of any sort, let alone a Colonel. His blond hair was long and unruly, past his ears and nearing his neck. He was dressed in blue jeans and a t-shirt. He reminded Linda of a middle-aged surfer.

"Hey, how you doing?" said Colonel Phelps with a smile and a nod.

Linda did not respond to any of their greetings. She focused on Rice. "So, you're not really Edmonton. And given your behavior here today, I can also assume that you're not really one of my agents." She indicated the others with a sweep of her arm. "And these gentlemen? Who are they pretending to be today?"

Rice stuck his face into the President's. "Your worst nightmare!" he scowled. His head fell back and he laughed again, delighted at his own cleverness.

Gellow shifted his great weight in his chair and cleared his throat. "Stop playing with her, Rice," he said, his voice surprisingly high and delicate. "Get to it."

Rice considered that, then shrugged. "Okay." He turned back to Linda. "Mrs. President, let me begin by saying that your life, and the universe in general, will from this day forward no longer be what you thought it was. Until the end of your days, you will be able to look back and remember this meeting as the moment your world changed forever."

"Not if you never get to the point," Linda answered.

Rice licked his lips. "Right." He motioned toward Colonel Phelps, who grabbed for a remote to dim the lights. From a recessed control panel on the table before him, Rice flicked on the plasma screen that hung on the wall behind Lowell and Phelps. The two men swiveled their chairs to face the screen, which glowed a soft, contented blue.

Rice touched a button on the panel. On the screen came a blurry black and white photograph, almost impossible to make out. Rice turned a knob and the picture came into better focus, though still poor quality. There were two figures: one unmistakably Dwight David Eisenhower and the other a very small man, dressed in a Hawaiian shirt and a huge straw hat that covered his pale, seemingly bald head. Most of his face was hidden behind a large pair of sunglasses. The two figures sat in canvas folding chairs on what looked to be the rear deck of a yacht. Rice leaned over, mock-whispered to the President. "I love this part!"

Linda ignored him.

Rice advanced the slides. Eisenhower again, with his odd friend. The little man had taken off his hat for this picture, revealing a strangely deformed, hairless head, quite large and very pale, with no ears to be seen.

Linda looked at Rice. "You've got to be kidding."

"What?"

"Is this whole thing a joke? Did Bickle put you up to this? Are you guys with the *Weekly Daily News*?" Linda started to stand.

Rice held out a hand to stop her. "No joke, ma'am. Please, sit down. It always goes like this. Just give it time."

The President stood anyway, pushed back her chair. "I'm outta here!" She took a step for the door but it opened before she could touch the knob. In stepped the woman she had seen before, her pistol out and aimed at the President's forehead. Linda stopped. "You're not going to kill the President of the United States in the White House," she said, looking around. "You are not that stupid."

Rice was at her side like a lawyer. "She doesn't have to kill you. She can just make it hurt. Come and sit down."

Linda looked at the woman. Her pale, oval face, a model's face, was surrounded by long, straight, honey-hued hair, and studded with eyes that froze her heart. There was murder in those eyes. And something else: space. The President shuddered involuntarily and did not resist as Rice led her back to her chair.

Rice advanced the slide. There was a close up of the smaller man, sunglasses now off, holding up a fish and a pole.

"What is this?" Linda asked, her voice now hoarse. "Who is this freak?"

Rice patted the President's arm gently. "That's Asimov," he said. "He's not from around here."

## 4.4

Linda's eyes darted around the room, looking at each of her captors before turning back to the image on the wall. "What are you saying?" she demanded huskily. She dropped her gaze to the table.

General Lowell cleared his throat and spoke for the first time. "Mrs. President, the government of the United States of America has been communicating with, and working alongside of, a group of alien beings from a star many light-years away from our own for the better part of seven decades now." He nodded shortly and turned back to stare at the wall.

"Yeah. Right." Linda snorted. "And you guys are their best buddies."

"We are known to them," chirped Gellow in his vague Slavic accent. In the darkened room, his face cast in skewed shadows from the projector, Gellow looked just like Jackie Gleason in a fright wig and beard.

The President waved a hand at the wall. "And this guy, this thing here, Asimov, he lives in some big government mansion and rules the whole world with his death ray?"

"No, Asimov died in 1956," explained Rice.

Linda shielded her face with her hands. "This is absurd."

"It always has been," said Lowell, still facing away. "We make it work."

"You have no proof. Just a couple of photos my niece could make in Photoshop. This is all just bullshit."

In response Rice picked up the controller again, started clicking rapidly through a series of slides. Linda stared at the images, unable to turn away, her fingers fluttering nervously in her lap. There were photographs of Eisenhower and Asimov in the Rose Garden. Photos of Kennedy, Nixon, Ford, Bush, Clinton, Bush the 2nd, all posing with more of the small, gray, bulbous-headed creatures. Linda looked at Rice as he pulled back from the control panel, leaving a full color image of George W. Bush hosting a trio of these alien things in the Oval Office frozen on the wall. "No proof," she repeated.

"Soon enough," said Rice. "Tomorrow." He nodded to Colonel Phelps, who touched the remote to turn the light back on as Rice flicked off the screen.

"They come from a planet which circles a star in the Canis Major dwarf galaxy," Rice stated matter-of-factly, "a galaxy which human scientists finally managed to detect in 2003, even though it's right next door. We made first contact with them on November 3, 1938, when one of their scout ships landed in a cornfield near Port Huron, Michigan. In a hilarious display of cosmic humor, their arrival came just a few days after Orson Welles' Scare-the-Rubes Halloween Radio Party. There was a brief meeting between the aliens, the local authorities, and representatives from a nearby Army base, at which time, according to the aliens, a "great gift" was given to humanity, though none of the humans attending had any memory of receiving anything.

"After that first contact they disappeared until 1941, at which time they began appearing in the skies over many parts of the world. Though we didn't know it at the time, those sightings signaled the arrival in the solar system of their entire population. In 1946, they re-established contact with the U.S. government and struck a deal. We have had a continuous relationship with them since, as we've worked out the details." Gellow nodded agreement from time to time, but said nothing. The General had not yet turned back to the table, but sat picking at his fingernails as he faced the wall. Colonel Phelps seemed to have fallen immediately to sleep. Rice's watch began to beep but he did not move to stop the sound. After half a minute it stopped by itself.

Linda sat in silence, looking down at her hands. They had shown her nothing. No proof. Just a bunch of terrorists with a pack of lies. Yet Linda knew, below her conscious thoughts, in a place where words were not allowed, that these pictures were not lies. She was neither happy nor surprised to see those strange faces on the wall.

She had seen them before.

## 4.5

The autumn night air had grown damp and cool, seeping into the house through the sliding glass door that Cole had cracked open, and covering the floor like wet leaves. The woods were quiet now, save for the occasional chirrup of a cricket and the distant queries of a barred owl: *Who? Who? Who cooks for you?* The phone had not sounded since Linda had begun speaking, gracing the evening with blessed relief.

Cole sat tightly in the rocker he'd pulled away from the woodstove, concentrating on his fingernails, tapping his heel nervously on the floor. Linda sat across from him on the sofa, watching him in silence. There was something like hope in her eyes. "So?" she finally said.

"So what?" asked Cole, looking up. He knew what, but he didn't know how to respond.

"You think I'm crazy?"

Cole hesitated, checked his watch, scrunched his nose. "The thought has crossed my mind more than once today." An apologetic smile flashed across his face. It was not polite to say such things.

Linda nodded. "Good. If it hadn't, I'd think *you* were crazy."

"So, you're saying that all this UFO stuff is true. And the government knows all about it."

Linda offered a soft sigh of agreement. "You're half right."

"This is very hard for me."

"Tell me about it. I had a gun pointed at me."

Cole cleared his throat. "So did I," he said, his voice low and sad.

Linda's mouth dropped open. She hadn't seen the similarity until that moment. It scared her, to realize how far desperation had driven her. "Oh, Cole," she said, almost moaning, "I'm so sorry. Please forgive me."

Cole started to reply but stopped when he heard a noise from upstairs. Down the steps came Grace, her hair mussed, her eyes full of sleep, dragging her Minnie Mouse behind her. Minnie's head thudded lightly on the steps as she descended.

Grace reached the bottom of the stairs and walked straight for her father, climbing onto his lap and nuzzling her face in his chest. Cole smoothed her hair and whispered into her ear. "What's up, Boo?" he said.

"There's a kid in my room," she said, sinking quickly back toward sleep in her father's arms.

"A kid?"

"He tried to take Minnie."

Cole lifted Grace and laid her gently on the sofa next to the President. "Watch her for a second," he said. He hurried up the stairs.

Grace wiggled to get comfortable on Linda's shoulder. Her breathing softened almost immediately. Linda sat quietly, listening to the sounds Cole made as he searched Grace's room above, to the grumpy complaints of Emily when he turned on the light, to floorboards creaking and doors pulled gently shut. She listened to the slow even music of Grace's tiny inhalations. How wonderful it would have been, to have had a daughter of her own. Not that they hadn't tried. But after three unexplained miscarriages, she and Earl had given up. The emotional cost was too high. She ran a hand along Grace's back, stroked her hair.

Cole continued to clunk around overhead, whispering a curse. Linda left him to it. She knew what he was going through. And she knew that he had to go through it. After a few minutes, Cole crept softly back down the stairs.

Linda looked up to him. "Did you see anything?"

"Nothing," answered Cole. He sat down, holding his still-shaking hands close to his stomach. His nose wrinkled and relaxed and wrinkled again. "God! I thought ... you know, those eyes, and ... and the things you've been saying. I just knew that one of those things was in her room."

Linda hugged Grace tightly to her shoulder. "One probably was," she answered sadly.

"You don't seem particularly alarmed by that," Cole growled.

Linda dropped her head, noting the smell of Grace's freshly shampooed hair. She looked up at Cole blankly.

Cole looked Linda in the eye, shook his head. "I don't believe any of this," he said.

Linda raised a finger to her lips. "Listen." Immediately the phone in the bushes began to ring again.

"Oh, come on!" said Cole.

"Go answer it," said the President evenly.

Cole stared at her in disbelief. "I'm not going out there!"

"I thought you didn't believe in any of this."

Cole shot the President an angry glance.

"Just go answer it," said Linda again.

Cole rose, stood, and looked down at the injured woman on his sofa. Fear and responsibility struggled for possession of his feet. Looping through his mind was a memory of Ruth hugging Grace at the airport, telling her daughter that she'd see her when she got back. With a fierce intake of breath, Cole walked across the living room and through the dining room to the front door. He opened it. The volume of the ringing swelled jarringly, as though the phone had leapt back into the room. Cole switched on the security light mounted near the door, illuminating a wide circle of walkways and bushes and trees. Grabbing the chef's knife from the block by the sink, he stepped out, leaving the door open behind him. His knees felt wobbly as he walked. Fear trickled down his throat.

From inside, Linda could hear him push aside the various roses and viburnums that lined the cobbled walk. Thirty seconds later came a loud ringing crash, the sound of the phone smashing down upon the stone walkway. Cole came back inside and stood in the center of the room. His arms hung limply at his sides.

"Cole?" asked the President. Cole's face was slack and white.

"Asimov," said Cole, his voice far away. "The voice said 'Asimov'."

The President looked down at the sleeping child, then back up at her host. The look on her face was that of quiet acceptance.

"They know you're here?"

Linda nodded and pointed up. "They do. They always know. But not the other ones, not the People I told you about." The President shook her head. "Not yet. They don't know yet." She prayed she was right.

The two of them sat in silence, sipping their tea, watching the dark woods beyond the windows. Linda glanced at the clock on the kitchen wall. Ten-thirty. Grace snored quietly, curled up on her lap. Cole had tried to put his daughter back to bed but Linda had asked him to let her stay. The weight of her innocence on Linda's legs and stomach was comforting, a reminder of simpler times. Rice had been right. Linda could trace the moment her old world ended to that briefing in June. She kissed the top of Grace's head. She would have given anything not to have brought such peril to this young child's life. Yet she could not do this herself, especially now. And this child's whole future could depend on what she did in the days ahead. She. Maybe Cole, if he would help her. And then there was Keeley, if Linda could find her.

Cole broke the silence, his voice soft and low. "So who are these people? The ones who briefed you?" he asked. "Tell me what happened. I need to know."

"They call themselves 'the People.' To distinguish themselves from the aliens, I suppose. General Lowell - they all just call him the General - seems to head up the whole group. I think he's for real. Military, I mean, though I could never find anybody in any branch of the service who had any record of his existence. Gellow's a scientist. Astronomer, maybe. Same story. Nobody's ever heard of him. Phelps I don't know about. I never did see him again. Rice is one of their special agents, as is the woman, Bob. Her real name's Roberta Reese. They're both pretty high up in the organization, I think."

"How did this all happen, Linda?"

"Well," she gently pulled a lock of hair from Grace's face. "I got the whole story after the screen was turned off."

## 4.6

Rice handed the President a thick, unmarked folder. Linda picked it up, started to leaf through the pages. "This is the history of our organization," said Rice. "You can read it tonight. I'll stop by at 8 tomorrow morning to pick you, and it, up."

Linda thought of her mother, Ellen, with whom she was scheduled to meet for lunch in an hour. What would she say? And how could she read this all tonight? Wasn't there some dinner she had to attend? "I can't tonight," she said. "There's no time."

Rice shook his head. "All taken care of, Mrs. President. Dinner tonight canceled. Mrs. Warren occupied. We're very thorough. You'll have time. But let me give you the highlights." He nodded at Phelps, who went to the door and spoke in hushed tones to someone outside. A moment later Phelps returned with a glass of iced tea. He placed it in front of the President and returned to his seat. Linda ignored the drink.

Rice continued. "You've heard of Project Blue Book?"

Linda nodded. Of course she had. Everybody had.

"Before Blue Book were Projects Sign and Grudge. You may have heard of those as well. These 'official' projects collected information, filtered reports, interacted with the public, and interfaced with various scientific and academic groups. The projects were designed to ease fears and speculation by pretending to investigate and explain the UFO situation." Rice leaned back in his chair and stretched his legs out under the table. "But even before Sign, we'd begun to take the real investigation offline. Majestic was the first working version of what has now become 'the People,' but by the time Majestic was discovered and made public in the mid-80s, we'd long since left it behind." Rice reached out and grabbed Linda's iced tea and took a sip. "Basically, over the course of the past eight decades, the alliance between human groups and the aliens has sunk deeper and deeper underground, far out of reach of most of those who think they govern. Almost from the beginning, there has been a secret group working behind the scenes, dealing face to face with the aliens and their spacecraft, both of which were, as far as the 'bewildered herd' was concerned, still huge mysteries.

"There was a great deal of disagreement early on regarding how much the public should be told. Eventually the orders came down that any and all information about UFOs and aliens should be kept away from the masses. The various study groups of scientists and politicians and military leaders were ordered to write the whole thing off as nonsense, and were then dissolved. Blue Book was closed up. Files, artifacts, and biological materials were gathered in from every intelligence organization, every branch of the service, even NASA, and were either destroyed, or stored in a centralized location in Nevada, in what has become known as Area 51. Most personnel with ties to official agencies were removed from those assignments and brought in full-time. Some were ordered to maintain their dual positions, creating shadow bureaucracies within such groups as NASA and the CIA, since we knew that reports would continue to come to these official agencies. Years of disinformation campaigns, harassment, threats, assassinations, public ridicule, and bureaucratic bullshit made the whole process easy enough to carry out. By 1970, the government and military were officially 'not interested' in UFOs. The alien situation was left in the capable hands of our group, the People, with no links whatsoever to those government or military powers that would try to control the show." Rice sat up straight and looked Linda in the eye. "We are invisible, unsupervised, and totally in control. We form the hub of that hidden elite who really run the world. All true power held by humans today is held by us."

Linda looked Rice dead in the face. "You, Mr. Rice, are the most arrogant man I've ever met."

Rice smiled. "I come by it legitimately, Mrs. President." He leaned back again, crossed his arms over his chest.

"Really. And how did you end up in this fine little club, Mr. Rice?"

"Life chose me from the very beginning. Life prepared me, tested me, guided me, groomed me. And here I am now, having shown my worthiness."

"Life prepared you?  What the hell does that mean?"

"Life is that of which we speak.  Life is that which has come to our planet to guide us from the fiery path." As Rice spoke his eyes closed. "Life is that which leads us and loves us and shows us the way." Rice stopped, his eyes still closed, his face a mask of pure bliss.

Gellow rolled his eyes. "He means the aliens, Mrs. President."

Rice blinked away his bliss and flicked a hateful look at his colleague. "It is we who are alien," he said sternly.

Linda interrupted. "So why are you telling me?  Is that the rule?  All the Presidents get to be in on the fun?"

Rice resumed his cheerful expression. "Not all, Mrs. President.  Johnson was never told.  Neither were Carter or Reagan.  Funny, given that both of them claimed to have seen a UFO.  Bush was brought into the loop as Vice-President, which helps explain how he won in '88."

Gellow began to chuckle deeply. "A thousand points of light.  If the voters only knew.  He'd seen 'em!"

Rice went on. "Clinton was told.  And Bush Junior.  But neither Obama nor Russell was brought in.  Now you know."

"I'm not sure that I really know anything," said Linda. "All I have is your words and those pictures.  The only thing I *know* is that I've been held against my will at gunpoint by a group of people who, if this works out my way, are in very deep shit."

Rice rose from his chair, walked around the table, and whispered briefly with the General.  Then he returned to his chair and faced Linda again. "That's it for today," he said cheerily. "You can go."

Linda stared, unbelieving. "*I* can go?  Who the hell are you to tell me I can go?  I want some answers!"

"Nope.  Sorry." Rice shook his head like a father talking to his whining child. "We're done.  I'll see you in the morning.  Lots of time tomorrow for questions.  We've got a big day planned." With that Rice rose, gathered his papers, and left.  The General followed without so much as a glance toward the President.  Gellow rose and walked around the table, tapping Phelps on the shoulder.  Phelps woke with a start, oriented himself to the situation, smiled at the President and rose to follow Gellow.  They both left without a word.

Linda sat, dumbfounded. What was going on tomorrow? Nothing! To hell with them all, she was not going to play their game. She'd tell Bickle right away. Arrest these crazies. And she would not stop until she got to the bottom of this whole meeting. How could her own security have failed her so? How could these idiots do what they did?

Rice stuck his head back in. "Oh, yes, Mrs. President. Just in case you're thinking of saying anything about this meeting to anybody, you need to know that your mother is, well, let's just say we know where she is. If you know what I mean." Rice's smile faded, pushed aside by a look of utter sadness. "One other thing, Mrs. President. Some very sad news. Very sad."

Linda rose from her chair. "What?"

"It's Mr. Bickle, ma'am. He, uh ... met with a very tragic accident. Just twenty minutes ago. I'm afraid he's dead."

Linda flung herself at the door, shouting as she ran, and slammed into it with all the force she could muster. But she was unsuccessful. Rice had already pulled his head out of the way.

# Chapter ⏀ Five

## 5.1

*Bob swept above the tree line, pulled to a stop at the sight of the massive objects drifting dark and mute over the house. Instinctively, she folded into a ball and dove back toward the house. She buzzed past the President's face, through the window behind her, and back to the sky. The Prez was still a blur. Nothing to fix on. The tugging at Bob's back grew stronger. She'd been gone long enough, and the woks were pulsing with an inscrutable menace she'd never before encountered. She looked to the stars above, preparing to reconstitute.*

*Something sparkled underfoot. She glanced down just in time to see a whirling form come crashing into her, flinging her high into the air. At the end of her energy, Bob didn't stick around to see what had hit her, but let the cord pull her back. The Cosmos zipped past, a torrent of color and vibrations. In a moment she fell back into her body.*

Bob opened her eyes. Mary was there, sitting quietly at the side of her bed, ready to hand Bob the glass of water from the night table. Traveling always made Bob thirsty.

"Ma Kettle's got another guardian," Bob said, her voice pebbly and poorly controlled. Her body never felt like her own when she first fell back.

Mary frowned. "How could she have a guardian? Ellen's on a slow drip. Who else knows? And how could they ever find her?"

Bob shrugged, draining the glass. "Whatever it was 'bout knocked me on my ass. Thought I'd regroup here before I took it on. I may need some help."

"Don't look at me," said Mary. "I gave it up for Lent."

"Maybe I'll take Alice."

Mary rose and walked to the window, switching the sim to a daylight pastoral that she always enjoyed. Forcing a smile to her face, she returned to her chair. "So, any luck?"

Bob lowered her eyes. "No. But Spud's there. He's got the whole gang out for a bit of fun, looks like. They didn't seem happy to see me. But the Angels are gone, which is good. Anything from your side?"

"Badges all over the country are looking for that old Cutlass. We told 'em it had been seen in connection with the kidnapping and that the driver may have important information. They'll find it. We've also found a guy in the little town of Spalter, Pennsylvania, up near the northern state line, who swears he saw somebody that looked like the president come in to his station in the middle of the night and pay for gas. He didn't see the car. Said it was after midnight. He didn't think much of it until he heard the reports on the radio in the morning."

"Pennsylvania. Knotweed. She's heading north. Any way to step up the search in the Northeast without raising suspicion?"

Mary nodded. "We're working on it. But we have to be careful. We don't actually want the badges to find her."

Bob agreed. "If they get to her first, she'll have a chance to talk. Which would make for one huge fucking mess. I wonder why she hasn't gone to them herself?"

Mary turned away, sighing. "Whom can she trust?" she said, her voice low and cheerless.

Bob flashed Mary a pouty lip. "Poor Mrs. President."

## 5.2

Rice opened the door wide before entering. "Good morning, Prez. How are we doing today?" He brushed a bit of lint from his gray, vicuña wool suit and walked in, closing the door behind him.

Linda sat in an overstuffed chair by the window, looking out over the city. She wore jeans and a yellow cotton blouse, and her hair was held back in a short ponytail. In the distance stood the Washington Monument, tall, unyielding and milky-bright against the clear blue sky, like the America she'd known as a kid. She spoke without turning around. "Why did you kill him?"

"Who, ma'am?" Rice walked across the room, took the seat opposite the President's. He smiled and flashed his eyebrows, as if it were all a joke to him.

Linda gave Rice a look of studied contempt. His cool condescension, so over-the-top it felt forced, offended her at every level, as if the future of the whole world had been put in the hands of a spiteful child. Real power would not need to belittle her. Maybe there was a weak spot in the edifice of authority he seemed so intent on building around her. "Fuck you," she said matter-of-factly.

"Is this about Bickle, ma'am?" said Rice, his face filled with concern.

"You know what I'm talking about. And don't call me 'ma'am.' You don't have an ounce of respect for me or my office." Linda turned back to the window.

Rice crossed his legs, picked at something on the bottom of his shoe. "You're right, you know."

Linda held silence and continued to stare out the window.

Rice cleared his throat, waited for a moment, straightened his legs and smoothed his slacks. At last he went on, as if she'd taken his bait. "I think you're a complete ass, Mrs. President: a dumb-shit farmer's wife who hasn't got a clue about how the real world works. It still amazes me that you managed to get elected. And if it were up to me, you'd never be told any of this."

Linda turned to face him again. "So who's it up to?"

"Life commands it."

Linda's eyes narrowed. "Life! More bullshit. It looks to me like you don't give a damn about life. I think Bickle would back me up on that assessment."

A smile came to Rice's face. "That was the problem, wasn't it, girlfriend? Bickle backing you up, making things difficult. Life decided to remove him. It's all part of the Plan."

"I'd like to hear what his wife and daughter think of your *plan*."

Rice shrugged. Linda glared.

"Where's Mom?"

"The Queen Mother? Oh, she's off sailing today with Mrs. Engle. Got a whole fun-packed day planned." Rice grinned. "She could use a rest, don't you think? All those parties and dinners and photo ops. The poor dear."

Linda rose from her chair and walked to the worktable in the corner to retrieve the folder Rice had given her the day before. She dropped it into Rice's lap. "Fuck you again," she said quietly.

Rice leafed through the folder. "Did you read it?"

"Fairy tales."

Rice slapped the folder shut. "Really?" he said, rising and walking toward the door. "C'mon, Mrs. President, ma'am. Let's go meet your Fairy Godfather." He stepped through the doorway, laughing. Linda listened as he walked down the hallway. After a moment, she pulled on her tennis shoes and followed.

## 5.3

Cole stood at the top of the stairs, breathing deeply. Grace was back in bed, out like a light. She hadn't even awakened when he'd pulled her from the President's embrace and carried her upstairs. The girls' room was clear. He'd searched every dark corner of both bedrooms, every hiding space, even the attic. Nothing. And the windows were both locked. As were those in Iain's room.

In the living room below, Linda Travis, the President of the United States, waited for him to return. Because she needed his help. Because there was more to the story. But Cole didn't even know what to do with what he'd heard so far. Should he be scared because she's crazy? Or because she's right?

The memory of those orange-red eyes haunted him. His face twitched. His fingers stretched and reached and curled into fists. What the hell had been out there? What the fuck was that thing? Cole was scared. Scared for the kids. Scared for himself. Scared of screwing up. He had no idea what he was dealing with, what the President was dealing with. Just that it was big and powerful and dangerous. Tomorrow morning, he would take the kids up to his father's house. Beyond that, he didn't have a clue what to do. Maybe with the kids safe, he'd be able to think more clearly.

It was true, what the President had said about Bickle. The Chief of Staff had died back in June. Cole had read about it in the paper. Bickle had run his rented Lexus off a bridge.

Cole started down the steps, able to move now that he had a plan. He would protect his children above all else. If they could take out Bickle, why would they hesitate with his children? Or with himself? Or with anyone?

And just who the hell were *they*?

## 5.4

Rice drove the President for an hour, west, away from the city. How they managed to get her out of the White House *and* out of the district without raising a stink with her staff and security Linda did not know. But they'd left without a hitch, as though the President leaving in a Jeep Cherokee with a single Secret Service agent was the most natural thing in the world. It was their ability to do things like this that most impressed upon Linda the seemingly unlimited nature of the People's power and influence. It should be impossible to do what they did. Impossible to take over a meeting within the White House and threaten her at gunpoint. Impossible to just drive away with her in the light of day. Impossible. Yet they did it.

Linda wondered at their methods. Why the cloak-and-dagger, why the gun, why the arrogance and anger, why the *murder*, if they were trying to recruit her to their team? She tried to imagine some other way they could have brought her in, but ultimately failed. What they were bringing her in *to*, if what Rice said was true, was not only criminal, it was ... Earth-shattering. They said they'd done this before. No doubt they thought they knew what they were doing.

Rice drove on, unusually silent. Linda watched him from the passenger seat, staring at his face, his hands, watching the tiny movements of his arms and legs and head as he piloted the car through the traffic. She would not be intimidated by this man. Not if she could help it. Rice had seemed yesterday to revel in his power, smirking and laughing at the President like a playground bully. But not now. There was perspiration on his forehead and his skin looked pale and waxy in the early morning light. Nervous, Linda thought. A good sign. Maybe there was a chink in the armor. So Linda stared, attempting to add to Rice's unease. It was something she could do.

The route Rice took was a mystery to Linda. He drove unerringly: on the freeway here, off to a side street there, down major boulevards and along silent residential streets, never once checking a map or doubling back, and never once getting snagged in the gridlock that could still haunt this city, even with gas at over nine dollars a gallon. Linda sighed her surrender. If knowing her location was crucial to her survival, she was screwed. She would never remember this route. She'd seen very little of Washington D.C., or its crumbling suburban buffer, before she had come here as the President. And in the months since her inauguration, chauffeured and flown everywhere she went, she still hadn't seen very much of the city.

What she saw now amazed her. She'd known it with her head, of course. She'd read the reports, seen the photos, heard the briefings. And she'd toured Memphis after the March flooding, so it was not as if she hadn't already seen for herself the full force of the past decade's economic meltdown as it had manifested in a major American city. But driving through the streets of D.C., it was hard to believe she was still in the U.S. This was far past decay. This was death. This was desiccation. This was desolation. The body of this great city had long since expired. And the spirit – still coursing through the hearts of those who walked and worked the city's engines of government and commerce, still pumping through the lungs of the systems and habits that kept the city standing, still flitting through the minds of the ever-fewer men and women and children who remained in their homes and jobs and lives, eager for a miracle – that spirit refused to let go of the corpse. Away from its padded, peopled, postcard-preserved center, Washington D.C. felt like a ghost town.

City and suburbs finally gave way to more open country. From the frequency and low altitudes of the flights overhead, Linda figured they were close to Dulles, somewhat south and to the west. The road before them was two lanes, paved but not very wide, lined with newer homes and the occasional farm. They passed a sign reading "Kelton - 6 Miles." Half a mile further brought them to an old gas station on the left, the defunct corporate logos plastered over with cardboard signs reading "Dave's Oil Company." There were two pumps, a single garage and a tiny store, all finely layered with dust.

Rice pulled into the station, parking carelessly between the cracked and faded white lines that defined the spaces in front of the store. An overweight man in a stained t-shirt and torn jeans stepped out from the door in front of them and walked past the Cherokee without a glance, climbing into the battered pick-up that sat at the pumps. Rice opened his door. Linda could see the beads of sweat on his forehead glisten in the cool morning sun. His hands twitched erratically at his side, looking for something to do. "C'mon," he commanded in a low voice. Linda opened her door and stepped out of the Jeep.

She could run now, she thought. Flag down that guy in the pick-up and tear away from Rice and all his crazy shit. Go to the police, the FBI. Go to the damn Joint Chiefs to get Rice off her ass. Rice wouldn't shoot her in broad daylight, would he? Not with a witness. Not so close to gas pumps.

But Linda didn't run. She knew already that she could not confront the situation that way. Whatever it was that Rice and his friends had, it gave them incredible power. She could never hide. And whom could she trust? If what Rice had said was even partly true, then anyone around her could be a part of it: the military, the

CIA, the ND, even the Secret Service. The agents of this "Life" could be anywhere. Everywhere. The guy in the pick-up could be one of theirs, a test to see how compliant she would be. Running wasn't the answer. Not yet. Better to watch, and wait, and learn just what the hell was going on. It seemed unlikely they would harm her at this point. Why go through all of this if that was their plan? Linda walked around the front of the Jeep and followed Rice into the store.

Rice picked up a bag of cheese puffs, opened it and began to eat. He nodded at Linda. "Want something?" he asked, his voice muffled by a mouth full of crunchy orange. Linda looked down the aisle, chose a packet of gum from a display on the top shelf, not really knowing why. Rice nodded and walked to the back of the store without a glance at the attendant, a young woman with a large blue bow in her hair who sat looking bored or stoned on her stool, watching a game show on a small TV. Rice stopped at the gray metal door next to the soft drink cooler and opened it, motioning for Linda to follow. Feeling guilty about the gum, the President pointed to the girl behind the counter. Rice rolled his eyes. "It's okay, Mrs. President. She doesn't even know we're here." He walked through the door, letting it swing closed behind him. Linda glanced again at the girl, then slid the gum into her denim pocket and pushed her way through the door.

The storeroom was stacked high with cases of soda and boxes of snack-foods. To the right was a door which, as far as Linda could see, must lead straight to the side lot, given how small the store looked from outside. Rice stepped back as he pulled the door open, motioning for Linda to walk through before him. His hand quavered as it held the knob. Linda stepped forward to peer out the door, hesitant, not knowing what to expect. She was right: a rutted, gravel parking lot surrounded by scraggly pines, with a rusty dumpster in the corner. Linda flashed Rice a look of bewilderment and stepped through...

...into a small gray room, the ceiling so low that Linda had to duck her head. She turned around, looking for the door and Rice. The door was gone, but there was Rice, standing hunched over right behind her. His eyes were closed, his face slack and still, his half-eaten snack dangling from his fingers.

Linda turned back around, scanned the room. No chairs. No tables. Nothing but a small wire magazine rack in one corner, filled to overflowing with magazines and newspapers. Linda stooped to pick one up: *Time*, March 17, 1958, Lyndon Johnson staring back at her from the cover, and a banner shouting *Spaceport USA: Beyond the Gates of Cape Canaveral.* Linda put it carefully back into the rack.

There was only one door, directly across from the spot where, it had seemed to Linda, they had entered the room. Behind Rice there was now only blank gray wall, like poured concrete but without the pockmarks or bubbles. Linda stepped back around Rice to feel the wall. It was solid and cool. The floor was tightly woven, gray carpeting. The ceiling glowed dull and gray, as if it were composed of solidified fog. She crossed back to the other side of the room and tried the door. It would not open; the handle was frozen and unyielding. There were no windows. Linda walked back, stood in front of Rice. "Hey," she snapped, "Rice! You wanna wake the hell up and tell 'em we're here?" Rice gave no sign that he had heard.

Linda put out a hand, touched Rice's shoulder, and gave a slight push. Rice did not react, did not tense up. Linda pushed harder. It was like pushing on a statue, as if he were held in some sort of force field. Rice didn't move at all.

The door clicked open behind her. Linda whirled at the sound of the latch to see an empty hallway beyond the door, brightly lit from above, as gray as the room. From down the hallway came the faint sound of music, as though an orchestra were tuning up a few rooms away. Linda walked to the door and pulled it fully open, half expecting to find someone standing there. There was no one. She stepped through the door.

To the right the hallway came to an abrupt end. To the left, the gray carpet stretched on and on, seemingly into infinity. Linda glanced back at Rice, then turned left and started slowly down the low-ceilinged hall, following the sounds of instruments as they plucked and bowed and blew their A's and B-flats. Fifty feet or so down, on the right, was another door. Linda pushed and it swung inward.

The President walked into her high school auditorium.

5.5

"Program, Linda?" It was Martin ... Anderson, she remembered. He'd been in her French class. He looked just like she remembered him, lanky and oily, still only eighteen years old. Linda nodded, struck dumb, absently taking the booklet he offered her.

She walked down the aisle of the Pierpoint High School auditorium. There was the stage on which she had played Abigail in *The Crucible* in the fall of her senior year. On the walls hung huge paper banners from the glorious 1989 football season: *Go Muskies*! Underfoot was the red carpeting over which Mr. Blood – and oh the grief they had given him about his name! – had fussed so vocally, shouting until his face looked as if it would pop whenever somebody spilled a drink or dared to walk through with muddy feet. Overhead hung the chandelier she remembered, a gift from the senior class of 1962. Half the little bulbs were still burned out. Linda stood and looked around, knowing that she was in that very auditorium, knowing that she was not. It had been torn down in 1996, after a new one was built.

Another young man came toward her up the aisle. She recognized his face. Jon Shea. God, Jon! Linda's stomach dropped to make room for her heart. She remembered all over again the night she had called it quits. She was off to college and wanted the freedom to date other guys there. Jon had smiled and said he understood. And Linda had promised that she would be back. But she had never returned.

Jon walked up to her, smiling warmly. He leaned in and gave her a gentle kiss on the cheek. "Hi, Linda," he said.

"Jon," Linda managed to say, her throat heavy and full. "Jon." He was a vision from her distant past, a time of youth and possibility and freedom. He was no more real than the auditorium, she knew, but he was still Jon, untouched by time, smooth and clean and strong, unsuspecting of the hard life that awaited him, and the cancer that would kill him before he was even thirty.

Jon took the President gently by the arm and guided her towards the row of chairs to his right, a spot about halfway back from the stage. "Have a seat," he said. Linda obeyed, picking the second seat in, hoping that Jon would sit next to her. Jon smiled and winked and took off down the aisle toward the stage without another word. He ascended the concrete steps at stage left and disappeared behind the maroon velvet curtain that hid the entire stage from view.

Linda sat back, stretched, made herself more comfortable, forgetting for the moment the briefing and the gun and Mr. Rice in the room down the hall, thinking only of Jon and the times they had shared.

The house lights dimmed just as Linda thought to look at the program in her hand. LIFE: A PLAY IN ONE ACT was printed on the cover in a script she should not have been able to read. Before she could open the pamphlet the auditorium went fully dark. Behind the curtain Linda could hear whispers and giggles and movement. A yellow glow seeped out from underneath.

The pit orchestra leapt into song, a big band sound, a show tune vaguely familiar. The curtain parted slowly. On the stage, four or five rows deep, forty or so members of the senior class of 1990, her class, sang loud and strong, their faces beaming under the lights. Jon was in the middle of the front row. And here and there in the troupe, strange little fellows danced and sang along with the students, slight and pale, with large bald heads and fluid black eyes full of stars.

## 5.6

Cole pried apart the last remaining pieces of the phone and tossed them onto the pile on the floor before him. As the President had recounted her story, the phone, smashed on the rocks as it was, had started to ring again. Cole, so angry that he'd forgotten to be scared, had run outside, grabbed the phone, brought it ringing into the kitchen, and had proceeded to take it apart piece by piece with a hammer and screwdriver. There was nothing left to make a sound. "Ring now, you bastard!" he said, rising and wiping his hands in self-satisfaction. He looked down at Linda, who was watching him with amusement from her seat on the sofa. "Let 'em bother us now!"

The President smiled weakly. "I wish I could tell you that that will help," she said.

Cole spun around. There were no lights in the woods, no eyes at the window. "What? Are they—?"

The President shrugged. "They do what they will, Cole. We can't stop them with a hammer and a screwdriver."

Cole thought again of Grace's account of the little kid in her room. Given what he'd seen, Cole was willing to take her story seriously. He grabbed the big night watchman's flashlight from its spot near the toaster and bolted upstairs, checking the kids' rooms again. But there was nothing there. And no sign of entry. The windows were whole and tight.

He made his way warily back downstairs.

"Everything okay?"

"Yeah." Cole came to a stop across the coffee table from the President, looked down on her for the longest time. Catching himself staring, he took a seat. He sighed deeply and smiled. Linda was beautiful in the warm glow of lamplight. Her hair blushed and pulsed, as if goodness and caring were flames that flickered in her soul. He wanted to get lost in those flames. Cole blinked, shivered, checked his watch. It was after eleven. They were both tired, but there was no way he could sleep now. Not until the President made sense of this. "I'm confused," he finally said.

Linda shifted her weight, rubbed at her leg, stretched her shoulders. Her eyes were soft and clear, as if the hardest part were over. "About what?"

"What's with this whole school play thing?" Cole asked. "I thought ... why are you telling me about your high school and your old sweetheart?"

Linda shrugged. "That's how they told me."

"Those alien guys?"

"Yeah, those alien guys." Linda finished her tea and put her cup on the table at the sofa's end. Slowly she swung her legs off the table, first the good left leg, then the splinted right leg.

Something was odd. Both legs felt strong and pain-free. She pushed herself up gingerly from the sofa and put some weight on her right foot. It felt impossibly normal.

Cole was at her side in a moment. "Can I help?"

Linda waved him off. "Something's not right here," she said, her voice trembling.

"What?"

Ignoring the question, the President pulled down her borrowed sweat pants and started yanking at the gauze-and-tape bandage that covered the puncture wound in her thigh.

"What are you doing?" Cole reached out as if to stop her. Linda ripped the dressing from her skin with a quick jerk. They both stared at her leg. There was no sign of a wound at all.

Linda looked up at Cole. "I think the break is better too," she said quickly, bending to the task of releasing the Velcro straps that held the brace together.

"Wait," Cole cautioned, stepping around to the President's side to help her. "Sit down first. Then we'll check."

Linda sat with Cole's assistance and placed her leg on the coffee table. Together they undid the straps. Cole pulled off the brace and Linda unraveled the elastic bandages. In a minute her broken leg was bare.

Linda reached out and ran her hands down her leg, rubbing the area just below her knee. "There's no pain at all."

Cole reached out. "May I?" he asked. Linda nodded. Cole took her right foot, noticing the electricity that flowed between them the moment he touched her. Gently he lifted her right ankle. "Does that hurt?"

"Not at all."

Cole grabbed her right calf with his other hand and pushed gently down on her foot. "How about that?"

Linda leaned out and put a hand over Cole's. "It's healed," she said, a slight smile conveying both puzzlement and relief.

"How?"

Linda's eyes lost their focus in an instant, as if his question had ignited a firestorm of recollection that surged across her awareness, as if Cole were a hypnotist who'd just snapped his fingers.

Her head started to loll slowly forward. Alarmed, Cole put out a hand to stop her. Before he could touch her, Linda jerked her head back like she'd been struck. Frightened and disoriented, she looked around the room as though it were filled with wasps. She drew back her hand to ward her face. "The bugs," she whispered, trembling. Her eyes searched the air.

Cole pulled back on his haunches. "What bugs, Linda?"

The President looked at Cole as though unsure who he was or why he was there, her eyes clouded with forgotten encounters and half-remembered secrets. She frowned, started to speak, stopped, then closed her eyes and breathed deeply. After a few moments her face relaxed. Her frown dissipated like a passing storm. When she opened her eyes again they were clear and more focused. She managed a weak smile. "I think that's what those moths were," she said at last. "I think they were here." She pointed toward the sky.

"You're fucking kidding me..." Cole's jaw dropped and he rose slowly, staring out the window behind the sofa. The pasture had lit up suddenly like a stadium.

Linda glanced over her shoulder to watch as the lights flickered back out, returning the farm to darkness. She turned to face Cole, smiling with encouragement. "Would you take me outside please?" she said, her voice shaded with meanings that Cole could not decipher.

"Outside?" asked Cole. The disbelief on his face was almost comic.

Linda's smile broke apart into a short laugh. "It'll be okay, Cole. There's something I want to show you."

Cole returned her laughter with a frown. He didn't know what to do. Outside were strange lights and red eyes and alien creatures. He didn't understand it, and it scared him. But the President asked him to trust her. There was something about this warm, strong woman that could not be denied. "Okay," he said with a heavy swallow. "Let's do it."

The President rose, pulled up her sweatpants, and stepped slowly toward the door, testing her leg. Satisfied that it was whole and hale, she took Cole's hand and pulled him eagerly into the night.

Cole pushed through the gate by the barn and into the star-lit pasture. The family's horse, Fanny, a black Welsh pony almost invisible in the night, met them with a snort and a stamping of hooves. The goats and sheep shifted in their stalls but did not emerge. Cole reached out and patted the horse's neck, nuzzling her with soft words of comfort, as much for himself as for her. He looked up to find Linda walking steadily to the pasture's center, searching the sky as she picked her way across the uneven ground. Stepping away from the sense of protection he felt with the horse, Cole marched out to join the President. He stopped beside her and matched her gaze. The sky above was dark and sharp, the stars dazzling in their clarity. The sliver of moon had long since set.

They watched for a full minute, letting their eyes adjust to the night. After a while Cole noticed how some of the stars blinked out, stayed out for a time, then winked back to life. Whole groups of stars flashed in and out in unison. After a moment, Cole understood. "Oh my God," he muttered.

He turned to the President at his side, whispered harshly. "What the hell have you brought here?" In the starlight he could just make out Linda's face. What he saw there was deeply disturbing. Awe, and fear, longing, even love, had gathered in her soul and were welling up through her eyes.

He turned back to scan the sky. Overhead was a swarm of objects, huge ovals and discs and triangular shapes, black against black, moving slowly and randomly across the sky, blotting out the stars as they moved. There must have been twenty or more. Their immensity moved him profoundly, as if their massive presences were tugging on the fibers of his heart.

Linda spoke into the night. "They are the Life, Cole. They have followed me since I left the ranch yesterday. They come from very far away. And they do not seem to want the people of this planet to know that they exist."

"At least not all of us," Cole said.

"Not all," Linda agreed.

"Will they hurt us?" asked Cole, peering up into the sky, his eyes wide. The objects overhead looked to him like a frenzy of sharks waiting impatiently for his boat to sink. Some swam over his house, as if they could smell the blood of his children in their bedrooms just below. His heart skipped with alarm. He almost shouted out. And yet he did not. Below his conscious awareness there was something else, something unexpected, something he could not put into words, something that is known only when one falls into the dark, dangerous ocean of the unknown: in the presence of the predator, the prey is reminded that it is alive. And that reminder is precious beyond reckoning.

"I don't think so, no," Linda answered, glancing at Cole. "They won't hurt us as long as they need us."

"Need us?" Cole did not like the sound of that.

The President exhaled slowly and deeply and tilted her head back once again to scan the sky, eyes wide with expectation.

"What are they trying to do?" asked Cole. "Need us for what?"

Linda opened her mouth to explain, but was interrupted when the ships overhead flared as one, bursting forth with light and joy and music so rich and so full it was as though a host of angels had suddenly appeared to sing the glories of God. An image formed in Linda's mind, of a French fry hovering before her, touching her forehead. Absently she reached up to swat it away. Then the image and the music and the UFOs fell away to darkness and quiet, leaving her momentarily deaf and blind. Staggering, she reached out to grab Cole's hand for support, biting her lip against the tears that burbled unbidden from her heart. Her hand trembled.

"I don't know," she whispered at last.

## 5.7

The singers held their final note, their arms thrust up and out, while the music rose skyward through its concluding measures. It ended with a crash of cymbals and the actors bent low in unison in an exaggerated bow. Linda stood and clapped enthusiastically. As one the troupe stood straight and filed off the stage. The stage lights dimmed and flickered out as the house lights came up with a distant clunk. Linda sat back in her chair, a huge smile smeared across her face.

How long had it gone on? She had no idea. Hours, it felt like, judging from her sore bottom. Hours in which they had sung and danced and told her the story of the Life, complete with the stilted acting and botched cues one might expect from a high school production. And now she knew their tale: how the Life had come from a dying planet that was called, simply, Home, a planet dying because "our" galaxy was consuming "theirs" in a cosmic collision so vast it was beyond comprehension; how, traveling across the light-years, they had searched for a new place to live, finding no suitable habitat until they had chanced upon the Earth almost eighty years ago; how their arrival had triggered an interstellar war with a race of evil, exploitive aliens who had long ago assumed ownership of the Earth; how the Life had been working with the human governments of the world since that time to make it possible for them to live with the humans, slowly changing their bodies to better handle the peculiar atmosphere and gravity of this planet, using genetic materials from humans to transform themselves into a race that could walk amongst us as equals, though it was clear that their abilities and technology put them far ahead of us in many ways; how humans were helping the Life in exchange for their help, in return, in ridding themselves of their evil alien overlords, and in solving the myriad energy, resource, and environmental problems that were upon them. It all made such perfect sense to Linda that she was not upset in the least when she heard how the American government had given permission to the Life to conduct their genetic projects in secret, abducting humans and performing experiments on them as though they were rats in a cage. It was Jon who had spoken of that. Jon. It didn't even occur to her, until later, that the language spoken on stage was not of this Earth. Yet she'd understood perfectly what had been said.

Linda heard footsteps behind her and turned. There was Rice, walking slowly toward her down the carpeted aisle. His steps were uneven and erratic, his face hard and flat, his eyes dead. He stopped at the end of Linda's row. "Come with me," he said, more like a robot than a man. He turned and started back up the aisle.

Linda looked toward the stage, hoping to see Jon, finding only darkness and silence. She rose and followed Rice, her body subtly buzzing. She could feel the workings of every individual cell. Something had struck her like a mallet strikes a gong and had left her ringing. Her outrage at Rice had ceased to matter. As had her fears. As had her expectations. She followed Rice with simple curiosity and openness, as if, having been hit by a truck, she was walking now in the land of the dead, stunned, but ready to meet the gods. She stopped at the back of the auditorium, tossed one final glance at the darkened stage, then turned to watch as Rice pushed into the hallway. On a small stand at the door was a stack of programs. Without a thought she placed her copy on top and then pressed through the double doors. Immediately her nose and eyes were assaulted by the rich, greasy smells and bright lights of a McDonald's restaurant.

Rice was nowhere to be seen. Without conscious volition, as though swept along by a tide far stronger than her own will, Linda took her place in line: three people back from the counter. An aching nostalgia filled her heart as she scanned the room. The dining area was small and cramped, brightly lit by overhead fluorescents, the tables plastic and metal, the floor old linoleum tile, black and white in a checkerboard pattern. Outside, two giant yellow arches came down from above the store and plunged into the sidewalks at the front corners, one right in front of an old Chevy Nomad. This was a McDonald's of forty or fifty years ago. Linda guessed that there wasn't one like this still standing anywhere in the world.

The line moved forward and Linda turned to focus on the menu. The counter before her was stainless steel, small, with two antique cash registers on top. The menu offered only hamburgers, cheeseburgers, french fries, soft drinks and shakes, all at ridiculously low prices. Linda wondered what she should order. All around her were people out of the past, young women with their hair piled high, young men with their jeans fit tight. None gave her so much as a glance. It didn't seem to matter that she was their President. They didn't know her.

The customer before her grabbed his bags and headed off, leaving Linda to confront the cheerful young brunette behind the counter. Linda opened her mouth to speak but the girl cut her off. "You're order's all set," she said, turning to grab a tray from the shelf behind her. She slid it toward the President with a sunny grin. On it was a cheeseburger, an orange drink, and a regular fries.

"Don't I need to...?" asked Linda, fumbling in her pockets for some cash.

The brunette smiled even wider, shaking her head and pointing out into the dining area. "All taken care of, ma'am," she said.

Linda followed her gesture. The girl had indicated what looked like a tiny monk sitting alone at a table near the door, his face buried in a copy of the *Washington Post*. Linda turned to ask the girl a question but she was already busy with another customer. With a sigh of inevitability, Linda picked up her tray and headed across the dining room.

She put her tray on the old man's table and took the seat across from him. The little man lowered his paper and stared at her with huge teardrop eyes, black and fluid: the eyes of an insect, or a demon, shining like hot tar and patent leather and deep space. He folded his paper neatly and placed it on the table before him, then scratched absently at the huge bald dome of his misshapen head with the long, white claws of his four-fingered hand. "Hey Linda," he said, "I'm Spud. What's shakin'?"

Linda looked around the restaurant, expecting some reaction to this creature in their midst. But the others acted as though nothing were amiss. She closed her eyes, wondering at her own response. She could see that there was terror in her pounding heart. And rage. She knew that her body wanted to get up and run away as fast as it could. But none of that seemed to matter. Her feelings were cut off from her willpower, locked away in a glass-walled vault for which she had no key, and replaced with the gentle reassurance that everything was just fine, it was all exactly as it should be, and she should just stay calm and know that nobody wanted to hurt her and that soon she would be back home, safe and sound.

Spud picked up the half-eaten hamburger before him and nibbled at its edge with his incision of a mouth. Then he crinkled that mouth slightly upwards at the ends, as if attempting a smile. He scrunched his tiny, vestigial nose. "I'm a regular here," he said. He nodded his permission, indicating the President's food.

Linda felt suddenly ravenous and reached out to unwrap her cheeseburger. The rich odor leapt into her nose as she took a bite. Nothing had ever tasted so glorious. She took a second bite, and a third, then started to unfold her napkin. There was a blot of mustard on the corner of her mouth.

"Permit me, Mrs. President." Spud reached out and dabbed the mustard away with a long, tan, leathery finger. He wiped his finger on his garment, some sort of rough, brown fabric, like the robe of a medieval friar. "I assume you have some questions?" He leaned over to sip from his soft drink without lifting it.

Linda couldn't help but stare as she spoke. "Questions? Jeesh," she finally said. "Yeah I've got questions. Where the hell are we?" She indicated the restaurant around her with a wave of the arm.

Spud leaned back in his chair, stretched his arms over his head, and gave the President what looked like the wink of a bullfrog, the eye folding backward into the skull, the skin of the forehead bulging out like a balloon. Linda felt a shard of memory poke her from the inside, looked away, took a long sip through her straw. "McDonald's," said Spud, hoiking his clavicles as if it were obvious.

Linda nodded. Oh. She knew that none of this made any sense at all, that none of it could really be happening, that she was being jerked around like a dog on a short leash. But those thoughts were playing happily behind the same thick glass wall through which she could not feel. On this side of the glass everything was great.

And Spud wasn't really speaking, was he? He made a giggling noise now and then, and moved his lips slightly from time to time. But he wasn't really forming words. Wasn't really talking. The words were just in Linda's head. Linda looked down at the paper that Spud had been reading. On the front page was a bold headline : TRAVIS RE-ELECTED. A paper that had not yet been written. She took another bite of her cheeseburger.

"And Rice?" asked Linda, chewing. She hadn't seen the red-haired agent since right after the play.

"Waiting patiently for you in the parking lot like a good boy," said Spud.

"So, why are you telling me all this?" she asked with her mouth full. She motioned back toward the auditorium she'd just left with a wave of her hand. "What was that all about?"

"Need a favor," said Spud. "Thought you might be able to help." The creature pointed towards Linda's tray. "You gonna eat those fries?"

Linda shook her head, pushed the tray toward Spud. "Help yourself."

"Thanks."

Linda stuffed the last bite of cheeseburger into her mouth, followed that with a swallow of orange soda. Outside, a family hurried to their car, the father fishing in his pocket for his keys, the mother carrying a large white bag. A pair of pre-teen girls, both with long blonde ponytails, carried the drinks. They climbed in and drove off. Linda leaned back in her chair, brushed crumbs from her shirt, and closed her eyes. The afternoon sun was creeping up her leg, warming her, soothing her. She felt herself drift away for a moment, tried to shake it off, then wiggled to get more comfortable and closed her eyes again. That family, she thought as she fell asleep. It was hers. Though it could never have happened in this time, she had just watched herself as a girl, and her parents, and her best friend Keeley, drive off down the road.

## 5.8

"When I woke up, I was in the back seat of that damned Jeep, with Rice up front at the wheel and Bob on the passenger side. Rice didn't say much, just some smart-ass crap about how Spud and I were gonna be best buddies and all. Bob didn't even turn around. They drove me back to the White House, just dropped me off at the gate like a taxi, if you can believe it. Nobody said a damn thing. I couldn't even get the guards at the gate to admit that there was anything out of the ordinary." Linda stopped to massage her neck. She'd been talking non-stop since they'd gone back into the house and her voice had grown threadbare around the edges. She looked up at Cole. "Could I get some more tea, Cole? Please?"

"Sure." Cole rose and walked out to the kitchen.

"Mom was there when I got back," the President said, loud enough so that Cole could hear her.

"What did she say?" Cole called back.

"She didn't know a thing. She'd had a wonderful time with Bess Engle. Hadn't even heard about Bickle."

"What exactly happened to Bickle?" asked Cole. "I remember something about a car and a bridge."

Linda nodded. "Yeah. He drove off the Douglass Bridge. They say he was dead before he hit the water. I hope so, I guess. I mean, God, drowning in a car.... But why he should be dead before he hit the water was never quite explained. And the funny thing was, Steven Bickle hadn't driven in years. Didn't own a car, didn't have a license. Nobody could explain just why he was behind the wheel that day. And nobody had any idea where he was headed. It was a mess."

"So what did you tell your Mother?" Cole asked from the kitchen. He walked carefully back to the living room carrying two cups of tea.

Linda took her cup and sipped it. "Nothing."

"Nothing? You didn't tell your mother?"

"No." The President raised a hand in self-defense. "I wasn't ... I wasn't myself. It was like ... some sort of drug or something. A side effect. I spent the rest of that day thinking that Rice was a pretty good guy. And how nice it had been to see Jon again. And what a great cheeseburger they used to make in the old days. I wasn't thinking. I mean, Jesus, I hate McDonald's. Telling Mom what had happened never even crossed my mind. It would have been like telling her about my trip to the mailbox. She was off to some dinner in Detroit and I had a meeting with the Ambassador from Denmark and a commencement address to finish."

"But this all wore off," urged Cole.

Linda nodded but did not speak at once. She stared down at the cup in her hands. When she raised her head again there was a tear streaking down her cheek. "Spud came to me that night. Woke me up with a slap to the face. Scared the shit out of me. Said 'touch my robe' and I did and zoom we were off like Scrooge and the Ghost, soaring over the city. My guts felt like they were going to fall right out." Linda dropped her head, weeping quietly now, tears spilling down her face.

Cole came and sat next to her. She took his hand and squeezed it firmly. "Keep going," he said softly.

Linda spoke through her tears. "He took me on a people hunt. I watched as some of his buddies invaded a home and took a small child. God, Cole, a little girl. Hardly older than Grace. Took her from her bed in the middle of the night and up into their ship. Strapped her to a table and poked and prodded her, stuck her with things. And all the time ... she didn't make a sound. But her eyes ... they were so full of pain and fear and they were asking me, 'Why? Why are you letting them do this to me? Why?' They took this long needle thing and shoved it right up her nose, hard, til it broke through fucking bone. Put some sort of electronic tagging device up in her brain. And I just stood there, Cole. Paralyzed. Not able to move. Or talk. Or even turn my head. Just watching."

Linda stopped and tried to bring her sobbing under control. Cole took the tea from her trembling hands and placed it on the end table. The President breathed deeply and went on. "He took me all over the country. Showed me team after team of these creatures abducting humans from their beds, their cars, right from their office cubicles. Bringing them into their ships and terrifying them. I asked Spud how they had the right. He said I was projecting. Asked me how I had the right and said that I had to help."

Linda's voice had evened out, and the tears had stopped. She took a tissue from the box Cole offered and wiped her eyes. "He took me to their ... facilities. Gigantic installations. Mostly underground. Some out under the ocean. A couple up in space. One right under God-damned Washington D.C.! All full of these creatures working on God knows what. And right beside them humans, checking out their ships and testing their machines. Like we'd sold our souls for some high-tech toys." Linda blew her nose into the tissue. "Fucking idiot."

"Who?"

"Spud. He never should have shown me that girl. His mistake. I might have gone along. He never should have shown me that girl."

Cole handed the President another tissue. "Did he ever say what the favor was?" he asked.

Linda stopped, looked away to think, then shook her head. "Not that I recall," she said, perplexed. "And the gum was gone from my pocket when I checked later."

Something thumped on the floor above them. Cole stiffened, then took off, running up the stairs, tossing out a strangled shout as he ran. "Grace!"

# Chapter Six

## 6.1

"You wanna come with me and see for yourself?" Bob spiked a limp french fry and shoved it into her mouth. It was pasty and cold but the salt was wonderful.

Rice, sitting across from her in a rumpled suit, his eyes red and crusty from being awakened in the middle of the night, shook his head. His stack of pancakes sat untouched before him, the syrup congealed. He looked around the cafeteria, acting as if it mattered whether anybody heard what he said. Bob followed his gaze. The room was almost empty, save for the pair of guards at the corner table near the salad bar. She smirked at the General's precautions. Like they needed more soldiers down *here*. She looked back to Rice. The overhead fluorescents, combined with his two-day growth of beard and his lack of sleep, gave his face a gray-green sheen that made him look like a plague victim.

Rice reached out for his cup. "You know it makes me sick."

"Oh, right. I forgot you had that little ... problem." Bob laughed, running her fingers through her long, honey hair. She knew that Rice's travels were usually followed by a couple of days of puking. She didn't care. She hated Rice, and any chance she could get to let him know that was worth taking.

Rice sipped his coffee but did not respond.

"You think I'm lying?" asked Bob. Grabbing the ketchup from the cheap plastic condiment holder, she proceeded to cover her fries. "You think I'm playing an angle?" She reached for the shaker and added more salt.

Rice smiled. "I'm just surprised to hear that the great Roberta Reese, Master of the Universe, Demon extraordinaire, has been knocked out of the sky." He flashed her a look of sarcastic disdain, pointed at her plate. "You and your salt," he said with a shake of his head. He pointed through the ceiling, through the hundreds of feet of rock overhead, to the heavens above. "So, whatcha got up there, Bobby-girl? Ol' Zeus up to his tricks again? Or maybe you fucked with Jesus H and the Big Guy this time."

Bob stuffed another fry into her mouth and stared at Rice, trying to decide what to say. "That's what I like about you, Rice," she said at last. "You keep your balls in your mouth so you can always find them."

Rice reddened, slid his chair back to leave. "Well," he said, rising, "you let me know if you need me to hold your hand."

Bob reached out, seized Rice by the wrist. "Wait!" She let go and Rice sat back down.

"What?"

"I don't know who or what it is." Bob looked down at her plate, then up at Rice. She knew that the only way to work Rice was to play into his bullshit. She flashed a look of helpless need across her clear, oval face. "It's not like anything I've ever dealt with. Very small, and it doesn't seem to be very fast, but it's got some field around it, some force I've never felt before. It's following the Prez everywhere she goes, and I can't get close without it trying to push me away."

Rice smiled.

"It's getting stronger, boss. I need your help."

Leaning back in his chair, Rice let out a huge sigh. Perhaps this was one of those times when he had to go look for himself. Mork had gone dormant and Spud had disappeared and the General was chewing his ass on a regular basis. He was tired of flying blind. But the alternative – a full day of vomiting – seemed an awful price to pay. And could he afford to be so incapacitated right now? He looked at Bob. Her hair was a mess. And there was a stain of what looked like real fear in her eyes. He hadn't thought her capable of that. Leaning forward, he picked up his coffee and took a sip. He cradled the cup against his chest. "I'll make you a deal," he said at last.

Bob's eyes tightened. "What sort of deal?"

"You try again today. As often as you can. Take Mr. Random with you. Or Alice. Or even Mary if she'll go. See what a couple of you can do. If it doesn't work, I'll join you tonight."

Bob nodded. It was all she'd wanted. He was an asshole, but there was no denying it; if you needed something killed, anything, then Rice was the man for the job.

Across from her, Rice stood again, his face flush with self-satisfaction. He smiled down at Bob. "I'm off. We're tracking down all of Ma's known contacts in the Northeast. Maybe we can beat her there ... wherever she's going."

Bob licked the salt from her finger. "Good luck."

Rice turned to leave, then stopped. There was Phelps in the doorway.

"Mr. Phelps?"

"Dude!" said Phelps, stepping into the room, "They found the car!"

## 6.2

"Where's Grace?" Cole's voice was loud and a bit angry. His nose twitched.

Emily grabbed her book bag. "I don't know. She was getting dressed last I saw her."

Cole walked to the bottom of the stairs and shouted. "Grace!" There was no response. He took a step up. "Grace?" He looked back at Emily. "Go ahead and get in the car." He headed up the stairs.

Emily lifted her backpack onto her shoulder, grabbed her brown paper bag half-full of DVDs, and stuffed a piece of cold toast into her mouth. She pushed through the door and stepped out onto the porch, the morning air cold and moist around her. She glanced at the car. The President stood by the back door of the Subaru, dressed in the jeans and red cotton sweater her mother used to wear, a bundle of blankets and a pillow in her arms, her green bag slung over her shoulder. Next to Linda stood Iain. He was showing her his new MarioKart game on his DSX3. Emily rolled her eyes and started down the steps.

Seeing his sister approach, Iain scrambled around the car to take the front passenger seat.

"Hey!" Emily ran forward, attempting to stop him but dropping her bag. DVDs spilled out onto the gravel.

"Jerk!" she spat, kneeling to pick up her movies.

"Idiot." Iain plopped down into the front seat.

"Hey!" It was Cole, walking out toward the car with an old sweater in his hand. Grace was at his side, her head bowed low, seemingly asleep on her feet.

"What?" Iain protested. "I was just—!"

Emily lifted her bag and stepped up to the car, jerking open the right rear door. She crawled in behind her brother, managing to kick the back of his seat more than once. Cole and Grace circled around to the driver's side and Cole opened the other back door. Grace just stood there so he picked her up and sat her in the center seat, next to her sister. Grace looked around as if in a dream as her father bent down to buckle her seatbelt. Satisfied, Cole tugged a latch by the headrest, pulled the rear seatback forward a bit, and stuffed the old sweater in behind to keep the mechanism from re-latching. Grace leaned back. Her eyes fell shut immediately.

"What's wrong with Grace?" asked Emily, now seated with her bag on her lap.

"She's just very tired, sweetie," answered Cole, trying to sound like he meant it. Cole shut the door and turned to face the President, who waited patiently at the hatchback door, watching. For a brief moment he imagined kissing her. He backed up a step, struck by the absurdity of the image, frowning as if he could stuff the thought back into unconsciousness with his eyebrows.

"You okay?" she asked.

The open concern in her voice and the incongruence of his secret thoughts almost undid him. He was about to abandon his own children when they most needed him and Linda Travis was asking about *his* well-being? And he wanted to *kiss* her? He did not deserve such care and support. He was leaving his kids. Nodding stiffly to hold back tears, he opened the hatchback and slid back the retractable cargo cover. Linda tossed in the blankets and pillow, then put a hand on Cole's shoulder. "She's going to be okay," she said.

Cole swirled to face her, anger flaring to shield the guilt and fear. The President held up a hand in defense, then motioned toward the kids with her head. "They're not going to hurt your children, Cole."

Cole laughed without humor. "Who're we talking about here, Linda? The bug-eyed aliens or the secret government agents?" He looked up at the bright morning sky. Not so much as a cloud. He turned back to Linda. "Let's remember that you're on the run, Mrs. President. It's not like you're in control of this."

Linda sighed and nodded, glancing down at the ground. "Yeah," she admitted softly. "I guess you're right." She raised her face to his and looked him right in the eyes. "Thank you, Cole," she said. "You're a remarkable man."

Cole flushed, caught off-guard by her acknowledgement. She'd taken his anger and given him back more kindness. He motioned to the cargo compartment, as if he could bury his discomfort in a bit of legerdemain. "I unlatched the back seat so you could push your way out in an emergency," he said, twisting his face nervously. "You ready?"

"Let's do it." Ducking her head, Linda crawled onto the pile of blankets, checking to make sure her hands and feet were clear. "Okay," she said. She smiled courageously, defiantly, as if, in control of the situation or not, she could still do that.

Cole pulled the cover closed and lowered the hatchback, latching it firmly with a solid whump. He stepped around to the driver's door and opened it, forcing a smile to his own face before taking his seat.

"Everybody strapped in and ready for blast-off?" he called out, like he always did.

"Yes," the kids replied in rote, Grace's voice notably absent.

"Good enough," he said, completing the ritual. Cole inserted the key in the ignition, hoping that his kids wouldn't ask any more questions, wondering if his answers were the truth. The night before, when Grace had fallen out of bed, she hadn't even awakened. Nor had she stirred when he lifted her up and put her back under her covers.

He hadn't thought much of it at the time. When he went back down to finish his conversation with the President – with Linda – he'd found that she had already taken a couple of her high-powered pills and was fast on her way to sleep herself. With a promise to figure things out in the light of a new day, she was out. Cole went to bed shortly thereafter, once he checked the locks on all the doors and windows. He'd called for Dennis, who'd gone missing shortly after those eyes had peered through the window. Cole had even screwed up his courage enough to step outside and look at the sky. But the huge black objects were gone. The night was quiet and cold and Dennis, who was afraid of his own shadow, let alone strange people and monsters and UFOs, was nowhere to be seen.

The remainder of the night had been quiet, but Cole had hardly slept. Alert to every snippet of sound, he had achieved little more than a hovering doze, an endless treading of water in the dark ocean of sleep. When dawn slammed through his eyelids it felt as if just moments had passed since he'd closed them. He woke with the vague memory of a dream tickling his mind. It quickly evaporated. Something about a Frenchman on a train.

Grace had slept through the alarm clock and had to be awakened by her sister. And she had fallen asleep at the breakfast table, dropping her toast peanut-butter-side down on the dining room floor. She barely spoke. When Cole announced that the kids would not be going to school, that they would go spend the day at their grandfather's house, Iain and Emily had been full of questions. Grace only smiled and closed her eyes. "Good," was all she'd said.

Cole started the engine and put the car in gear, glancing over at Iain with a faint smile. "You okay, Dad?" Iain asked.

Cole nodded, touching the gas. The car moved out onto the gravel drive, propelling them all into a future that he could not divine. After breakfast he'd attempted an explanation. Iain and Emily were too old, and too damned smart, for him to try to hide things. He knew they could see right through him: see his fear, his exhaustion, his confusion. So he'd told them what he could: that the President of the United States was in trouble; that there were some very mysterious forces involved; that she needed his help in getting to a friend's home in the Northeast Kingdom; that he'd be taking them to their Grandfather's for the day, while he gave her what help he could; and that he'd be very, very careful. The older kids had been unusually helpful, packing up their things and bringing a bag full of items they knew Grace would want. Grace had fallen back to sleep.

"Dad!" called Emily from the back seat. "What about Dennis?"

Damn! He'd forgotten the dog. "Did you guys see him?" he asked. Neither of them had.

"I'll bet you twenty bucks he's up at Jake and Cat's house again," he said, hoping to satisfy them. "He's such a chicken." He forced a chuckle. "He just couldn't get used to having the President of the United States in his house."

"But he liked her, Dad!" answered Emily.

"Tell you what," said Cole, knowing that his daughter would never give this one up. "I'll get your Grandpa to come over and pick him up later. After we get you guys settled in."

"But Dad!"

Iain turned to his sister. "There's no time," he said, his voice both stronger and more gentle than Cole would have expected. Iain nodded toward the back of the car where the President was hidden. "They have to get going."

Emily scowled, then tapped her father on the shoulder. "You promise?"

"I promise."

Cole made his way out to the main road, thinking back on the morning as he drove. Linda had stood in his bedroom doorway. It was her knock that had awakened him. She'd asked if there was a car she could borrow, but the thought of her just driving away without him had grabbed his gut. There was no way he could allow that. Sure, Ruth's old Toyota still ran, though with the hard economy Cole had done little to maintain it. And with her leg healed, Linda could now continue on as she had planned, as if nothing had happened. But something *had* happened. The President had revealed to him a world he'd never imagined: a world fraught with dangers that threatened his children; and a world filled with wonders that drew him toward them, even as he pushed away in fear. How could he just sit back and let others face this danger? These were *his* children.

And how could he resist the adventure that stretched out before him like a trail of blank pages? He was off script now, for sure. Ruth was the one that had known where she was going, and she was dead. It was time to find his own right work in the world. He could feel that now. He was no farmer. He sure as hell wasn't a painter. He didn't know what he was. But he knew he was just running on fumes at Harmony, once again playing out the story somebody else had written for him. Even though it meant leaving his kids, he knew he would always regret it if he did not see this through.

And there was more, a piece Cole could only begin to think out loud. Just as the Little Prince had done with the fox, in the short, intense time they'd spent together, Linda Travis had *tamed* him. Her problems were now his problems. If she had to go somewhere, Cole Thomas would be the one to accompany her. He was not at all clear exactly who or what they were facing, and he was scared as hell, but he was certain of this: he would do everything in his power to protect this woman.

But while he might endanger himself to oppose this threat, he would first take his kids out of the line of fire. He would leave them with their grandfather before he did anything else. Cole chuckled to himself as they headed toward his father's house, the car now gaining speed on the paved road. The President thought she had problems, with her aliens and her crazy government agents. At least she didn't have to deal with Ben Thomas.

## 6.3

Though Ben's house was less than a mile away as the crow flies, the task of getting the kids there required a three-mile drive on the main roads. Sobered and cautioned by the President's story, and certainly alerted by the events of the previous night, Cole was nevertheless surprised to see the flashing lights up ahead as he neared the intersection of Gray Mountain and Boston Spoke. His guts turned immediately to gazpacho. Christ! How'd they find that car so fast? Frantic, he searched for a turn-off, but his car delivered him in moments to a line of stopped traffic three cars deep, a surprising number given how few cars traveled this route these days, with gas so spendy. There was no turning away. Not without being noticed.

Cole expelled a huge sigh of fear. "Don't say a thing, guys," he said, not daring to look at his kids. Up ahead, Ken Fairly, the younger and slimmer of Hindrance's two policemen, waved the cars through with an orange-tipped traffic wand, stopping to speak to each driver. Anticipating his turn next, anxious to appear normal, Cole lowered his window. He knew Ken from the community substance-abuse prevention meetings they both attended every month. The car before him pulled ahead. Cole inched up to the officer.

"Mornin', Cole," said Ken. "Looks like you're getting a late start this morning." He bent down to look inside. "Hey, kids."

"Watcha got here, Ken?" asked Cole, hoping to cut off any response his children might make, hoping any nervousness he exhibited would be chalked up to their running late, hoping Ken wouldn't notice the new dent in his fender. Just up the road a tow truck was winching the President's battered Cutlass from its hiding place in the bushes. Beyond the tow truck sat two state cruisers, their lightbars broadcasting both warning and excitement. Across the road sat another state cruiser, Ken's local black & white, and a shiny black Lincoln. Two state troopers stood by the tow truck, watching.

"Don't really know, Cole," said Ken. "I just got here. Cyndi and Marissa found this car. Just before dawn. Saw the dome light. Tommy was on then but he's gone home now."

Cole took a deep breath and smiled, motioning toward the action. "You sure got a lotta uniforms here for a car in the ditch." He forced a knowing chuckle. "Things getting too slow in the police biz?"

Ken shook his head, glancing nervously over his shoulder. He poked his head into the car, speaking in confidential tones. "I, uh, can't really say, Cole, ya know? It's big. That's all I know. It's something big. You heard about the President, right?"

Ken suddenly straightened and took a step back. A tall, thin red-haired man in a slick gray suit was approaching, stepping stiffly around the tow truck. He headed right for Cole's car, a big smile on his face, as if Ken were an old friend. "What do we have here, officer?" he asked. His tone was expectant, his delivery formal.

Ken cleared his throat, obviously nervous. "Just my friend Cole and his kids, Mr. Edmonton." He motioned toward Iain. "His boy and mine play on the soccer team."

The man stepped up to the car, displacing the policeman, and offered his hand. Cole took it. "Nice to meet you, Cole," said Edmonton. His smile was warm and genuine, his handshake solid. "Really nice." He leaned to look into the car, catching Iain's eye. "And you too, son. You're a soccer player, are you?"

Iain waved slightly and looked down at his feet. "Yeah," he muttered.

Edmonton noticed the girls in the back and smiled even more broadly. "Oh, and nice to meet you girls as well." Emily just stared, giving nothing away. Grace was asleep. Winking at Emily, Edmonton withdrew his head. With a quick step to his left, he leaned out over the front windshield and starting drawing in the dirty haze on the glass with his finger: a circle the size of a tennis ball bisected by an inverted capital L. Finishing, the man rapped three times on the glass with his knuckles, grinned broadly, then started to leave. A dozen steps from the car he turned and waved. "See you later," he said with a smile. He turned and walked away.

"Ken?" asked Cole, perplexed and wary, watching as Edmonton disappeared behind the tow truck. An old blue pickup pulled up behind them.

"Like I said, Cole. Something pretty big." The policeman noticed the pickup and started waving his flashlight. Cole eased the car forward, an automatic response to the signaling wand. Skirting the tow truck, he saw no sign of the red-haired man in the slick gray suit.

## 6.4

It was all Linda could do to keep from screaming out. Edmonton? That was fucking Rice! Her heart hammered and her guts gritted and her legs raged with the need to kick something. How had that motherfucker found her so quickly? And now... Jesus! Cole! And the kids! Scrunching her face tight, she worked to control her breathing. Though every bit of her body wanted to kick the door open and run, she knew that she had to stay silent and listen. Somehow these poor people had already been noticed. It was too late to leave them out of it. Too late.

The aliens must have sold her out.

Rice's voice cut right through the kids and the seat cushions and the engine noise, stabbing her repeatedly as she lay folded and crumpled in the cargo compartment, unable to defend herself. She could see him in her mind, standing at Cole's window, his eyes all over the kids, his fucking smirk soiling them with his smug disdain. She heard him greet Emily and she knew, in that moment, that if he tried to hurt that child she would reach right through the seat and strangle him where he stood.

Emily did not respond. Linda held her breath. Three rapid knocks sounded on what she supposed was the front windshield. Rice said something she could not make out. Cole spoke. Then the policeman spoke. The car began to move. Linda let out her breath. For some reason, they were being allowed to pass through. As if maybe Rice had found her car but did not yet know about Cole. Linda felt a spark of hope catch hold in her heart. Was it possible that the aliens had not sold her out after all?

No. That was stupid. Wishful thinking. Linda Travis would not get caught hoping again. But then what had just happened?

Linda thought furiously as the car picked up speed. She had to get to Keeley. That's the only plan she had, as wild and meager as it was. She couldn't let Cole and his kids get dragged into this any further. Not these beautiful children. She just couldn't. She had to get to Keeley. Keeley owed her.

If only she hadn't gone into the ditch. She'd be there already. And poor little Grace would be playing at school right now, instead of lost in ... she couldn't even finish the thought. There was something deeply disturbing to her about Grace's slumber. She did not know what it meant, but she knew that it wasn't right. And she knew that it had something to do with her. Linda sighed. She had to find a way to make the world right again.

Her plan, if she even dared call it that, had come to her the morning after Spud had abducted her. Linda's mind had finally cleared and she could see them all – Rice, Bob, the People, the Life – for what they were: traitors, psychopaths, mobsters, monsters. She was going to stop them. That was her job.

Keeley had been in that high school play. Dancing and singing with the rest. But this was not the Keeley she had last known, the sad, defeated teen with the limp blonde hair. She was older, this Keeley. Brighter of spirit. Stronger. Her eyes glinted once again with that rebellious edge that had immediately enchanted Linda Warren when they first met in fifth grade. Keeley played shortstop and Linda covered first base and they'd become a team of two from there on out. But then Keeley had moved away in their senior year, not long after one of her uncles had been put in jail. Soon thereafter she stopped answering Linda's letters. Linda went off to college and met Earl, married him and moved away. It seemed that Linda and Keeley would be lost from each other forever.

But there she was, onstage, singing and dancing, stronger than ever. It was as if the answer to Linda's predicament was contained right in the question. The President of the United States had begun to plan her escape.

The car made a quick left turn and Linda tensed against the cargo space wall to keep herself from sliding. Not long after that the pavement ended and the sound of tires on gravel filled her ears. The road inclined. After a couple of long curves and a very steep hill the car slowed to a crawl and turned to the left again. Linda heard puddles splashing underneath, more gravel, and tall grass sweeping the underside. The car eased to a stop. The engine went silent.

They were one step closer. And Rice was hot on her trail.

## 6.5

His father was right where Cole expected him: standing, waiting on the concrete stoop like a guard dog on a short chain. The message was "you can't come in," which suited Cole just fine. He'd carry Grace inside and then leave as quickly as possible. The police had found the President's car. They were so close he could feel them watching. Cole had to get Linda out of here as quickly as he could.

Cole stopped behind his father's old Land Cruiser and put his Subaru in park, then turned off the engine. He swung his head around to talk to his kids. "You guys remember what we talked about, right?" he asked.

Iain rolled his eyes but spoke gently. "We got it, Dad."

"You just let me do the talking. After I'm gone, you just repeat what we agreed on and keep everything else to yourself. You know how your grandfather...."

"Dad." Emily grabbed her backpack and opened her door. "We got it."

Cole nodded, glancing at Grace in the rearview mirror. She was still asleep. A small trickle of saliva seeped down from the corner of her slack and heavy mouth. He glanced out at his father, waved perfunctorily, and opened his door.

Iain and Emily got out and collected their things. Cole opened Grace's door and shook her gently. "Grace, honey? Time to wake up."

Grace stirred, opened her eyes for a moment, then closed them again. "I'll need Grandpa to guard me," she mumbled.

"Okay, sweetie. He will." Cole unlatched Grace's seatbelt and pulled her to her feet, then lifted her into his arms. Worried and confused and filled with urgency, Cole carried his youngest to his father's home. Catching up with Iain and Emily, the four of them approached Ben Thomas on the porch, his bantam legs spread wide, his hands on his hips.

"Hey, Dad," said Cole, an awkward attempt at normality that neither of them was buying.

"You mind telling me what the hell this is all about?" asked Ben. At five-foot-nine, with peppered black hair and a deep tan, Ben Thomas looked nowhere near the sixty-nine years he had under his belt. He'd aged like the scratch golfer that he was and still dressed like the banker he'd been. His was a face that allowed for no bullshit. And you just knew that he was the one who determined what bullshit was.

Cole frowned, coming to a stop at the bottom of the steps. He'd never figured out how to handle his father, but he just didn't have time for it today. He was about to retort when Emily stepped forward.

"Hi, Grandpa," she said sweetly.

Ben's hard face softened as he looked down at the kids. "Hey, kiddoes," he said, smiling. He reached around, opening the storm door behind him and swinging it open. "C'mon, in."

"We brought the cribbage board," offered Iain, stepping up to his grandfather's compact, well-appointed and very tidy ranch house.

"Glad to hear it, boss," answered Ben with a chuckle. He reached out to tousle Iain's hair and Iain stopped him with a sideways glance and an index finger in the air, a bit of theater they'd performed hundreds of times. Ben laughed and winked. Iain smiled and followed his sister inside. Ben turned and stepped aside to watch as Cole carried Grace up the steps and through the door. Grace didn't rouse at all.

Cole took Grace down the hallway to the left, past the bathroom and into the bedroom she slept in when they stayed over. Drawing back the covers, he lowered her gently into her bed and pulled off her shoes, then leaned over and kissed her on the forehead. She opened her eyes for a moment, smiling crookedly at her father. Something in her expression caught Cole in the throat and he choked back a sob, whether from love or dread he could not tell.

Grace whispered something that Cole could not quite make out, her voice full of sleep. "Take care of cornfed," it sounded like. She grabbed his hand and squeezed it, then closed her eyes again. "G'bye, Daddy," she muttered, rolling to her side. Cole pulled the covers up and turned to leave. Ben Thomas stood in the bedroom door, watching silently.

Cole pushed past him and back to the living room, where Emily stood waiting and Iain sat with his DSX3. Cole stopped long enough to hug his older children goodbye, then stepped back out onto the stoop and hurried down the steps, his father right behind him. A good thirty feet out into the yard, Cole whirled to face the unavoidable. Ben was right in his face.

"I can't tell you, Dad. It's not—"

"Bullshit you can't tell me, Cole!" Ben's eyes were wire and steel and he used them to get what he wanted. He'd had long decades of practice. "You call me up and tell me you're keeping the kids out of school today and can I watch them and you've gotta go out of town and Grace won't wake up and you can't tell me? Bullshit. Something's off here."

Cole opened his mouth to respond when Ben held up a hand to stop him. Nodding over Cole's shoulder he said, "There's somebody in your car, Cole."

Cole turned to see the Subaru's back seat door swing open. Linda Travis crawled out over the seat, pulled her legs around, and stepped out, straightening her clothes. "Can I help?" she asked.

"You've gotta be fuckin' kiddin' me," said Ben. He looked at Cole, his jaw slack, for once bereft of words. "You gotta be fuckin' kiddin' me," he repeated.

Linda strode forward with all the confidence and power one might expect from a head of state, sweeping aside Ben's steely glare with one of her own. "Nobody's kidding anybody here, Ben," she said, thrusting out her hand for a hearty shake. "I'm in need of a great deal of help. Cole's helping me. And now we need yours. You up for that?" The President rocked back on her heels and crossed her arms. Every inch of her stance conveyed this message: *You don't scare me a bit.*

Ben Thomas looked her up and down, cleared his throat, glanced down at his feet and then looked the President right in the eye. Cole watched, remembering when, as a teenager, he'd witnessed his father buy a new car from the local dealer. He'd seen that little dance before. He'd seen it a million times. And he knew what it meant; his father was calculating his relative position in the situation, assessing his advantage, and figuring out his next move. His father was looking to make a deal. Or a sale. Or a kill. Ben Thomas cleared his throat again and spoke. "Lotta people looking for you right now, Mrs. President."

Linda responded with a derisive laugh. "You don't know the half of it."

"Yeah, well, I guess I don't, Mrs. President," answered Ben, his chin jutting defiantly. "Obviously things are not what they seem." He glanced sidelong at his son. "My boy Cole here sure ain't no gang of terrorists."

"I'd agree with you there, Ben," Linda answered, using his first name like a knife. "Things are not at all what they seem. For instance, you might notice that Cole is not a boy."

Ben smiled, as if in acknowledgement of a worthy opponent. "I'm just watching out for my loved ones, Linda," he said, tossing her first name back at her. He motioned toward the house, reminding them all of the children inside, as if nobody could argue with a man protecting his family. "I'm guessing you're in a shitload of trouble right now, ma'am. More than any of us here is up for. And I'm not too keen on you bringing that trouble to my home. I think you need more help than that. Real help. From the people who's job it is—"

Linda had had enough. She stepped right into Ben Thomas' personal space and cut him off. "Listen to me. You will not threaten me under the guise of protecting your family. You have no idea what's going on here."

Ben took a step backward. "Hold on," he said, hands out in protest.

Linda stepped right back into his space. "I'm calling the bullshit here, Ben Thomas. You think I'm coming in for a loan on a used car? The President of your country is standing right in front of you requesting your help. This is a national security issue the likes of which you cannot even *begin* to imagine. And the futures of those precious children inside are at stake. Now, you gonna get in my way here, Ben? Or are you gonna step up to the plate and take care of your grandkids while Cole and I go see what we can do about all this? 'Cause I'm telling you, Ben: You're right. There's trouble right on my heels. If you don't help us, it's gonna be right on your doorstep."

Linda stopped, her eyes hard, her breath somewhat ragged. Ben stared her down for a moment, then dropped his gaze and retreated another step. The President didn't follow this time. She just stood her ground. Cole held his breath, his eyes focused on a spot between the President and his father, unable to look either of them in the eye. Off in the distance the sound of car tires crunching on gravel intruded into the birdsong and rustle of leaves. Linda twisted her neck to measure the sound, then turned back to Ben. "We gotta get out of here, Ben," she said, her voice tinged with trepidation and need.

Ben looked up again, his eyes now softened with acceptance and respect. "Can you tell me what this is about?" he asked.

The President shook her head, relaxing just a bit. "I can't, Mr. Thomas. I'm sorry. There's simply no time. You're going to have to help without understanding why. Can you do that?"

Ben nodded, scratched his neck. "Yeah."

The front door swung open with a squeal and Emily stepped out onto the stoop. "Don't forget about Dennis," she pleaded.

Cole saw the way out of this. Stepping forward, he grabbed his father and pulled him in for a stiff hug. "We gotta go, Dad," he said into his father's ear. Ben pulled away but Cole kept hold of his shoulders. "We couldn't find Dennis this morning. Can you get somebody to go look for him?"

"Yeah. I can do that."

"Thanks. Try Cat and Jake first. Okay?"

Ben offered a slight smile of acquiescence. "Okay, Cole." He turned to Emily. "We'll find that little mobster, Em," he called out. "Don't you worry." Satisfied, Emily nodded. She glanced at her father, a look of love and fear in her eyes, then stepped back inside. Ben turned to Cole and Linda. "You'd better go."

Cole nodded, then shrugged, tears welling up in his eyes. "I don't know what's wrong with Grace, Dad," he said.

"I'll get the doc over here. Have her checked out." Ben smiled. "She probably just didn't sleep much last night, given the excitement."

Cole smiled back. "Yeah. Maybe. Thanks, Dad."

Linda reached out and took Ben's hand. "Thank you, Mr. Thomas," she said gently. With that she turned and walked quickly to the car, slamming the back door and walking around to the front passenger door instead.

"Don't you think –" Cole called, following. Linda shook her head decisively, opened the door and climbed in. Cole pulled open the driver's door, then glanced back at his father. Ben stood where they had left him, looking both smaller and larger at the same time.

Ben smiled. "You be careful, Cole," he said.

"I will."

Ben nodded. Cole climbed into the car and closed the door. He started the engine and backed up to turn around. With one last wave to his father he put the Subaru into first gear and headed up the drive.

He stopped at the mailbox and twisted toward Linda. "You can't ride up here. There are police all over the place."

"That was Rice," she responded. There was a fatalistic air to her that scared Cole. As if something deep inside of her had been defeated.

"What was Rice?" he asked. "I don't—"

Linda raised a hand to stop him. She motioned down the road, a sad, vague gesture of devastation and bitterness. "Edmonton. The tall red-haired guy that spoke with you. That was Rice. He's here."

Cole's stomach cramped as it sunk. "Fuck."

"Yeah. Fuck."

"How'd he find us?"

The President sighed heavily, glancing up and down the gravel road as if the answer were there. When she turned back to Cole there was a tear on her cheek. "It's possible they found the car and connected it to me. More likely, they sold us out."

"Who?"

"The aliens. The Life. Whatever the fuck. Spud. That's the only way I can think of that Rice could've gotten here so fast. And how he could have known to come talk to you."

"Christ." Cole's thoughts went racing back to his kids. The trouble was already here. Cole pictured Rice at his father's front door, staring in at Iain and Emily, watching Grace as she slept. The images made him shudder. But something was off. "So why did he let me go?" he asked. It didn't add up.

Linda shrugged. "I don't know," she replied. "Sometimes I think it's all just a game to Rice. Maybe he's playing with us. Or maybe he knows less than we fear."

"So what do we do?" he asked.

Linda leaned back and closed her eyes, astounded at her own stupidity. Her escape? Her miraculous healing? Had she actually thought the aliens were helping her? Was that insane or what? The one thing you could count on was that the aliens would follow their own agenda, no matter what. Had she learned nothing? There was no help. She and Cole were on their own. If they were to survive this, it would be due to their own efforts. It was that simple. And that simplicity gave her the strength to go on.

She looked at Cole. The defeat in her eyes had turned to something softer. Acceptance. Resolve. "We get the fuck out of here," she said.

"But what about Rice?"

"We have to draw him away from your kids." Linda opened her door and crawled out of the car, leaning back in to finish the conversation.

Cole nodded. "Yeah. We do."

"So, I think I might know how to do that." Linda closed her door and stepped around to the back of the car to open the hatchback. Cole got out to help. Linda crawled into the cargo compartment, adjusting the pillow and blankets to find what comfort she could. "Just drive north, Cole," she said. "Up to Keeley's place in Eastbound, like I showed you on the map. I'll take care of the rest."

Cole reached up to grab the door handle. The President of the United States was smiling up at him. It looked neither false nor forced, as if she'd found something inside herself that would keep her going. What that might be Cole did not know, but he was thankful for it nonetheless. He realized that he was in the same situation as his father; he would have to help her without really understanding why.

He smiled warmly in return, his body tingling with deep respect and growing affection. This beautiful soul needed him to trust her. He could do that.

Cole pushed the hatchback shut and climbed back into the car. He looked up at the clock. It was going on nine. Slightly more than a day since that old Cutlass burst out of his rearview mirror and smashed into his life. He shook his head with wonder, then slipped the Subaru into gear and pulled out onto the road.

He drove north.

## 6.6

*She couldn't quite figure it out. Sometimes when she looked at her hand it looked like a hand. But sometimes it looked like it was made of fuzzy white light, like a rabbit she'd once seen, or like a cloud, or a wad of cotton. And sometimes it shone so brightly it was like looking at the sun. She was thankful that when she needed a hand, she had one. That was all that mattered, really. There was a scary person here, a beautiful woman whose face would sometimes melt and distort in hideous ways, and she was threatening her new friend, Linda. Already she'd had to push the scary woman away. She would need her hands.*

*She drifted downward, toward the pulsing heart that stood alone in a field of glowing grass. She knew this to be her grandfather, who watched over her body in the dense level below. Nearby was the building from which she'd just come. And inside were the glowing hearts of the two souls she knew to be her brother and sister, with whom she felt deeply coupled. The tough, flexible cord she could sense at her back kept her tethered to a body lying in a bed inside this building. And more lacy filaments reached out to these three souls, and between them, and back again, and outward. It occurred to her that this network of connections was what some would call love. She glowed with satisfaction at this knowing. There was so much to remember here.*

*She sent her grandfather a shimmering parcel of courage for the times ahead. Casting outward, she discerned that her father and Linda were nowhere near. They must have departed without her noticing. Concerned for their safety, she was about to go find them when something bumped her from behind. The world became swirling colors and stars and music as she whirled and rolled in reaction. She righted herself, twisting to see what had hit her, but found she could see without turning. It was a dazzling orb of light, smaller than she but bright with the tendrils of love.*

*"Dennis!" she called out, the greeting flowing from her like laughter and cool water and the joys of bees. The little ball of light became the dog she knew and wrapped himself around her legs, wagging his tail. She could feel his fear evaporate like rain on a summer sidewalk and knew, in that moment, that she had been afraid as well. Dennis disengaged from their embrace, dancing around her as he always did. He had no words, but she knew love when she saw it. And she knew it would make her stronger, that love. She was glad of that. Her new friend Linda would need her to be as strong as she could be.*

*She called her dog, beaming an image of the two of them walking in the woods, sending him a vibration of consciousness and memory from their life together in the physical realm. "C'mon Dennis! We've gotta go!" Together, without even knowing how, they flickered out and back in, traversing the distance between where they were and where they wished to be in an instant. The tugging sensation at her back held firm, and she knew that that was good. Below them moved a white, boxy something speeding noisily through what looked like a thick sludge. It took her a moment to realize that this was a car on a dusty gravel road. Until that moment she'd forgotten all about cars and dust and roads. She darted in for a peek, leaving Dennis behind in the sky that was not really a sky at all. They were in the right place. Her father's unyielding love, and Linda's fierce courage, could not be mistaken. She beamed her own love at the two of them, bathing them in the vibrations of her being. Then she rose through the ceiling to take her post just above the car, side by side with her beloved Dennis.*

*She remembered then that her name was Grace and that she lived in the body of a five-year-old girl on the planet Earth. She smiled. Yes. Grace. That was right. That's exactly who she was.*

# Chapter Seven

## 7.1

"She's in a car. A white Subaru, I think. So we know she's on the move. Alice flashed on the word 'squirrel' and Random kept chanting 'beach, beach, beach'." Bob stuffed another handful of potato chips into her mouth. She'd earned it.

"Alice says. Random says. What about you?" Rice's voice was rich and full in her ear, the product of alien technologies she no longer questioned. The fact that he sounded like he was breathing over her shoulder didn't even creep her out anymore. Bob noted the irritation in Rice's voice. That she had not reported her own experiences had not escaped him. They both knew she was the best.

Bob smiled. "I got the ocean, the sign, the boat, the dock, and the cottage," she answered, swallowing, taking her time. She loved to make Rice squirm. "I think Ma Kettle's on her way to the island. Her intent is clear."

"You think. C'mon, Bob, did you get in or didn't you? And if you got in, why the fuck didn't you blow her mind? And where the hell was that guardian you were so worried about?"

"The guardian was a no-show, boss. Must've just been a tourist. As for the Prez, she's got those fucking pills in her system, Teddy." Bob had a sharp edge in her voice. "I don't think you understand how disorienting that is. And she's learning to say 'no.' It was all I could do to get what I got. But it's clear enough, I think, given what Alice and Random got."

"Alice is a newbie and Random's half crazy, Bob. You're the lead here. They're just support. Don't send me to fucking Maine unless you know."

"I—"

"And don't call me fucking Teddy."

Bob sat down in the chair next to Mr. Random's crib and closed her eyes to think. Both Alice and Random worked with externals. Helpful but rarely conclusive. What made Bob so valuable was her ability to sneak inside without being noticed. Nothing like thoughts and memories to give you the real dirt. But the benzos in the President's bloodstream fucked everything up. Even when Bob could get in, it was like snorkeling in mud.

Bob tallied the evidence. Alice and Random both had her in a moving car. They got 'squirrel' and a beach. Add her impressions of a ferry ride and her match of the dock and the cottage, both of which she'd visited less than two months ago, and it seemed to fall together: the President was bolting for her favorite summer getaway. Bob opened her eyes and stepped away from Mr. Random, not wanting to disturb him any further, forgetting that she could not disturb him at all. "I'm pretty sure, Rice," she said. "That's all I got."

"So why the hell would she run to Squirrel Cove? I mean, it's not like we wouldn't think to look there. She's gotta know that."

Bob shrugged, then realized that Rice was not there to see her gesture. As good as this technology was, it was still voice-only. "Who knows? I'm guessing it's just Fred there right now. Late-season and all. She and Fred go back a long way."

Rice laughed. "Yeah, that's who'd I'd turn to if I had the Life and the People on my ass: a seventy-two-year-old ex-hardware-store clerk."

"It's what we saw, Rice." Bob stepped to the room's single sim-window and looked down on the image of a manicured lawn. It was so quiet down here. She grabbed the bag of chips from the table and dug out another handful.

Rice sighed and Bob could almost feel his hot breath on her neck. "Okay. Fine. There's nothing here anyways. It's gone cold."

"So where are you?" Bob packed the chips into her mouth.

"Some little bookstore-slash-bakery thing in Rochester," he answered, derision in his voice. "Watering hole for the local cattle."

"Nothing in the car?"

"Well, there's blood, so you were right about the injury. How the fuck she got out of that car and all the way to fucking Maine on her own with a bleeding whatever is anybody's guess."

"She is a day ahead of us, you know."

Rice snorted. "Golly, Bob, I forgot about that. She must've hobbled up to the road and flagged down a bus. Nobody would've recognized her. It's not like Americans watch television or anything."

"Screw you, chief. You know what I mean. She's got help."

"The Subaru."

"Not just the Subaru, Rice."

"Yeah, what the fuck is that all about anyways? Spud says 'bring her in' and then he helps her escape?" Bob heard the sound of Rice's fist pounding what sounded like a cafe table, that unmistakable jangle of a rattled coffee cup and spoon. "This is fuck-all hard enough as it is without getting jerked around by the bugs...."

"God, Rice!"

"Fuck 'em, Bobby-girl! I'm tired of this. They want my help they're gonna ... oh fuck."

Bob stopped chewing so she could hear. There was the sound of glass breaking, as though somebody had tossed a brick through a window. And was that a table toppling over? She couldn't tell.

Rice did not answer her hails.

Bob crossed the room and stared down at Mr. Random for a time, waiting to see if Rice would come back online. When he didn't, she reached down to adjust one of the leads attached to Random's temporal bone. On the way out, she switched off the sim, revealing the raw rock behind it.

Dead men did not need a view.


## 7.2


Cole turned into the gravel parking area next to an abandoned gas station, stopping parallel to the road, with the driver's side of the car closest to the pavement. He peered up at the rusted sign, which insisted that a gallon of regular was only four thirty-nine. He smirked. Those were the days. He unbuckled his belt. He'd been driving for well over an hour without a word from Linda and, whether it disturbed her or not, he had to stop. His coffee was ready to be released on its own recognizance. He stepped out into the cool October air and inhaled deeply, then headed toward the tree line. After relieving himself, he made his way back to the car and sat down behind the wheel.

"Cole?" Linda's voice was faint and careful.

"Yeah?"

"Can I come out for a bit?"

Cole scanned the area. There wasn't a house or car in sight. And he hadn't seen a single cop since turning onto Highway 2 back in East Montpelier. "Yeah," he said, turning around. "I think it's safe enough for a bit."

He popped out and hurried to open the hatch. Linda shielded her eyes for a moment, letting the light soak in, then smiled and swung her legs out to stand. Without a word they both hurried to their respective front doors and climbed in. Linda reached out and grabbed Cole's hand from the steering wheel, squeezing it for a moment with glad greetings, shared danger, and warm affection. She let go of his hand and glanced up the road. "Where are we?" she asked.

"We're heading into a little town called Marshfield, if my map is right." Cole noticed how the late morning sun reflected off

Linda's hair, how her eyebrows rose when she asked a question, how her ponytail bobbed as she spoke. It made him a little giddy. He reached out and gripped the wheel tightly, clamping down on the impulse to touch Linda's face. What was he thinking? This was the President! And they were *on the fucking run*. Cole relaxed his hands to his lap, forcing himself to take this break from driving. He'd been white-knuckling it since they left. He searched the President's face. "You, uh, have any luck?" he said.

Linda nodded. "I think so." She rested her head on the passenger-side window and looked up at the sky for the span of a few long breaths. To Cole, she seemed a bit dazed, as if she'd spent the last hour sleeping.

"Can you tell me about it?"

She nodded and closed her eyes. "One day ... I had an hour between meetings. So I laid down for a brief nap. And I got to thinking about Earl and the good times we'd had. And I ... I kind of imagined him lying in bed with me, like he was still alive. Like he was there with me in the White House. I don't know, it was just ... nice. To feel him with me. Even ... well ... you know. It was nice. And I fell asleep and dreamed about him some more." Linda glanced cautiously at Cole, as if it felt risky to speak of this. She closed her eyes again and continued. "Then there was a knock at the door. It was Mary, the agent who'd been assigned to 'watch over me.' This was a few weeks after I'd been brought in. And ... it was strange. She came in all sweet and helpful. Saying it was time to get ready for my meeting, as if I didn't already have people that reminded me when to take my next breath. She walked around the room, checking things. She even looked into my closet. And then she asked me if there was anybody else in the room. I told her no and she left."

Linda's eyes flashed opened and she sunk down into her seat as an old Honda passed them from behind. The car sped by without slowing and she sat back up as it faded from view. She looked at Cole. "There's so much I haven't told you yet," she said, her eyes soft and haunted.

This time Cole reached out and took her hand. "I know. Just keep going." His reassuring touch told her that they were going to be okay. Believing because she had to, she squeezed his hand, let go, leaned back again, and closed her eyes.

"That stuck with me. I mean, you have to understand how out of it I was. I was a basket case. We buried Bickle, and Rice and Bob pretty much disappeared, and this Mary shows up dogging my heels. Every attempt I made to find some answers met with a blank wall. At the funeral Rice comes up to me and puts a gun to my side. Right there in fucking public, though he kept it hidden. And he whispers into my ear that if I tell anyone at all, they're gonna kill my mother." Linda stopped long enough to choke back the memory of it, whether rage or grief or both Cole could not tell. "I was ... frantic. And it just stuck with me: Mary asking if there was anybody else in the room. For days, that scene played over and over in my mind. Finally it fell into place. Somehow, they were seeing into my thoughts, or into my dreams. They'd gotten into my head and seen Earl lying there next to me and they came in looking for him, wondering what the hell was going on." Linda looked over at Cole. "Does that sound crazy?" she asked, as if she truly didn't know.

"It might have. A day or two ago." Cole smiled, to soften his words.

The President took a long, slow breath and continued, her confidence somewhat revived. "I started looking for it. Noticing it. Trying to figure out how it worked. One night I had a dream about being sick and throwing up. I remembered it because it reminded me of how sick I'd been with the flu during the campaign. The next morning, while escorting me to a meeting with some Senators, Mary asks me if I'm feeling better. But she had no reason to ask that. I hadn't been sick the day before. Another time I sat at my desk. I'd decided to start writing some things down. You know, notes about what was happening. To help me think. But then I thought better of it and crumpled them up and tossed them in the wastebasket. Soon enough, there's Mary again. Comes in all smiles and greetings to tell me about some meeting or another, then kneels down and snatches the crumpled notes from the trash as if it were the most natural thing in the world for her to be doing. It was things like that. Eventually I figured out that they could somehow 'watch' me at any time, day or night, but that it was only when I was sleeping, or nearly so, that they could get into my head, my thoughts."

"That's why the pills?"

Linda nodded. "That's why the pills." She gestured with a nod toward her shoulder bag in the back. "I think the pills fog my brain up so much that they can't see inside."

Cole twisted in his seat to get more comfortable. "And all of this has something to do with what you were doing?" He gestured toward the cargo compartment.

"Yeah. I think Mary genuinely likes me. It's made it easier to get things past her. So I started teaching myself to get really calm. I remembered a phrase my mother picked up at a workshop she'd gone to, some astral projection thing. 'Body asleep but mind awake,' she said. Something like that. So I started playing with that idea. As I said, I was frantic. I didn't want these monsters getting in my head. I didn't have the pills yet. I figured if I could control my thinking, or my sleeping, or something, I could find some way to keep them out."

"So you were asleep back there?"

Linda smiled, as though proud of herself. "My body was. So they could get in closer. But not my mind. My mind was filled with thoughts and memories of the summer retreat I go to in Maine. Thoughts of the cottage and the boat." She allowed a slight chuckle. "I'm pretty sure I got 'em."

"They think you're going to Maine?"

"I think so. I hope so. I mean, they must know we're in a car right now, but they probably can't tell where we're headed unless they get into my thoughts. I just spent the last hour believing we're headed to Maine. If they picked up on that, and I've got this gut feeling that they did, then maybe they'll focus there for a while. Give us a chance to shake them."

Cole thought about his kids back at his father's house: Grace, asleep in her bed; Emily, worried about her dog; Iain, wanting to be strong but not yet trusting himself. He allowed himself to hope that Linda was right, that maybe Rice would now leave them alone. His shoulders loosened and dropped and his chest filled with the first full and easy breath he'd taken all day. Unbidden, a stream of tears spilled down his face, as though his inhalation had opened a spigot in his heart.

Linda put a hand on Cole's forearm. "Tell me," she said.

Cole sat for a full minute, staring down at his lap, letting the tears flow. It took him that long, to feel his way down to the source of his sobbing. He looked up at Linda with wet, red eyes and forced a brave smile to his face, as if hoping not to add to her problems. "I left my kids," he said at last, his voice a mere whisper.

Linda's heart broke wide open and she put a gentle hand to Cole's cheek, wishing she had the power to whisk away his anguish. But she knew she could not. She had her own guilt to deal with, in allowing Cole to join her, in standing there and watching as he walked away from his family. She had her own doubt. Her own shame. And she could guess, gazing ahead to the confrontation that she could see coming, and at the forces bearing down upon them even now as they sat here on the roadside, that there would be much more than this to grieve before it was all over.

The path she had chosen would require tough choices, sacrifice and loss. It already had. Now Cole had to feel the consequences of the choice *he'd* made: to stand beside her as an ally as they confronted those who would threaten their world. And maybe there were deeper consequences for them both to face. Deeper choices they *had* made. Deeper choices *the whole world* had made, even though they might never have felt like choices at all. They lived in a world chock-full of consequences, it seemed. It was only right, that she and Cole should bear their portion of acceptance and responsibility and loss.

For now, there was little she could think to do but to tell the truth as she saw it. *I left my kids*, Cole had said. "Yes, you did," she replied. She ran her fingers down to his chin, then let her hand fall away to her lap. "So it's now our job to make that count for something." She held his eyes with her own, letting the raincloud of fears and thoughts and wants and wounds that pulsed and churned between them break apart and dissipate in the bright sun of her regard. A warm, joyful sensation bubbled up from her heart and kindled a smile on her face. A great peace washed over her soul. They could do this. They could stand the pain and doubt. They could feel the fear. They could walk the path they'd chosen. There was no grief that could last forever. The human face was simply too eager to smile.

Another car approached, slowing a bit as it neared them, before zooming off. Cole followed it as it passed, then looked over to see the President hunched low in her seat. She winked. "I'd better get back in the dungeon," she said, rolling her eyes. When the car was gone, she opened her door and did just that.

### 7.3

Five miles down the road the President started laughing uncontrollably. Curious, Cole got the idea to fold the back seat forward so that they could talk while he drove. That would require a stop. Glancing down, he noticed that they needed gas anyway, so he continued into the next town, Marshfield, and pulled into the Quik-E-Stop there.

Linda quieted as he pulled up to the pumps. He swiped his card and set the nozzle on autocut, then stepped around to lower the seat back on the right side. As soon as Linda saw him she started laughing again. Cole couldn't help himself and laughed along. "What?" he said.

She waved him away, shaking her head in an attempt to stop herself. "Just ... pump the gas," she finally managed to say. Cole lifted an eyebrow and went around to finish the task, then got back into the driver's seat and started the car. He adjusted the rearview mirror downward and they caught each other's eye. Linda laughed even harder.

"What?" he demanded, grinning broadly.

The President drew in a huge breath, wiping the tears from her eyes. That seemed to control it a bit. "Your father!" she managed to say before laughing again. "I can't believe I called bullshit on your father!"

Cole pictured his father standing there and taking it as the

President of the United States got in his face. "That was some-thing," he answered with a sigh. Something Cole never thought he'd see.

Linda's laughter sputtered out and she wiped her eyes. Cole glanced at her in the mirror. She looked peaceful. The laughter had released a great deal of pain. The shadows that had haunted her eyes since their first meeting had faded away.

Linda noticed him looking at her. "I'm sorry," she said.

"For what?"

"That was your dad, Cole! I had no right to—"

Cole shook his head and laughed. "I could fill a stadium with people who would have paid good money to watch that."

"Yeah, but—" Linda closed her eyes, as if replaying the scene. "I hope the kids didn't witness it."

"I don't know. It's like, maybe it'd be good for them. You know?"

Linda shrugged. "Looks like your father dotes on them."

"Yeah. And they really love him. But they know that things are off between their Grandpa and me."

Linda adjusted the pillow under her head and closed her eyes. "You wanna talk about it?"

"About what?"

"About what's up with your father."

Cole turned his attention to the road. The interstate was com-ing up in a mile and he knew that they'd have to take it for a bit, to catch route 114 up to Eastbound. The thought of that fright-ened him. They were more likely to encounter the police on the interstate. "Um, Linda?"

"Yeah?"

"Check and make sure you can pull that seat back up, okay? We gotta get onto the interstate for a bit. I need to know that we can close it in a hurry."

Linda scooted back and reached out to grab the seat. She pulled but it barely moved. "I can't get it," she said. "The angle's wrong."

Cole reached back with his right hand and lifted. Once he got it started Linda could pull it the rest of the way. "I can't get it to latch," she said, her voice muffled.

Cole glanced back. "It looks closed. Good enough."

The President pushed out enough to get an arm through and shoved her shoulder bag under the seat back to keep it from going all the way forward. Then she pushed herself back out a bit, wriggling around to get more comfortable. They caught each other's eye in the rearview mirror and Linda smiled courageously. Cole sighed. "So," he finally said, "my father."

"Your father."

Cole took the ramp up to the interstate. His heart lurched to see a state cruiser speeding southward, its lights screaming. He eased into northbound traffic and checked his speed, watching the cruiser disappear in his side mirror. "My father," he repeated.

"You don't have to tell me," she said, her voice warm with invitation and kindness. She'd settled in once again, eyes closed, a slight smile on her face, as if she could hear anything Cole had to say and not be undone by it.

"Yeah, well. It's ... complicated. My father has always been..."

"Hard?"

"Well, you know *It's a Wonderful Life*, right?"

"Yeah."

"Let's just say dear old dad was more Mr. Potter than George Bailey."

Linda looked up to catch Cole's eye. "That must have been rough," she said.

"Yeah, but, you get used to it, you know? And he's softened over the years. You saw him with the kids."

"So what did you do wrong?" she asked.

Cole flinched. A tandem rig blew by on his left, rattling the car. Cole slowed a bit. What did he do wrong? Where do you start? And how do you speak of it? "I told you about, you know ... how Ruth died."

Linda nodded. "NewAir 413," she replied.

"Right. So. About a week before that, I told Ruth that I thought that, you know, that maybe we should separate."

"Oh, Cole," moaned the President, in sympathy with Cole's obvious distress. She shook her head slightly. "Jesus."

"Yeah. It was a mess. I was too. It was like, well, we talked all that week. And cried. And then she had to go to London and … and…."

"And her plane went down."

Cole nodded. There were tears welling in his eyes but he held them back. Knuckles white on the wheel, he stared out over the road. After a moment he could speak again. "So at the funeral, I'm standing there, just watching as the people file in. Dad comes up from behind and says to me 'Well, Cole, at least this'll save you on legal bills.' And then he walked away." Cole's chest heaved as the deep hurt welled up once again. Tears flooded his cheeks.

"I'm so sorry," said Linda from the cargo compartment.

"I didn't even know she'd told anyone, least of all my father." Cole's voice was wistful, aching, choked with regret and bitter with betrayal. He could never get that week back. Never make it right. Never work it out. Ruth's cold smile and quick peck would remain forever in his mind, the last moments of their time together, fraught with unfinished business and hope and anger and misunderstanding, a song stuck in his head that would never fade to silence.

"I didn't know she'd told anyone," he repeated.

He glanced up to see the cop in his rearview mirror just moments before the siren sounded.

## 7.4

He could see the Lyndonville exit just ahead. He could see the road that would take them to Keeley's house, to whatever plan the President had in her head, to what safety they might find there. Two-tenths of a mile and they'd have been off this god-damned interstate, and the goddamned state trooper now sitting in his car right behind them as traffic zipped past, the goddamned state trooper with his goddamned clipboard and his goddamned sunglasses and his goddamned attitude that didn't have a clue what was going on or what was at stake, that goddamned trooper would have gone zipping past just like the rest of the traffic and he and Linda would have been free. Fuck!

Cole's guts squirmed as he watched the trooper climb slowly from his cruiser, all stern caution and confidence. He could feel the eyes of every passing motorist slide over his face as he sat there: exposed, trapped, caught, with absolutely no way out. The trooper walked slowly toward his Forester, stopping for a moment at the hatchback door and bending down to reach for the latch, as if he knew the President was lying in the cargo compartment, as if he'd been told exactly what road, exactly what time, exactly which car, exactly which door. As if he were not a state trooper at all but some sort of alien, a robot, a Terminator, with the power to read minds and see through walls. Cole would not have been surprised to see the trooper morph into some huge and lethal machine, to see him raise his rocket-launcher arm and blow them both straight to hell. After a moment the trooper rose to his feet and walked around to Cole's open window. He hadn't touched the hatchback door. Cole glanced back quickly, to make sure Linda had pulled the seat back up as tightly as was possible.

"License and registration please, sir," said the trooper, his voice a caricature of every movie cop Cole had ever seen. The trooper stood at his window with his hand outstretched in self-assured anticipation that Cole would give him exactly what he had requested. Cole reached for his wallet and his glove box and did just that.

"Uh ... was I speeding, officer?" Cole managed to ask, wincing inwardly at how nervous he sounded.

The policeman glanced at Cole's documents and then handed them back. "Your speed was fine, sir," he said stiffly. "But you have what looks like a blanket hanging from your back door, dragging on the road. It's obscuring your license plate."

*Fuck fuck fuck fuck*, Cole cursed inside. *Fuck!* He struggled to catch his breath before the gasp welling up inside of him got out where the trooper could hear it. Clenching the steering wheel to keep his hands steady he looked up at the trooper and smiled. "You're kidding me," he said, scrunching his nose again and again. It was all he could think to say.

"Excuse me?" said the cop.

Cole winced, smiling all the harder, sure that his face was more rictus than grin. "I mean ... it must have been ... I think one of my kids must have left it there."

The trooper nodded, looking out over the traffic for a moment before returning his gaze to Cole. A tanker truck slammed past, flapping the trooper's jacket sleeves in its wake. "No doubt, sir," he said, when the noise had died down. When Cole continued to just sit and smile he added, "So shall I fix it for you, sir?"

Cole staggered inwardly, twitching as if he'd just been slapped. He was sure the trooper could see it. His mind raced to Grace, lying there in that deep, mysterious sleep, waking one day to learn that her father was in prison. His foot pressed lightly on the accelerator, ready to punch and run. He could feel his heartbeat in the space between his fingertips and the steering wheel, as if his life was bleeding out before him. Only seconds left. He opened his mouth to speak, gagged on his own words, and cleared his throat. "I, uh, no. Sir. No thanks. I'll get it." He knew then how people could wet themselves in such moments. His body was barely under his control. His fingers stretched and curled on the wheel like worms in the rain.

The officer nodded, clicked his tongue, wrinkled his nose, as if he were matching Cole's words to the Vermont State Police Official List of Reasonable Responses, as if he were walking Cole's answer along a straight line to see if it wavered. He took a single step backward. "So, then, you'll be getting out and fixing it yourself. Is that right, sir?"

Cole nodded quickly. The trooper stood and stared. There was no way out of this. They were dead. Cole thought he heard a faint clunk come from the back and flashed immediately on his memory of the President bursting forth to confront his father. His heart began to hammer. He opened his mouth to speak. He had to say something. But he could not seem to make his mouth move.

A black ball appeared just inches above his hood. Cole didn't see that it had come from anywhere. It was just there. Six inches across, maybe. Black like a crow is black, slightly shiny, tinged with blue. It didn't hover, really. Hovering implied some small movement and this was so still that Cole could sense the Earth itself moving underneath. He stared.

"Sir?" asked the trooper.

Cole glanced at the trooper, then back at the ball. "Do you see that?" he asked, his hands flourishing like a game-show hostess.

The trooper glanced over at the ball, then back at Cole. "The black ball, sir?" he asked, his voice unfazed.

Cole laughed with bewilderment. "Yeah. The black ball," he said, as if the trooper had just noted the end of the world with nothing more than a nod.

"I see it, sir," replied the trooper. "So, about that blanket...."

Cole was about to respond when the light from an explosion ahead blasted his eyes, followed immediately with a roar that shook the whole car. The trooper was almost flung to the ground, catching himself with a side step and a hand on Cole's luggage rack. Cole peered up the road as a fireball punched the sky. He thought for a second of the tanker truck that had passed only a moment before.

Traffic was coming to a standstill, taillights flashing a line of warning, as if the fireball needed any help. The trooper dusted himself off, his attention on the explosion. "You have a good day, sir," he said absently, not even looking at Cole. He returned to his car as quickly as he could and lurched out onto the interstate, speeding toward the blaze while the road was still clear enough to do so. Cole started the Forester and shifted into gear. In seconds he was on the ramp, veering away from the interstate, the trooper, and whatever it was that had just happened.

It was only then that he thought to wonder where the black ball had gone.

### 7.5

Cole pushed through the convenience store door carrying two bottles of juice, a chocolate-covered donut, a bag of cheddar-cheese popcorn, and a vague twinge of guilt: first, because while many countries were dealing with food riots and rationing, Americans could still seem to get all the junk food they could afford and, second, because the money in Cole's pocket had come from the wrongful death settlement that had resulted from his wife's dismemberment. He looked up at the sky, squinting against the brightness and wondering if there was anyone looking back down on him. He chuckled at the thought. It was all just too much. And the "too much" was piling higher so swiftly now that he'd lost all hope of keeping up. He sighed his surrender, remembering one of his father's favorite phrases: he would simply have to "summer on." There was never time for winter in Ben Thomas's kingdom. That's just the way the world works, m'boy. Nobody ever said it was fair.

Cole ducked into the car and handed a drink and the donut back to Linda, slamming the door on his father's unsolicited advice. "Orange juice and chocolate." He shook his head in mock disgust. "I don't know how you can stomach it."

Linda laughed, then gestured with a quick toss of her head. "How's it look out there?"

"I think we're good for a while," Cole mused, peering out the passenger side window at the fire, now a couple of miles behind them. Black smoke hung in the sky like a dirty towel on the back of a chair. "Must've been diesel fuel in that tanker. And it looks like every cop and emergency crew in the state has gone to check it out. So we may have a clear shot to Eastbound." On the drive into Lyndonville he'd seen three police cars shoot past them toward the interstate. Since pulling into the Gas 'n' Get, he'd seen two fire trucks. "The sirens must be driving you crazy," he said.

"Well, I am kind of in the dark here, Cole," she said. "You okay?"

Cole inserted the key and started the car. "I'm doing good, Mrs. President," he said, pressing his lips in thought. "My heartbeat's down to around two hundred and my pants are starting to dry." He turned back to Linda and flashed his eyebrows with good humor.

"I was about to come out and talk to that trooper myself, you know."

"I *do* know. Which is why I'm so glad your little friend showed up when he did."

Puzzlement slipped over the President's face. "My little friend?" she asked.

"Yeah. Little black ball. About the size of a grapefruit. Came and just sat there over the hood till the tanker blew." Cole noticed the look on Linda's face. "Not a friend of yours?"

Linda shook her head. "I don't know what you're talking about, Cole. The seat back was up. I didn't see it."

"Weird." Cole frowned. It all just got stranger and stranger. "Well, whatever. I thought we were caught for sure. Didn't know whether to hit the gas or beg for mercy. Then that little guy shows up and the tanker blows and here we are."

"Maybe we have more help than we know about." The words had spilled out of Linda without conscious thought, as if spoken by someone else. "You know?" she added, seeking acknowledgement. If she was going to start hoping for something, she was damn well going to have his agreement in the matter.

"Maybe we do, yeah," he replied, glancing again at the sky. He turned to look at Linda. "I'm sure not gonna complain." He gestured toward the highway. "You ready?"

"Let's do it," Linda said with a quick smile. She took a bite of her donut.

Cole faced forward and opened the bag of popcorn, chewing his way through the Mylar like a starving raccoon and stuffing a handful of the salty snack into his mouth. He put the car in gear and pulled onto the road. They were on 114, which would take them almost all the way to Keeley's house. Cole straightened in his seat, relaxed his shoulders. There was something new in his blood. He could feel it. A nonchalance. A bit of devil-may-care. Maybe even power. He felt ... happy?

It's the last thing he would have expected, but there it was. For the first time in a long time, Cole felt fully alive, as if the state trooper had given him a blessing instead of a fright. He could still feel the Earth moving majestically beneath him. And he could imagine himself standing straight and true on this slowly-spinning ground, as if, finally, *finally*, he belonged here. There were huge forces at work all around him: spinning underneath, flitting overhead, stirring deep inside. There was some vast story being enacted in the universe. He understood very little of it, and he was scared as hell. But he was also needed. He was involved. He had a role. His actions now mattered in a way they never had before. Like a pupal moth beginning to form its wings, Cole could feel the first hints of some new purpose he might serve in the wider world, some grander meaning he might discover beyond the quiet caretaking of his family. Rather than finding the right script to follow before he could live his life, Cole now found himself thrust onstage with no script at all. It was ... exhilarating.

The President took another bite of her donut and spoke around the chocolate, interrupting Cole's reverie. "So why do you call it 'he'?" she asked.

"What?"

"The black ball. You referred to it as 'he', and then called it 'the little guy.'"

Cole stopped chewing long enough to think for a moment. "It seemed ... friendly somehow," he finally replied. "Like a person. Not just a thing."

Linda smiled. She wasn't going to question it either. They would use all the friends they could get right now. She took a swig of the orange juice, savoring that mix of tangy and sweet she'd learned to love as a child. Keeley had eaten dog kibble. Linda had drunk OJ mixed with chocolate milk. As so often happens with children living at the far ends of the normal curve, shared eccentricities had drawn them closer together.

"So tell me about Keeley," said Cole from up front. Linda flinched in defense. Great! Now *Cole* was reading her thoughts *too*? She'd had enough of that to last her a lifetime. After a couple of long breaths she calmed back down. Of course he'd ask about Keeley. She'd told him almost nothing, and they were getting closer to her house.

Inhaling deeply, as if breathing new life into old memories, Linda's mind inflated with images. "I met her in school. Fifth grade. We played on the same team in Little League: the Wildcats. We were best friends until she moved away, when we were seniors. I haven't seen her or talked to her since."

Cole nodded, trying to take it all in and form a picture of the situation. "So how is it that we're now driving to her house?"

Linda caught Cole's eye in the rearview mirror and grinned, her heart opening to this brave man who was helping her, who was trying so hard to comprehend, to give comfort, and to hold it all together without coming unraveled himself. Gratitude welled up in her eyes. She'd been alone in this crazy situation for so long. She wanted more than anything to reach out and hold his hand in hers, to take their growing connection and make it manifest. "Keeley was in that play," she said at last, searching for the shortest route to understanding. There was so little time.

"With the aliens?"

"Yeah. And an image of her stuck in my mind." Linda finished the donut and swallowed some more juice. Done with her snack, she could rest her head again on the seat back. "Those few weeks and months after Rice brought me in...." her voice drifted. "It was a really strange time. On the one hand, here I was, the President of the United States, attending meetings and dinners and parties and press conferences and more meetings. Dealing with senators and congressmen and cabinet members and all that. Nothing had changed. The machines of government just kept on chooglin' all around me, whether I was paying attention or not. It was as if that briefing had never happened. As if the memory of Spud was just a horror movie I'd seen long ago."

"And on the other hand?"

"On the other hand everything had changed. Mary was there, my new shadow. Every now and then I'd see Rice, pretending to be Edmonton, part of my Secret Service detail. It was always from a distance and we never spoke. He wouldn't even look at me. But the feel of his gun digging into my side, his voice in my ear - it haunted me."

"You couldn't afford to just react out of hand. He might hurt the people you love."

Linda closed her eyes to see further. "Yeah. He'd certainly given me clear enough warning. I never did tell Mom anything. I just couldn't bring her into it. But there was something more essential going on, Cole. There was something shifting inside of me. Something coming alive. Like, there was a voice in my ear, constantly whispering things I couldn't quite understand. There was something I was supposed to do or say or think or be or ... I don't know. Something."

"So, Keeley?"

Linda nodded. "Right. For the longest time I was just plain stupid. I look back on those first few weeks and it was like I was drugged or something. But eventually I came back to myself. Or woke up." Linda paused for a moment, searching for the right word. "I guess you could say I started to hide myself. Hide my thoughts. Hide my actions."

"Like when you were figuring out how they could get in your mind and you started testing that."

"Yeah. And I started to see that I needed a plan. I knew that I had to get out of there. I knew that I had to tell the world what was going on. But, how does the President escape? I mean, every time I thought of telling somebody, well, they'd think I was crazy, wouldn't they? And who could I trust? I mean, the People had to be everywhere, to be able to do what they did, to drag me from the White House whenever they wanted, to put Mary on me with no questions asked. And they'd threatened my *mother*. So, it was like, to whom could I turn? I mean, I was at a fucking Joint Chiefs meeting one morning and when it adjourned I grabbed Xander's elbow and took him aside. I tell him there's something I need to talk to him about. He looks around to make sure we're alone and then starts laughing. He tells me that I have to take it up with Spud! This is the Chief of Staff of the god-damned U.S. Air Force!"

Linda stopped. The memory of it still grabbed her by the guts and she hugged herself tighter, to feel what little protection she could. The Forester hit a hole in the road and the unexpected jolt almost made her scream. She took a deep breath, let it out, and continued. "I kept seeing Keeley in my mind, up on that stage, singing and dancing with the aliens. The expression on her face was amazing. She looked so ... mighty. So I got online one day and Googled her. Found her website. She's got a little farm up in the Northeast Kingdom. Up near Wallace Pond. Almost on the border. Married to a guy called 'Pooch.' They sell raw milk and eggs and vegetables in the summer. Pooch apparently fixes motorcycles and Keeley does dog grooming and flower arrangements."

"And they don't know we're coming, I take it."

Linda chuckled quietly. "No. I think they're in for a bit of a shock."

"I'd say so." Cole smiled. He asked his next question, fearing the response. "And so, when we get there ... what next? *Do* you have a plan?"

Linda looked away, as if ashamed. "I have a long shot," she finally said, her voice defensive and hesitant. "But I'd rather wait until we're at Keeley's before I talk about it."

Cole nodded. A long shot. Of course. The world he'd known was crumbling around him, just as it had crumbled around the President. The old rules were no longer valid. Long shots would be as good as it gets from here on out. There could be no real plan. The question that remained was this: what do you do when you have no plan? With no answer to that immediately forthcoming, Cole stuffed another handful of popcorn into his mouth. "Ah well," he said, searching for comfort in a philosophical tone. "I guess we'll just do what we do."

"I guess we will," answered Linda. "I don't really know what we're walking into, you know? Whether Keeley will be pissed off, or grateful, or what. I don't know that she can help."

Cole glanced into the rearview mirror, one eyebrow raised. "Why would she be pissed off?"

Linda thought for a moment, frowning with confusion. "She just ... moved away," she said, shrugging. "After I saved her from her uncle. We never really had a chance to talk about it."

Cole understood immediately, having grown up in a world where schoolgirls sometimes needed to be rescued from uncles. The road made a hard right turn and he slowed to take it, noticing in his side mirror that he could no longer see the smoke in the sky. He allowed himself to hope that their problems were as far behind them as that burning tanker.

He suspected, of course, that they were not.

## 7.6

Cole turned left at the intersection, unsure that he should. There was no street sign at the corner. The new road was gravel and it stretched northward, down into a valley and then back up. That had to be Canada just ahead. The thought made him feel better. He picked up speed, creating a cloud of dust behind them.

Linda, now sitting up front, pointed at the windshield. "What's that?" she asked. She was scrunched down in the front seat, her head held just high enough to help Cole find Keeley's farm.

"Oh!" Cole glanced at Linda, then reddened with embarrassment. "I forgot to show you. Rice did that."

The President reached up with a hesitant finger to follow the symbol Rice had drawn in the grime: a circle with a vertical line through it, another line coming off the top of the first in a right angle. She'd expected to feel something. Some sort of energy, maybe. A tingle. A jolt of memory. But there was nothing. No magic. No force. No wild ride. Just glass and dirt and a little drawing that didn't mean a thing to her. "When did he do that?" she asked.

"At the end," Cole shrugged. "After he'd spoken to Emily. He just stopped and leaned over and drew that on the window and left."

"And you've been looking at it for hours now and you didn't say anything?"

Cole leaned toward his door, defensiveness rising up inside. "Hey!" he barked. "It's been a crazy day, you know? There's tons of stuff we haven't talked about!"

Linda stopped him with a hand on his elbow. "I know," she said, her voice firm but gentle. "I know. We're under a great deal of stress. We're doing our best." She removed her hand and ducked back down as a car approached. It rumbled past, cloaking them further with dust.

Something else had come to memory and Cole shuddered at the thought of it. "I can't believe I didn't tell you this," he said. He slammed his forehead with the flat of his hand. "Stupid!"

"We don't know what it means anyway, Cole," said Linda.

"No, no," answered Cole with a bleak smile of humiliation. "Not the sign. After that. Rice walked away and then turned back. Looked me right in the eye and smiled and said, 'see you later.'" A muddled expression of guilt and confusion and pleading clouded Cole's eyes. How could he have forgotten that? Stupid!

Linda turned away abruptly, stared out the side window for a moment as open fields ended and woods began. *See you later*? Jesus! What the hell did *that* mean? The apparent normalcy of the outside world clashed with the bizarre nature of their journey. The dissonance threatened to unmake her. It almost felt as if that's exactly what somebody was trying to do: unmake her, tear her to pieces, take everything away. Linda shuddered at the thought of Rice's hands on the glass, as if that bastard had touched *her*. She wanted to stop the car and wash his mark away with bleach and cold acid and bitter curses. But she suspected that it wasn't just Rice. In the end, as dangerous as Rice could be, he was probably just the errand boy. In the end, hiding somewhere in the invisible fissures of their society, there must be powers far more lethal than Theodore Rice.

Linda turned back to face Cole, offering him a smile of apology. This was *not* his fault. "They can do that, Cole," she said. "Make us forget things. Make us stupid." She reached out and took his hand. "So we have to help each other be smarter. Okay? We can't afford to go to sleep."

Cole nodded in obvious relief. "You got it, Mrs. President." He hit the brakes and brought the car to a full stop. The road had come to a dead end. An iron gate painted in orange and yellow held two signs. The first, a red circle with a white horizontal bar, said, "DO NOT ENTER". The second, black lettering on a white background, read, "REPORT TO PORT OF ENTRY. AVOID HEAVY PENALTY." Cole put the car in reverse and turned around.

They finally found Keeley's little sign, hanging lopsidedly on a single length of chain from a battered mailbox that had long since given up its numbers. *"Fiche le camp!"* it read, purple letters on a dull yellow background, a faded iris to one side.

"Get lost," Linda murmured.

"Excuse me?"

"Get lost. That's what the sign means in French. Get Lost Farm. I read about it on the website."

"Nice."

Cole pulled onto the drive, picked up a bit of speed as the car plunged into the woods and across a culvert. The mountains here receded, rolling down into farmlands and woodlots. The driveway took them out of the trees and past open fields on both sides. They saw the farm: the small white Cape, the red barn and outbuildings, the gardens, the pasture with half a dozen disinterested cows and a gang of curious goats.

Linda held her breath. So much rested on this moment, so many months of pain and fear. As if all the troubles of the world had flocked to this one corner of the planet like so many vultures, to perch in the surrounding trees and await her arrival. Were they here to help her fly, or to tear her to shreds? Linda guessed that she'd find out soon enough. She rubbed her eyes with a shaky hand. All she wanted was to rest. She feared that she might never rest again.

Cole pulled up to a two-track parking space in front of the barn and turned off the engine. Linda took Cole's hand and squeezed, then opened her door. Cole followed suit. Starting toward the house, they both jerked with surprise to see the front door swing open. Out stepped a tall bear of a man in blue overalls and a green flannel shirt, his huge black beard flecked with gray. He looked at them, nodded and smiled, then called into the house, his words thickly accented in French.

"They're here, *mon cœur*," he said. There was such laughter in his face that Linda's heart pounded. The bear stepped down from the porch and strode forward to greet them, pulling them into his embrace. "Call me Pooch, eh?" he said.

Linda burst into tears.

## 7·7

*She could feel the warmth of his glow from where she was and knew that he was good. Another heart came out of the house and joined them: a woman. It was just as the Elder had said back on the highway, before He joined with that tanker and let loose the energy within: "If the President and your father make it to their destination, they will find some help." Grace beamed a packet of love toward the four of them and retreated a bit, giving them the space and time they would need to create their web of connections. Dennis hung at her heels, wagging his tail.*

*Grace practiced her maneuvers and fine-tuned her discernment, watching from what felt like "above" as the four souls "below" her appeared as shimmering orbs, then solid bodies, and then orbs again. Slowly, she was figuring out how to perceive and make sense of the kaleidoscope of shifting, swirling levels and layers and vibrations that ran through every facet of reality. She enjoyed her new mastery. If she put her mind to it, she could see the physical plane almost as she remembered living in it. And she could see so much more, from the far corners of the Cosmos to the buried ages of time and the innermost secrets of space, to other realities as real and solid as the world from which she'd come.*

*She'd been here before. She knew that much. But the specific memory of that time was closed to her. She could access the young mind she was still entangled with, as it slumbered on in that little girl's head. In some very real sense she was that little girl. And yet, she could sense that she was much, much more. That little girl was only the momentary expression of a self that had lived for a very long time. Hidden in the folds of her being was a more essential nature, an eternal spirit that had access to experience and information far beyond the confines of that brief, embodied life. She smiled at the boundless possibilities that lived within her.*

*But she would have to be careful. Because this realm was filled with other beings, and not all of them were nice. And because she was still that little girl. Her perceptions were limited. Already she'd made a mistake. Earlier, when the scary people had come, she'd thought to repel them, as she had before. She was just about to flicker in to help when Linda signaled for her to stay back. That had surprised her. She hadn't realized that Linda even knew she was there. So she'd caught herself and pulled back just in time, enfolding herself into a ball, holding her vibrations calm and quiet, and watching as Linda drew the scary ones in.*

*There were three of them now, three scary beings: the warped and distorted woman from before, a tiny girl, and a monstrous, skeletal madman. Grace stayed hidden, ready to help, as Linda focused and opened, filling these strange beings with images of an ocean and a cottage and a boat, scenes that made Grace's whole being pulse and ache with love and longing, remembering how her mother had so loved the ocean before she had died. Grace could sense Linda's concentration, her intelligence, and her skill as she maintained her glow even when the car bounced and jerked around her. Soon enough the scary ones departed. Linda rejoined her body and the car sped on.*

*"It will not be so easy the next time," the Elder had told her before He left. She shuddered at the memory of Him. The Elder's love was so hot, so demanding, so fierce, that she could feel herself dissolving in His presence. His glow sliced the universe, a knife-edge of conscious light that could not be misconstrued, piercing the hood of her father's car and reaching down through the planet, and up to infinity. "These dense ones are very clever," He cautioned. "They will learn from this defeat and return even stronger."*

*Grace had opened to the vibrations of the 'dense one' that stood at her father's car door, discerning his patterns of fear and suspicion. She thought she might share her heart with him, fill him with love and understanding. But he was closed to her, and she had no other ideas. She could feel her father's terror. She could feel Linda's growing anger. But she did not know how to help. It was only when the Elder had flickered over to ignite the tanker, and the dense one followed to investigate, that she could begin to relax.*

*Dennis beamed her an image of fur and fingers, and she reached down to scratch behind his ears. His presence grounded her, kept her in touch with her other self, connected to the realm of bodies and houses and cars and trees and dogs who needed petting. She was glad of that. This world of light and vibration threatened to enchant her into staying. And she was not ready for that. Even now, even here, she could feel her grandfather's heart bathing her body with love and sadness and regret. He was sitting right there, beside her bed, reading out loud from a book his mother had read to him when he was as young as she. She wanted to hear how the story ended.*

*Linda and her father followed their two new friends into their home. Grace beamed Dennis an image of a bumblebee and together they took to the sky, spiraling around in a series of loop-the-loops and curls that left her laughing and Dennis barking for more. Promising another run later, Grace settled down to a spot above the roof. Dennis took his place at her heel.*

*For now, she had work to do. She scanned the sky for more dangers.*

# Chapter Eight

## 8.1

"Fucking Vermont!" Rice cursed, tossing his cell phone out the window. He laughed as it clattered to the middle of the other lane, where it would get smashed under-wheel. He'd bought the damned thing at a gas station in some stupid little cattle-town called Bethel. One of those pre-paid pieces of shit the domesticateds used these days, as most no longer had the money for a real phone. But he'd charged it for over an hour and it still didn't fucking work! He yanked the charger from the cigarette lighter, gathered up the packaging, and threw it all into the road, glad to be rid of any memory of it. There didn't look to be one decent phone store in all of New England, as far as he could see. How could these people live like this?

A gas station appeared out of nowhere up on the left and he steered his Mercedes rental lazily across the center line and past the pumps, making a bee-line for the pay phone in the corner of the lot, not giving one good-goddamn for the oncoming car that mashed its horn as it swerved to miss him, dopplering past like the whiny little baby that drove it. "Bite me," he muttered as he slammed to a stop, just missing the crow that yanked at whatever-the-fuck dead rodent lay slow-cooking in the afternoon sun. He pushed open the door, lifted the handset and swiped his card.

"Hello?"

Mary's voice sounded galaxies away, weak and scratchy. Fucking phones. "I need to talk at Bob," he said impatiently. Fucking Mary as well.

"She's working, Rice," said Mary, warily.

"Off hunting?"

"As far as I know. When you went missing she grabbed Alice and Random and took off to see what's up. I haven't been in to check on her since. The General and I—"

Rice cut her off. "What's up is that Spud and his homies blasted me and melted my com implant. Which is why I'm talking on a pay phone here in the fucking wasteland."

"Blasted you?"

He could hear the scorn hidden in her voice. Bitch. It was her fault he was out here in the first place. "Yes, Mary," he said, as if explaining things to the village idiot. "A Martian tripod in the middle of Rochester-fucking-Vermont. The Spielberg version, no less. Nasty fucker blasted the front picture window of a local coffee shop. Behind which I was sitting, thank you very much." He picked at the dry blood crusting the small hole behind his ear. It still hurt like fuck-all, even with the medkit. He pulled another chip of tempered glass from his jacket pocket and hurled it at the crow. "Another fun bit of theater from Spud and the gang."

Mary sighed in that "tsk, tsk" way she had. "That'll be hard to cover, won't it Rice?"

"Probably. So what? Not my job. My guess is that I'm the only one who saw it. No doubt the provincials are still standing around slackjawed, scratching their noggins and wondering 'Hey, Rufus, why'd that-there window shatter?' and what was that light they saw? I mean, hell, the bugs can ram the Pentagon on 9/11 in the middle of broad-fucking-daylight and people still swear they saw an airplane."

"You're pretty free with the epithets when there's nobody around," Mary said, her voice now cold.

Rice was past caring. "Yeah, well. I've about had it with the games." He glanced at the sky, flinching at his own words. He had more than one implant. *They* could still listen in any time they wanted.

"So where's your agency phone?"

Rice was tired of the stupid questions. "In my other pants, Mary. I wasn't expecting to need it. Listen, I need you to take a message."

"Okay," Mary said perkily. "Just let me get my steno pad. You want coffee?"

Rice slammed the handset against the Plexiglas wall. And again. Taking a deep breath, he returned the receiver to his ear. "Sorry," he said sweetly. "Dropped the phone. Say again?"

"What's the message?"

"Tell Bob I'm on my way to the Squirrel. Since they've never figured out how to build straight, level highways in New England, it's going to take me six hours instead of four. So I'll be lucky to get there before dark. A charming little time warp that could have been avoided had the General not insisted I play it human and just signed me out a goddamned wok."

Mary's condescension oozed through the phone lines. Holy Mother of God, he'd like to smash her fucking face. "I'll talk to the General about that," she said.

He knew she wouldn't. She was probably fucking him. Or Spud. She lets Ma Kettle slip away and nobody says a goddamned thing. "I bet you will, sweetheart," he said.

"Anything else I can do for you, Theo?" she asked.

"Yeah," answered Rice with a sigh, actually meaning what he said. "Can somebody please explain to me what we're doing here?"

## 8.2

The President was bringing Keeley and Pooch up to speed, but Cole hardly heard a word, enthralled as he was by the way Linda's throat bobbed and danced as she spoke, captivated by the way she massaged her own ankles. She sat next to him on the sofa, her feet drawn up underneath her bottom. Her fingers, long and exquisite, were just inches away from his own. Images drifted across his consciousness, like memories sent back from the future; he was nuzzling that throat, drawing in her rich scent, caressing her ankles and shins and thighs, drawing her into him, drawing himself into her. His heart hammered inside its cage of ribs, shouting to be let out. Some part of him judged these thoughts as ludicrous. He hardly knew her. They were on the run. His kids were in grave danger. But ludicrous or not, it was all he could do to not reach out and pull her to him. In the warm and relaxed respite of this simple, cozy living room, the strange attraction that had been nibbling at his soul since the night before had blossomed and grown to a fever pitch.

Cole shook his head to clear the images. "Uh, what did you just say?" he asked, reaching down to scratch the chin of the Border Collie named Chapin that had adopted him in exchange for his constant attentions. In his daze he had missed something important. He scrunched his face into a knot.

Keeley stopped and looked quizzically at Cole. "You talking to me?"

"Yeah. You just said something." He gestured at Linda. "You called her something."

Linda smiled and nodded. "Cornfed. She called me Cornfed."

Cole shivered. "Yeah! Why'd you call her that?"

Keeley shrugged. "I don't know. It's what I used to call her. Back when—"

"What's up, Cole?" Linda could tell he was onto something. Her fingers crawled a bit closer to his. A spark flew between them.

Cole stood to break the connection, hoping to keep his head clear. He walked to the window and gazed for a moment out over the front lawn, his long arms hanging awkwardly at his sides. The early October sun was fading into late afternoon, kissing the distant tree line with gold before turning in for the night. "It's something Grace said," he answered, stepping back to face them all. "Just before we left. She said 'watch out for cornfed.'" He walked across the living room and sat back down, again sharing the sofa with Linda.

Linda's voice hummed with remembrance. "We had these names for each other. I was Cornfed. Because I grew up on a farm and was a goody-goody. Keeley was Vinegar. As in 'piss'n'vinegar.' Because she was the wild one."

"So how did Grace know?" Cole said.

Keeley raised her mug and took a sip of the home-made witbier that Pooch called *"pisser des dieux"*: piss of the gods. "You say she just wouldn't wake up this morning?"

"Yeah."

"My guess is that she's involved somehow. Got dragged into this. She's not in her body."

Cole laughed nervously. "Wow! That's wonderful! Great! So glad to hear that." Chapin nudged at his ankle and Cole scratched the dog's ear with his toe, thankful to have something he could do. He exhaled noisily. "She's five-fucking-years-old!" he cursed.

Linda reached out to him with a gentle hand and he looked over to take it in his own for a brief squeeze. For a moment their eyes locked, and the energy that passed between them – despondency and rage, worry and fascination and crazed, panicked passion - came together in a dazzle of electric power that threatened to split him open like a lightning strike. He let go of Linda's hand and shook his head, mistaking his own guilty thoughts for hers. "It's not your fault," he said.

Linda held his gaze. "I know," she said. "And neither is it yours."

"Those fuckers," he spat. He drew a couple of long, deep breaths and rubbed his face, as though he could wipe away the anger with his fingertips. Chapin nudged him again and he leaned forward, to scratch the dog with his fingers.

Linda turned to Keeley, who sat across from the sofa in one of two massive club chairs. The deep blue chenille, speckled with white flecks, reminded Linda of a star field, a night sky, a fitting setting for Keeley's "Earth Mother" vibe and flowing floral scarves. "So it's your turn, Keeley, my dear. How about telling us how you know shit like that. And how you knew we were coming. You said something about a dream?" Linda scrunched around on the sofa a bit, tucked her feet up enough to let them accidentally rest on Cole's thigh, knowing it was no accident, feeling the heat of his body, trying to keep her mind on their plight while letting the energy flow between them. She took a sip of tea to soothe the pounding of her heart. "I saw that look in Pooch's eyes," she added, catching Keeley's glance toward her husband, who was sitting in the chair beside her. "He knew we were coming. He wasn't surprised one bit."

The big French-Canadian buried his head in his hands for a moment, breathing softly through his fingers. The couple's other Border Collie, an older female named Betty, tunneled in from beneath and licked at his nose. Pooch looked up at Keeley with an expression so heavy with love and sorrow it was a wonder he could hold up his head.

"When I saw you in the auditorium, I knew it wouldn't be long," said Keeley at last, still watching her husband. She turned to face Linda. "It wasn't a dream, Mrs. President. It was real. Just like always."

Linda wrinkled her nose with distaste. "I'm not following you," she said.

Keeley sighed deeply, as if releasing decades of loss and regret, then slid out of her chair and dropped to her knees at Linda's feet, reaching out to take both of her old friend's hands in her own. She settled back onto her heels and smiled bravely, glancing back at Pooch for just a moment before speaking. "You really don't remember, do you?" she asked gently.

Linda shrugged. "Remember what?"

"Why I left."

"You left because of your uncle. You left because...." Linda stopped when Keeley started shaking her head. Linda looked around the room. At Cole. At Pooch. It had grown suddenly dark, as if the sun had passed behind a cloud. An image of Earl driving his boat into the pier flashed across her mind, the lightning in the cloud. She shook her head to clear it but it only felt darker. A shiver passed through her like a restless spirit. The window seemed too far away.

Keeley drank in a long, cool breath. "C'mon, sweetie. Slow down. Close your eyes. You remember."

Linda pulled back. "I don't know what you're talking about," she said tersely, anger rumbling on the horizon. "You left because of your uncle. You—" She looked off toward the corner of the room, as if seeking an escape route.

Keeley put a finger to her lips. "Hush, darlin'. My uncle went to jail and you helped put him there." She reached up, put a hand to the President's cheek, pulled her face around. "You saved my life, girl. You put that fucker in jail. And I will be forever grateful to you, even though it tore my family apart. But that's not why I left. And you know it."

Tears spilled from Linda's eyes and she wiped them away. "C'mon, Keeley. I *don't* know it. I don't. I *can't* know—" Linda sputtered out, as though an unseen hand had just hushed her with a touch. She looked at her lap, at the floor, at the windows, anything but her friend.

"Oh, baby, yes." Keeley's eyes welled with tears in communion with her old friend. "You can know. You do know. It's okay, now. To know. It's okay. That's why you came to me. So you could know."

Linda doubled over suddenly, as if punched in the gut, her inhalation a wrenching gasp of pain that brought both dogs to their feet. They came forward quietly, lending their noses and warm breath to Keeley's gentle touch. Linda sobbed and sobbed. The storm had broken. Keeley rose and sat beside the President on the sofa, making room for herself between Linda and Cole, hugging Linda with one arm while reaching out to Cole for strength with the other.

"They came for us, Cornfed," she said softly, as if speaking in a chapel. "Just like they had so many times before. Since we were little. You remember? They came again. We were just starting our senior year. And we were so beautiful. So beautiful." Keeley's own face was wet now with tears and she let them run freely.

Slowly Keeley went on, as if letting the story tell itself, at the pace it needed to go. "They came for us. Took us away to their ship or lab or whatever the hell it was. Put us on those tables and stuck us with those fucking needles. We were naked and you ... you were so afraid. And I couldn't help you. I couldn't move." Keeley hushed for a second as Linda cried, making some room for the memories to drip down into Linda's soul. "They brought this young man in," she continued softly. "He was ... dazed. A robot. Naked. They brought him in and he laid down on top of you."

Linda's sobbing had quieted to a soft staccato shudder as Keeley spoke, the lighter patter that followed the cloudburst. In the shelter of Keeley's love, she could let the whole truth soak into her conscious memory, knowing without knowing that the rain of her grief would wash away the grit and dust of so many years of forgetting. Betty licked the tears as they continued to fall, doing what she could to help sluice away the pain.

"I couldn't help you, sweetie. I wanted to, but I couldn't. They held me ... frozen ... unable to even turn my head. So I saw it all. I saw your eyes. How animal. How terrified. How ... assaulted. And I knew that pain. But all I could do was lie there and watch," Keeley paused and swallowed, as though her grief and shame were welling up in her throat. "You were my sweet Cornfed." Keeley's own tears joined the rainfall, mingling with Linda's, soothing their parched souls. "I felt like I failed you."

Linda shook her head and sat back to look at her friend. "You didn't fail me," she said, her eyes willing to brook no argument.

Keeley smiled sadly. "I know, baby. I know. But I was young. I didn't know up from down. I felt bad about everything. It happened just after I told you about my uncle and ... I couldn't even look at you. I couldn't. I was so ashamed. I mean, we could barely remember that something had happened, you know? But we sure as fuck could feel it. And that whole year turned out to be just one mess after another. You got pregnant and we panicked and told your folks. You sounded completely fucking crazy, swearing you hadn't gone all the way with anybody. And then luckily you miscarried. Christmas came and you told my Dad about how his brother was messing with me, and Daddy beat the shit out of him right there by the tree. Daddy filed charges. There was the whole investigation, and all the questions, and everybody, and I mean everybody – family, friends, teachers – everybody was looking at us. Lordy! No wonder we were drinking, Cornfed. It's amazing we survived it at all." Keeley shook her head in wonder. "After the trial, when Daddy said something about moving ... I jumped on it." Keeley leaned back onto the sofa cushions, hugged her arms against her chest, rested her face on her clasped hands and exhaled quietly, as though she were in a confessional. "We didn't know what had happened, Cornfed. It was like we'd both had this horrible nightmare that we couldn't quite remember. But our bodies remembered. And I didn't know how to help. All I knew was how badly I hurt." Keeley looked up at Linda. "All I could think to do was to run away. And I'm so, so sorry. I ran away. I failed again."

The President pulled away from Keeley and rose slowly to her feet. Stiffly, she walked to the living room window, moving past Pooch as if guarding a wound, as if she'd just had surgery, though whether something had been removed or added she could not tell. The setting sun lit the distant treetops with flame, autumn reds and golds crackling in the blaze. Linda felt like her whole world was on fire. Lightning had struck and ignited the sky and everything was burning away. Time. Distance. Self. The blood in her veins and the molecules in her cells. Everything she'd ever known and believed and cherished. Shifting. Twisting. Lurching. Boiling away. The fire of memory that had sparked and smoldered since that high-school play so many months before raged brightly now in the safe and gentle spirit of her long-lost friend. Keeley had been the only hope and comfort she could find in those far-flung nights of horror and pain.

And yet, in the end, even Keeley had abandoned her. Linda turned to face her friends. The flames of memory left a bitter ash of determination and truth-telling in her mouth. "Yeah, Keeley," she said, her voice little more than a raspy whisper. "You left." Her face reddened. "It was ... Jesus! We were on the track team, for chrissake! We were popular! And then I'm pregnant and you're getting fucked by your uncle and the trial and my parents and we're getting drunk every night ... and ...

everybody looking at us like we were freaks! And you fucking left me." Linda turned away and grabbed the window latch as if she were losing her balance. She took a long, slow breath. "And now you tell me we were abducted." Her voice had hardened and grayed. "What the fuck am I supposed to do with that?"

Keeley leaned forward on the sofa as if she might rise and join her old friend. "I know—"

"You don't know shit!" Linda screamed, whirling back. She took a couple of steps toward them. "I'm the goddamn President of the United States, Keeley! And these motherfuckers can just rip kids from their beds and force them—" She stopped for a moment, to choke down her grief. "Force them to...." She closed her eyes. "And there's nothing I can do about it? What the hell was I thinking? *I* shouldn't be President. I can't control this. I couldn't control it then and I sure as fuck can't control it now!"

"Oh, baby," said Keeley.

Linda turned away. "Those bastards took away everything I was, and I had to just lay there naked and let them do it."

Keeley rose and crossed the room, engulfing Linda in her flowing embrace. "I'm so sorry," she whispered.

"*I* let them," Linda stiffened, shaking her head against Keeley's apology, her voice still keen with hatred. "You didn't let them. *I* let them."

"Yes, Cornfed. We both let them." whispered Keeley.

"Those fuckers," said Linda. She let out a long, sputtering moan, like the wind gusting through an old barn. She relaxed a bit in Keeley's arms. "There was no fighting them."

"No, there wasn't."

"There wasn't anything we could do," Linda's voice was softer now, the voice of a child in her mother's arms.

"There wasn't anything we could do," agreed Keeley.

Linda stood silent for the longest time, just breathing into Keeley's shoulder. Pooch and Cole sat still and attentive, as if in church. Chapin and Betty had taken up positions on either side of the humans. They scanned the room like security guards. At last Linda looked up and disengaged from Keeley's embrace, wiped at her nose with the back of her hand, and turned to face the others.

"I, um ... I don't really know what to do with all of this." She reached up absently to smooth her hair. "I think I always knew. That night, when Spud took me people-hunting. I think I knew that that little girl was me. In the end, I think that's why I ran. Why I'm here now. I needed this missing piece." Linda looked down at her feet, then up at her friends. "But, Jesus, it hurts." Her heart pounded, terrified of being judged by those she loved most. The shame of her helplessness at the hands of the aliens, hidden for decades in an old bureau drawer in the attic of her memory, threatened now to dismantle the strong, capable identity she'd managed to create for herself in the world. She looked Keeley in the eye. "I'm sorry, too," she said. A slight smile washed briefly across Linda's face, the first soft touch of sun after the storm had passed. "Turns out I'm just a human being after all."

Keeley returned her smile. "I think maybe we're all we've got, Mrs. President," she said. "Human beings like you and me and Cole and Pooch. Whatever happens next, I think it's up to us."

Linda looked up at the ceiling, as though she could see right through it to the sky above. Then she looked back at her friends. Cole's eyes were moist and warm with shared feelings. Pooch wore a grin as big as his beard. Keeley's eyes, huge and fierce and defiant, seemed to stare right through her, as though she were seeing the work still before them. Linda shrugged. "I just want to hide," she said.

"Well you came to de right place, eh!" said Pooch heartily, lifting his beer and finishing it off. He wiped his mouth and beard and grinned even wider, his eyes as star-filled as the club chairs. "*Fiche le camp*, dis is," he said. His voice was so full of laughter and good cheer that Linda couldn't help but smile. "You get lost here!"

Linda stepped up to Pooch's chair and leaned down to hug him from behind. He reached up and rubbed her head roughly, the camaraderie of a teammate, or a fellow soldier. "Oh, Pooch," she said, kissing the top of his head. "What did we ever do to deserve you?" She looked up at Cole, and then Keeley, who had returned to the sofa. "I so want to get lost here."

Cole nodded, knowing just how she felt. But something was disturbing him. His long, thin arms wove about his sides awkwardly, his hands stretching and twisting like radar dishes, looking for answers from deep space. His face twitched involuntarily as his nod turned to its opposite. An image of Grace, lying in her bed as evil aliens swarmed about her, rose in his mind. There could be no rest. Not yet. Not for them. "We can't, can we?" he said, his voice rife with resignation and resolve. "We can't get lost here."

Linda stood and stretched her neck, then stepped around Pooch's chair. "No, Cole," she said sadly. "We can't." She squatted down to scratch Betty's chin. Betty raised her muzzle to show her just where to put those monkey fingers, the old covenant of domestication still in force. A wave of well-being washed up around Linda's heart and she buried her face in the long fur of Betty's neck. Chapin, calculating an opportunity, rose from Cole's feet and wandered nonchalantly over, nosing his way in for a share.

Keeley cleared her throat as if to call everyone back to work. Linda looked up. Keeley's face held one last secret. "You know who that was," she offered, statement and question wrapped as one.

Linda frowned. "Who?"

"That boy on the ship. The father of your miscarried child."

The words brought the whole thing into sharp focus, turning nightmare and memory into metal and flesh. There really had been a ship. And a beautiful boy. Linda closed her eyes and then opened them again so many years ago. The table underneath was bitter and slippery, the walls around her curved away in directions she couldn't quite grasp. A small, gray-white being stood next to her shoulder, looking down at her with his huge, black almond eyes. He held a long, silver wand over her forehead, the tip almost touching her skin. Every now and then he blinked, both eyes folding backward into his skull, like a frog swallowing. Two more beings, taller and thinner than the others, their mirrored eyes yielding nothing, brought in a naked young man. The young man towered over them by a good foot, his hair dark and tousled, his face blank, his eyes elsewhere. She saw now that she knew that face, and tears spilled once again down her cheeks.

She opened her eyes and looked at Keeley. "Earl?" she said.

Keeley nodded. "Yeah, baby. It was Earl."

## 8.3

Linda saw Cole's huge grin and breathed a sigh of relief. "Good news, I take it?"

Cole nodded, stepping in from the hallway. He surveyed the room. Keeley was on the sofa now, Chapin and Betty book-ending her in wet tongues, cold noses, and black and white fur. Pooch hummed in the kitchen, making a fresh stir-fry straight from their garden for dinner. His vaguely familiar tune filled the room with cheer. Linda sat in one of the huge armchairs, her legs pulled up underneath her. A fire burned in the woodstove, an old Jøtul #4 that looked like one of those statues from Easter Island. "Doctor says Grace is fine. Dad says she's been awake since mid-afternoon, acting like her usual self."

"Did you talk with her?" asked Linda.

"Nope. Right now she's up at Cat and Jake's with Emily. They found Dennis." Cole crossed over, reaching out to pat Chapin's head as he took the other chair.

"He okay?" said Keeley.

"Dad says he called Cat not long after we left, at Emily's insistence. They hadn't seen him. But later Cat got the notion to go look for him. She found him in the crawl space, under their back deck. She thought he was dead but when she wriggled in to get him she found that he was just asleep. Couldn't wake him up. Just like Grace."

"Jesus," said Linda, her voice almost a whisper.

"Apparently he won't wake up at all. So Dad walked Emily and Grace over to Cat and Jake's and they're watching over Dennis now."

"And Iain?" asked Linda.

"He's beating the crap out of his grandfather on the cribbage board. So far Dad owes him two pizzas."

"And no sign of this Rice guy?" asked Keeley. She'd argued against Cole's calling home, worried that a call might lead the People to Cole's children. And worried that it would lead them to her home as well. Pooch had assured her that it would be fine, insisting that Cole make the call. Keeley had looked fit to burst at the notion, but Pooch had held her in his arms and she'd finally agreed.

Cole shook his head. "No sign at all. And Dad has hired a security service he worked with in St. Cloud. Turns out they have a branch in Burlington. So he's now got round-the-clock armed guards at the house."

Keeley laughed. "Your Dad doesn't fuck around, does he?" Betty woke up with the laughter and curled around to lick Keeley's hand.

"No," Cole answered, letting his relief wash over him. "He doesn't."

"I like your fadder, eh?" Pooch called from the kitchen, obviously listening to every word.

Linda got up from her chair and seated herself on the rug at Cole's feet, leaning against his leg. "That's really great," she said with relief, smiling up at him. By unspoken agreement, they'd both given in to the undeniable force that had drawn them together, as though they'd each had lodestones implanted in their hearts. In ways they did not yet comprehend, they had become a team. There was little use in fighting it; they would meet this challenge as one. Here, in the brief reprieve of Get Lost Farm, in the warm before the storm they both knew was coming, they reached out to each other for comfort and support. Tentatively, Cole began to massage Linda's shoulder. Tentatively, Linda let him. All the evil aliens in the world could not overpower the tenderness and affection in that touch.

Cole cleared his throat, checking his impulse to sink utterly into his heart. Linda had told him they had to help each other be smarter. He did not intend to let her down again. This was a time to stay focused. Cole turned to Keeley, picking up where they had left off. "So, you do this out-of-body thing whenever you want?" There was determination in his query. If they were going to stay a step ahead, they had to know how this all worked.

Keeley shook her head, jangling the huge gold hoops that hung from her ears. "It's not something *I do* at all, really," she replied. "It's more like it's done *to* me. And then only rarely. A hand reaches down and pulls me out and away we go."

"And it's because of these aliens?" he asked.

"Yeah. I think so. Being with them has somehow loosened me from the flesh. Something the Nabbers are good at."

"The Nabbers?" asked Linda.

Keeley laughed. "Sorry. My name for them."

"They steal our baby!" Pooch spat, disgust in his voice. Linda turned to see him standing in the doorway, a wooden spoon held high like a cutlass. He nodded decisively, as if nothing else needed to be said, then went back to his work.

"And that was twelve years ago, you said?" asked Cole. Keeley's earlier recounting of her experience had shuddered through his heart. To lose a child, a baby, to these creatures: he could hardly begin to comprehend. His face twitched in empathy.

"Yeah. He'll be twelve in November. We call him Jack."

Linda shifted a bit, put a hand on Cole's calf, a further connection made manifest. She sighed. "Keeley, why don't you hate them?"

"Oh, sometimes I do." Keeley smoothed her curly hair, now much redder than Linda remembered. "But ... it's complicated. Nothing is as easy as it seems like it should be."

"No argument from me," said Linda with a bleak smile.

Cole frowned in concentration, continuing to draw Keeley out. "So you've had these experiences throughout your adult life. Abductions ... what have you. Out of body episodes. They took your baby. And you and Pooch bought this farm to ... what? To kind of just ... hide out? See if you could escape somehow?"

"They take Pooch too, you know," interjected Keeley. "That's how we met."

"You're kidding," said Linda.

"They fuck wit me!" called Pooch from the kitchen, stirring in the tempeh. "But I fuck wit dem back!"

Keeley stared at her husband for a moment, lost in undis-closed thoughts. A solitary tear rolled down her cheek and she let it hang, as if honoring its presence. She turned to Cole. "We haven't been hiding, Cole. There is no hiding." She let her gaze fall to the President, seated on the floor at Cole's feet. "We've been waiting for you to show up."

Linda let that sink in for a good long while, watching how her whole being wanted to push back against Keeley's words. Yeah, right. Like *I* know what to do? It just got stranger and stranger. She felt like she was trapped in a sci-fi novel; there *was* no hiding. But Rice, and Spud, and those ships in the sky, were no mere fiction. And all of those forces seemed to be revolving around *her*. As if being the President of the United States actually *meant* something here. Linda scoffed at the thought, then caught her-self. Perhaps it did mean something....

Chapin yawned and stretched, rolling over to negotiate a belly rub. Keeley complied with the dog's request. "So how did you know we were coming?" Linda finally asked.

"Spud told me. The year you would arrive. With whom. Even the type of car you'd be driving. He told me the night you were sworn in as governor."

"Jesus!" said Linda. That had been ... what? Over six years ago! The implications slowly sank in. "You know Spud?" The President winced. She did not want to hear the answer.

"Well, that's what they call him, these People from whom you're running. He told me once. Said he thought it was funny." Keeley frowned. "I don't know his real name. I don't even know if they *have* names." She stopped petting the dog and leaned for-ward, bringing her face closer to Linda's. "Think, Cornfed. Go find those memories. You've known him most of your life."

Linda turned away as if struck yet again, closing her eyes, let-ting the blow reverberate in the privacy of her own soul. As if she were falling, she reached up and clutched Cole's hand, grasping it for strength. She breathed deeply, letting the images surface, letting the feelings wash over her soul, working to simply accept, to stop resisting, to let the whole truth of her past find a place to dwell in her conscious mind. The worst of the pain passed and she looked up at her friend. "Yeah," she husked. "I know. He was there. That night. With Earl."

Keeley shooed the dogs off the sofa as Pooch came into the room with big crockery bowls.

"You want more beer?" he asked Cole as he offered him the food.

"Sure. Thanks." Cole handed the first bowl down to Linda and took the second. Pooch returned to the kitchen for the beer and the other two bowls, handed Cole the beer, then sat next to Keeley on the sofa.

"One day I will break dat leetle fucker's neck, eh?" Pooch said, with a smile that let you know he meant it. He forked a chunk of tempeh into his mouth.

"You know Spud too, Pooch?" asked Cole.

Keeley smiled. "Spud and Pooch have had a ... let's say a 'special' relationship." She picked a large wedge of bell pepper out of her bowl and plunked it into Pooch's. "For some reason, they brought the big guy here along to witness the implantation, when they put that fetus in me. When Pooch realized what had just happened, he managed to break free of his paralysis long enough to snap Spud's arm."

Pooch gestured as Keeley spoke, as if he were breaking a twig. "Next time his neck," he said again.

"Not surprisingly, they haven't abducted him since," said Keeley.

Cole and Linda looked at each other and grinned. The warmth of the Jøtul and the intimate connection with these two amazing souls overpowered the growing darkness just outside. For now, comfort and sanctuary. They would drink it deeply.

But the darkness was growing, covering the world. And Cole knew that sometime soon he'd have to step back into it. For now, he needed to understand, and so he asked another question. "You said something about the fetus. Implantation, you said. What does that mean?"

"Oh, yeah," Pooch answered sadly. "Dat's what so piss me off. De little boy Jack. He is not all human, eh? Poor leetle bugger."

## 8.4

"Man!" Cole yawned. The food, beer and radiant heat had gone straight to his head and he was struggling to stay awake. He stood and stretched. "I shouldn't have had that second beer."

Pooch raised his bottle in salute. "The gods think maybe you should rest, eh?" he said.

Cole shook his head, trying to dispel his weariness. It would not so easily surrender. "Yeah. A little nap might not be a bad idea." He sat back down, avoiding Linda's eyes. The thought of lying down for a nap set his heart pounding, because he imagined lying next to *her*. He tamped the image down. He had to be smart and stay on task. He looked at Keeley. "So tell us how these People can know where Linda is. How do they get into her head? Do you understand how that all works?"

Keeley shrugged. "I know what I've read. And I know what I've experienced. But all I'm doing is guessing, really."

"Guesses are better than nothing," said Linda.

Keeley nestled her head in the crook of Pooch's arm and took his hand in hers. Chapin and Betty slept in a pile at her feet and she reached out to rub them with her toes. "I imagine it's like out of body travel. Or remote viewing. These 'People,' these agents, go into a deep trance and their consciousness leaves their body and they go do whatever they need to do. They probably have some way of homing in on Linda's energy. Some knowledge of her pattern or something. So they can get to her instantly. I read once that important people, like Presidents, often have, like, psychic guardians, you know? Like an out-of-body Secret Service detail that stands guard over their psyches. So maybe they watch you and follow you and get inside of you all the time."

"But it makes a difference whether I'm sleeping or not," said Linda. Stiffly she rolled around and got on her knees, then stood, letting the blood flow back into her legs. She'd sat on the floor all through their meal. Now she needed the comfort of the other club chair. And she needed to concentrate. "So, they can follow me when I'm awake, but they can't get into my head?"

"Probably. On one of *my* astral journeys I visited my sister, Beth. She was awake, sitting on her sofa and knitting while watching a movie. But she knew I was there. She looked up at me and said 'Hi, Sis.' And she reminded me about my niece's birthday. All while her body kept knitting and watching TV. Her waking self wasn't aware of me. When I called her the next morning, she didn't remember a thing. So, it's like, there's all these layers going on at once." Keeley laughed. "The language gets really convoluted, doesn't it?"

Cole agreed. "So when Linda's awake, Rice and those guys can view her from the outside, and even talk with her from the outside? Without her even knowing it? But they can't get into her thoughts and know what she knows?"

"I guess," answered Keeley. "But my experience is that this other realm – Itzhak Bentov calls it the astral – or maybe it's more like that physicist ... what's his name?" She looked to Pooch, and then recovered his name herself. "Bohm. David Bohm. It's like Bohm's implicate order. All this quantum stuff, this whole realm, it's really confusing. Like, I didn't recognize Beth until she spoke to me. I couldn't tell I was in her living room, even though I'd been there many times. And I couldn't see what movie she was watching. There was just this energy thing, almost like a volcano, spewing out these hot, toxic gasses, and I just knew it was a TV. It's all so ... different. It's vibration and thought and energy and color and movement and it really takes some focus to map that onto the physical realm and move around with any sense of where you're going, without just getting totally lost. So, like, even if this Rice fucker is hovering right here in the room with us, he's probably pretty limited in what he can know."

"Unless Linda goes to sleep without her pills," Cole added.

"Right. Unless that. We seem to be most vulnerable when we're asleep."

Cole shifted in his chair, a hidden fear rumbling through his body before coming to consciousness. He closed his eyes and took a deep breath and the words came to him. "And you say maybe Grace ... that this is where she's been when she was so deeply asleep?"

Keeley leaned toward him. "Yeah, Cole. That might be what happened. When the Nabbers are around, people just get caught up in it." She breathed deeply, resonating with Cole's fear. "It's really scary, isn't it? Your little girl—"

Cole jerked his arms up in defense as both dogs started furiously barking. The two Border Collies leapt to their feet and raced from window to window around the living room. The protectiveness in their voices was palpable. Keeley pushed forward to stand but Pooch held her back, gesturing with a hand for her to wait a moment. He got up and checked the windows, but saw nothing that could have set the dogs off. He watched as they circled and barked, then raised his voice just enough to be heard. "Enough, eh?" he said. The dogs stopped barking immediately but remained on alert. Betty headed straight to Linda's chair and sat before her, watching over the four of them. Chapin slowly circled the room. Pooch sat back down.

"Whew!" said Cole.

"Sorry," answered Keeley. "That's *their* way of saying 'get lost.'"

"Pretty effective," said Linda.

"That's why we have 'em." Keeley settled back into her husband's embrace. "Chapin's got a nose for Nabbers."

Linda noticed how gentle Pooch was with Keeley. The love between them felt as hot and fierce as the fire in the wood stove. She remembered how it had felt, to have that with Earl: that sense of being known so deeply that there was nothing left to hide. What a relief that had been. Keeley and Pooch had that. But there was something else between them, something in their eyes when they looked at each other. As if they shared a secret they dared not tell. Or a grief. Or a terror. It would flit across Keeley's face like a moth on a bulb. And it fueled the good cheer that Pooch exuded, as if he could sacrifice himself on the altar of hospitality and courage to save them all, as if he could drive out his hidden sadness like the Jøtul drove out the cold. Linda doubted that she would ever know that secret. There simply wasn't time.

"So they probably have your mother on some sort of sedative," Keeley said, interrupting Linda's thoughts.

"I'm sorry?" said Linda, confused.

"Didn't you say she's in some non-existent hospital? Your mom? She was probably guarding you in the astral realm. Probably wasn't even aware of it. But they took her out."

Linda pulled her feet up, warming her toes in the chair cushion. She sighed thickly, giving up any hope of understanding or control. There was just too much they didn't know. "You think she's okay?" she finally asked, her eyes pleading.

"They wouldn't hurt their best bargaining chip, Cornfed. Don't you worry."

Cole rolled out of his chair and onto his knees, curling up on the rug next to Betty. He patted the floor and Betty sank down beside him, twisting a bit for maximum contact. Cole flopped his arm over Betty's belly and closed his eyes. Just for a few minutes. That was all he needed. He was so tired.

Linda smiled weakly. "Thanks, Vinegar. I hope you're right." She watched quietly as Pooch got up to lay another log on the fire and then step out onto the front porch, Chapin at his heels. Keeley rose and went to the kitchen, returning with a teapot to place on the woodstove before settling back into her spot on the sofa. The two women sighed as one, holding each other's eyes with love and regret and glad hearts, re-forging the connection so long broken. We hold secrets together too, Linda thought, Keeley and I. Their cold, strange nights together in the dominion of the aliens had bonded them in ways neither distance nor decades could erase or interrupt.

Pooch and Chapin came back in from outside. Pooch walked up behind Linda and put his huge hand on her head. "De clouds are moving in t'night, eh?" he whispered.

"Everything quiet out there?" asked Keeley.

Pooch nodded. "Is quiet fer now," he whispered again. "Maybe some t'under an' rain later. I put in de goats."

Linda looked up. "Why are you whispering?"

Pooch grinned and pointed down. Cole was asleep on the floor.

## 8.5

Emily lay curled up with Dennis, stroking his fur, her eyes closed. Grace sat in the chair at the foot of the bed, watching them. It felt right to her, that Emily should protect Dennis now. Dennis needed it, and Grace needed to take care of herself. She took another bite of the grilled cheese sandwich that Cat had brought her, washing it down with a big gulp of milk. She could feel how much her body loved it. She was thankful. She'd been so hungry.

Emily opened one eye. "You okay?" she asked.

Grace nodded, speaking around another bite. "I feel good," she said. "Are you okay?" She noted a sensation in her body, a warmth in her chest as she looked at her sister, as if they were connected heart to heart. It occurred to her that this was love, but it did not occur to her how strange it was that she thought this. She could not see how her older soul had followed her back to this physical life, as if those separate selves had newly coalesced in this small human body. And she could not feel how, already, she was sinking back into the limited mind of that child.

"I'm worried about Dennis," said Emily.

Grace could see that worry in her sister's face, but she did not share it. It was odd for Dennis to be sleeping like this, sure, but she could sense that he was fine. She just knew. "He'll be okay," she said, understanding that Emily would still be afraid.

"I hope so."

"I was asleep," Grace offered as justification. She'd awakened, hadn't she? They'd told her she slept most of the day. And yet she was fine, right? Grace stopped and scanned her body. She smiled. Yes. She was more than fine. "You wanna hear my dream?" she asked. Emily loved stories.

Emily sighed and closed her eyes. "Okay."

"I met the Little Prince," Grace said.

Emily opened her eyes just enough to roll them. "Right," she said.

"No, really." Grace put the last bite of grilled cheese into her mouth and swallowed it. "I was taking a walk with Dennis and we were standing outside this old farmhouse and the Little Prince came and asked us what we were doing. I told him we were guarding the house and the Little Prince said that he would guard it for us for a while so that I could go home and rest. And he was so nice, and he really wanted to help, so I let him."

"That's a pretty weird dream, Gracie," Emily said, smiling.

"Oh, and Dennis said he wanted to stay and play with the Little Prince. So he did."

"Dennis talked in your dream?"

"Yeah. And you know what?"

"What?"

"The Little Prince's name is Jack."

# Chapter Ø Nine

## 9.1

The fact that Rice was taking a Coast Guard boat filled him with delight. And that this particular boat was a twenty-five foot Zodiac that they called a "Short Range Prosecutor" was perfect. He wasn't sure why, really. He knew the President wasn't at her cottage on the Squirrel. That fucking bitch had duped them all. He knew he had to get back to Vermont as soon as possible. But there was something he needed to do first. Short Range Prosecutor: he liked the sound of that.

The lights of Boothbay Harbor receded behind him as he pushed the small craft southward. He smiled to himself, thinking back on his conversation with Bob. He'd commandeered the OC's office – some Bos'n's-Petty-what-the-fuck with a bad crew cut and cheese for brains – sat at the fucker's desk with his feet up, and made his call in style. When you're a Secret Service agent and the President has a retreat nearby, you get to do shit like that. When the President has been kidnapped by terrorists, you get to do pretty much whatever the fuck you want.

Bob had been so excited. She'd finally caught a break. Their infonets had unearthed a uniform in Vermont who'd reported a suspicious incident involving a white Subaru Forester and a tanker truck explosion. The police report had a plate number that lead to some fuckwit named Cole Thomas who lived just around the corner from where they'd found Ma Kettle's ride. A couple of tech-supports wokked out and pillaged the house, bringing back enough bio for Bob to get a make on his pattern. She was on him like a yuppie on a gingerbread latte. Fuck Linda Travis and her goddamned pills; Bob now had a back door. He was sitting right next to the good Mrs. President. And clearly they weren't at the Squirrel. So where *were* they?

Rice laughed as he rounded the point, his progress slowly revealing the sparse lights of Squirrel Island. He could just picture Bob stalking them, hovering right in their midst: the President and her hero and whoever the fuck those other two were. The woman was talking about "oh how confusing the astral realm was," and Bob was right there, laughing in her face the whole time. The bitch didn't have a fucking clue. Bob buzzed the dogs, making them crazy with rage. She loved that part. And she had to scare off a neomorph. But, God, it must have been a blast. Almost worth the puking.

And then the hero falls asleep and gives them all away.... Priceless.

Rice laughed out loud and gunned the engine as the water opened up around him. There was little boat activity this time of night, which was nice. Less to cover up. He checked his watch. At top speed it would take him about six minutes. Tie up to the dock. A ten-minute walk to the cottage. Maybe twelve. Twenty minutes tops. Surely he could spare twenty minutes?

His mission played out just as he'd imagined. Nineteen minutes later he rang the front doorbell, still not exactly sure why he was there. His gaze wandered up to the night sky as he waited. Clear just overhead, but a line of clouds spilling in from the west. It was probably already raining in Vermont. He noticed the wok parked in front of the garage. They were tracking him. Of course. Rice smirked. Finally he was getting some decent backup. And this was a seventeen-footer with a bubble, not one of those cramped twelves with nothing but a helmet. The seventeens could blind an Angel. The General must have been as pleased with Bob's success as Rice was.

The front porch light clicked on and Rice turned to the opening door. "Mr. Edmonton?" said Fred, rubbing at his eyes. The sole winter caretaker of the President's favorite summer retreat must have been asleep in front of the goddamned television.

Rice stepped in and with a quick jab crushed the old man's windpipe. The President's dear old friend fell to the floor like a steer in an abattoir. Rice rubbed his hand as he repeatedly kicked Fred's body, slowly pushing it far enough inside that he could close the door. He flicked off the porch light and headed toward the wok, hoping he remembered how to start the damned thing. The controls, designed by beings from another galaxy, were not exactly intuitive.

He stopped for a moment for one last look at the sky. He sighed deeply. He felt much better now, even though his knuckles hurt like hell. His hand was no bolt pistol. Next time, maybe he'd use a gun.

Short Range Prosecutor. Indeed.

## 9.2

"Let me look," said Linda, pushing Keeley's hand away. She swung around to stare in the mirror, plucked at her new bangs. "Jesus, I look like Liza Minnelli."

"Oh, you do not!" said Keeley, swinging Linda back around. "You look like Audrey Hepburn in *Sabrina*." She snipped at the edges near the President's ears, then stood back to assess her work. "You're beautiful."

"Can we make it any darker?"

Keeley shook her head. "This'll have to do, sweetie. It's all I got."

Linda stood and brushed the clippings from her red sweater. "We'll have to do the rest with make-up and clothes."

"Yep. Get some old hippie threads on you. A few layers. Some scarves. Something with a hood. Ain't nobody gonna notice you."

Cole stepped into the bathroom and smiled. "You look great," he said.

Linda chucked him on the shoulder as she stepped out into the hallway. "Yeah, well, you got it easy, mister. Nobody knows what you look like."

"Let's keep it that way," said Keeley, starting toward the kitchen. "Pooch!" she called ahead of her. "You off the phone?"

Pooch stepped into the hallway, another beer in hand. "Is all set," he said.

"You gotta quit drinking those, baby. You gotta drive!"

Pooch's face melted, as though he'd just failed her miserably. "I'm trying to make it not hurt so much, eh?" he said, a plea for understanding. Keeley swept him up in her arms and buried her face in his neck, discharging her dread in quiet tremors and mute weeping. Pooch handed Cole his beer and engulfed her in his arms. "I will drive so safely, *mon cœur*," he cooed. "They will make it. I know dis, eh? They will make it."

Keeley pushed herself away and wiped her face with her sleeve. "I know, baby." She strode past him and into the living room. "It's all gonna be okay." She found her purse at the end of the couch and rummaged for her keys. She looked up at her husband. "Everything's set with Elly?"

"He is leaving dere now," he said. "He will wait where we said."

Keeley nodded and turned to Linda. "And this Legrand. You know he's in Ottawa right now? Parliament's in session?"

'Well, it's not like I could call ahead and tell him I'm coming. But I saw him just a week ago and he said he was headed home for the fall session."

"And you know where he lives?"

"Jesus, Keeley!" Linda said, harshly. "I don't *know* anything! But he's all we got, you know? You got a better idea just say so!"

Keeley recoiled, raising her hand to slow things down. She took a deep breath. "I'm sorry, baby. I'm not judging your plan. I'm just ... worried." She wiped away some tears with her sleeve. "Terrified, actually."

Linda came in and sat beside her on the sofa. "Yeah, I know. I'm sorry I snapped. We're all terrified, I think. But it may be the only chance we have. Guy's brother works for the CBC. He can put me on live."

"I can't wait to see dat, eh?" said Pooch with a grin. Keeley looked away.

Pooch shrugged and turned to Cole. "We go get you some clothes now," he said. The two of them headed down the hall toward the bedroom.

Keeley listened as they pulled out drawers and opened the squeaky closet door. Pooch's cheerful patter and Cole's eager responses filled the house with normalcy. These two could have been good friends, she thought. In another time. Another universe. But all they had, all they would ever have, were these few moments. Pooch used them wisely, giving this man what gifts of courage he could, this man whom the Cosmos had chosen for this journey. Soon Linda and Cole would step through her front door and into the night, and Keeley had no idea where their path would take them. That knowledge had not been given to her. And the foresight that Spud *had* given her would soon run out, leaving her stranded on the dark and lonely trail that would take her through her own coming days. She did not wish to walk that path.

Keeley stood and pulled Linda to her feet. "C'mon, Cornfed," she said. "Let's get you made up."

## 9.3

"You can be so fucking stubborn!" shouted Linda.

Keeley stood her ground. "It has to be done."

"Like hell it does. You said it yourself. You don't know how it all plays out from here!"

Keeley reeled back as if slapped, then stormed across the room and yanked her jacket from the closet by the front door. She whirled to face them. "We have to assume they know everything, Mrs. President. Who you're with. What kind of car you're driving. Everything. If I can draw them away, if I can keep them in Maine longer, I will. I am not just going to sit here while you three go off and get yourselves—" She stopped, turned away, fished for her hat on the closet shelf, as if she was done arguing.

"Vermont's a fucking state-wide Subaru dealership, Keeley," said Linda coldly. "You don't have to drive Cole's car to fucking Portland. If they're checking out white Foresters, it's gonna take them a while to get here!"

The phone rang in the kitchen and Keeley went to get it, stepping quickly past Cole and her husband as if ready to knock them over if they got in her way. She grabbed the handset and barked. "Hello!"

The three of them listened as she took the call. Pooch put on his jacket. Cole, dressed in jeans and a blue flannel shirt and one of Pooch's raincoats, lifted a duffel bag filled with extra clothes to his shoulder. Linda sighed impatiently, standing near the woodstove. She was dressed full out in what Keeley had termed "nouveau glam hippie-chick," long skirts and layers and dangling earrings and lots of eyeliner. She felt stupid and vulnerable, but Cole had said he liked it. She sure as hell didn't look like the President.

"Fuck you!" Keeley shouted from the kitchen, slamming the handset into its cradle. She stormed into the room.

"Anyt'ing we should know about dere?" asked Pooch.

Keeley cast a withering glare at her husband and marched back to the closet to grab her boots. She sat on the floor. "Just some dipshit wrong number from Duluth," she said, pulling on a boot. She looked up at her husband and her face softened. "Said his name was Obie. Got mad at me because he said I called *him*!"

Both boots on, Keeley stood. She put on her hat and pulled the hood of her raincoat over it. Checking to make sure she had her keys, she crossed the room to her husband. She started to speak, stopped, shook her head, and pulled his face to hers for a quick kiss. "I'll see you again one day, my Pooch," she said, her voice almost a whisper.

"Hep!" she called. Both dogs sprang to their feet. Turning, almost running, Keeley headed out the front door, Betty and Chapin close to heel. She ran into the rain. And the night. And the uncertain days that lay just beyond the future she already knew.

The three of them watched as she departed, speechless. They heard the Forester start and watched as the car lights swung around and headed up the drive. Pooch sighed but said nothing.

Cole cleared his throat. "I have a brother called Obie in Duluth," he said.

## 9.4

"I don't even know who the bad guys are anymore," said Linda, watching out the side window of Pooch's van, an old recycled ice cream truck now used for transporting motorcycles. The lights of oncoming cars and the heavy rain made it hard to see the road, and Pooch drove slowly.

"I know what you mean, eh?" said Pooch from the driver's seat. Cole sat beside him up front. Behind them, in the cargo area, Pooch had created a makeshift "tent" out of two old Honda street bikes. The idea was that Linda would wedge in between them, under a pile of tarps, when they neared the border. "De whole worl' is become insane," he added.

Pooch followed 114 and headed southeast into Canaan, picking up speed as he veered past 141 on the left. Keeley had argued that they should take 141 up to the Hereford Road crossing. Closer and smaller, little more than an old gas station and some orange traffic cones, she thought Hereford Road was their best point at which to skip over the border. But Pooch was determined to go through Canaan and skim the New Hampshire line, crossing into Canada on 253. Even though the Beecher Falls station was brand new and more fully staffed, having been rebuilt in 2012 as part of the ever-tightening dictates of Homeland Security, Pooch felt like he was better known there. He'd fixed the station chief's old Harley more than once, and he'd crossed there many times, picking up and dropping off. New or not, it was still a very small station, and this was still a sparsely populated corner of the planet.

Linda sat on a milk crate and watched the road as they slowed into Canaan. Her guts were twisted tight with fear and anger and uncertainty. Too many questions had gone unasked, let alone unanswered. There had not been time. The dogs' agitated barking had spooked them. And Cole's falling asleep. Everything had changed after that. They'd been gripped with an urgency they hadn't felt before, as if they could hear Rice coming down the drive, as if they were being watched by unseen demons. Keeley had dragged Linda into the bathroom to cut and dye her hair, and Pooch woke Cole to share what plans he and Keeley had made to get them into Canada, and to pack some supplies. Then Keeley ran off into the night with her scheme to hide Cole's car. Why had she been so angry? And that phone call. They'd run through the rain and into Pooch's van and they were now less than five miles from the choke point for the whole endeavor. The country's borderline had become her own. She was crossing into her greatest test. She was coming around that oft-dreamt corner, right here in the real world. And she did not have a map.

Linda reached forward and put a hand on Cole's shoulder. Cole turned to face her, his expression distant and distracted. He was as terrified as she. "Tell me about your brother," she said. They had to think about it sometime.

Cole grimaced. "It couldn't have been Obie," he said. "Obie doesn't have a phone. It must have been the aliens. Like those strange calls at my house."

Linda nodded. "Possible. We shouldn't assume anything."

The van lurched as Pooch crossed the New Hampshire line and turned left onto Route 3. Linda braced herself on Pooch's shoulder. He reached up to pat her hand. "We be dere soon, eh?" he said.

Linda breathed deeply in an attempt to calm her pounding heart. She thought back with confusion to Keeley's departure, how she'd stormed out the door. Her old friend hadn't even said goodbye. It didn't make sense. "Did you guys have it all worked out?" she asked. Linda caught Pooch's eye in the rearview mirror. "About Keeley ditching Cole's car, I mean."

Pooch shrugged. "She come up wit dat at the last minute," he replied. He rolled the steering wheel to the left, taking them back into Vermont on 253. "You'd better go under de tarps now," he advised. The van pushed slowly northward, past a row of sleeping houses and the vast remnants of some old manufacturing plant. There were no other cars. Linda started to move back.

"Fuck," spat Cole.

Linda stopped and peered through the rain-spattered windshield. The Canadian crossing was less than half a mile ahead, lit up like a box store. Parked right next to the station were two police cars, gleaming under the blazing lights. Their lightbars, though not activated, reflected the van's headlights like possum's eyes. Linda ducked down as quickly as she could, sliding under the cold canvas and wedging herself between the motorcycles.

"Looks like maybe somebody tell dem we are coming," Pooch said. He didn't slow the van for a moment, as if he knew that to do so would only draw suspicion. Cole looked on in amazement as Pooch grabbed another beer from a bag beside his seat and opened it. He leaned back for a big gulp, then winked at Cole. "*Pisser des dieux!*" he shouted out in defiance.

Cole looked ahead to the border crossing, noting the customs signs in both English and French. A thought struck him and he turned to Pooch in panic. "What about passports?" he asked.

Pooch nodded, patting his shirt pocket. "We tink of dat too," he said with a grin.

The station's canopy, studded with high-pressure sodium vapor lamps, loomed over them like the entrance to hell: glowing orange, with nothing but blackness beyond, and raindrops falling through the light. Pooch brought the van to a stop. Apart from the provincial cruisers and an old Saturn in an employee space, their van looked to be the only vehicle there. The place felt deserted.

"Eh, fuck dis," said Pooch, pulling back again on his beer. He honked his horn. "C'mon, you fuckers!" he shouted again.

Cole shrunk into his seat. "Christ, Pooch," he said. It was all he could get out past the terror.

Pooch started rolling down his window, ready to shout again, when the station door opened. Out came a uniformed officer, the golden maple-leaf arm patch declaring him a border services agent. Pooch smiled and waved. It was Luc ... Pomerleau, if he remembered correctly. Not one of the regulars, but he knew Luc from a poker game he'd sat in on a year or so ago. Luc walked stiffly around the front of the van.

"You run dis crossing like you play cards, Luc," he said with a grin. He held up his beer. "I gotta piss."

Luc smiled briefly. "Seems like I remember winning, though, eh?" he said. "Pooch, right?" Luc kept his hand on the leather holster at his belt. Beads of perspiration dotted his forehead. He was barely twenty-one. A kid.

Pooch nodded. "Dis is my friend Doug," he said, motioning toward Cole with his beer. He reached up to dig the passports from his shirt pocket. Cole, his heart pounding, nodded slightly and stared.

Luc glanced at Cole for a second, then back at Pooch. He ignored the proffered documents. "Where you headed, Pooch?" As he spoke, three more officers, two from the Sûreté du Québec and another from Border Services, slipped out of the station and walked toward the van. The CBSA officer stopped about eight feet from Cole's window, far enough ahead that he and Luc had a clear line of sight between them. The two provincial policemen stepped around to the back. All three wore full riot gear and hard, tense faces.

Not even glancing at the troopers, Pooch took another swig of his beer and gestured with this thumb to the back of the van. "Gotta couple of bikes for Louis up in Cookshire, eh? You know Louis? He run de *dépanneur* dere." Pooch looked over at Cole. "De convenient store," he explained.

Luc glanced nervously at the trooper across from him.

Pooch followed his gaze. He'd never seen this fellow before. Looked really angry. He smiled at the man and turned back to Luc. "You guys must be all riled up like bees, eh? What wit de President gone missing." Luc frowned but did not respond. The trooper shifted his stance, flipped open the strap on his holster. Pooch finished his beer and tossed the bottle over his shoulder. "You gonna pass us t'rough, Luc, or do I piss right here, eh?" Pooch grabbed the handle and started to open his door.

"Stop!" shouted the trooper in front, gun suddenly drawn and aimed. Cole flinched, raising his arm as if to ward off a blow. The station door flew open with a bang, revealing a tall, thin, red-haired man in a gray suit and hat. In his outstretched hand was something small and black, a cube or tiny box the size of a golf ball. Cole could barely make him out through the raindrops, but he knew instinctively who this man was.

"Punch it!" Cole shouted to Pooch. Pooch complied without hesitation, slamming his door shut as he hit the gas. The van pitched forward, the engine much more lively than Cole would have guessed. Cole watched in the side mirror as the patrolman to his right turned, took a stance and popped off a pistol shot that grazed the side of the van as they sped away. Two more shots sounded, no doubt coming from the provincial troopers behind them. Cole ducked, but nothing seemed to hit the van. "That was fucking Rice back there!" he shouted.

Pooch looked over and grinned. "I guess so, eh?" he said. He weaved back and forth in his lane a bit, trying to confound the troopers' aim. The station lights jiggled and shrank in his rear-view mirror. Ahead lay straight black road, steady rain, and the dark of night. He floored the accelerator and finished his beer.

"Cole?" came Linda's voice from behind.

"Elly's just a mile ahead, *mon trésor*," said Pooch. "We make it!" He laughed wildly and rolled up his window.

"We're okay, Linda," added Cole. He turned to watch the road as Pooch pushed them onward. The wipers could barely keep up with the rain. The road was too black to be seen. There was no other traffic. Cole looked back through the van's rear windows. The station lights were sinking into the distance. There was no sign of pursuit.

"Ah," said Pooch. "So dis is it, eh?"

Cole faced forward and peered into the darkness. "Oh, no," he muttered. A blot of light reflected faintly in the headlights. Was that...? Rice again! The van punched through the rain. Rice grew larger in their field of view. Pooch did not slow. Rice raised both arms. A huge black gun. A blinding flash of green at the barrel. A hole the size of an orange punched through the windshield. Cole turned to his friend. A hole the size of an orange had been punched through Pooch's chest. The blunt nose of the van smacked into Rice with a sickening thud, slinging his head against the windshield with a vicious crack before dragging him under. The van veered to the right and tipped to the left, sliding and sparking on its side along the pavement before plunging over the gravel shoulder and into the ditch. It came to rest just short of the tree line.

Cole yelped for breath against the seatbelts that held him hanging.

The rain continued to fall.

## 9.5

Is that my blood? Linda pulled her hand out and reached for her forehead. Not blood. How could it be my blood? It's dripping on me from above. Another drop hit her fingers. Cold. Not blood. Not blood. Water. Rain. Cold. She could hear rain. She could hear wind. No, not wind. Breath. Breathing. Hard and labored. Cole. Fuck. "Cole?" No sound. "Pooch?" Who's Pooch? She thought she was speaking but she didn't hear the words. She focused on her mouth, her lungs, her throat, her lips. She tried again. "Cole?" She heard that, but it did not sound like her voice that said it.

She listened. There was a distant flapping sound like hands and handles and panic and pain. A shout of rage and effort filled the darkness, followed by a loud click and a zip and a thud and a huge intake of breath.

"Linda?"

Linda opened her mouth and spoke again, hoping her words would make it up and out of the deep well into which she had fallen. Everything felt so far away. And what was this sticking into her back? She'd fallen onto a pile of bones. "I'm here!"

"Oh my God," said a voice.

It was Cole. He must have fallen in too. Into the well. No. Not a well. Nobody had fallen. They'd been driving. In a van. Cole. Pooch. There was movement overhead. The rustling of bats. She raised her hand in defense. Bats. No. Not bats. It was Cole. He was coming. Another drop hit her forehead and she flinched.

"I'm here," she said again. She didn't know if Cole could hear her. Everything was so far away. "Are you okay?"

A hand reached down under the canvas and found hers, grabbing and squeezing. "Linda. It's Cole. I'm okay. Are you alright?"

She checked her body, testing her extremities with her mind. No bad pain. That thing in her back. She felt trapped, her legs wedged in tightly, wrapped in something cold. She moved her head. It moved. "Cole?" she said again.

"I'm right here, sweetie. Are you okay? Can you move?"

Hands pulled at the canvas, drawing it back and away. The cold air swept in. She shivered. But she could move her leg a bit more easily. "I'm here."

"Can you move?"

"I can move." She raised her right knee, freeing her foot. Cole's hands worked in under her shoulders and lifted her up. "Where's Pooch?"

"Does that hurt?" he asked. "Can you move?"

"I can move." She felt around in the darkness, her hands questing for something real. There was cold metal and oil. There was Cole's neck, warm and alive. The rain continued to fall outside, the patter on metal reminding her of summer nights at her grandparent's house. Did he call me "sweetie"? *Where's Pooch?*

"We've gotta get out of here," said Cole in the dark. He pulled her to a sitting position. "Can you walk?"

She wrapped an arm around his bare neck, using his warmth to guide her when there was no light. She could feel his heart pulsing and she buried her face against his throat. The warmth melted her tears and she started to sob. The raindrops hovered in mid-fall. The world hushed. Time itself stopped in sacred observance. There were her tears. There was Cole's beating heart and warm, wet neck. There was breath and grief and darkness. That was the whole of reality.

"C'mon," Cole whispered, patting her back. "We gotta go."

"Pooch!" she shouted, her heart pounding. He'd been driving. They were on their way to Ottawa. Rice was there, Cole had said. Rice! They'd been in an accident. "Where's Pooch?"

Cole crawled over her in the darkness, feeling his way past the jumble behind her. She reached out to her right. The handle of a motorcycle. That's what had stuck in her back. "We gotta go, Linda," Cole repeated. He pushed at the back. A door fell open, but it was wrong. She could see in the faint light from outside. The door fell down. The van was on its side.

Cole lifted the top door with one hand and pulled on the layers of canvas with the other, flipping them away and freeing both of her feet. Cold air and rain blew in through the doors. "Can you move?" he asked again. He glanced over his shoulder, back down the road.

"Okay," she said. She pushed herself forward on her bottom, her skirt catching momentarily. Cole grabbed her feet and helped her as she neared the door.

"Watch your head," he cautioned. His voice was still too far away.

She lowered her legs over the edge, bare skin sliding over cold, wet metal, her feet slipping down the door that now formed a ramp. Cole grabbed her elbows and pulled her forward until she was standing on the grass. Rain fell on her face and Cole reached around to pull up the hood of her raincoat. "We need to help Pooch!" she said.

The lights from the Beecher Falls station cast a faint glow across the sky, like the radiance of a distant city. She could see Cole sag at her words. *He didn't make it?* The tears came again.

"He's dead, Linda."

She started forward on the slippery grass. "I need to see him."

Cole grabbed her arm. The wind was picking up. It sounded like a tent flap, flailing in a storm. Cole looked up at the sky, then turned to the President. "No, Linda. We have to go."

"I need to see him!" she snarled. Jerking free of his grip, she kept moving, running her hand along the edge of the van to guide her. She made it to the front, then realized that Pooch's window was now buried in the mud. She started for the front windshield but Cole grabbed her arm again.

"We have to go!" he shouted over the growing wind. He pointed to the sky and she looked up, rain pattering her face.

Directly overhead was a light, a round, ghostly blue-white disc that glowed steadily in the rainstorm. It grew to the size of the moon as she watched. It was coming down right on them. Coming. For her. Coming like they had always come. In the confusion of night. In the cold and tender hours of her life. Coming....

Cole tugged on her arm, pulled her toward the ditch. She lost her footing and fell to one knee, feeling the cold grass and mud soak through her gauzy skirt. Cole lifted her back to her feet and walked her across the ditch until they were on the gravel shoulder. She looked up, eyes shielded with a hand, expecting the aliens to set upon her like starving dogs.

The cloud ceiling, high and featureless, began to glow and flicker, as if lit from above by dozens of powerful searchlights. A helicopter dropped suddenly out of the dark mist, cast in silhouette by the flashing clouds. It rushed toward Cole and Linda like an eagle diving for its prey, its forward spotlight scanning the ground. The glowing blue disc, almost on top of them now, jerked quickly aside, then circled the helicopter as if readying to strike. The entire cloud ceiling flashed daylight-bright and the tiny disc pulsed brightly, waggled back and forth in the air, then streaked away into the night, as though it were terrified. The helicopter settled down onto the pavement as the sky went dark again.

"Run!" shouted Cole over the clamor of the rotors, grabbing Linda's hand and dragging her away. He peered into the darkness, searching frantically for the yellow Toyota pickup that Pooch had said would be meeting them.

Linda yanked herself free of Cole's grasp and cried out, pointing. There in the road, lit by the chopper's running lights, lay a body, its face horribly mangled, its arms splayed at revolting angles. The wash from the rotor blades picked at the fabric of the man's gray suit.

"Rice!" Cole shouted over the noise.

The cockpit door swung open. They could see the pilot inside, his grim face dimly lit by the blush of an instrument panel. Cole stepped backwards, reaching out to pull Linda away. Linda shook off Cole's hand and turned back to the chopper. The man inside smiled and Linda knew in her heart that he was their friend. She grabbed Cole's hand and tugged at him through the noise and the rain and the twisting air, then jerked open the cabin door and climbed inside, her head bowed low, as if in surrender or obeisance or both. Cole hesitated, glancing over his shoulder at the distant headlights approaching from the north, then back at Linda in the cabin. With an exaggerated shrug he threw off his doubts and fears and followed his President into the copter, pulling the door closed behind them. The roar was deafening. The whole cabin shook. Before they could even sit down the helicopter had leapt into the night sky, forcing them to grab hold of each other to avoid falling.

The pilot reached over and flicked on a cabin light long enough for them to take their jump seats and find their seatbelts. Cole and Linda strapped themselves in and the light flicked back off.

"Welcome to Canada, Mrs. President," said the pilot over the rattle and hum.

"Are you Elly?" asked Cole, shouting to be heard.

"I am," said Elly, concentrating on the controls. The copter lurched to the left, swinging around in a tight sweep that jostled them all.

"We thought you'd be in a truck."

"The Toyota would not start." He reached down to his left and the helicopter shot up toward the clouds. "The electrical system was totally fried. So I came in my other car."

"Pooch is dead," said Linda, her throat thick with loss. She noticed her hand in Cole's and squeezed it tightly.

Elly stared ahead, focusing on his mission. When he spoke there was anger in his voice. "He said he probably would be."

Pooch was Elly's cousin, Linda remembered. And he'd died to get her across the border. No wonder Elly was angry. As she had so many times before, the President cursed the damned aliens, and the People who served them. Pooch had broken Spud's arm. Linda vowed, in that moment, to exceed him. She reached forward, placing her hand on Elly's shoulder. The pilot flinched but did not turn around. "I'm sorry," Linda offered. It was all she had to give. For now.

Elly pointed out the cockpit window to the sky before them. "Your welcoming party is here," he said.

Linda stretched her neck to better see. Moving across the sky in a seemingly random pattern was a multitude of lights - globes and discs and triangles and straight lines - some as small as basketballs, others as massive as aircraft carriers. As the helicopter approached, the UFOs fell into a circular formation thousands of feet in diameter, looking like the mouth of a wormhole to a distant galaxy, or a wreath of lights hanging in the air. Linda took a deep breath, to help calm her fear and excitement. She couldn't tell whether these were the jaws of a monster ready to snap shut, or an honor guard to see them on their way.

"Pooch said to expect them, but I didn't believe him," said Elly over the rotors. His hand steady on the controls, his eyes focused on the task at hand, Elly pushed them forward toward the lights.

## 9.6

*She focused on her father and flickered out to go find him. The sky flew to pieces around her, flinging her through the hearts of galaxies and the flutterings of butterflies. There was her mother, boarding her plane. There was Emily, bored in class. There were the dead living, the living dying, the lights of birds and the mutterings of boulders. A screaming woman grabbed at Grace's cord. A distant sun burned her face. Her universe whirled like a midway ride, lifting her to the clouds and tossing her back to Earth. And there was her father's car, speeding below her through the night.*

*A cry rose up from the car. A scream. A howl. That woman from the house. Keeley. It was she in the car. Grace feared that Keeley's grief could cause her to have an accident, so she settled in beside her and cast a warm glow of love and peace over her. Keeley sighed and kept the car on the road.*

*Her father was not here. Linda was not here. For some reason Grace had missed them. She rose and enfolded and scanned the Cosmos for her father's pattern of love and flickered again. In an instant, there he was.*

*The Little Prince zipped away as she approached. He stopped in the distance and turned to watch, a fawn seeking the safety of woods. Grace smiled. He was so shy! Grace beamed him a packet of gratitude, thankful that he'd watched over her father and Linda while she was away. She turned to look for Dennis. Her little dog was flying excitedly toward her from below, almost tripping over his own legs. Dennis jumped into her arms and slathered her face with love, then wriggled down and took his place at her feet, proud to be helping. She reached down and scratched under his chin. The little dog closed his eyes and thumped a hind leg.*

*Grace noted how differently she felt here, how clear was her mind, how distant was that little girl whose body she inhabited. She focused her awareness on her surroundings and peered into the densest layers. She frowned. This was not the house where she'd left them. This was a lone highway. A decrepit white truck lay on its side. An Elder disentangled himself from a battered body in the middle of the road and flickered out without a word.*

*Linda and her father crawled out of the truck. Grace sent them a parcel of love and dove into the vehicle to see what had happened. The big man from the house would not be crawling anywhere.*

*She rose up to a spot overhead, scanning for dangers. The sky was filled with beings, with voices and intentions and wants and needs and plans she could barely begin to comprehend. A flutter of metal and wind came in from the north, pushing the multitude aside. She could feel the good heart of the man inside and drifted away to observe.*

*Her father and Linda climbed into the metal thing. She knew what it was ... a helicopter! Grace smiled and started to follow.*

*A furious knot of dark, blinding power flew out of nowhere and knocked her from the sky.*

# Chapter Ten

## 10.1

Mary keyed her way in and shut the door quietly behind her. She glanced at the clock over the sofa and sighed with exhaustion. God, it was after midnight. Making her way across the room by the diffuse haze of city lights filtering in through her window, she pulled aside the sheer curtains and slid open the door to the promenade. She stepped out into the night. After two hours down in the Rock with Bob, she found the view comforting. Buildings full of people, working through the night, sparse traffic winding its way between those buildings, the lights on the Monument: these things all connected her to the normal world. Alone and afraid on the third floor of the White House, Mary needed that connection.

She let the curtains fall and made her way to the bathroom, pulling her sweater over her head and slipping out of her shoes as she walked. Feeling her way through the darkness, she sat on the edge of the tub and turned on the water, letting it get hot before she stopped the drain. The situation below, and Rice's failure, had left her feeling soiled and worn. Cold. Old. Beat up. Used. She lit the votive candle that sat on the tub's edge, then unbuttoned her silk blouse and let it slide to the floor. She sat and let the bathtub fill, thinking of nothing at all. Standing, she slipped off her skirt, panties and bra, making a heap on the floor. She lowered herself into the tub and turned off the flow. The comfort of warm water brought tears to her eyes and she let them gather and slide down her cheeks. Here in her own room, here in the dark, she got to cry.

Had it all made sense at one time? She couldn't quite remember. The clock on the living room wall had said it was 12:07 a.m. Seven minutes into day four. Fifty-three hours and change since the President had run. Hardly enough time for Mary's whole world to have unraveled. And yet it had. The reports from around the world had come in no more than an hour ago. A few of the Life had gone completely dormant. The rest of them had fled, leaving their facilities behind as if they'd just popped out for a smoke and then never come back. Not even Spud would answer the call. The General was holed up in his office, drunk and angry. The President was lost in the night. Rice had failed to bring her in. And that failure had brought to Mary's conscious mind something she hadn't allowed herself to know before: she was in love with Linda Travis. Fuck. That's just wonderful. Rice's last words clung to her like a song, playing over and over in her mind: what *are* we doing here?

Mary grabbed the soap from its dish and pulled it across her stomach, sighing at the touch, the simple joy of lather and fingers and skin. They didn't touch. The aliens. She sniffed bitterly. After all this time they still hadn't found a better term for them. Decades of contact and they were still alien. They might call themselves the Life, but they didn't feel like Life to her. They felt like concrete and stainless steel and wet leather gloves.

Now that they were gone it was easier to see: humans had never been able to get inside of them, to know them, to feel who they were and what they wanted and where they were headed and why. Behind the words, the treaties, the actions, the information, the promises, and the Plan, the inner world of the Life remained as essentially unknown as the Earthly bugs they resembled. Rice had figured it out sooner than she: she, too, had had enough. But she had no idea what that meant. Despite the fact that she hated his guts, she wished Rice were here right now, to talk to. He would have understood.

She had thought they loved her, the aliens. She'd thought *she* loved *them*. She laughed bitterly at the notion, the echo of her voice on the cold tile bouncing back to slap her face. Right. Like *she* knew anything about love. She could barely feel her own heart. She remembered when they'd brought her in, almost two decades ago. They abducted her right in the middle of one of her father's beatings, freezing the moment in time and space like a dandelion puff in a Lucite paperweight. They floated her through her second-story bedroom window on a beam of blue butterflies, up to their waiting craft and a room full of old pinball machines and boxes of yarn. With fussy precision, they wrapped her with long, silver ribbons and poked her with tiny, black batons, as though they were tailors, fitting her for a new outfit. Whether by luck, providence, or sheer force of will, Mary had managed to break out of their damnable fog. The aliens just stood there, surprised, mouths comically agape, as Mary begged them to take her with them. A full minute passed. Then the tallest of them nodded once, a single, silent gesture that had changed the course of her life. She'd never gone back. Not once. The bugs had saved her. They would be her family now. Even a bug was better than her father.

Mary took a deep breath and slid her head under the water to wash the pain from her short, black hair. She'd thought the People were saving the world. She'd thought this was the only way: trade a small piece of the planet for the knowledge humans needed to get out of the mess they were in. But that piece of the planet kept getting bigger and bigger, and the promises never quite came true. And now the Life were *gone*. And so was Linda. And the mess was getting out of hand. Fred was dead. And that poor kid at the border crossing. And those troopers! God, Rice, you crazy bastard! The President was still running, zooming off into the night in a helicopter, according to Bob. Leaving Mary behind to clean things up. Leaving her....

Mary came up for air and screamed into the darkness. The Vice-President had cornered her in the hall and yelled at her!

The fucking Vice-President! She splashed at the water with both hands, sending ripples of loneliness and rage over the rim of the tub. The *whole world* had gone out for a smoke, and left *her* in charge! The press would be bleating come morning. The General would chew her out once again, pickled in his own powerlessness. Mork would sit there in her resting-box, as still as a gargoyle, mocking her with her silence. Bob and Random and Alice would keep trying because that's what they did, whether it made any sense or not. And she would ... what? She didn't know who she was anymore.

The departure of the aliens was a game changer, and Mary was not sure that she wanted the game to change. She'd been so happy these past twenty years. To have found other human beings involved with the aliens, other humans who seemed to know what was going on, who seemed to be in control, who actually *wanted* her ... it had been intoxicating. All of a sudden, at fifteen years of age, she'd been brought into the most important project the world had ever known. And in a grand display of Cosmic irony, her childhood of violence and abuse at the hands of her father, when coupled with her lifelong experience as an abductee, had left her with a rare gift: she could interface with the Life in real-time normal reality like nobody's business. She was hired.

It hadn't mattered to Mary that somewhere behind the People, in some nebulous, far-off somewhere, there existed a network of hidden powers that controlled the world. She'd known all along that they were there: the elite, the rich, the powers that be. After all, who signed her paychecks? She'd heard that, behind the layers of secrecy there were just more layers, that for every Bilderberg Group and Skull & Bones "secret society" that frightened the bloggers like bedtime boogeymen, there were older, richer, more deeply hidden circles that used these "known" groups as fronts and screens. She'd been told of families and bloodlines that stretched so far back into the ancient mysteries that they made a mockery of "history." She'd known all along that these were the people who really determined the course of the future for all of humanity, unbeknownst to the vast majority of regular folk, and certainly unbeknownst to the bozos in Washington who imagined that *they* were in charge. She'd known, but she hadn't much cared. If her father had taught her nothing else about life on Earth it was this: people needed somebody to rule them. They were not up to the task of ruling themselves.

It had all been fine by Mary. *Let* these guys run the show. Lord knows somebody has to. And she was doing fine. The People took their orders from the highest and most hidden levels of power on the globe, helping to enact the secret Plan that had been devised to guide them all into a great and glorious future, humans and aliens alike. You couldn't get better work than that.

But now it was shifting, and enormous cracks had appeared in the foundational assumptions of her life, revealing her own felt sense of things to her conscious mind. The aliens had departed. It had never before occurred to her that such a thing was possible. And without the aliens, without their strange powers and astounding technologies, without their assistance in this grand scheme to help humans solve the greatest challenges they have ever faced, without the Plan and its promise, the People themselves were nothing: a ragtag collection of wounded souls and insane, power-addled egos. If the Plan were to fall into doubt, if the People found themselves suddenly "redundant," the real money and power would cast them aside as a fail, redesign their goals, and do things the old-fashioned way. War, conquest, and chattel slavery had been around long before media manipulation, economic control, wage slavery, and alien technologies came on the scene. If the game was to rule the Earth, and, in the end, it was, these old tactics would still do fine in a pinch. Sure, climate change and the oil problem would be a mess, but they'd muddle through somehow. They sure as hell wouldn't need the People for that. If the People could no longer deliver the aliens, and if they could not even keep the President under control, they may as well pack up their show and hit the road.

Mary sighed and submerged her head again. She didn't even know *why* the Life had departed. But it was worse than that: Linda was lost now too. And without Linda, Mary may as well just curl up and die.

## 10.2

Linda reached out and nudged Cole's shin with her toe. He opened his eyes. "We can't go to sleep," she said over the noise. She glanced out the window. There were no strange lights in the night sky. Their extra-terrestrial honor guard had scattered as soon as the helicopter passed through their circle of ships.

Cole smiled and nodded. They knew, after the fiasco at the border, that they had to assume they were both under constant surveillance. No sleeping without one of Linda's pills. He looked at his watch: half past midnight. Another thirty minutes to go, if Elly's estimate was correct. Was it really only this morning that Linda had knocked on his bedroom door? How could that be possible?

The old Sikorsky hit an updraft and lurched, rattling its contents. Cole surveyed the cabin. Obviously, Elly was a pilot for a medical evacuation service. The tools and equipment of emergency medical transport lined the compartment, everything in its right place. The gurney was clamped solidly to the floor. The drawers and cabinets were well secured. It occurred to Cole that this was likely *not* an authorized flight, and he thought ahead to their eventual landing. He turned to the pilot. "Elly? How are you going to explain this when you get back?"

Elly smiled grimly. "That should not be so hard," he said, his accent less pronounced than was Pooch's. "I will explain to the dispatcher of Medicopter Quebec that when I heard of my cousin's accident I go a bit crazy and take off without even filing a flight plan. Since the dispatcher of Medicopter Quebec is my wife, I think she will accept my story, eh?"

Cole cringed. The mention of Pooch hit him in the gut. The whole thing was just too surreal for words, moving much too quickly for him to keep up. He wondered if he might awaken at any moment, his children arrayed around his bed, and Dennis too, attending him in his delirium. He looked across the cabin at the President and his insides twisted again, a pain of a very different sort: his heart was broken wide open. Snatched from the D.C. world of business suits and sensible shoes and power hair, and made over in Keeley's hippie-goddess image, Linda Travis caught in his throat, a vision of grace and power and vulnerability so magnetic that he could not turn away. He hoped *she* wasn't an hallucination.

"You okay?" asked Linda.

"I'm fine, Mrs. President. You?"

Linda smiled. "I'm okay," she answered. Her eyes welled up. "I'm really sad."

Cole nodded, wishing the jump seats weren't opposite each other, wishing he could hold her. "Yeah," he said quietly. "Me too."

Elly called back, pointing out the cluster of lights in the darkness ahead, a small city surrounded by farmlands. "Montmagny," he said. Cole pushed up from his chair to see. Their destination looked larger than Elly had indicated, and the St. Lawrence River, upon which Montmagny was situated, was a vast ribbon of blackness beyond the city lights. Elly continued. "If I land at the hospital, you know, there are too many people there, eh? You should not be seen. So we meet Stephan at the house."

Cole relaxed back into his seat. He just had to trust. Apparently, Pooch and Keeley had seen this all coming and made ready for it. There was a plan in place, a plan unfolding, a plan that included helicopters and trains and people named Stephan who would appear in the night and take them another step along the way. It sunk in then that Cole's life was no longer his own. It was being shaped by forces outside of himself, by forces great and small and far beyond his ken, by motorcycle repairmen and secret agents and aliens from outer space. He was an actor in some grand drama he did not comprehend. This is how it must feel to be President, he thought, letting his gaze fall on Linda as she stared out the window, seemingly lost in thoughts of her own. Feeling his attention, she turned and smiled. He reached out and took her hand. They would both have to trust.

Cole turned to Elly. "Did Pooch tell you where we are heading, and why?" he asked.

Elly shrugged. "He didn't know, eh? He said for me to get you to the train. Dis is the best way."

"So who's Stephan?"

Elly glanced back for just a moment, long enough to grin. "He's my son," he said.

Linda straightened. "Why are you doing this, Elly?" she asked.

"Doing what, Mrs. President?"

"Why are you helping us?"

Elly took a moment to pilot his craft. The lights of Mont-magny were growing near, spreading out to the port side. He was flying in just to the south, descending over an area of dark, partly-cloudy night, flecked with the occasional speck of illu-mination. The headlights of a lone car crawled along a roadway below. Elly shrugged. "Because Pooch asked me to," he finally answered. "Over a year ago, it has been. Because he said that one day you would go missing from the White House, and that you would come to his house. He said that the televisions would be telling lies. He said you would need help. He said the sky would be filled with strange lights."

Elly pushed the collective lever and the copter descended into the darkness. A patch of pavement rose up underneath: a two-lane road with open fields on either side. The road was dry, the rain having passed to the south. Elly sat them on the ground and throttled down. The noise subsided a bit, allowing him to speak more quietly. He turned to face his passengers. "I help you because Pooch was my friend. And because everyt'ing he said has come true." He looked at Linda with eyes that almost pleaded. "I am so tired of the lies, you know?"

The cabin door swung open. Cole and Linda turned to see a young man in jeans and a black leather jacket, with the same curly dark hair as his father's, though longer. All of seventeen, he stood as tall as Pooch had, but was much thinner.

"Welcome to Canada, newlyweds!" the young man said, clutching his cap.

10.3

Slowing only slightly, Stephan turned left onto a gravel road. The car skidded in the loose stone, jostling Cole and Linda in the back seat. Stephan floored the accelerator, reached down to grab a cigarette, and poked it into his mouth. "You guys okay with me picking up my girlfriend?" he said, with no trace of his father's accent.

Cole frowned, though the expression was lost in the darkness of the back seat. "Your girlfriend?"

"Yeah. Roxanne. She said she'd hang out with us if you guys were game."

A protective urge welled up in Cole. Linda was exhausted. They were on the run. *Pooch had been murdered by a psychotic government agent.* "Uh, what do you mean hang out?"

"Well, your romantic wedding-day helicopter getaway to Canada comes with one little snag," Stephan smirked. "We got three hours to kill before the train gets here."

Cole and Linda looked at each other. Whatever story it was Elly had given his son, they would just have to go along with it. "What time is it now?" asked Linda.

Stephan tapped on the digital clock on the dash. "One-sixteen, Julie," he said. He glanced over his shoulder. "It is Julie, right? Julie and Doug?"

"Yeah," said Linda with a nod.

"You're friends of Pooch's?"

Linda recoiled. No doubt Stephan would not hear about his father's cousin until morning. She took a deep breath. "Yeah. Friends of Pooch's. From Vermont."

Stephan nodded. "So you're cool with Roxanne?"

"Sure," said Linda, grabbing at Cole's hand and giving it a squeeze. "That'd be fine. Where are we going to hang out?"

"The Animal Recycler," Stephan shrugged. "The only place in town that's open all night. You guys are buying, right?"

Linda looked on in wonder. How Cole could eat that junk was beyond her. It was disgusting: a huge, drippy blob of fat and steroids and industrial chemicals called the Hereford Deluxe. She shook her head. Cole winked and took another bite. Linda sipped at her tea. She'd eaten a great many awful things in her travels but she would draw the line at factory-farmed fast food. She'd rather just fast.

"So you guys just got married," said Roxanne, taking a slug of her strawberry shake. It wasn't a question, though the singsong quality of her voice made it sound like one. They'd told her all about it in the car. But she was nervous. She pulled absently at the neck of her t-shirt, as if it were cutting off her oxygen.

Linda smiled and nodded. "Yep," she said. She was so tired her bones hurt. And these hard plastic benches would not warm up no matter how long they sat on them. She thought ahead a few hours, imagining herself and Cole on the train, maybe catching a few hours of sleep in coach. It was all she could do to keep from screaming.

Roxanne shoved a wad of fries into her mouth and bobbed her head while she spoke. "So, like, is this your *wedding night* then?" she asked, not hiding in the least where she was heading.

Cole cut her off at the pass. "We've been living together for a while now," he said, avoiding Linda's eye.

"Oh." She scanned the dining room for another question, finding one near the trash receptacle. "So where are you guys headed?"

Cole opened his mouth but no response rolled out. Linda jumped in. "Toronto."

"Really?" said Roxanne. "My friend Del grew up there."

Linda smiled. "Really? Wow."

"Yeah. He lives in Beaumont now. Do you know him?"

Linda couldn't help but laugh. "No, Roxanne. I don't." The girl's question comforted her. Here Roxanne was, sitting for hours in a brightly lit restaurant with the U.S. President, and she didn't have a clue. Keeley's disguise worked. If Roxanne was any indication, Linda could stroll around the National Mall at this point and go unnoticed.

As if reading Linda's mind, Roxanne spoke again. "So we heard about your president," she said. She shoved more fries into her mouth and spoke around them. "Man, that's some crazy shit."

It was Cole's turn to jump in. "Yeah, Roxanne, it's pretty disturbing." He reached out for Linda's hand under the table. "It's a crazy world we live in."

Stephan roused from his disinterest and lethargy long enough to comment. "Yeah," he said. He hadn't eaten a thing, preferring instead to pop out "for a dart" every ten minutes. Apparently Canadians didn't smoke in public places either.

Cole checked his watch. He sighed and looked at Stephan. "What time should we get to the station, boss?" he asked.

"What time is it?"

"Almost two."

Stephan waved a hand. "You got lots of time, Doug. Don't sweat it."

Cole held his anger in check. He knew he was totally reliant on this young man. "Okay. I won't. But it would help me to know a time. So I can plan it out in my head."

"So you think you should have a plan, eh?"

"Yep."

Stephan pulled another cigarette from his pack. "It's a flag stop," he said.

"Meaning?" Cole took a deep breath.

"Meaning it doesn't stop unless they know there's a passenger to pick up."

Cole glanced at Linda for a moment, then back at Stephan. "So do we need to tell them?"

"Already taken care of," Stephan said.

"You called them?"

"My dad did."

Cole pulled out the pamphlet Stephan had handed them earlier. It was a schedule for a train called "The Ocean." He checked it again. "And the train stops at 4:09?"

"That's the plan." Stephan got up, flicking his cigarette with his lips. "Off for another cig," he said.

"Do they run on time?" Cole asked as Stephan walked toward the door.

The young man stopped, rumpling his eyebrows as if questioning a doubting child. "Wouldn't that be nice?" he said. He laughed derisively and pushed his way outside.

Roxanne smiled, looking from Cole to Linda and back again. "He's just mad because he thinks his papa didn't pay him enough."

It was just after three in the morning when Stephan dropped them off at the Montmagny station. He and Roxanne were headed back to her house "to skronk," he said before driving away. Cole could guess the meaning and was glad that the young man's gonads had taken over. One more story from Roxanne about her and her friends and the great times they had would have sent him over the edge.

Alone in the night, Cole guided Linda from the parking lot and up the walk, his hand on her elbow. Pooch's old duffel bag was slung over his shoulder. A solitary flickering floodlight lit the walkway. They reached the station, a huge two-storied affair that reminded Cole of an ornate barn, and passed through a rusty chain-link gate. They stepped out onto the platform and Cole pulled on the station's front door. As he'd anticipated, it did not open. A sign taped to the glass said in both English and French that the building was no longer offering service to passengers. The light fixture on the building itself, a small yellow bulb under the overhang on the far corner, left most of the waiting area in darkness. That was fine with him. He didn't much care to be observed right now.

There was no bench so Cole took off his jacket, threw the duffle against the wall, and sat on the paved platform, motioning for Linda to join him. She cuddled up beside him and he pulled his jacket over them both, tucking it around their knees and necks as tight as he could to keep out the cold. Thankfully, the duffle blocked the cold air from behind. An October night in Canada could easily bottom out near freezing. He was glad they only had an hour to wait.

"They're young," Linda whispered into his neck. She sighed deeply.

"Yeah, they are," he agreed.

Linda pulled back enough to see him, looked Cole in the eyes for most of a minute, studying him, drinking him in. It was all so fucking strange. She could not deny his quirkiness: his goofy stance, his facial tics, the way his head tilted and gimballed when he spoke. He wasn't her type at all. But there was a fire inside him as well, a flame that blazed with sure and undeniable power.

She felt like the Universe itself had sent him to her, a gift of aid and companionship in an uncertain time. Cole flicked his eyebrows playfully as she stared, as though reading her thoughts. He seemed to know and even like the fact that he was a bit odd, and that was powerfully attractive to her. Linda's heart missed a beat and then picked it up. She settled back in beside him.

Cole stared out over the landscape. The moon had risen, to cast its wraithlike radiance on the tracks. The sky was mostly clear here, faint wisps of high cloud drifting along, in no hurry whatsoever. The air at ground level was still. Cole watched the horizon, feeling like a rabbit in an open glade. Could they make it to safety before the hawks struck again? There was no way to know. For now, only this: the empty platform, the cover of over-hang and darkness, and the tracks glinting off to infinity in both directions, promising them another day, and another journey. It would suffice.

"Any chance we're gonna fall asleep?" Linda murmured the question into Cole's chest.

"Nope."

"How do you know?"

Cole smiled. "Because I'm going to sing to you."

Linda pulled her head from the warmth of his neck to look him in the eye again. "You're gonna sing to me?"

"It's how I always stay awake. On long drives at night."

"Hmm," smiled Linda. "What are you going to sing?"

Cole chuckled softly. "You're going to laugh."

"It's going to be hard to keep it a secret if you plan to sing it to me."

"Yeah. I guess so."

"C'mon, mister," she said, punching him playfully in the side. "I could use a laugh right now."

Cole blushed in the dim light. "When I was a kid, I really loved Bowie. I memorized every word of the Ziggy Stardust album."

"And that's what you're going to sing?"

"Yep."

Linda kissed him quickly, blushingly, and settled back in, burying her face in his neck. Cole cleared his throat and started to sing. Softly, because he did not want them to be discovered. And yet with the full intensity and wild abandon of hope and joy and love that coursed unexpectedly through his veins. He sang until the train arrived.

And it really *was* paradise.

## 10.4

"Monsieur?" Cole looked down. A tiny white poodle was pulling at his pants leg. He didn't have time for this. He'd been looking all night for his room and hadn't found it. He was exhausted. And where was Ruth? She said she'd meet him in the cafeteria, but she was nowhere to be seen. With the exception of the tiny old man who'd been following him all evening, the cafeteria was empty. The old man cleared his throat and spoke again, his weird eyes winking backward into his head like a frog's. "Monsieur?"

Cole opened his eyes. The train had stopped. It was light outside. And here was the porter shaking him awake. The older man's gentle, doe-eyed, patrician face conveyed both amusement and concern.

"*Nous sommes à Montréal, monsieur*," he said with a smile. "Montréal."

Cole smiled in return. "Thank you," he said, his voice rough and dry.

The porter left. Cole turned to watch Linda sleep, her knees tucked up to her chin, her head propped at an awkward angle against the window. In Montmagy, under the dark overhang, they'd both taken a sleeping pill fifteen minutes before the train was scheduled to stop. "The Ocean" had actually arrived ten minutes early and they'd boarded without incident, purchasing their tickets with the wad of cash Keeley had stuffed into Cole's hand before she left. They also purchased tickets to Toronto, Buffalo and Detroit. Even though the aliens and the People could apparently track them at will, there was no reason to make it any easier for them. Maybe they could throw them off the trail for a while.

The car had been half full, if that, and they'd fallen like rag dolls into their seats, the porter bringing them pillows and blankets almost instantly. While "service" was deteriorating around the planet, the trains in Canada were clean and well-staffed, as if things there had actually improved. Cole and Linda relaxed instantly, feeling like they'd been transported to some safer, saner universe. They fell eagerly to sleep, trusting that the porter would wake them in Montréal. He had. Cole hoped that their trust in the pills was similarly justified. It was bad enough, if what Keeley had said was true, that these People must already know that they were on a train. He did not want them to know their destination.

Linda was lovely in sleep. The cares of her world had fallen away, leaving simple beauty and grace to radiate from her face in a soft, even glow. In the course of just two days, this President, this woman, had become precious to him as few people ever had. She'd given him the gift of needing him, and of needing him to be exactly who he was. He longed for the time to savor that. He wanted to take care of her. He wanted to whisk away the pain that had already found her, and spare her the hard days he knew were still coming. He wished he could just let her rest.

"Linda?" he said softly, taking her hand. Her fingers flexed but she did not stir. "Linda?"

Cole watched over her as her breathing slowly grew deeper with each inhalation. After a minute she opened her eyes, focusing on some distant land. "I was dreaming of Earl," she whispered.

"I'm glad," Cole said.

"He was ... he was in a park. Or the woods. Walking a couple of his old black Labs. Tossing a tennis ball for them to chase. He said he was okay. And he told me to remember to wear my mittens because it was going to get cold." She smiled, looking into Cole's eyes. "Are we there yet?"

"We're in Montréal."

"What time is it?"

Cole checked his watch. "Eight forty-seven."

"Hmmm." Linda sat up and stretched, her hands reaching the overhead compartment. "You sleep?"

"Yeah. Yeah, I think I did."

She looked around the car. "We're the last ones."

"Yeah. The porter was just here. Woke me up. We've probably been here ten minutes or so."

"And we've got til ten?"

"The 33 to Ottawa leaves right at ten, yeah. So we've got time for breakfast. And maybe I should call the kids."

Linda frowned. "Is that a good idea? I mean..."

Cole hiked his shoulders as if to protect his exposed neck. Linda's question brought the previous night's cold horrors crashing back in on the warm comfort of the present moment. He exhaled his frustration and closed his eyes. "How can we know?" he said, rubbing his face. His voice was dark and heavy with anger, fatigue and helplessness. "Like, can they crawl into the telephone and follow the lines right back to my kids? Are those bastards already there, at my dad's house?" He looked at Linda. "Fuck! Who the hell knows? I mean, even with Rice dead ... there's more of 'em, right? More of them," he motioned to the air around them with a wave of his arm, "just, I don't know, swarming all around us, ready to pounce."

"I wish I knew," answered Linda softly.

"It's fucking killing me," Cole said bitterly. "Not knowing if the kids are okay." His face was tight and angry, furrowed with helplessness and hardened with the need to protect his children.

"Yeah," said the President. There was a loud banging sound out on the platform, followed by some distant shouts. Linda took a long, slow breath and glanced at the door of the railroad car. She squeezed Cole's hand. "I think we need to get going," she said.

Cole nodded, then got up and pulled the duffle bag down from overhead. "We need coffee," he said, as if they might both find their answers at the bottom of a cup.

"Hell, yeah, we do," answered Linda. She unfolded her legs and pulled herself to her feet. Together they made their way off the train.

Economic instability had been good for the railroads; the #33 was packed to the rafters with mid-week commuters. With the Economy and Business class seats sold out, Cole and Linda ended up paying for first class tickets. That was fine by Cole. If they got through this alive, he intended to present a hefty bill to the U.S. Treasury, the thought of which made him smile. The coffee in the snack bar had been surprisingly good, as had the croissants. Add in three hours of sleep, the preferred seating, and the complimentary newspaper, and all-in-all he was feeling pretty good. Sitting side by side now on the leather sofa in the lounge car, watching the Canadian countryside pass by through the panoramic windows, Cole and Linda had time to simply sit and catch their breath. And to look at each other.

"Tell me about your brother," said Linda. Ten minutes in the rest room had left her looking fresh and alive and whole again. Keeley's clothes, purples and yellows in gauzy layers and flowing designs, made for a wonderful disguise. With her eyeliner and lipstick retouched to perfection, Linda was a forty-something flower goddess seeing the sights. The President of the United States was nowhere to be seen.

"Okay. Jeez. Let's see." Cole shrugged. "I'm not sure where to start."

"Well, let's see," said Linda playfully. "He's your brother ... which means he had the same parents as you do. And he lives in Duluth. And his name's Obie?"

"His name's Carl. OB stands for Older Brother. I never really got to know him as a person, by name. I just knew him from the stories my folks told. It was 'your older brother' this and 'your older brother' that. I started calling him OB and it stuck."

"But he's in Duluth?"

"I guess. I haven't seen him in years."

"How many years?"

"Maybe ten."

"Really? Close family, huh? Why did you never get to know him?"

Cole nodded. "Yeah, well, he was fifteen when I was born. He was the oldest and I was the third-born. So we never really knew each other as kids. He was pretty much out of the house by the time I was walking."

"I see," Linda said. "And he moved off to Duluth and you stayed in ... where was it?"

"Carville. Up north of St. Cloud."

"You stayed in Carville. And you just lost touch?"

"He joined the military right out of high school. The Air Force. Ended up in the ISR, down in Texas."

"The ISR?"

"Intelligence, Surveillance and Reconnaissance Agency. He got into computers in high school. One of those whiz kid types. Got caught up in the whole 'air and space superiority' thing. And then he went nuts and disappeared off the face of the planet."

Linda twisted to face him. "He what?"

Cole sighed. "Well, that's a kind of shorthand way of saying I have no idea what happened. He was career Air Force, all the way. Then about the time I'm graduating from high school my dad gets a letter saying Obie's in a hospital in Turkey. Some sort of mental breakdown. Before Dad can get there to see him he disappears. He's been living on the street ever since, as far as we know. He was in Chicago for years, but then started heading farther north in the summer. Dad says he loved Duluth as a kid."

"I see." Linda stared out the window for a bit, letting the information sink in. Just past Alexandria now, the train pushed through agricultural lands and wooded parcels. The morning sky was clear and crisp, the sun bright. It was only a couple of hours to Ottawa. Hardly enough time for thinking. She turned to Cole. "He must be involved," she said.

"Who? Obie?"

"Yeah. Keeley said that he was angry because *she* called *him*. Somebody made that connection. Somebody wants *us* to talk to him."

"Oh. Right." Cole made a soft, sardonic snort. Of course. He knew that. He just hadn't taken the time to know that he knew it. Somehow his brother was involved with all this. He shrugged. "Something funny there, though. If he's living on the street he doesn't have a phone, right?"

"Yeah. You'd think."

Cole rose. "Fuck it. We need to know. And I need to talk to my kids. I'm gonna call Dad. Maybe whoever the hell it is that likes to play with telephones hooked *him* up with Obie too."

Linda stiffened at the thought of endangering the kids, then calmed herself with a breath. "OK," she said. "If that's what your gut tells you is right, let's go with it. This might be the perfect time. Maybe Rice's death has thrown the People off our trail. And you need to let your kids know that you're okay."

Cole smiled courageously, relieved to have Linda's blessing. He looked around the lounge car, then back down at the President.

Linda pointed to the doorway behind him. "There's a phone in the dining car."

Cole grabbed his wallet from his jacket on the seat. "I'll be right back."

### 10.5

Linda's heart started pounding with fear when Cole returned to the lounge car. His face was tight with worry. He sat beside her and took her hand. "Grace is asleep again. Wouldn't wake up this morning. Dad's got the doctor coming."

"Jesus. I'm sorry." Linda shifted in her seat and pulled up her legs so she could give Cole her full attention. "It's really scary, isn't it?"

"Yes. It is." He waved his arms around his head in exasperation. "I mean, is she like ... here? Right now? Hovering around us? Is she running into those freaks, those fucking People? Meeting them and ... I don't know ... having to fight with them or something? In whatever the fuck astral fucking realm they're all in? Christ!"

"It doesn't make any—"

"Fuck all, Linda! She's my little girl!" Tears welled up in his eyes and he wiped them away with the back of his hand.

Linda just sat quietly and let him feel. Her attention and acceptance was all she had to give him in this moment, and it seemed to be what he most needed anyway. She fished a Kleenex out of her purse to daub his face, letting her fingers come to rest on his twitching nose and cheek. After a while his face relaxed and his breathing slowed. Linda smiled warmly. "We're going to stop them, Cole," she said softly.

Cole returned her smile through the remnants of tears. "You fucking got that right, Mrs. President." He flinched, looking quickly around the car to make sure nobody was listening. The few passengers in the lounge were reading their papers and books, paying them no attention. "Sorry," he whispered.

Linda smiled. "We're almost to Ottawa. Guy will help us. By the end of today, if I have my way, we'll have brought this all public."

Cole sighed. "Yeah, well, I hope you're right about that. I hope you're right."

"I hope so too."

Cole's smile brightened. "I got to talk to both Emily and Iain. Iain's up five pizzas now. And Emily's joined forces with the security guards. She's been peppering them with questions and they gave her an ID badge. Made her part of the team. She's ecstatic."

"I'm glad," said Linda.

"Yeah." Cole sat in silence for a moment. "Dad hasn't heard anything from Obie."

Linda shifted in her seat, stuffing the pillow between her hip and the armrest. "It was worth a shot," she said.

"Yeah."

Linda pointed to the duffle at Cole's feet. "We got any fruit in there?" she asked.

Cole grabbed the bag, pulling it onto the seat next to him. "I don't know. I know Keeley put some food in here."

"I'm amazed we still have that bag. With the accident and all."

"Yeah. Me too. I had the strap around my neck in the van, the bag in my arms. Ready to run, you know. When we went over it almost pulled my ears off. I didn't realize I still had it until we were on the copter." Cole fished in the duffle. Under the extra clothes and the maps was a plastic container. He lifted it out and pulled off the top. Inside were sandwiches and carrots and a couple of homemade cookies, but no fruit.

"What's this?" Linda reached into the container and drew out a white envelope from underneath the sandwich. On the cover were two words, written in green ink in Keeley's florid script: *"for later."*

Linda placed the letter gently in her lap, closed her eyes, and breathed deeply. Cole put down the container and reached out to take her hand. Glancing at Cole for support, Linda opened the envelope and pulled out a single sheet of notepaper. She unfolded and read it. As she read her eyes filled with tears. "Oh, Keeley," she sighed. She handed the letter to Cole.

*Cornfed,*

*I don't know where you are now. Whom you're with. Where you're headed. I only know that my love is dead by now, and my heart is in pieces.*

*I have to leave because if I don't I'll tear you apart, with anger that does not belong to you. And because if I stay I'll stop you before you leave and tell you everything. And then you won't go. And I can't do that. I can't fail you again. We have to go through with this, even though our help will come at the cost of my love.*

*Our mutual friend told me. That night, so long ago, when he told me you were coming. He told me my husband would die. And there was no hiding that from him. We both knew this was coming. But we've never known how or why or what. By now those details have no doubt been filled in. I don't want to hear them.*

*I don't know if or when I'll go back home. That's why I took the dogs. I'm gonna ditch your car and get a rental and head down to my sister's. I'm sorry I didn't say goodbye. I'm sorry I couldn't be stronger. But I've lived with this for more than six years now. I think that's fucking strong enough.*

*Follow this through, Cornfed. I have no idea what this is all about. I don't even know whom to hate. But my flesh already craves revenge, even though my sweet husband is still alive, down the hallway, going over the map with your traveling companion. I know I'll see him again. I know that death is an illusion. But my body is going to have to live without him for the rest of its days. Please. Make that loss mean something.*

*I pray that this man you have found is still with you. He is yours now, you know. And you are his. You'll realize that in time. I wish you both the love you deserve.*

*If, on your travels, you happen to run into a twelve-year-old boy with funny eyes and a pointy chin, give him a hug for me, and tell him that I love him.*

*I'll see you again one day, my girl. Until then, you have my love.*
*Vinegar*

Cole finished reading and put his arms around the President, hiding both their faces in the embrace. Silently and together they sobbed as the train underneath beat its gentle rhythm. Eventually they ran out of tears.

## 10.6

"She didn't use any real names," said Linda.

"Yeah?" Cole sat watching the passing countryside. Linda leaned against him.

"Yeah. Like she didn't know who'd see her letter."

Cole sighed. Keeley was a smart one.

"I just can't imagine it, Cole. I mean ... Jesus. All that time they knew. How do you hold something like that?"

"I don't know," Cole replied. He kissed the top of Linda's head, breathed in her smell. "I don't know."

"Jesus," she said again.

An announcement came over the intercom system. They were coming to the Casselman stop. "That puts us maybe half an hour out of Ottawa," Cole said. He began to think ahead. "What do I need to know about this Legrand?" he asked.

Linda sat up and stretched. "He's a member of Parliament. Province of Ontario. In his thirties. He's got a couple of young girls. Looks kind of like Tom Cruise. Nice hair."

"How'd you meet him?"

"He came to find me. Back in ... I think it was February. Not long after I moved into the White House. He was in D.C. with his girls, touring the museums. Turns out he's married to one of Earl's nieces. So he looked me up, used that connection to get a message through to me. He and the girls came in and we did the whole Oval Office thing."

"And you said you saw him recently."

Linda nodded. "Yeah. About ten days ago. He'd been in New York. A climate change meeting. Popped down to D.C. to stop in and say 'Hi.' Brought me some maple candy."

Cole folded Keeley's letter and put it back in the envelope, then slipped it into the pocket and zipped it tight. "He's a good guy?"

"Yeah," Linda nodded. "I think so. And he's got that brother at the CBC." She stood. "You ready?"

Cole frowned. "For what?"

"To go back to our seats."

"Do we need to? All our stuff is here, isn't it?"

"I left my hat and gloves under my seat."

Cole gazed kindly into Linda's still-reddened eyes. "How about I just go find them?"

Linda smiled. "Sure. I'll use the rest room and then meet you."

Cole leaned out to give her a quick kiss, his heart pounding. It lasted longer than he had imagined it might. He took her by the elbows. "We're gonna have to talk about what Keeley said in her letter," he said, his voice open and gentle.

Linda smiled shyly. "I know. Later." She grabbed her purse and headed toward the dining car. Cole headed the other direction, back toward their seats.

Cole stepped into the lounge car.

Linda looked up as he approached. He'd been running. "Hi," she said, concerned.

"I thought we were meeting at the seats!" he said, almost frantic.

"I thought we were meeting back here," she replied. "What is it?"

"You need to come see this."

Linda grabbed her things and slipped back into her shoes. Cole turned and started down the aisle, pushing through the connector doors as quickly as he could. The train lurched underfoot as they made their way, through one car and into the next. Rather than head to their seats, Cole opened the rest-room door. "I had to go too," he said.

The door slid open easily and the light blinked on. Cole stepped in and motioned for Linda to follow. He pointed at the mirror. Scrawled across the face of it in what looked like red lipstick was a symbol, a circle with an upside-down capital L through it. The same symbol Rice had drawn on his windshield.

"Oh my God," breathed Linda.

"That just about says it," agreed Cole.

## 10.7

*Grace pushed up against the glass but it would not budge. She tried to make her hands as solid as she could. It didn't make any difference. She turned and tried another direction. There were no other directions.*

*It wasn't really glass. It just looked like glass. But even the word "glass" didn't quite work. It was also like ice. And like electricity, though she did not really know what electricity looked like. Whatever it was, it was all around her: a whole house made of glass, drifting in an ocean of blackness that stretched to infinity on all sides, as if the stars themselves had all been snuffed out. The walls kept shifting and crossing over each other, through each other, moving around and around, reminding Grace of that place full of mirrors she'd walked through with her Grandpa at the carnival last summer. There were layers and layers, growing larger and smaller, copies upon copies in every direction, and she couldn't get out of it. Even her cord got lost in the maze. She could not follow it back. She'd never seen anything like it.*

*The scary woman with the melting face had come out of the dark and knocked her to the ground and the skeleton had grabbed her wrists and flung her across the sky. He was astoundingly quick. The scary woman appeared behind her and grabbed her arms and held her tight. Grace tried to make her own arms disappear, but she couldn't. The woman's grip held her in focus. They flickered together and the next thing Grace knew they were next to the glass and the skeleton was pushing her backwards. She rolled end over end and when she stopped she was stuck inside.*

Grace peered out through the shifting layers of glass. The scary woman hovered just beyond the farthest wall, looking back in at her. Her beautiful face melted and distorted into a hideous mask and Grace pulled back, afraid. The scary woman laughed and said something Grace could not hear. In the distance behind her, the skeleton danced gleefully. Then he and the distorted woman flickered and were gone and Grace was alone. Even Dennis had disappeared. The skeleton had kicked at him, but Dennis had dodged the skeleton's bony foot and run away, barking madly, into the blackness beyond. Grace hoped he'd escaped.

Grace surveyed the house of glass.

She sat down to think.

She thought for a very long time.

Then a new light came and she stood back up. It was an odd light, strikingly white yet full of colors she could barely make out, like a distant starburst, a lone jewel set on the velvet blackness of the sky. The light grew larger as it circled in toward the house of glass, the colors growing more distinct. As it neared, Grace began to sense that this light was also a person: a woman whose heart sparkled with goodness. Grace watched through the glass as the woman of light approached, and smiled as the sound of soft humming reached her ears. It was the song of someone happy and at peace. Grace had not heard the melting woman before, when that scary one had laughed and spoken, but she could hear this light woman now. "Alouette," the woman mumbled and hummed, as she drifted slowly toward the glass house. Soon the woman of light was standing right outside. Her heart was a swirl of glittering flecks. Her glow bounced back and forth between the shifting layers, filling every corner.

The woman raised an arm and pounded on the glass. Grace was not afraid, even though the walls of the glass house shook and twisted and rolled over each other. She could sense the light woman's good intentions. The woman pounded again and cracks of light crinkled along the glass. The woman pounded and pounded and the cracks of light grew larger and longer. At last and at once the house flew apart, and the black void with it, the pieces crumbling around them, or flying off to the now-visible stars, in the sky that was not a sky. The light woman approached Grace, humming still, the melody *one that Grace had heard before, in a place called school. Grace stared up into her face. The woman was really old, and very beautiful, her pale white skin wrinkled and radiant.*

*"Hello, little one," said the light woman. As Grace watched she changed from a woman to an old black man in tatters, and then back to a woman, but young now, with Japanese eyes. Her form was unsure of itself; she kept changing as she spoke. "How did you get stuck in here?" she asked. Her head was still an old woman's but her body was that of a young Indian boy. Briefly she took the form of a deer and then an infant and then settled back into the old woman for a while.*

*"A skeleton put me here," said Grace. "And a scary woman with a melting face."*

*The old woman's bushy eyebrows lifted. "Are there many such beings here?" she asked.*

*"More than I want," answered Grace. "And they are very strong." She watched the woman of light for a moment as she shuffled through more bodies, as if searching for the right one. "Who are you?" Grace asked at last.*

*The old woman flowed into the body of a big white man with dark hair and a beard, then into that of a pale young man in a business suit. He hesitated for a moment, as if thinking about her question. At last he responded. "I'm not really certain," he said. He flowed back into the form of the old woman.*

*That made sense to Grace. With so many bodies, it must get confusing. And yet Grace could sense that, even amongst these varied forms, there was a Somebody at the center, a spirit who held them all together. "What can I call you?" asked Grace.*

*The old woman wrinkled her shining brow in deep concentration. Her eyes brightened and her wrinkled mouth stretched into a wide grin. "I am told my name is now Evlyn," she said. "The living light."*

*"Told by whom?" asked Grace.*

*The old woman cocked her head, puzzled. "A voice from somewhere else." Her eyes drifted off to the stars. "It is not yet time," she continued, her voice deeper and more resonant than before, tinged with authority and finality, as if some distant god were speaking through her. She returned her focus to Grace and blinked her eyes. "I'm sorry, little one," she said. "That's all I know."*

*Grace nodded. "That's okay," she said. "I like the name Evlyn." She looked around them. "Have you seen my dog?" she asked.*

*Evlyn slowly shook her head. "No. I'm sorry."*

*Grace sighed. "He's run away." She beamed her heart, bathing the old woman in her essential vibrations, in order to share who she was. Evlyn did the same. "Ah," said Grace. "It's you." She was so glad to know. She'd been worried.*

*"Shall we go look for your dog?" the old woman asked.*

*"Yes," said Grace. "And then I have to go find my father and Linda."*

*Evlyn brightened and Grace could feel the strength of her love. "I shall help you," the old woman said.*

*Together they went to find Dennis.*

# Chapter ⌀ Eleven

## 11.1

Alice had agreed to meet in Mr. Random's room. It helped them, Bob thought, to be together in the physical, and this was the only place that worked for that. Random's mummified corpse wasn't going anywhere.

Though only six, Alice was proving to be far more gifted than Bob had been at even twice her age. She was one of the first of her kind to display the talents of both species, while also maintaining a viable physical existence on Earth. Bob shuddered, to think of where Alice could end up. Even now, her facility with the written word while stalking the astral realms was especially keen. Her potential as a weapon was unlimited.

And Random would do anything. Absolutely anything. And they were at a point now where "absolutely anything" was justified. Even necessary. With Mary gone to who knows where, with Rice's failure still resonating through the Rock, with the General's flagging confidence, it was up to the three of them, only two Stalkers and one Demon, to hold it all together. They were all they had. The trainees would be of no use at this point, and the General would never agree to call in their foreign counterparts. Not if there was any way to avoid it. There was too much risk in that much loss of face.

Bob pulled the two armchairs closer to Random's crib, and then dragged over a stool, to place in front of hers. Alice always sat cross-legged. Most hybrids preferred it that way. Folded in on themselves, they felt protected. Their disrupted socialization schedules, and their inborn deficiencies with regard to touch, left them skittish and hesitant, almost catatonic at times.

The door opened and in walked Alice. Though Alice was strangely beautiful, Bob's flesh still quivered, at times, to see her; Bob's primate genes were still programmed to repel the extraordinary. Alice's hair, so like Bob's, was luminous, straight and pale, like milk-and-honey cascading from a fountain. Her perfect features sat delicately on her head. But those eyes, so large and so black. Bob could see the Milky Way in their inky depths. If Alice was any indication of where the aliens could take them, it was worth every bit of the pain. Humans were done for. Alice was the next step in their evolution, the beta test for the next new thing. Which was exactly why Rice hated her.

Bob watched intently as Alice crossed the room and stood next to Mr. Random. As was her ritual, Alice leaned over and kissed the papery skin that covered portions of Random's skull. Then she turned and smiled at Bob, an awkward expression that made Bob's intestines turn to pond water and cold soup. Bob smiled back. "Hi, Alice," she said. "Did you sleep?"

"How could I sleep?" answered Alice. Bob had to add the question mark herself. There was not enough inflection in Alice's speech to put it there on its own. Communication with hybrids was often very tricky, if you were confined to the spoken word.

Alice sat in the second chair.

Bob took the conversation inside. CAN YOU WORK?

YES.

DO YOU WANT TO?

WE HAVE TO.

Bob nodded. She knew what Alice meant. There were too many unknown factors at this point, for the People to deviate from the primary goals. Bob and Alice would have to trust that it was all in the Plan.

YOU UNDERSTAND THAT IF I CAN GET INSIDE THE PRESIDENT I HAVE ORDERS TO KILL HER?

YES. YOU'VE NEVER KILLED BEFORE.

NO, I HAVEN'T, ALICE. AND I MAY NEED YOUR HELP WITH THAT.

I WILL HELP.

Bob smiled. Alice never hesitated when it came to the Plan. YOU KNOW HER GUARDIANS ARE IMPRISONED NOW, JUST AS SHE IS?

YES.

IT'S ONLY A MATTER OF WAITING.

I UNDERSTAND.

RICE'S PLAN MAY YET WORK OUT.

YES.

Bob relaxed into her chair. Alice crossed her legs. They both closed their eyes and slowed their breath, in preparation for their journey.

MR. RANDOM WILL MEET US? Alice asked.

HE'S WAITING FOR US NOW.

HE WORRIES ME.

YOU NEED NOT BE FRIGHTENED OF HIM, ALICE. HE WILL NOT HARM YOU.

I WILL ACCEPT YOUR WORD OVER MY OWN SENSE OF THINGS.

WHY IS THAT?

BECAUSE MY MOTHER WOULD NOT LIE TO ME.


11.2


The taste in Linda's mouth reminded her of the dentist's office: blood and smoke and the memory of metal. She reached up to rub her temple, where Rice had hit her. Rice. That fucking bastard. She wanted to scream, but knew that she would not. He would not have that satisfaction. She would not give it to him.

"So do you," Cole had said. His last words. And those three words dogged her like a toddler, begging to be listened to. "So do you." Something about those words had stirred a terror deep inside. But then Rice had shot Cole in the stomach and he'd crumpled to the floor and the last of her hope had crumpled with him.

How could she have been so stupid? It had gone too easily. She should have seen it coming. "There's no escaping," Keeley had said. But Linda hadn't believed it. She'd pretended otherwise. Even though she knew how powerful the People had proven to be. Even though she knew that the aliens were following their own agenda. She'd been caught hoping once again. Hoping that the aliens were helping them. Hoping that somehow they were being guided or protected. Hoping that because they were standing up against an evil in the world, the gods themselves were on their side. Linda sighed and sat up in the utter darkness of her holding cell, anticipating that a change in posture would spill the tears she knew must be inside. But no tears came. It was far too dark for tears.

She thought back on the day. The train had pulled into Ottawa right on schedule. They caught the #95 bus up to Albert without a hitch, then walked to the Visitor Welcome Centre just like any other tourists, invisible in the sunshine and the crowds and the business of government. They learned that Legrand's office was not on Parliament Hill but on Bank Street, and made their way over to his building. Despite their fears, it had gone as easily as if they were meeting friends for lunch. They found the nearest pay phone and Linda placed a call.

"MP Legrand," answered the receptionist, a young woman by the sound of her voice.

"Uh, hi," said Linda, momentarily surprised to be so close so quickly. She'd expected a succession of operators. "May I speak with Monsieur Legrand, please?"

"May I say who is calling?"

This was the crucial moment and Linda had already decided how she would play it. "No you may not," she said.

The receptionist, young or not, was unruffled by Linda's response. "Then I cannot put you through."

Linda spoke quickly, before the woman could hang up. "Tell him I still have Ally's scarf. She left it in my office."

That stopped the young woman. After a long silence she came back. "Let me put you on hold," she said.

Thirty seconds later the phone clicked again. "My God! Linda?" It was Legrand.

"Hello, Guy," Linda had said. Then she started to weep.

Legrand had come down, picked them up in his car, driven them into the underground parking garage, and taken them up a back elevator. He was gentle, sympathetic, concerned, and helpful. They stole unseen into his office through a back hallway and he told his staff to leave him undisturbed until further notice. Then he locked the door. He motioned to Cole and Linda to take the leather armchairs opposite his desk, then sat in his own.

"You need to tell me what's going on," said Legrand. His voice was kind but firm.

"Well, obviously I have not been kidnapped by terrorists." Linda laughed nervously. There was no easy way to tell her tale.

"I can see that. So what *has* happened?"

Linda shifted in her chair, glanced over at Cole, reached out to take his hand. She looked at Legrand and his expression of kind concern put her at ease. She could do this. "Does your brother still work for the CBC?" she asked.

"Paul? Yeah. He's somewhere in the Sports division now. Why?"

"Can he put me on tonight? A live feed to the whole world?"

Legrand sat back. A slight smile flickered across his face. "You really think that'll help?"

Linda's guts twisted. "Guy?" she said, her voice little more than a squeak.

Legrand reached out and punched his intercom. "You can come in now," he said. He looked at Linda. "You really are a very stupid woman," he said.

The door opened. In stepped Rice, a large, black pistol in his hand. He closed the door behind him and smiled, looking at Linda. "You look different," Rice said with scorn.

Cole rose from his chair and started for Rice, putting his body between Linda and the gun. "So do you," he said.

Rice fired without even bothering to look. Cole fell. Rice stepped over his body. Linda rose slowly, not even in control of her own movements. Cole!

Rice came face to face with her. "You've caused me a great deal of trouble," he said. Pocketing the pistol, he lashed out with his right hand.

The blow to Linda's temple didn't hurt his hand at all.

## 11.3

There was no way to fill in the blanks. The loss of time. The change of venue. The current situation. There was not much she could know just lying there in the dark. She'd been knocked unconscious and taken someplace. Rice was alive. And Legrand. Jesus! Even Guy! There really was no place to turn for help. Linda moaned and sat up. The loss of Cole sat heavily in her gut, a rock, a brick, a tumor locked away from her heart. It would have to wait.

She felt the area around her. The "bed" was just a couple of sofa cushions thrown on the floor. The blanket was rough and heavy. The floor itself was cold tile or stone, soiled with dirt and sand. Gritty. Waxy, even. Very strange.

With no idea how high the ceiling was, Linda rolled onto her knees and stood up, careful of her head. That proved to be a wise move. The ceiling was low and uneven, forcing her to crouch slightly. She ran her hand overhead. The ceiling was cold and rough to the touch. Carved rock, she guessed. She was underground.

Linda reached outward in all directions. Nothing. She started out in a straight line, taking one step at a time. After three steps she touched a wall. She ran her hands along the carved rock but found nothing. No pictures or hangings. No light switch. She took a step to the left, running her hand along the wall in front of her in large arcs, investigating high and low. The utter blackness was an assault on her senses, as though she were being waterboarded with buckets of night. Linda pushed on her eyelids, trying to force her eyes to see something, desperate to squeeze out the dark. Her hand found another wall. She turned to the left and followed it.

After a few steps her foot bumped up against something hard. She stopped. Squatting, she reached out to examine what had blocked her way. It was a box, smooth and cold and metallic, a couple of feet wide and maybe three feet tall. She stood, running her hand along the edge. The top was open. Slowly, she reached down to explore. Her hand found something round and leathery, pebbled like a basketball. It gave a little when she pushed against it. She ran her fingers down the side, then pulled back with a start. Jesus! An image of Spud flashed in her mind. It was an alien! She waited, holding her breath. No response. No movement. Nothing. Maybe it was dead.

Minutes passed like hours. Eventually she was ready to move again. Feeling her way with her foot she inched around the box, certain that at any moment long spindly fingers would reach out and grab her. But none did. She made it back to blank wall and kept on. Her hand found another corner that turned to the left. She followed the new wall. She appeared to be in a square cell maybe ten feet on a side and five feet high.

The next corner brought her to the final wall, assuming this was a square. If there was a door out of the cell, it had to be in this wall. Had to be. She moved forward slowly. The rock wall ended abruptly and her heart pounded. An opening! Slowly she moved to face it, feeling into the black openness. This could be it.

Her hand brushed against fabric, smooth and soft. She grabbed at it, her fingers knowing what she'd found before her mind caught up. She pulled back from the explosion of laughter, screamed as she tripped on the cushions on the floor. Her elbows cracked and slid on the cold stone floor. Her head struck the back wall with a thud.

"I love this part!" said a voice in the blackness. The room was suddenly filled with blinding light from glowing strips on the ceiling. There stood Rice, hunched over so as not to hit his head, a small black remote control in his hand. "You up for Chinese?" he asked.

## 11.4

Linda had launched herself at him, fit to burst with rage, but Rice had sidestepped and turned off the light with the remote, tripping her as she passed him, sending her sprawling on her face into the blackness beyond her cell. She could hear him step past her and walk away, down a hallway she could not see. Crawling, crying, gasping, cursing, she'd returned to her cushions and curled up in a ball, shivering in the cold. She'd lost her jacket in Legrand's office.

After what seemed like an hour, Rice returned. The odors announced his arrival. He had, indeed, come with Chinese food. He switched on the light.

"Hungry?" he said, raising an eyebrow.

Linda stayed curled up on the cushions. She would give him nothing. She opened her eyes a crack. "Where's Cole?" she asked, her voice a dark monotone.

"Six feet under by now, I imagine," he said cheerily. "He was starting to stink."

Linda took a long, heavy breath. "And my mother?"

"You do have trouble keeping track of people, don't you?"

"I want you to die," she said.

"Oh, don't be silly," Rice replied, sitting cross-legged on the floor by her bed and unpacking the white paper bag. He set the cartons and plates and plastic silverware in the space between them. "If I die then you just stay lost down here in the darkness until you rot. Egg roll?" He opened a carton.

"As long as we're rotting together," Linda said.

"Got up on the wrong side of the straw pallet this morning, did we?" Rice smiled and plopped an egg roll on her plate.

"Why aren't you dead already?" Linda asked.

"Because nobody's killed me yet." Rice shrugged.

"I saw your body on the highway."

Rice frowned. "Twernt me, Prez," he said. "I was dogfighting that fucking helicopter. You sure your chauffeur didn't run down a vagrant? That's gonna put some points on his license."

Linda ignored his joke. "You killed Cole."

Rice scoffed. "Oh, please, Mrs. P. You hardly knew the guy." He spooned some fried rice onto his plate and reached for another carton. Then he looked up at Linda and smiled, shaking his head. "You fell in love with him, didn't you?" he said, chuckling.

Linda looked at the floor, attempting to give nothing away, failing miserably.

Rice threw his head back in laughter. "Damn, Prez! What're you, a thirteen-year-old schoolgirl? Grow the fuck up."

"Fuck you."

"Yeah, well, me and everybody else, apparently." Rice scooped some cashew chicken out onto his plate, picking out hunks of green pepper and tossing them over Linda's shoulder. He shoved a spoonful into his mouth and chewed. "Not bad," he said. "For Canadians."

"So we're still in Canada?" Linda pushed up onto an elbow, ignoring the food put before her.

Rice pointed at her plate. "That's gonna taste a lot better hot than cold," he said. He ate another bite. "Look. Daddy's eating."

"I want you all to die," said Linda. Her voice was dead already.

Rice sighed and put down his plate. "Look, Linda. It's like this: there're rules to this game and you need to learn them. We brought you in and you don't like it. Fine. Most of you assholes don't like it. Big fucking deal. Nixon cried like a baby for three days. Fine. Ford went on a drunk. Fine. Ike actually wet himself the first time he met Asimov. Fine, fine, fine. But like it or not, this is how the world works. Alien beings collude secretly with the government. Wah, wah, wah. Get used to it. Like all of those other bozos did. All except JFK. Because you really don't have any choice in the matter, girlfriend. And if you keep fighting us, we're gonna have to take you out just like we took Kennedy out. And I hate Dallas this time of year." Rice smiled at his own joke and picked up his plate. He took a bite of his egg roll.

Linda simply stared at him. She knew it would unnerve him. That seemed worth doing, if nothing else did. But that game had its limits. She needed information as well, and Rice seemed to be her only source right now. After a long time she pointed at the metal box behind her. "What's wrong with your friend?" she asked.

"Ya got me, Prez," answered Rice. "Heartbreak of psoriasis, maybe? Hangnails? Gas? I thought maybe sharing a room would cheer her up, but she still looks rather sad."

Linda turned to look. The box was open on the top and front. The alien sat inside, her knees pulled up to her chin and her arms wrapped around her shins. She looked lifeless. Fossilized. All but her open eyes. Though glassy now, and covered with dust, they gave off the impression of something not quite dead, as if a fire smoldered somewhere in the basement of her being. How Rice could tell it was a female was beyond Linda's knowing.

Linda turned back to Rice. "It's pretty quiet around here," she pointed out.

"Would you stop with the whole I'm-gonna-figure-this-all-out shit? Let me save you the trouble. You're in a cell at the end of a hallway that extends off the central workspace of an alien facility carved out of solid rock two hundred feet below the surface of Ottawa. Up until I arrived there were half-a-dozen humans working down here. I sent them all home. The Life, the aliens, left of their own accord two days ago. Nobody knows why, and the Life aren't saying. Two or three dormant ones got left behind in each facility, like our friend here, who seems to have missed the bus. Otherwise, the place is empty. Well, there's you and me and egg rolls make three. Anything else you want to know?"

Linda sat up. There was something about Rice's arrogance that was exhilarating. She'd seen such confidence before. It could lead to mistakes. "How do I get out of here?" she asked.

"You cooperate with me."

Linda shook her head. "No. I mean alone. How do I get out of here after I kill you?"

Rice laughed. "Hmm. Well, let's see ... after you kill me, you make your way through the utter blackness, down the hallway and into the central chamber. Watch out for that pit in the floor! There are another dozen hallways off the central chamber. You choose the correct one, in the darkness because the lighting system is keyed to my prints, make your way to the elevators, and then ... and then ... then you sit down and fucking die because the elevators have all been deactivated." He smiled at Linda. "Sorry. I thought I could help."

"No. No. That was good. Thanks."

Rice pushed at Linda's plate. "You really should eat," he said. "Keep your strength up and all that. I won't be back until morning so this is your only chance."

She was hungry, having eaten nothing since breakfast on the train. It must be evening now, given Rice's last comment. And he was right. It would do her no good to starve. She reached out for the plate.

Rice finished his food and stood to leave. "I've got to get back to work," he said, packing his plate in the paper bag. "Should I leave you the leftovers?"

Linda nodded.

"I've got some folks working on a little treat for you," he offered.

Linda ignored him, continuing to eat.

"Anything else you need?"

Linda looked up. "A bathroom?"

"Directly across the hall. Human friendly. Everything you need."

"Can you leave the light on?"

Rice looked for a moment like he might go for it, then wrinkled his nose. "I don't think so, Mrs. President. I'd love to but ... I don't trust you."

Linda nodded. "Fair enough."

"Anything else?"

"I still want you to die."

Rice laughed as he left, switching out the light. "Just like Kennedy," he said.

Linda sat in the darkness and finished her egg roll.

## 11.5

Nausea forced Linda to wakefulness and she rolled over to vomit on the floor. Hot juices splattered onto her face and neck. When she went to wipe her mouth she noticed how badly her arms and hands hurt. The fingers of her right hand would hardly move, so swollen were they. She pressed them lightly against her thigh and almost passed out. The pain was excruciating.

She rolled onto her back and breathed deeply, wincing at the sharp sting in her left ankle. Her head was so heavy she couldn't lift it. The food must have been drugged. Her eyes felt glued shut. She tried to open them but could not tell if she succeeded. It was too dark to know. The cold had soaked into her bones, but she was past caring. If Rice intended to kill her, let him go ahead and do it. She was ready.

The light came on and she raised an arm to shade her eyes. She waited and listened but heard nothing. After a while, when her vision had adjusted, she tilted her head to look toward the door. There sat Rice on a folding chair in the entranceway, reading a tablet computer.

He noticed her gaze and pointed at the tablet. "Says here in the Post that you've been kidnapped by terrorists, Mrs. President. Towel-heads, most likely. And look what they've done to you." He motioned toward her with disgust, shaking his head in a tsk, tsk, tsk.

Linda raised her head slightly, her eyes following his gesture. She gasped. Fuck! She was dressed in a filthy old bathrobe, untied and partly open, naked underneath. Her left leg was covered with bruises. She had raised welts and cuts on her stomach and the undersides of her forearms, as if she'd fended off some weapon. The fingers of her right hand bent backwards in a way they should not. She wretched again.

Rice stood and walked over to her, looking down with sadness. "The real shame is your hair," he spoke gently. "After all the time and energy you put into your makeover."

Linda reached up. Her hair had been brutally chopped away, leaving bald spots and tufts and long strings and bleeding wounds in her scalp. She turned away, squeezing her eyes tight. "Just kill me," she said, her tongue thick, her throat dry.

"They tried to, Mrs. President. They almost succeeded. But thanks to the diligence and hard work of police, FBI and military officers and agents, those too-often unsung heroes who put their lives on the line to find and rescue you, you've been delivered from the hands of those evildoers. Or something like that. I don't write the news, I just make it."

Linda started to weep, though she had no tears left to shed. Rolling to her left she pulled her knees toward her chest and shook uncontrollably, wheezing for breath. She could not stop.

Rice knelt beside her, reaching out to cover the nakedness that her rolling over had exposed. "At least I knocked you out first," he said, his voice soft and sad. "At least I didn't rape you." He put a hand on her shoulder.

Linda recoiled, knocking his hand away with her arm. The pain from doing so evoked a scream but she cut it off. She breathed deeply, over and over, finding, in her ability to focus her breath, what peace she could.

After a while Rice departed.

He left the light on.

## 11.6

"I need you to look at this," Rice said. At least a day had passed since he'd last been there.

Linda sat in the corner farthest from the doorway, in a little nest she'd made between the alien resting-box and the walls. She'd formed a small fort with the cushions and sat curled inside it, her feet pulled up underneath, everything but her face covered with the bathrobe. She did not look up when Rice entered.

Rice raised an eyebrow at Linda's fort, then sat on the floor in the middle of the room and booted his iPadX. He looked up at the President, huddling in her corner. "We don't get out of here until we work this out, Prez. I don't know about you but I'm not having a fun time. Come look at this."

"Fuck you," said Linda hoarsely.

"Yeah, yeah. Fuck me, fuck you, fuck everybody. Ma Kettle's mad. Boo-fucking-hoo-hoo-hoo. I'm all hurt. Now get your ass over here."

Linda ducked down so that Rice couldn't see her face. After a moment she untucked her legs and started to move. Slowly, her pain obvious and debilitating, she crawled out into the room on her knees and left hand, cradling her broken right hand to her breast. She got to within a couple of feet of Rice and sat back on her thigh, keeping the pressure off her tender, weakened ankle. She looked up at Rice. Her eyes were cold.

Rice smiled. "Got some options for you here, Mrs. P," he said. He touched the screen and a video started playing. Linda watched.

It was an ACN news bulletin. Stendahl Banks, jubilant but somber, was reporting on the daring rescue of the American president. In the background, video of her, Linda Travis, her body beaten, her hair cut to shreds, being wheeled out of some godforsaken Middle Eastern hut and into an ambulance. Stendahl Banks worked up a single tear for his president as he assured the American people that she would recover. He let the teardrop slide dramatically down his cheek. Linda gawked at the screen. It looked just like her!

"That's option one," said Rice. He switched pages with a touch and hit play again. "Here's option two."

Another video. Stendahl Banks again, but this time grim, reporting on a disc that had just been received by the State Department, with a video depicting the brutal murder of the President of the United States. This scenario came in two versions, the first with Banks in front of a waving American flag, the second with actual footage from the video in question. Linda was shown naked on her knees in a room full of dark and evil looking men, one with a sword in his hand. She was beaten and broken, her hair chopped away. The man with the sword raised his arm and the video cut away.

Rice hit pause, forgoing the last bit of Banks' report. "We haven't decided whether to go with the video in that one or not. Not sure the public will buy your murder unless they see it."

"How did you—?"

Rice cut her off with a wave of his hand. "One more," he said, touching the tablet.

The third video was another ACN report, again with Stendahl Banks, this time with file footage of Ellen Warren, Linda's mother.

Banks reported how, after collapsing just days earlier, the news of the President's execution was too much for her already-weakened heart. Ellen Warren was dead. A nation mourned.

Rice cleared the tablet's screen and faced the President. He rubbed at the fatigue in his eyes. "So how much do I need to explain to you, Linda?" he asked. "We've got more coming, you know. There's a team tracking down your old school chum, for instance. Vinegar, is it? She should be easy enough to find. Good for another story. 'Despondent old friend of the President commits suicide by cop,' or some such nonsense. We've got good writers."

Linda looked at the floor. "You found the note."

Rice rolled his eyes. "It was in your fucking duffel bag, Linda."

The President looked Rice in the eye. "How can you do this?" she asked.

Rice shrugged. "You know. A room full of nerds and all the storage space they need. We've got the graphic capabilities at this point to create an exact facsimile of you if we wanted to. We could kill you off right now and as far as the public was concerned you'd still be alive, because they'd see you on TV." Rice sighed wistfully. "Maybe one day..."

Linda shook her head. "No. I mean ... how can you *do this*?"

Rice smiled sadly. "I hope one day you understand that, Linda. I really do."

"I don't think I ever will," she answered, just as sadly.

Rice yawned. "Oh well. So which is it gonna be, Prez? Door number one? It's the only door that takes you out of here alive."

Linda looked at Rice, letting him see the desolation in her eyes, noticing how defeat and vomit had the same flavor. "I think I want you to kill me," she said. She thought the words would make her cry, but they didn't. There was relief in her heart, rather than grief. For the first time since she'd got there, she smiled.

"Well, it may come to that, girlfriend. It just might. Of course, it won't be me."

"What do you mean?"

"Well, we've got Bob on standby for that little duty. You haven't been on your benzos for a couple of days now, you know."

He reached out and rubbed her head. "Bob's pretty much moved into the ol' noggin here." Rice laughed, picking up his computer and standing to leave.

Linda stared as he left.

At the door he turned. "I mean, damn, Linda! Ziggy Stardust?" He laughed heartily as he walked away.

## 11.7

*"Some of us thought it best to start with the lie," said Spud. Linda opened her eyes to let him know she was listening. The overhead fluorescents of the McDonald's dining room bounced off Spud's huge black eyeballs, giving him an insectile appearance. "So we showed you what we showed some of your predecessors. The same tragic story our Mr. Rice would recognize as the truth: the cosmic collision, the dying planet, the search for another home, all of that. But there's a reason you're here alone with me now." Spud poured Linda's fries out onto his tray and started to push them apart with his clawed fingertip, studying them intently, as though they were yarrow stalks or sheep's entrails.*

*"What's the reason?" asked Linda.*

*"So I could tell you that that story's not really true," said Spud, without looking up.*

*"Ah," said Linda. Curiously, Spud's news did not come as a surprise. "So what's the truth?"*

*"You're going to have to find that out for yourself," said the little gray man, choosing a long, bent french fry. He looked up at Linda and smiled his stiff, peculiar smile. "That's part of the favor."*

*Linda watched with interest as Spud lifted the french fry and held it in front of her face. "Of course," he said, "I can't let you remember any of this yet." Leaning forward, he touched the french fry to Linda's forehead and turned off her mind.*

Linda shook herself awake. But not awake. She hadn't been dreaming. She was sure of it. She'd been *there*. As if the aliens had lifted her out of space and time and deposited her back in her own past. As if they had decided that it was finally time for her to remember this. The scent of french fries echoed across her cold, black cell. Spud's eyes lingered in her mind, just as cold, just as black. The story the Life had told was not really true? Then what *was* true?

The lights had been turned back off, though Linda did not know when that had happened. She had no idea whether it was night or day. Perhaps she *had* been asleep. Her heart began to hammer but she didn't know why. She rose up into the black. Had she heard something that had awakened her? Had she heard something just now? She held her breath and listened. Silence for a full minute. And then ... footsteps. Rice! He would kill her after all. And here, in the darkness, so that he would not have to see his own dirty work. Linda pulled her robe around her and hunkered down in her nest, pushing her shoulders up to guard her neck. The darkness left her more exposed than any light ever could.

The footsteps were so faint she could barely make them out. That didn't make sense. Rice's arrogance would have him stomping down the hallway, singing a work song. The footsteps stopped right outside the doorway to her cell. Was that breathing she heard? After a moment the steps continued. Whoever it was had stepped inside. The breathing was clear now. Linda's heart pounded. She thought she'd been ready to die, but now that death had come, she wanted to flee.

"Hello?" came a voice, a whisper, a question. It was Cole! Her love had come for her! But she did not call out. She did not even breathe. She'd been fooled before. How like Rice, to trick her with love just before he killed her.

Another footstep. "Hello? Linda Travis? Are you here?"

It *was* Cole. It had to be. Linda took a breath and answered. "Cole?" she asked, her voice a wobbly moan.

"It's Obie, Mrs. President," said the voice.

## 11.8

*Evlyn, the old woman of living light, hung quietly in the sky that was not a sky, keeping her essential light to herself, watching the dark ones from a distance, feeling their hatred and pain* and confusion. There were three of them now, and the old woman could sense them even through the rock.

The young one, Grace, had left abruptly, just after they'd found her confused little dog. He'd been standing sentry over his own body in the physical realm, as if he'd known to go back to where it had all begun and wait there for his human to find him. The little one and her dog had shared a joyful embrace, and then they'd both flickered away. The old woman knew that they had merely awakened into their physical bodies. This kind of thing happened all the time around here. People came and went. Just as she had come and gone, so many, many times before.

While she watched the dark ones, Evlyn's form shifted into that of a young black girl. A few moments later her form flowed back to that of the old woman. She did not notice the shift herself. And with no one else observing, it hadn't really happened. They were all the same to her, all one, all her. Too many lives she'd lived. Too many to worry about, or remember, or even keep separate. The journey had lasted ages, eras, eons, and she was so very ready to move on.

The young one, Grace, had revealed her heart when they first met, and in so doing had shared her concern, and her purpose. So after Grace departed, Evlyn had stepped in to take the little one's place, following after Grace's father and the woman, Linda, as they traveled across the dense, physical landscape below. The old woman knew how to find them; their glowing patterns were easy enough to track. And she knew how badly they still needed her help. It was the President and Grace's father that the dark ones were after.

She'd found Cole and Linda in a huge city filled with souls. They seemed happy enough, so she held back. But then the Black Heart had caught them and the father had fallen and the dark ones had arrived. She'd thought herself strong enough to confront them, but Grace had been right: these beings were stronger. The skeleton was wild. His insanity had set him free. The pretty girl with the distorted face was colder than anything Evlyn had yet experienced. And the strange, tiny girl with the huge, black eyes: the old woman couldn't read her at all. It was as if her heart was hidden, or hiding.

Evlyn had been forced to flee. The skeleton had surrounded her with his bony arms and legs and had almost squeezed the light from *her. His voice filled her, battering her heart with shrieks and howls of astounding fury. It was only when she remembered who she wasn't that she was able to slip away. She enfolded and flickered and was gone.*

*When Evelyn crept back later, she did so without being seen. Somebody needed to watch over Linda. Even if from afar. Even if they couldn't help. Perhaps when Grace returned they could find a way together.*

*Evlyn dimmed. First she would have to tell the poor girl about her father.*

# Chapter Twelve

## 12.1

Mary flicked off the television before the pundits could start pontificating. Like they knew anything. Albert Singer had as much as declared the President dead, from what she could tell. He'd danced the requisite steps of "hope" and "determination" and "retribution," of course, playing the humility card, just a good ol' Virginia boy trying to keep things together until their President was rescued, God have mercy. But his actions said otherwise. Five days had passed since Linda Travis' "violent abduction by unknown terrorists," with no real leads. How could there be leads, since it hadn't really happened? It was clear that Singer was holding very little "hope," and that his "determination" centered on redecorating the White House. As for "retribution," well, the fun would come later, wouldn't it? There was always somebody needing a little smacky-face.

The hotel room was as ugly as she'd ever seen, some little Interstate mom'n'pop in Coxsackie, New York, with hard, thick pillows, a fiberglass tub, and a cheap green polyester bedspread the color of rotting avocados. It was the sort of hotel that had barely registered the economic meltdown, even as its giant corporate cousins had taken huge hits. And it would do just fine for

Mary. It would have to. Without the General signing her expense sheets, this was on her dime. And her dime was pretty fucking thin. Mary rolled her shoulders to relieve the tension from hours of driving. What had she needed money for? Everything had been covered with the People. Everything. She'd sent her black-budget salary to her little brother, Gordon. Anonymously. It was the least she could do, after leaving him with their father.

Mary sat back on the bed and lit a cigarette. Her first ever. Something about running away made her want to break all the rules. She sucked in a lungful of smoke and started coughing. It was awful. She didn't know how people could smoke these things for as long as they did. She took another drag and immediately felt dizzy and sick to her stomach. She inhaled once more, doubled over in a fit of coughing, and then inhaled again, as if hoping that the physical pain might distract her from the ache in her heart.

When she thought about it, it was really the General she had to thank, that cocksucker. Her promotions and assignments had all been clearly designed to keep her close by, and to get her eventually into his bed. Even when she'd first arrived, even when she was just a kid, his sleazy little eyes had been all over her. If he hadn't been such a chickenshit, his hands would have been as well. And there'd been a part of her that had sought that attention. It was familiar, if nothing else. And it had brought her side benefits. But the General's order to kill the President at the first opportunity had kicked her down the path toward clarity. If that was who the People were, she wanted no part of them. Saving the world was one thing. Killing the President was another. Especially when the President was someone you loved.

Yeah. Like that could ever happen. Mary sighed, too tired for tears. She pulled on the cigarette again, managing to keep the smoke from choking her. The dizzy feeling had abated a bit. She looked around for an ashtray, realizing after a moment that she would not find one. This was a no smoking room. There goes another rule. She rose and found a Styrofoam cup in the bathroom and filled it halfway with water, then dropped the half-smoked Merit in. She looked at herself in the mirror, noticing the tiny wrinkles around her sky-blue eyes. She took a deep breath of the stale motel room air. It was time.

Digging into her travel bag, Mary pulled out a scalpel, a tube of lidocaine, and some alcohol and gauze. She swabbed the skin behind her right ear with alcohol, daubed on the anesthetic, waited for the numbing to set in, and then started to dig for her implants. Having inserted them herself, she knew right where they were.

### 12.2

"Here," said Obie, handing Linda a long, yellow jumpsuit. "This looks like it might fit."

Linda smiled defensively as she took it, shying away. Her eyes had adjusted to the light given off by Obie's flashlight, now propped against the wall to reflect off the ceiling. She knew she looked horrible. Her bruises had blossomed huge and orange and purple and blue, and the welts and lacerations on her arms screamed their outrage. Her face felt swollen and misshapen. And her hair. She shuddered, to have anyone see her now, so beaten, so exposed. She motioned toward the door with her broken right hand. "Can you...?" she said, timidly.

"We need to hurry," said Obie with a nod. He turned and walked into the hallway.

Linda let the filthy bathrobe slip from around her and fall to the floor. With no place else to sit, she balanced on the edge of the alien's box long enough to step gently into the jumpsuit and tug it up over her feet and legs. She stood so that she could pull it up far enough to carefully slide her broken hand into one sleeve. Then she drew it awkwardly over her shoulders. The rough fabric, heavy and obviously synthetic, probably fireproofed, rasped her battered skin, pulling at her naked nipples like rough, calloused hands. She zipped it up, thankful, despite its abrasiveness, for the almost immediate sense of warmth it brought her. She'd been so cold. "Okay," she said, whispering in the dim light. She flinched at the sound of her own voice. To make a sound was to be noticed and found. She did not want to be found. Not ever again.

Obie stepped back in and Linda got her first good look at him. The dim, oblique illumination from the flashlight left most of his face in shadows, giving him a wild and furtive air that seemed to confirm Cole's story of his brother's mental breakdown. She took a step backward, her traumatized body seeking what safety it might find in distance, should her savior turn out to be a madman.

"I couldn't find anything for your feet," said Obie. "Sorry." He pulled the knit blue stocking cap off his head and stepped forward to hand it to her. "You ready to go?"

Linda winced as Obie approached but held her ground, and then reached out to take the cap. She smushed it onto her head with her good hand and nodded. "Do you know how to get out of here?" she asked.

Obie laughed, flinging his arms wide and spinning around, his long red robe twirling with him. He was dressed like a homeless person's version of a Jedi Knight, though Linda was certain that that was a gun stuck in his belt, rather than a lightsaber. Obie stopped dead still, holding up a finger to listen for a moment before responding. He grinned. "Are you asking whether I came down into the dragon's den without a plan for escape?"

Linda smiled slightly, uncertain how to react. "I guess," she said.

"Good question," he answered, pointing at Linda with a forefinger. His eyes flashed with good humor. "I've been wondering the same thing."

Linda's heart sank and she looked down at the floor. He was mad after all. Her chin began to tremble.

Obie stepped closer. "Fear not," he said with a gentle voice, reaching out as if to comfort her. "I've got an idea."

Linda ignored his outstretched hand. "You know that Cole is dead," she said, her voice nearly dead itself.

Obie cocked his head. "Maybe," he said, matter-of-factly. "But things are not always as they seem."

Linda looked up with eyes moist and hollow.

"C'mon," Obie said. "Rice has been sidelined for a bit, but there's no telling how long that'll last. We've got to go."

## 12.3

The layout was much as Rice had described. The central chamber was huge and circular, with various consoles and pieces of equipment forming an outer ring that faced an inner open space. None of it looked even vaguely human in design. The ceiling was much taller here, rising up into the darkness at least fifty feet. Obie pointed with his flashlight to the vertical air intake shaft through which he'd entered the Lodge. The loose end of his rappelling gear hung fifteen feet overhead. The shaft would not work as an exit. There was no way to reach it from below, and its walls were too glassy-smooth for Linda to scale in any event, as damaged as she was.

There was, indeed, what looked to be a huge, bottomless pit in the very center of the open space. And there were a number of hallways leading off from the central chamber, each roughly twenty feet wide and five feet tall. Linda explained that the elevators had been disabled, but Obie told her not to worry. He had something else in mind. He circled the chamber, standing still at each hallway entrance. He closed his eyes and stood quietly for a full minute or so, then moved onto the next. At the eighth hallway he smiled.

"Here we go," he said.

"Here we go where?" asked Linda, standing at his side.

"They left us a wok."

"And that is...?"

"Our way out of here."

Linda turned to face Cole's brother. Obie returned her gaze. "How do you know all this stuff?" she asked.

"I was Rice's most promising student," he pronounced with mock solemnity.

Linda recoiled, unhappy to learn that Obie and Rice were connected at all. She shook her head in confusion. "And you ... what? Flunked out?"

Obie grinned. "Yeah. Failed my final exam."

"Which was...?"

"I should have killed the fucker before I left."

Linda searched Obie's gleaming eyes, trying to assess this man who had come to help her. He was shorter than Cole by a couple of inches. Stockier. More muscular. And his long hair, tied in a ponytail, was very light, almost blond, where Cole's had been dark. But those were Cole's deep-set eyes. That was Cole's nose, and Cole's crooked smile, pushing out from behind a well-trimmed beard. This was surely Cole's brother, and though he was obviously very different, he felt as sane and good to her as Cole had.

Obie started down the hall, crouching forward as he walked. Linda limped along behind him, not wanting to lose the light, and beginning to hope that this man might be able to rescue her after all.

The hallway curved down and to the right in a sweeping arc. After maybe a hundred yards it opened out into another circular chamber, this one smaller in diameter but just as tall as the first. Obie and Linda sighed together as they emerged, thankful for the opportunity to stand straight. Obie shined his flashlight and Linda gasped. There was the "wok," a sleek metallic craft shaped much like its namesake. A UFO. It was twelve feet or so across, and made of what looked like burnished steel. Linda could not see any doors or windows in it.

Obie shook his head in wonder, his eyes soft and wide with a look that approached reverence. "She's beautiful, isn't she?"

"She?"

"Not just a sailor's convention, in this case," Obie said with a grin, stepping forward. "She's definitely a she, though I'm not exactly sure what that means." He looked at Linda. "This ship is alive, Mrs. President," he said.

Something old and long lost stirred inside her and Linda stepped forward, reaching out and placing her unbroken hand on the wok's side. She closed her eyes, then opened them and turned to Obie with a smile. "Jesus!" she said.

Obie reached out and touched the ship as well, then stepped back and laughed. "You two have met before," he said.

Linda didn't say a thing. It was too much. And the laughter hurt more than anything. Cole was dead. She did not want to laugh. She backed away until her shoulders touched the rough granite wall. Something inside her felt ready to snap. "I need her to get me out of here," she said, her voice a ragged whisper.

"I think that's why she's here," said Obie.

## 12.4

"You ever fly one of these?" asked Linda. They were lying side-by-side in the wok's inner cabin, Obie on his stomach and Linda curled on her left side, guarding her broken hand. Obie was searching for something in the darkness. When the door melted shut Obie's flashlight had gone dead and they'd been left in pitch black again. Linda was about ready to scream.

"Here it is," said Obie.

"What?" Linda could hear something metallic scraping against the floor.

"Flight helmet," said Obie. "I knew there'd be one somewhere."

Linda listened as Obie pulled whatever he'd found over his head. "You don't really have a clue what you're doing, do you?" she said.

Obie's voice was muffled. "Not really. But I've learned to trust my dreams."

"Your dreams?"

Obie pulled at a strap of some sort. Linda could hear the unmistakable sound of Velcro strips being ripped open and adjusted. "It's how I found you, Mrs. President. Why I'm here. I dreamt two weeks ago that you'd been imprisoned in the Ottawa Lodge, lost in the dark. There was this huge square drain in the floor, like a black hole, and you were being sucked into it and I stepped in to help. Then somehow you were in a wok, flying away. And there was a helmet like this, though you were wearing it." He tapped the helmet in the blackness. "When the news of your ... shall we say 'abduction' ... hit the airwaves, I knew there had to be more to the story."

"Jesus," said Linda. "So they knew all along I would end up down here?"

"Don't know, Mrs. President. When you start messing with

timelines, all bets are off."

Linda sighed. She could not wrap her mind around such things right now. "So then you came to find me?"

"Well, I didn't do anything until that pay-phone rang as I was walking by. That was your friend, right? You were there?"

"You mean that phone call at Keeley's? Yeah, Cole and I were right there."

"Wish I'd known that. Could've saved us all a great deal of trouble." Obie chuckled. "Maybe. Depends on how locked in the timelines are. It took me about ten minutes to realize that there might be more to it than a stray wrong number. I went back to that phone and ran a trackback. Got the ID and did a search at the library. Found your connection to Ms. Benedict and figured it out from there. I knew then that Rice had attempted to bring you in, and that something had gone wrong. When I called back, there was no answer. I guess you'd already made for the border at that point."

Linda reached over and grasped his arm with her good hand. "Keeley's husband was killed getting us across," she said.

Obie sighed again. "Like I said, I wish I'd known."

"Yeah, me too," Linda said. She took a deep breath. "So what did you mean when you said Rice has been sidelined?"

Obie stopped and flashed his eyebrows with delight. "I arrived in Ottawa yesterday, but wasn't quite sure how to proceed. Figured Bob and Rice were keeping pretty close tabs on you. But I took a chance this morning and buzzed the astral for a quick peek. Found Bob in D.C. and Rice still in bed. I didn't get too close, but it felt like he was sick. That was my cue to come get you."

"So where do we go from here?"

"Right down that pit Rice warned you about."

"Down the drain?" asked Linda.

"Down the drain."

The wok began to glow from the walls and ceiling, a faint blue-white light that cast Obie in silhouette. Linda breathed deeply, relieved just to have some illumination. Obie lay still for the longest time. Linda wondered if he'd fallen asleep. After a few minutes, she asked, "Obie?"

"Hang on," he said. "Almost there."

"Almost where?" asked Linda. They hadn't even moved yet.

Obie reached around with his left hand, looking for something. "I wish I knew how to make this thing transparent," he said.

In an instant the ship was as clear as glass. Linda covered her eyes with a gasp. They were underwater, rushing along what looked like a riverbed with full daylight overhead. After a moment the water disappeared. The wok was again opaque. They were back in the relative darkness of the blue-white light.

"Sorry," said Obie. "Should've warned you."

"Where are we?"

"The Lodge is right under Parliament Hill. Directly beneath the seat of government, as they like to say. The People love to do shit like that." He reached down to scratch his side. "We're currently making our way up the Ottawa River."

"You can see where we're going?" asked Linda.

"Yeah. That's what the helmet's for. Sorry there's only one."

"Why does it feel like we're not moving?"

Obie turned in the dim light and saluted. "Alien technology, ma'am," he said with a laugh. He turned back.

"Where are we headed?"

"I asked the ship to take us someplace safe."

"You can just talk to the ship?"

Obie shrugged. "Think of the ship as concentrated consciousness," he said.

Linda didn't know what that meant. She started to ask another question but Obie cut her off.

"We're here." He pulled off the helmet.

"Where's here?" asked Linda.

"Looks like a golf course."

## 12.5

"I should have thought to bring pain meds," said Obie, gesturing toward Linda's broken hand. "We don't have time right now for real healing."

Linda looked down. She'd been carrying her right hand against her chest, cradling it against the fabric of her jumpsuit, protecting it with her left hand when she could. The fingers were swollen and red and would not move. She could imagine Rice, kneeling over her unconscious body, breaking her fingers one by one, maybe with a hammer, maybe with his bare hands. What she could not imagine was the inner experience of someone who could do such a thing. That sort of emotional detachment was beyond her. It was evil. And it was very, very dangerous. She thought of Cole falling to the floor, then looked over at his brother. She waved her broken hand in the air between them. "I have way worse pain than this, Obie," she said.

Obie exhaled heavily. "Yeah. So let's talk about that, okay?"

Linda looked away. The wok had set down in a small pond at the golf course's edge. Transparent now, it looked to Linda as though they were lying side-by-side in a soap bubble, surrounded by mud and lost golf balls and the remains of last summer's water lilies. She looked back at Obie. "Okay," she said.

Obie nodded. "It may be true that Cole is dead," he said, choosing his words carefully. "I'm sure that's what Rice intended."

Linda closed her eyes.

"But he's also capable of making mistakes, Mrs. President. Shooting Cole proves that. I mean, if what he wants is to control you, then killing my brother was a stupid, impulsive move on his part. Cole would've been of much more use to him alive. So Rice *can* fuck up. But another mistake he might be making is to assume Cole dead, just because he killed him. I don't intend to make the same mistake."

Linda reached out and took Obie's hand. "I don't understand, Obie. I saw him die."

"I'm sure you did," answered Obie, gently. "But when you start hanging out with the Strangers," he pointed toward the sky, "the word 'death' kinda loses its meaning."

Linda opened an eye. "What are you saying, Obie?"

"I'm saying, Mrs. President, that from what I can see, the Strangers have gone to way too much trouble to bring you two together to just let Cole go now."

Linda raised her head. "What?"

"I'm saying that I think we need to go find my brother."

Linda's breath caught, her brow furrowed. "I don't—" Linda raised herself to her elbow. "Do you know where to find him?"

Obie nodded. "I have a pretty good idea."

"Then we need to go get him."

"It'll mean going back into danger," he cautioned.

"I don't care."

"I should just go myself."

"The fuck you will, Obie. Take me there. Now."

Obie lowered his head. "It may not be easy. To see him," he said.

"Take me there, Obie. Please. We have to get him. We can't let Rice have him." Linda held Obie's gaze with fierce, raw eyes.

Obie reached out and pulled on the flight helmet.

## 12.6

The afternoon sun was waning. The shadows reached out to Linda like cold, spindly fingers as she followed Obie across the roof. Her bare feet stuck slightly to the black, tarry surface as she walked. The wok had landed on a squat, flat-roofed building, part of a complex of such buildings that lay just to the north of downtown Ottawa. Obie had told her not to worry, that they wouldn't be seen. The ship knew what "she" was doing even if he didn't. They made their way to an entranceway and Obie pulled on the gunmetal door. It opened without a hitch.

Obie stopped and turned. "You have to remember: ultimately, nothing you see here is real. And at the same time, of course, it's all very real indeed."

"And you don't have time to explain that to me right now, do you?"

Obie grinned. "You got it, Mrs. President."

"Where are we?"

Obie shrugged. "As far as the locals are concerned, it's a hospital, a brand new facility specializing in the care and treatment of children with cancer. All of which is a cover for the Show."

"The show?"

Obie raised a finger. "Like I said, nothing you see here is real." He patted the gun at his hip, turned and walked through the entranceway. Linda followed, closing the door behind her. Together they headed down the stairway.

The fifth floor was as empty as the sixth had been: long, well-lit hallways lined with locked doors, the halls bending back on themselves to form rectangles. The elevators seemed to function properly but Obie insisted on the freedom of stairwells, even if they were harder on Linda's ankle. He started down the next flight. Linda stopped to rest. "Wait," she said.

Obie halted and turned. "Sorry. You okay?"

"I just need a minute."

Obie walked back up to her side. "I think Rice's biggest mistake is that things have changed and he hasn't caught up yet."

Linda frowned. "What does that mean?"

"Well, the Strangers – the Life, as he calls them – have departed. And without them, the Plan begins to fall apart. Without the aliens, it's a whole new ballgame."

Linda nodded. "Rice said something about that," she said. She gestured behind her with a vague wave of her wrecked hand. "Back there. Underground. He didn't seem to know where they've gone. Or why they've left those dormant ones behind."

"Well, with any luck, what Rice doesn't know will kill him. All I know is that I was expecting this place to be full of activity: labs and mad scientists and vats full of body parts and hybrid aliens on gurneys. Shit like that. But it's not. It looks like they've closed up shop."

"Will Cole be here then?" asked Linda. Hope clung like a small child to the edges of her words.

"I don't know where else he could be," shrugged Obie. "It's standard practice to store bodies topside. I doubt Rice would just stash him in Legrand's closet."

Linda reached out and grabbed Obie's arm. "Please, Obie. Please. This is hard. Please don't talk about him that way." She let go of his arm.

Obie nodded and sighed. "I'm sorry, Mrs. President," he said. "I, uh, don't even know Cole, you know?" He looked into Linda's reddened eyes. "He's not even real to me."

"He's very real to me," answered Linda quietly. "I ... I was falling in love with him."

Obie smiled. "Well, Mrs. President, we'd better go find him then, hadn't we?"


12.7


Obie pulled open the stairwell door to the third floor and stepped back. "Fuck me!" he said.

Linda pushed in beside him and looked around. "Jesus," she said quietly.

The third floor had been completely gutted, from the looks of things. Instead of blank white walls and hallways of locked doors and overhead fluorescents, they saw a single huge room, murky and cavernous, the ceilings much taller than they had any right to be, lit only by distant windows and the remains of the day.

Obie knelt down to feel the floor. "It's grass," he said.

Linda walked into the darkness so that her eyes could adjust. It sure felt like grass to her bare feet. She looked out across the room. Something huge took up a good third of the space, blocking most of the windows on the opposite wall. The room filled suddenly with bright light and Linda spun to see Obie, his hand on a switch. She turned back. That huge thing was the burnt-out tail section of a jet airplane.

Obie came up beside the President and exhaled, a low, whistling sigh. "Here's the Show," he said, his voice filled with wonder.

Linda started forward, then stopped. She pointed toward the plane. "Are those...?"

Obie nodded. "Bodies. Yes." He passed her on the right and walked toward the wreck.

There were flames still licking around the edges of the tail section, though there was no smoke in the air. The tail had split from the main cabin about thirteen rows from the back, a jagged maw of twisted metal and dangling cables and bent, burnt rows of seats. The ground around it, for this was soil and grass and weeds rather than hard, tile floor, was gouged and torn and littered with shoulder bags and coffee cups and shoes. And bodies. Obie counted thirty-nine, just on the ground. Who knew how many more they'd find inside the tail? Here were those body parts he'd anticipated. But they sure as hell weren't in vats.

"How can this be here, Obie?" asked Linda, her face frozen and hard. She stood beside him where he'd stopped at the closest corpse. "What the hell is this?"

Obie shrugged. "Some of the Strangers find it most effective to communicate with us with these," he gestured toward the wreck with a wave of his hand, "these theatrics. These object lessons." He turned to face her. "I've found that the best thing to do in cases like this is to breathe deeply, go very slowly, notice everything, and suspend any attempts to figure it all out until later." He turned back to the wreck. "Let's see what this is about."

Obie started picking his way through the bodies and luggage. Linda followed, working with her breath as Obie had advised, trying to quiet her mind and slow her pounding heart. She moved with measured deliberation, so as not to step on a body part with her bare feet. She told herself that nothing was real, that it was all just a show, but that got more and more difficult to do. The decapitated body of a young boy assaulted her at every level. When she saw the head just beyond the body, how it had rolled to a stop next to an intact bottle of hand lotion standing as if on display, she almost screamed.

A burst of laughter from Obie distracted her. Linda looked up to find him holding out a pair of hiking boots. "Looks like they knew you'd need shoes," he said. The boots were brand new, still tagged and laced together, and appeared to be about her size.

"I don't think I can take this," Linda said, her voice desperate.

Obie walked to her with the boots and led her away from the boy's head. "Let me help you put these on," he said, supporting her as she sat on the grass. He untied the boots from each other and pulled off the tags, jerking open the tongues so she could slip them on. He squatted before her, then guided each foot gently into a boot. He laced and tied them quickly and stood back up. "Better?" he asked.

Linda nodded.

"C'mon," he said, helping the President to her feet. "You're okay. Just take it in like you're watching a play." He led her to the plane.

A few steps along Obie bent to pick up a piece of paper. A ticket. He read it, then looked up toward the heavens and smiled. "Good one," he said, as if he were Tevye speaking with God.

"What is it?" asked Linda.

Obie handed the ticket to Linda. "New Air 413," he said. "This was Ruth's flight." Linda let the ticket fall to the ground and looked up at the plane with sad, wet eyes. Obie grabbed her good hand. "C'mon," he said. He guided her around to the open end of the tail section.

Linda gasped. There was Cole, sprawled along the aisle between the twisted rows of seats. He was lying on his back, his legs away from them, his head hanging over the torn edge of the aisle floor like a rag doll. The height of the wreckage put his face on a level with hers.

Obie squeezed her hand. "Linda? It's the Show. Remember it's the Show."

To Linda it just didn't fucking matter that it was the god-damned Show. She pulled off the stocking cap, clasped it to her stomach, and stepped toward Cole's body.

Obie passed her and heaved himself up through the twisted metal and over the first row of seats. He knelt beside his brother's corpse. The body was quite thoroughly dead, cold and stiff and resting in a drying pool of blood. He pulled open Cole's shirt but found no gunshot wound to the stomach or chest. What he found was that Cole's left arm had been severed just under the shoulder. He'd bled to death in a matter of moments. Obie looked around for the missing arm, found it wedged under a seat two rows back. There were three fingers missing. While he'd kept his distance from family affairs, Obie had paid attention when his brother's wife had been killed. These were the same injuries that Ruth had received in the real crash of Flight 413.

He stood and leaned out over the jagged open end. There stood Linda, cradling Cole's head on her shoulder. She looked up at him with puffy, vacant eyes.

"Let's get him out of here," said Obie.

## 12.8

Linda didn't think there'd be room for all three of them, but there was, as if the ship had grown larger while they were in the building. Obie lay on the far right with the flight helmet on. Cole's severed arm, wrapped in a white lab coat they'd found on their way out, was wedged between Obie and the wall. Linda was on the left. Cole's body, the upper torso wrapped in another lab coat and secured with duct tape to help contain the sticky, drying blood, lay between them. Linda rested her broken hand on Cole's stomach.

"You ready?" asked Obie. "Rice must know you're gone by now."

Linda shivered in the blackness. It had been dark and icy when they'd reached the roof, and Cole's body was colder than she'd thought it could be. She found unexpected comfort in that. She needed to be frozen right now. She needed the black. She needed the silence. If her heart warmed up even a bit she'd melt in a torrent of horror and grief. She answered with a voice from the far side of death. "I'm ready." The ship began to glow again, the faint blue-white light the color of cemeteries and nightmares.

After a while Linda spoke again. "Where do we go?"

Obie took a moment before responding. "It seems best to do something random and unexpected, so rather than plan our next move, I've asked the *ship* to take us someplace safe," he said. He adjusted the helmet strap and consulted the view screen for a moment. "It's dark, and we're very high right now, but we seem to be headed north."

Linda laid her head on the floor and closed her eyes. The sight of Cole's body was too disturbing to her senses for her to hold for long. Obie's mention of Rice had frozen her resolve to the same state as her body and heart. With icy determination, she knew she would kill him one day, or die in the attempt. His presence on the planet was an abomination that could not be tolerated. This time, she'd make sure he was dead. She had no idea how she would do that.

She reached out and touched Cole's thinning hair. He was gone. Totally and inexorably absent. She and Obie would bury him. She could see that far. But what came beyond that moment she could not see. She would look up at Obie and he'd smile his crooked smile and shrug and say something, but she could imagine no words that would make any sense. The path between the present moment and the moment she put a bullet in Rice's head was blacker than the cell in which he'd imprisoned her, and just as bitter.

"Linda?" said Obie.

"Yes?"

"I want to show you something."

"Okay."

"I'm going to ask the ship to turn transparent again," he explained, glancing back at her over his shoulder. "When she does, it'll look to us as if we're hurtling through space, which, in fact, we are."

"Okay."

"I just wanted to let you know."

"Thank you."

Obie turned and mumbled something. The ship disappeared just as he said it would. Linda breathed deeply to steady herself as she hung, seemingly unprotected and unsupported, in the depths of space, their forward movement impossible to discern in the vast distances around her. She looked down to see the Earth below, the dark surface lit by the quarter moon and sparse twinkles of electric light.

"Look ahead," said Obie, his voice soft with awe.

Linda complied. Ahead in the distance, against the field of stars, she saw two straight lines of illumination, slowly converging. As they neared, the lines resolved into perfect rows of blue-white lights, stretching before her as far as she could see. Ships. Woks, like the one she was in, waiting at attention as the three of them passed between. This time, Linda had no trouble seeing it for the honor guard that it was, a loving salute to a fallen comrade. Her tears spilled forth at last, and her quiet sobs of grief and gratitude filled the whole of her soul.

The ship landed on a frozen lake and the door melted open. Frigid arctic air burst into the cabin, freezing Linda even further. Obie scrambled out, feet first, and then helped Linda do the same. As soon as she was clear of the ship the door melted shut.

"Hey!" shouted Linda in the gale, but she couldn't even hear herself.

Obie grabbed her hand and pulled her back a few steps. The ship began to glow, faintly at first, then bright and clear, moving from yellow to orange to a deep, rich red. Linda could feel the heat of it through her jumpsuit and stepped back another few feet. Together they stood and watched as the ice beneath the ship melted and the wok sank down into the water-filled hole. In just a couple of minutes the ship was gone from sight, its glow pulsing up through the ice for just a moment before fading away. The water started to skim with slush. Cole was gone.

Obie pulled her away. She turned to face him, filled with questions but unable to ask any of them in the roar of the wind. He pointed over her shoulder and she turned.

There stood three figures, bundled in fur.

### 12.9

*Grace was thankful to find no scary ones lurking about. And thankful as well to find Evlyn nearby. Grace had used Linda's heart as a beacon to navigate this realm, found the President standing next to a man she did not know, with three others nearby, and more beyond that. Good hearts, all of them. Strong hearts. Hearts that could help. Grace vibrated with relief. She'd been gone so long. She reached down to scratch Dennis's head, grateful that he had come with her again. She was glad that Linda was safe. But where was her father? She beamed her concern.*

*The old woman flickered to her side. "You're back, eh?" she said, before sliding momentarily into the form of a young Chinese man. Grace could see that Evlyn's appearance was more stable now, less chaotic. Her transformations were fewer and briefer. She was settling into her essential self, integrating her lives, her lessons, her times. And she was more light, now, than woman. The power of her glow bathed Grace with peace.*

*Grace soaked up that light and love. "Where's my father?" she asked.*

*Evlyn dimmed, anticipating this young one's sadness. "He has become untethered from his body," she said.*

*Grace shifted down into the thickness of the densest layers to see for herself, then returned to the old woman's side. "Then where did he go?" she asked. "Shouldn't he be here with us?"*

*The old woman rolled in confusion, shifting to the body of the large, dark-haired white man, and then a young Hispanic girl, before settling back into her dominant form. "I do not know, little sleeper," she said. "His disappearance surprised me. The dark ones returned to follow your father and Linda, and in the physical realm they encountered a very black heart. Your father vanished in an instant. I did not see where he went, and I have not seen him since."*

*Grace watched as Linda and the others moved away across the snow and ice. "That is very odd," she said. She extended a hand into the physical. It was extremely cold there. "Is Linda okay?" she asked.*

*Evlyn beamed her assurance. "She is. The old ones have surrounded her. The dark ones have been forced to flee."*

*"The Elders?" asked Grace, searching with her heart, glad of the news, and yet wary.*

*"The Elders, yes. And the alive ones. Both are standing guard. And a few of the other ancient races are now present, observing from a distance. Much has happened since you were last here." Evlyn held steady in her old woman form. "Two days have come and gone for your friend Linda. Where have you been?" Grace slowly turned around, as if trying to see the path that had brought her here. Evlyn frowned, puzzled at what she now noticed. "And what has become of your own tether?" the old woman asked.*

*Grace stopped turning and folded in tightly to think, gathering her power around her like a cloak, trying to recall through the fog. It was so hard to remember, sometimes, that other life. Something about a doctor talking to her grandfather. Something about some medication. She remembered screaming at them to let her sleep. Emily cried. Grandpa fretted. Dennis was frantic at her feet. She pleaded to be left alone, but they would not listen. They didn't understand.*

*Grace searched through her entire being, scanning her pulsing patterns, feeling and sensing but finding no connection now whatsoever. She remembered the stretching she'd felt. The tearing away. The focus it had taken her. The pain. The loss. But that pain was gone now. All that remained was an absence. She beamed at the old woman. "I broke the cord!" she said.*

*Evlyn slumped. She did not think this young one understood what that meant.*

# Chapter Thirteen

## 13.1

Rice didn't know which was more humiliating: that he'd lost her again or that he had to sit here on the toilet with cramps and diarrhea. He wondered, as he always did at such times, whether he was really an alien himself, some advanced being from another galaxy living on Earth in a human body, an agent under the covers as well as above them. That would explain his disgust for these people. And his disdain for this weak, limited bag of flesh in which he had to live. Even with the enhancements that kept him feeling much younger than his one hundred and ten years, this body could not begin to match the full reality of who he knew himself to be.

He grimaced and pushed, feeling his flesh burn. Fucking take-out. And fucking Carl. He was really going to enjoy cutting that motherfucker into little pieces, one of these fucking days. Put him in the vats with the rest of the bungled and botched. Should've done that a long time ago.

Bob had recognized Carl right away, of course. She'd watched him enter the Lodge. Watched him find Ma Kettle. Watched them leave. She'd tried to call Rice to tell him before they got away. But Theodore Rice hadn't managed to get a new implant yet, had he? When had he had the time? He hadn't told Bob where he was staying, which was just plain stupid. And his fucking cell phone, hung on the back of the door in his jacket pocket, was set to vibrate. There he was, less than ten feet away, sprawled out in the agony of food poisoning on his fucking hotel bed, cramping and sweating and puking and shitting his fucking guts out, and he didn't hear Bob's calls. He'd figured the Prez would just sit cozy and tight in her dark little cage until he was back on his feet. He'd figured poorly.

Rice coughed up a bitter laugh, the movement roiling his stomach again. It's a crazy fucking universe we live in, where the fate of worlds can hang on one bad enchilada. What had he been thinking? Fucking Canadians can't make Mexican. And given the upheavals in world agricultural markets, it was probably fucking rat meat they'd served him.

Hot acids spilled from his bowels and he looked up at the ceiling, roaring to the heavens and pounding the wall with his fist. Holy fuck! He took some deep breaths to try to calm himself, realizing that he probably shouldn't make this much noise. The last thing he needed was somebody knocking at his door.

He'd already drawn suspicion. When he'd finally fallen asleep the evening before, Bob had been able to get in and implant a compulsion to call her, which he'd done at about two in the morning, when he awakened to puke. He'd emptied himself out as best he could, coked up on painkillers, and stormed out of the hotel, berating the young woman at the front desk just because she was there. Bad form, that.

Moaning, stumbling, doubled over with cramps, he'd made his way down into the Lodge and to the scene of the crime, cursing the tiny rooms, the low ceilings and the bare, cold stone as he made his way to Linda's cell. The President was gone. So was that little wok. All he'd found was Linda's filthy bathrobe on the floor. Like, what the fuck? Had she left naked? He could feel his own arousal at the thought of that. Should've fucked her while he'd had the chance.

The thing that really pissed him off is that he should have seen this coming. Ten minutes of Googling would have told him that the goddamned President's fuck-toy was goddamned Carl Thomas's goddamned little brother. The aliens loved to do shit like that. They're probably all yukking it up over beer and brats right now, while he sits here flushing half his body weight down a fucking toilet in the Ottawa Hilton. He breathed deeply and pushed, hoping this was the last of it.

Enough. It was all a test. To see if he could keep to the Plan. To see if the People were still worthy. As if they hadn't already proven themselves over and over. Rice sighed. So he'd choked on the true-and-false. So fucking what? Let's see how he does on the multiple-choice. Bob said the aliens were now blocking her from getting anywhere near Carl and the Prez. Fine. Play your stupid little games, buggy-boys. Theodore Rice was not without resources, even now. He still had his own wok. In a few hours this sickness would run its course. Soon enough he'd be back in the game. This was not over yet.

Let's see, kiddies. Today's problem: Crazy Carl comes out of nowhere and steals the President right from under his nose. Should Agent Rice:

a) go to the topside facility and grind up that fucker Cole's body for dog food,

b) head back to D.C. and get Bob and Random and Alice and whomever the fuck else they could find, and go kick some astral ass,

c) nab Cole's newly-orphaned larvae and toss them down into the Rock to use as bargaining chips or,

d) all of the above?

Rice smiled, grabbing a huge wad of paper to wipe his ass. This was a no-brainer. D it would be: all of the fucking above.

## 13.2

Linda opened her eyes. Obie was right where she'd left him, sitting cross-legged on the tattered brown recliner opposite the futon on which she'd slept. The only difference was that it was morning now. Soft gray light sifted like drifting snow through the closed blinds behind Obie's head, hiding his eyes in darkness, surrounding him with an ethereal glow.

Obie felt her gaze and opened his eyes and smiled. "You look better," he said.

The President reached up to run her fingers over her smooth scalp. In the middle of the night, consumed by grief and surrounded by safety and willing help, she'd insisted, before she could sleep, that they cut her hair and find her a hot shower. Rice's assault was lodged in her body. Though she would have to tolerate the bruises and broken bones, she would not collude with his attempt to humiliate and disfigure her. A short search at the vet's office had turned up some clippers used to shave sled dogs before surgery. Those would do. The hair had to go. All of it, save for the fine, velvety stubble the clippers left, the sparse promise of something new. She'd wear a fucking hat.

"Rather stylish, wouldn't you say?" She smiled weakly.

"It's appropriate," said Obie with a nod. "Around the world, shaving one's head symbolizes an intention to detach oneself from the old, material world, and to apprentice oneself to that which lies beyond the material."

Linda frowned. "I didn't realize I'd taken vows," she said, her voice edging on sarcasm.

"I think, before this is all over, you'll understand what I mean," answered Obie.

Linda let it go for now and swabbed the sleep from her eyes with gentle finger strokes, careful of the swelling and the bruises. "You sure I don't need my pills?"

"You saw the ships last night, Mrs. President. What does your heart tell you?"

Linda closed her eyes to see what she could feel, imagining herself voyaging around inside her body, then up through the sky and into the void. She pictured the multitude of ships patrolling the airspace over her body far below, just as she'd seen them in the night sky over the trailer in which she now sat. She felt no hostile eyes spying, no evil mind possessing hers, no ill will, no attack. She opened her eyes and nodded. "I feel pretty safe," she said.

"Then you are," said Obie.

Linda pulled back the down comforter and pushed out her legs, lifting her torso into a sitting position and resting her feet gently on the carpeted floor. She noted the dull throb in her right hand, now splinted and wrapped, as her heart rate increased in response to her movements. She breathed through the deep aching in her abdominals. She could endure this. The broken fingers. The ankle. The cuts and welts and bruises. The memories. She could take it all in, feel it as it passed through her in waves, live through it, let it go, and move on. She was the fucking President. She could do that.

But there was a black hole inside her now, eating her up from the inside out, a puncture, a tear, a grief so profound that it threatened to unravel her. The world was not as it seemed, not as she'd always believed. There was magic and wonder far grander than she'd ever imagined, and evil to match, it seemed. And Cole was dead. Rice had scoffed that she'd hardly even known him. He was right, but he was also wrong. She could feel in her body a truth her mind could not fathom: she and Cole had been meant to do something together. Some big work. And now it appeared that she'd been left to do it alone, to "follow this through," as Keeley had demanded. She did not know if she could do that. The black hole's pull was relentless.

She looked at Obie. "What time is it?" she asked.

"I don't know. Nine, maybe. You hungry?"

Linda shook her head. "Coffee?"

"I'll check." Obie uncrossed his legs and rose, stretching his arms to the ceiling for a moment before heading into the kitchen. Linda watched, noticing how the whole mobile home rocked slightly under his feet as he walked, how it rattled and groaned in the frigid winds that knocked at the doors and windows, insisting that they be let inside. The oil furnace kept the cold at bay, but she longed for a woodstove like the one she and Earl had installed in their living room, an Aztec god she could appease with a steady diet of well-seasoned logs. Just knowing she was sitting in a trailer on a side-street in a tiny arctic village chilled her to the bone, whether her body was warm enough or not. And she'd grown up in Michigan. So much for being cold hardy.

Obie scrounged the cupboards. "Here we go," he said, pulling down a jar of instant.

Linda grimaced. "That's not coffee," she said.

"Looks like your only choice, Mrs. President," said Obie.

"Do you have to call me that?" she asked. The title made her feel spoiled and demanding. The thought of that made her wince. Maybe she was.

"What do you want me to call you?" asked Obie.

"How about Linda?"

Obie nodded. "Okay. I can do that."

"And can I call you Obie? Or do you prefer Carl?"

He shrugged. "Obie's fine, these days. I've been using it since I went underground. It works for Duluth." He spooned some coffee powder into a mug and filled a teapot to heat on the gas stove.

"Aren't you having any?" asked Linda.

"Never touch the stuff."

Linda nodded. "Where are our hosts?"

Obie walked around to lean with his back to the bar while the water heated. "They left before daybreak. Headed up to their camp. Something about preparing for a ceremony of some sort. Payok said not to expect them until after dark, or maybe tomorrow morning. He said they'd bring Sinaaq to meet you as soon as they could."

As she had felt countless times since she'd run from the Ranch so many days ago, there was just too much she did not understand. Once again she had no choice but to put her life in the hands of others, of people like Obie who had showed up in the blackness and whisked her away in a UFO, of people like these Inuit who had stepped out of the past to bring her in from the cold and dark. These people seemed to comprehend far better than she what was going on. As hard and fast as she ran, she could only barely keep up. Her world had careened out of its former orbit. All she could do was hang onto her hat. She nodded out of habit, as if she should have understood.

Obie smiled. "Sinaaq, or Sina, as they all call her, is the young woman these people all work for," he explained. The teapot started to sing and he jumped around the counter to make Linda's coffee.

"And they're working on a documentary about climate change?" asked Linda.

"That's their cover story," said Obie, stirring the coffee. He opened the refrigerator. "You need milk?"

"Black is fine," said Linda. "Why do they need a cover story? What are they doing here?"

Obie stepped back into the living room and handed her the mug of steaming brown liquid. He sat back down in the recliner and flashed his eyebrows with delight. "They're reclaiming their lives."

"Which means what, exactly?"

"The Inuit peoples have had most of their culture systematically stripped away over the past couple of centuries. Something at which we Imperialists excel. You know the routine: send in the missionaries and bureaucrats, move people into cities, put them into schools, give them new names, kill off their sources of food, outlaw their customs, take away their identities. It doesn't take that long to obliterate an entire people, if you put your mind to it. And once you've got TV sets, it's easy as pie."

Linda shuddered. "And they're trying to ... what ... reclaim their old ways? Something like that?" She took a sip of her coffee and was surprised by how good it tasted, even as the heat of it burned her tongue.

Obie smiled. "Something like that."

"So why the cover story?"

"As far as I can make out, Sina is some sort of prophet or visionary, the last living descendant of a tribal group known as the Sadlermiut, who were thought to have all died out in the early 20th century. Apparently there were a few mixed-blood survivors. The Sadlermiut were said to be the last remnant of the Tuniit, an ancient people who populated the far north *before* the Inuit peoples moved into the area over a thousand years ago. The Inuit who encountered them described the Tuniit as a race of 'giants' and 'dwarves.' According to Sernartok, this does not just mean that they were shorter or taller."

Linda shook her head in confusion. "I can't keep the names straight, Obie. Who's Sernakok, or whatever? Who wasn't taller?"

"Sernartok is the middle-aged woman who shaved your head last night," Obie explained. "Her Western name is Genna Black. She works part-time with the local veterinarian and had used the clippers before."

"And these giants and dwarves?"

Obie's eyes flickered with excitement. "According to their prophet, the Tuniit peoples, of whom she is the last surviving descendant, remember, were good buddies with our friends up above." He gestured toward the sky. "Sina and Utterpok are working to re-establish diplomatic relations, shall we say."

"Jesus." Linda took another sip of her coffee, then cradled the mug against her stomach, letting the warmth seep through the flannel and fleece they'd given her to replace the jumpsuit. She hoped the coffee would warm her courage and soothe her aching muscles. "How do you keep all these names straight? Let alone pronounce them?"

"Babel fish."

"Excuse me?"

Obie grinned. "Just a joke. Sorry. It's a side effect of my training, I guess. Things just stick to me. I just ... know things I shouldn't. Or remember them."

"Nice trick."

"It comes in handy."

Obie crossed his legs again, pulling his long, heavy robe, the color of drying blood, over his knees. With his sandy hair now free of its rubber band, and his tight little Van Dyke, Obie had a dashing air about him. Linda would not have been surprised to see a rapier in his hand and a plumed hat on his head. The thought made her laugh: she'd been rescued by a Musketeer. Now if only she could find two more.

Linda exhaled heavily, trying to find some focus. "So what do we do now?" she asked. "Where are we exactly?"

"Times are so urgent we have to ask our questions two at a time, don't we?"

"I guess so," Linda smiled tightly. "So start with 'where are we?'"

"Bathurst Island. Close to the center. Roughly the same latitude as central Greenland. The people here call this place Akkituyok, which means 'costs much' in English. Many of these buildings were part of a mining operation that closed in 2011. Zinc and lead, primarily. A little silver. A small hamlet had built up around the mine and the Inuit who lived here were granted the right to stay. Most of them now work in one way or another to decommission the mine and reclaim the land. And with the effects of climate change becoming so apparent these past years, this has become a sort of base camp for people who are studying and documenting the changes, so there's lots of work with outfitting and guiding. The Inuit are more than a little pissed off at the U.S. for its refusal to take climate change seriously. We're lucky it was Sina's people that found us. Not everyone in Akkituyok would be glad to know that the President of the United States is here. Western civilization has, indeed, cost them much."

Linda nodded, sipping at her coffee. "I can understand that. The last few administrations have been major disappointments." She pulled her legs up and tucked them underneath her. "But I still don't understand what our hosts are doing here."

Obie nodded, acknowledging the missing pieces. "Sinaaq came on the scene about three years ago. Started having these dreams or visions, and began to write about them on the Internet. She says that the Strangers, whom she calls the Tuurngait or 'helping spirits,' have called her to lead her people back to the old ways, including back into relationship with the Tuurngait themselves, in preparation for the major Earth changes that are now upon us. Looks like she's attracted a rather dedicated following."

"And they're pretending to make a documentary."

Obie looked Linda in the eyes. "Not everybody here would look kindly on the whole alien thing. You need to remember that the Inuit are only now beginning to heal from the trauma of forced Westernization. Most of them are pretty stuck in the mainstream paradigm."

"Why do you call the aliens 'the Strangers'?"

"I needed a term that was not fraught with judgment," said Obie with a smile. "They just feel like strangers to me. People whom we don't know."

"Okay." She held the coffee cup against her cheek to soak in its warmth. "So how did Sina end up here?"

"Sernartok started reading Sina's writings and they resonated with her. Since most of the workers left after the mine closed, there was an abundance of housing here. Sernartok invited Sina and her group up about a year ago to use as its own base camp. They've been teaching themselves the traditional skills of hunting and cooking and preserving food and building shelters."

"If the whole place is melting, why are they going to the trouble of learning how to survive in the cold and ice?"

"That's a really good question."

Linda finished her coffee and placed the mug gently on an end table, managing the maneuver with her splinted right hand. She rubbed her head absently with her left hand, trying to get used to the smooth, suede-like feel of it. Everything was so new. She felt like she was in a dream. Obie smiled gently, creating a space for her next question. "So, if the Inuit are pissed off at the U.S., why do Sina's people like me?"

Obie paused for a moment before answering, as if unsure which words to choose. There was a sadness in his eyes that Linda hadn't seen before. "I don't think it's a matter of liking you," he said at last. "Apparently they're of the opinion that the survival or extinction of the entire human species may rest on your shoulders."

## 13.3

Obie's blunt statement slapped Linda into stunned silence like a blow to the temple. Panic ruptured her crusted heart like hot lava and searing gases, leaving her throat choked and clouded with volcanic ash. It was on *her* shoulders? That was just ... too fucking bat-shit crazy. Her mind reeled, searching for something to hang onto, something that she could wrap her intellect around, something that she could control. She grabbed the first thing that flew by. "Did you stay up all night, Obie? To learn all of this?"

Obie smiled thinly, as though noticing Linda's weak attempt to deflect what he'd said. "I did. Most of it."

"Don't you need some sleep? How can you—?"

Obie shrugged. "I got the rest I needed, Linda. Trust me."

Linda looked down at her hands and breathed a few slow breaths. She looked up at Obie with weary eyes. "I don't know how to hold this, Obie. I really don't. It's like ... here I thought I was just battling corrupt government agents who are colluding with evil aliens to take over the world, and you're telling me the extinction of the human race is at stake? And that it's up to *me*?" Tears welled up in her eyes as she spoke. "How do I process that? What do I do next? And who the hell are you and why are you telling me these things? I mean, Jesus, it's insane. It's driving me fucking nuts!"

Obie let her sputter out, then rose and crossed the room to sit next to her on the futon. He reached out and took her unbroken hand. "This is the expository section of your story, Linda," he said with soft humor and gentle firmness. "It's a time for explanations and understanding and the sharing of information. So we'll have to take these questions one at a time, and slowly."

Tears welled in Linda's swollen eyes as he spoke. She hung her head and let them spill. "We don't have time, Obie. There's a madman out there trying to kill me. Albert Singer has probably already buried me and moved into my office. My mother's been taken and who knows what those fuckers have done to her? And Cole's—" She stopped to let a single sob pass through her. "Cole's kids. And his father." She looked up at Obie. "*Your* father. They ... they need to be told."

Obie nodded in agreement. "You're right, Linda. They need to be told. So that's what we're doing here."

"What?"

"We're figuring out what to tell them. And when. And how."

Linda closed her eyes and took a series of slow, deep breaths.

Obie was right. Even if she held a phone in her hand right now she wouldn't know what to say to Cole's children. She would need more clarity before she could interrupt those precious young lives. The word "death" loses its meaning when the aliens are involved, Obie had told her. There was too much she did not understand. She'd have to breathe through her anxiety and go more slowly. She looked at Obie. "Where do we start?" she asked.

"I want to tell you who the hell I am," he replied with a grin.

Linda squeezed Obie's hand and released it, pushing herself around on the futon so that she could face him. "Okay. Tell me who you are."

Obie matched her movement, pulling his legs up to face her. "How much did Cole tell you?"

"He got to the part where you went nuts and disappeared," she said, smiling to let him know that she did not think he was crazy.

"All of which just left Cole confused, I'd guess."

"Pretty much. He said he hadn't seen you in years, that as far as he knew you were living homeless in Chicago or Duluth or someplace."

"Did he tell you about the ISR? Or the hospital in Turkey?"

Linda nodded. "He said you were in Air Force intelligence and that you had some sort of mental breakdown."

"Right. So, by now you'll understand what I mean when I say that the term 'mental breakdown' is just short-hand for meeting Theodore Rice."

Linda shivered. "Yeah. I do understand."

"Rice recruited me out of the ISR. I'd started to put things together on my own. About the Strangers, I mean. I was just a mid-level tech working with AFTAC in Florida. Apparently some of my reports and conclusions made their way to the People. As is standard procedure in a case like mine, they hauled my ass in and showed me the full monty, just as they did with you. I was young and stupid and this was a chance to finally learn what was really going on. I was in."

"And when was this?"

"The summer of 2000, I'm pretty sure. Just before George the 2nd was elected. I would have been thirty-three or thereabouts."

"Pretty heady stuff."

A strong wind buffeted the trailer and Obie grabbed the down comforter Linda had used as a blanket to spread over their legs. "Yeah. And I was one cocky son-of-a-bitch. Had a natural talent for deep-cover recon in the physical bands. They had high hopes for me."

Linda frowned, wanting to understand every word but not wanting to get in Obie's way. He had so much to explain, and she had too many questions. She sighed and let it go, trusting that it would all become clear soon enough. Or she'd figure out that Obie really *was* crazy. She didn't want to even *think* about that. "So it didn't work out," she said at last.

"Nope. Thanks to Dad."

"Which means?"

"Well, if Dad taught me one thing in this life, it's that things are rarely as they seem. I mean, he was a respected figure in our town. Loved, even. Local banker with a heart of gold. Created grants and endowments to fund good works. A member in good standing of the Loyal Order of the Water Buffalo, as I used to joke. He'd always have a car in the July 4th parade. People would clap and wave. And I'd watch them, wondering why. Because none of it was him. Not the him I knew. The him that wasn't even there. The him that calculated every move. The him that always got exactly what he wanted. The him that would buy me anything I asked for and take me fishing and build me a tree house, but who never once let me inside, to know how he felt, to share his dreams, to know what it all meant to him."

Linda thought back to her confrontation with Ben and wondered if Obie's father had changed much in the years since Obie had known him. "Do you know I met your Dad?"

"Yeah. I got the complete packet."

"I don't know what that means."

Obie sighed. "I don't want to get too far off track here, Linda. Let's just say that, on my way to get you out of the Lodge, you gave me a, like, a package, a mental package that contained pretty much your whole story since escaping the Ranch. And I just took it all in at once. So I got to see your take on the encounter with my father. It was … interesting." Obie smiled.

Relaxing a bit, Linda leaned back on the futon arm and pulled the comforter up to her neck. "Will there ever be time for me to understand all this stuff, Obie?" she asked.

"I don't know. Right now we have to stick to the task at hand."

"Which is?"

"We'll know by the time we finish."

Linda exhaled noisily. "Okay."

Obie untangled himself from the comforter and stood up, stretching again before walking to the kitchen for a tumbler of water. He gulped a full glass and poured another before returning to take his seat again.

"So things were not as they seemed," offered the President.

"Not at all, though it took me some time to figure that out. I was rather enamored of our Mr. Rice. His power was intoxicating. I mean, hell, I even got to sit in as Rice's assistant at one of the planning sessions for what turned out to be 9/11. You don't get more inside than that."

Linda's confusion was palpable. "Planning sessions?" she asked.

"We'll get to that. The point is I was enamored. He showed me pictures of himself and Truman. He's way older than he looks, and he's been involved since the beginning. And that blinded me."

"From what?"

"From the fact that the whole deal was a load of crap."

Linda sighed. "I wish you could just give me one of those packet things you were talking about. This all takes so long."

"I do too, Linda. But we need to do this in the physical. It's where it's playing out. And you're not checked out for anything beyond that. You're flying blindfolded right now."

"Oh, thanks," Linda said with mock gratitude. "I'll try to take that as a compliment."

"We have to start with what is."

"You're the boss, Obie. So what whole deal is a load of crap?"

"The People. The Plan. Rice's entire notion of what's going on. From the start, the people 'in charge' have tried to control and use the UFO phenomenon, interpreting what they saw through the materialist paradigm, and failing to notice that the non-human intelligences involved were up to something they could barely imagine." Obie stopped and raised an eyebrow. "You tracking this?" he asked.

Linda frowned. "Not sure." She thought for a moment. "You're just saying that the way we've thought about UFOs has been wrong from the get-go, right?"

Obie nodded. "There have been a few people who could break through the confines of our culture and see the phenomenon more clearly, but in terms of our government and military leaders, yes. They got it all wrong. And they've now built an entire system of institutions and structures based on this misunderstanding."

"I see." Linda took a deep breath. "I'll just assume that you'll eventually tell me *how* they got it all wrong. But we were talking about you. How is it you came to know this?"

"I started to figure it out the first time I met the Strangers." Obie twisted so that he could cross his legs underneath him. He closed his eyes. "You remember what I said about 'the Show,' right?"

"Sure. You said the aliens just adore the theater."

"It's a somewhat clunky way of sharing a packet in the physical realm, using words and images and music, old archetypal and mythic stuff that resonates with the physical bands and human vibrational levels, so that we can begin to understand them. I'd been with Rice for about six months. Lived down in the Rock. I was training with Bob and Random. And I'd met Spud and Mork, the two designated "ambassador" aliens that lived down in the Rock with us. But it wasn't until the Strangers grabbed me and took me for tagging that I began to understand that it was *all* the show, the whole of the UFO experience, going back centuries, maybe millennia. It's one vast piece of performance art, the world's largest and longest running off-Broadway play, with the Strangers directing, and Spud and Mork as seasoned actors."

Obie stopped for a moment, his eyes remaining closed as if playing out the scene in his mind. Just before Linda could prompt him he spoke again. "They took me through a classic abduction scenario. All the same stuff you went through. But every one of them was Rice. Every little bug, every walking stick, they all had Rice's face, Rice's hair, even Rice's voice. Three little Rices came and got me and floated me through a sliding glass door to a ship where a bunch more little Rices examined me and a couple of tall, spindly Rices spoke with me and told me about the end of the world. It was Rice everywhere." Obie opened his eyes and grinned at Linda. "Thinking about it now it was funny as hell."

Linda held up her bandaged hand. "You'll forgive me if I don't share in the joke."

"Sorry. But yeah, it was Rice everywhere. And that stuck with me. I knew they were trying to communicate something important, but it took a while to sink in."

"What was it that changed for you?"

Obie's eyes were closed again, to help him remember. "They took me apart," he said.

"Who took you apart?"

"The Strangers. The Rices. On that first encounter. They dismembered my body right before my eyes. Cut me up into little pieces and then put me back together. It was the most physically excruciating thing I've ever felt."

"Jesus."

"That's what I said. But Jesus didn't come and help me. Neither did anybody else. They cut me up and I died and then they brought me back to life and put me back in my bed. Life hasn't been the same since."

"I'll bet."

"Please remember that I was gung ho Air Force up until that point. This was all brand new to me. But I wasn't stupid. And I started to see that things were not as they seemed."

"Tell me."

"What I realized was that Rice and the People see the whole alien thing almost entirely in materialist terms. Sure, they'll do a bit of out-of-body universe-hopping when it suits them, but as far as they're concerned they live in a physical world of rocks and trees and dogs and cats, where the aliens come in metallic ships from distant planets to exploit the Earth's resources and battle for control of the world. In other words, they created the Strangers in their own image. They see them as being essentially just like themselves, which was the meaning of all of those Rice faces. The Strangers were telling me that, when we look at them, we're seeing ourselves."

"So something didn't add up. My experience of the Strangers was that they were far more bizarre than Rice, or any of us, could imagine. And the fact that, for some reason I didn't quite understand, the Strangers were trying to warn *me* of our misperception didn't align with the story of interstellar wars and evil aliens trying to rule the world. I began to question the Plan."

"Tell me about this Plan, Obie. What is the Plan? I'm not sure I really understand it. Who all is involved? How much do the People control?"

Obie smiled. "The Plan is for the People and the Life to ally against what they see as the 'evil' nations and ideologies on this planet, and those supposedly 'evil' alien species who are trying to control and exploit the planet, in order, they say, to protect the rights and freedoms of the Earth and her people. The Plan is to genetically combine the Life and *Homo sapiens* together into a hybrid species that represents the best of both. And the Plan is for the aliens to give us the technologies we'll need to keep our civilization going, despite how grim things look now."

"Wow. That's quite a mission statement."

"That's the short version that goes in the brochure. But once you hire on and read the fine print, you learn that, for the People, it has always been about power and control, about an occult technocracy of elite bankers, corporate power brokers, and world leaders enacting a long-term and carefully thought-out plan to manipulate the vast majority of humans into enslaving themselves while believing themselves free. They breed us like cattle, making compliant slaves who question neither the fence nor the abattoir. It's a plan for control at all costs, damn the consequences, which include, now, the possible extinction of most of the life on this planet. Somewhere in there you'll find a self-disgust so deep, and a death wish so profound, that it'll take your breath away."

Linda sighed deeply, thinking of the nation she had sworn to lead. How had we become so lost, that we would keep such things hidden in the darkness? And was there any way back into the light? She reached up and rubbed the short nap of her hair, basking briefly in the way it tingled, in how smooth and clean it felt, gently caressing the bruises and cuts that reminded her of those long days and nights underground. The touch of her own fingers soothed her exhausted mind and opened her heart, making room for Obie's strange tale to wash over her in such a way that she could feel how it resonated with her own inner knowing.

"That feels true to me," she said at last. She took a deep breath, to help her find her next question. "So how did it come to be like this?"

Obie nodded and raised his eyebrows, a teacher acknowledging a good question. "Well, you have to start by realizing that the framing conditions of our culture select for psychopaths, or were invented by them. The whole dominate-and-control game tends strongly to reward, and put into positions of power, people with little or no conscience, feeling, or empathy, people who are wired to lie, cheat, steal, and manipulate to get what they want, and to protect themselves from being discovered."

"Hmm. Another compliment. How nice." Linda smiled to show she wasn't really offended.

"Yeah, well, you're in office despite that system, Linda, not because of it. But I'm sure you understand my meaning. Your compatriots in Washington and around the globe tend toward the money-grubbing and power-hungry end of the continuum, rather than the compassion and service end of things. The government is morally bankrupt."

Linda nodded. "You've been to the same parties I've been to, I see."

"So these are the people who grabbed hold of the whole UFO/alien thing when the opportunity arose. They seized it and tried to shape it to suit their agendas. The rest is history. Or would be, if anybody knew about it. They're in it for the long haul, or think they are, these bastards, using fear and disinformation to control the comfort-addled masses. When the Strangers made their move back in the forties, the power elite simply subsumed them into their psychopathic worldview. And what a stroke of luck for them. Not only do you get some incredible new toys, you get some very convincing bargaining chips. When China starts squirming about propping up the U.S. economy, claims of an alien-designed missile-defense system give our threats to nuke them back to the Stone Age some real teeth, as Russell's team found out in 2013."

"So it was like with your father: what you saw behind the scenes did not match up with what the People said about themselves. You started to question their Plan."

"I did. That dismemberment was for real, as far as my psyche was concerned. The Strangers really did take me apart. Over the course of the next few months they abducted me six more times, each experience stripping away deeper levels of assumption and identity. It was ... fierce. But it swept the insanity of our culture right out of my soul, or most of it, at least. And it opened me up to this miraculous, apparently chaotic Universe in which we live. I don't regret a bit of it."

"I'm glad," said Linda. Saying this, Linda realized that it was really so. Obie felt pretty sane and free to her. She *was* glad.

"In my free time I started reading anything and everything I could get my hands on, about the UFO phenomenon, about paranormal experiences and lost ancient cultures and alternate spiritual systems and the quantum/holographic nature of reality. For the first time in my life, I felt like I could see, as if the gods had reached down and touched me with a larger view of reality. But of course Rice didn't want to hear about it. Neither did anyone else with whom I was working. As far as they were concerned, they had it all figured out. 'No need to ask such questions, my boy, we dealt with that decades ago.' Shit like that. There were hybrids to breed and ships to build and systems to deploy and there just wasn't time for that fairy nonsense. So I went underground inside an already deeply underground organization. I hid my thoughts and watched and waited, and felt more and more alone."

"And then you left."

"Not for quite a while, no. You don't jump paradigms overnight. I sure as hell didn't. But eventually I came to see that Rice and the rest of them had missed the real news: that the universe is made of consciousness; that the Cosmos is a place of magic and wonder and evolution. And I think I would have stayed with the People and tried to help them see what I saw, to transform the organization from the inside out, had it not been for 9/11."

Linda sighed heavily. "Tell me what you know."

"Well, basically, the 9/11 Truth movement has been right to challenge the official conspiracy theory with one of their own. And they've got much of it right. But what they are seemingly unable to see, because most of *them* are products of the dominant mainstream culture, is that humans were not the only intelligent species flying around over New York and Washington that day. And they don't see how 9/11 fit into the human/alien Plan."

"Jesus."

There was a knock on the door and Obie rose to see who was there, holding the door against the wind with his knee. An old Inuit woman bundled in Gore-tex and fur stood on the stoop, smiling and blinking in the windstorm, her face a web of wrinkles. She was holding out a covered iron pot. Obie motioned for her to come in but she shook her head. She shouted into the gale, a single, cheery word that Obie could not make out, then handed him the pot, turned, and walked away toward the center of the hamlet.

Obie closed the door. "Looks like breakfast has arrived," he said with a grin.

"Great." Linda pushed off the comforter and stood, slowly stretching her legs and back, twisting side-to-side to loosen her tight, aching stomach. The thermal long johns, moleskin jeans, flannel shirt and fleece jacket they'd given her kept her warm enough, but she'd taken off her wool socks to sleep and her feet were freezing on the trailer floor. She sat back down and worked to pull on her socks with her one good hand. It took her a while, but she managed it. She joined Obie in the kitchen. Already he was spooning a hot mixture into a pair of bowls, and there looked to be large hunks of fried bread as well. Linda's stomach reminded her how long it had been since she'd eaten.

"Looks like a fish stew," explained Obie. "With some berries of some sort. And seaweed, I think." He blew across a spoonful to cool it and then put it into his mouth. "Good," he said, chewing.

Linda took her bowl and a piece of the bread and limped back to the futon, favoring her sprained ankle. Drawing her legs up, she cradled the bowl on her lap and tasted the stew. "Oh, man," she said. "It's been...." She stopped for a moment to think. "Jesus, Obie! Was it just yesterday afternoon that you found me?"

"Yep."

"And I hadn't seen Rice since ... I don't know. It was pitch black most of the time. I lost track. I was sick for a long time. And then he left me alone for at least a day, except for those fucking videos. I don't even know what day this is. But I haven't eaten since he brought me Chinese." She spooned another mouthful, then another, the hunger building as she ate.

"It's Saturday," said Obie. "The seventh."

Linda stopped. They'd gone to meet Legrand on Wednesday. Which meant Cole had been dead for three days now. Three days. Where were his kids now? How was Grace? And Keeley? It was all so fucked. She couldn't keep up with the past, let alone the present. Linda caught a big hunk of fish with her spoon and shoved it into her mouth. The warmth and solidity of it soothed her anxiety for a moment. She returned to the conversation.

"So 9/11 changed everything?" she asked.

Obie nodded. He was back in the recliner, his bowl balanced on one knee, his bread balanced on the other. "It changed things for a lot of people, Linda. Woke them up to the reality of the situation. Not just about our government, but our economic, energy, and environmental situations as well. For me, there was no way I was going to remain in a group that could do such things. I'd thought the meeting that I attended was just scenario planning, you know? War games and shit. When I saw it play out in the real world, that was it: I was out of there. Hopped a transport to Istanbul. Shot up a bar and stole a truck, which I crashed through a fence and drove up onto the lawn of the some rich guy from Germany. I ended up in the hospital at Incirlik Air Base. It didn't take much acting to convince them I'd gone bonkers. As soon as I could I snuck out and disappeared."

"And you've been living on the streets ever since?"

Obie nodded. "Yep. Chicago in the summers. Sometimes Duluth. Usually someplace in California for the winters, though lately I've tended to stay in the Midwest all year long. It doesn't get much crazier than living on the streets of Chicago in sub-zero temps."

"And that's your goal? To look crazy?"

"You got it. As long as I'm crazy, it seems like Rice and Bob leave me alone."

"But can't they just, you know, get inside your skull and learn the truth?"

Obie tapped his head. "Not this skull."

Linda smiled. "Another nice trick."

"I'll teach it to you before we leave here," said Obie.

Linda finished her stew and started on her hunk of bread. "So didn't you blow your cover, rescuing me?" she asked.

"Yeah. I guess I probably did. Let's hope it was worth it, eh?"

They both ate in silence for a while.

"So what have you done since, Obie? This was all over fifteen years ago. I mean, the country's been slowly going to hell and Rice is still running the show and you're just hanging out in soup lines? It doesn't seem to fit who you are."

Obie considered Linda's question for a moment before responding. "We could say I've been in a long and rigorous apprenticeship."

"With whom?"

"All of the above," answered Obie. He pointed toward the heavens.

"And now you're, like, ready to hang out your own shingle?"

Obie smiled. "I think my work, now, is to help you do the work the world has given you to do."

## 13.4

*She'd searched the places she could think to investigate, but found nothing. No matter how much she focused on her father's heart, he was simply gone, as if he'd fallen off the edge of the Universe. His vibration was absent. There was nothing to move toward. And the Cosmos was much too big a place to explore blindly. So many layers. So many souls.*

*The thought of him gone forever dimmed her to a dull gray. Grace could feel her own heart fade into uncertainty and loss. But she also realized that she understood very little of this realm. Maybe he was hidden, somehow. Trapped by the scary ones, perhaps, as she had been. It was too soon to grieve. For now, she would continue to look.*

"We have a visitor."

Grace whirled in surprise, not realizing she'd returned to where she'd left Evlyn with Dennis. She opened back up and shared her heart, greeting her friends and noting that Linda remained safe. The President was talking with the man Grace now knew to be her uncle Obie. Overhead, old ones from many realms stood guard. That was good.

She discerned another heart floating in the distance, enfolded and sputtering, on the verge of flickering away. "Jack!" she blazed happily. It was the Little Prince! She moved joyfully toward him, then stopped as he pulled away. He was so shy!

"Easy, little sleeper," said Evlyn, holding her own form steadily. The light from within illuminated her essence like a Christmas tree angel. "He's torn by the conflicts of his existence. It is not easy for him to be here with us. Fortunately, his connection to his mother calls him to join our efforts."

"What conflicts?" asked Grace. Jack had rallied a bit and now hovered in place, glowing more steadily.

"He is born of two worlds, of both humans and alive ones, and can live fully in neither species' domain. His heart is confused, stretched between levels, trembling with vibrations that do not easily align."

*Grace rolled with gentle greeting. "Hello, Jack," she said. She watched him as he settled into his densest shape. He was taller than she, but much thinner, and his large, almond-shaped eyes were blacker than space.*

*"You need my help," he said, his voice tremulous. "You need it." Jack shared his heart briefly and pulled away. Grace understood.*

*"Are you afraid of the scary ones?" asked Grace.*

*"Yes."*

*"Me too," said Grace.*

*"Me too, eh?" said Evlyn. Dennis wagged his tail at her feet, pretending to be brave.*

*"Can we all be afraid together?" asked Grace. She knew that the scary people would return. Why else would the old ones stand guard?*

*"I think that's what we're supposed to do," said Jack. He pulsed a wave of his whole being toward Grace and the woman of light.*

*Grace received his packet and all at once glimpsed his life. So that was it. She felt the truth of him. He was bound with obligations, resentments, and hopes to the beings who had created him, so was almost paralyzed with anger and grief, bereft of belonging in any realm and yearning always and only for an existence that had some meaning. Like himself, his mother, the one named Keeley whom Linda loved, had been used for purposes beyond her ken. So now Jack would help those whom she had helped. It was the only thing he could find to do that might ease his loneliness and anguish.*

*Grace let her heart expand, reaching out with love and kind acceptance. Jack flinched but held steady, allowing her soul to touch his own. She offered him the belonging of a single heart. Perhaps that would suffice. Jack's heart may be confused, but she sensed that it was strong, and good, and that he wanted to help.*

*The scary ones would return. Strong hearts would have to be enough.*

# Chapter ⦰ Fourteen

## 14.1

Cole Thomas's house was easy to find but difficult to approach. Mary had no idea what Rice had stirred up here and she didn't want to end up in the hands of the local constabulary. Especially when she didn't really know why she'd come. Rice had initiated the standard containment procedures before heading to Maine, but Mary knew that local cops were the most difficult to control. Given the missing President, the car in the ditch, and the incident at the bakery, the reeves of this shire were likely on high alert. There had probably been a good number of UFO reports as well. And then there were friends and neighbors. The techs had reported some sort of commune or something. Those people did Neighborhood Watch like nobody's business. With Cole gone for four days now, who knew what to expect?

The techs had taken extensive notes, including stills and video, which she'd downloaded to her laptop before she fled. But Mary needed more. She needed to get her hands on things. She needed to taste the place. She needed to draw it into her lungs. The air. The feel. The memory. The moment. There was something she needed to do. She could sense it. But the only way to get from here to there was to walk the path that unfolded before her. And she had to walk the path in her body. Years of astral trekking had taught her, paradoxically, to trust the flesh, the animal, the physical. Trekking had almost driven her mad.

Ten minutes of Google Universe on the bakery's Wi-Fi had shown her the layout of Harmony Farm and Cole's home site. It showed her the nearby gravel road that wound up through the hollow from the main road, taking her less than a half-mile from Cole's house, where it sat near the farm's northern edge. It had even shown her the little stream she had just crossed, where she'd soaked her tennis shoes when she slipped. Mary smiled. Google Universe was more accurate than Bob.

Cole's house was just up the hill now, less than a hundred yards away. She could see it waiting warily amongst the fall-colored trees, flecks of afternoon sun squinting off its tin roof. Mary stood and watched, listening for any sounds of activity, feeling for any eyes that might see her. The house was empty and still, deserted, abandoned, alone. Mary could sense it. She started up the hill.

There were back steps up to the side deck and she took them, hoping to avoid the front of the house and the prying eyes of passersby. The deck's sliding glass door was unlocked. She slid it open, entered the house, and closed the door. The silence encircled her like a lonely aunt, anxious to tell her what it knew. Mary stood and listened.

Linda had been here. This was the home Bob had seen on her trek the morning after the President escaped. This was where the tall man named Cole lived. This is where the two, then strangers, had met and spoken, where Linda had told her story, where Cole had agreed to help. Mary felt a pang in her stomach, not so much jealousy as simple sadness and regret: that things had gotten so out of hand; that she had not been as clear and strong as she could have been; that Linda was lost to her. The President and Cole had fled to Canada, the last she'd heard, with Rice no doubt nipping at their heels. Even if he managed to drag Linda back to D.C., nothing would ever be the same.

Mary stepped out into the middle of the room, turning slowly to take it all in, noticing the signs of children: the clothes, the schoolbooks, the toys. Cole and Linda must have taken the kids somewhere safe before fleeing. Probably not far. With any luck Rice would ignore the children. Mary prayed for that. There had already been too many mistakes.

Slowly she wandered the house, sitting on the leather sofa, leafing through the newspaper on the table, looking out the window at the horse in the pasture. In the trashcan she found bloody blue jeans and pieces of a telephone. In the sink she found unwashed breakfast dishes. The dog bowls were empty. The kids' beds were unmade. On the boy's room wall was a Star Wars poster. On the floor of the girls' room lay a copy of *The Little Prince*.

A great weariness came over Mary as she looked down on the little bed by the window. The words *wait here* surfaced in her mind but she had no idea what that meant. She sat on the mattress' edge, running her hand across the bedspread, smiling at the pastel flowers. She laid down, burying her face in the soft pink pillow, breathing in the scent of the young girl who had slept here, tasting the life that remained, wondering for a moment just what the hell she thought she was doing.

And then she fell asleep.

14.2

Obie stomped the snow from his boots and peeled the mask from his face.

"How is it out there?" asked Linda.

"Balmy!" he said with a laugh. He pulled the rubber band from his ponytail and shook out his long, sandy hair.

Linda smiled. "Yeah. Right. So how is it really?"

Obie unlaced his boots and kicked them off, then ducked into the kitchen for a large glass of water. Downing it in one huge draft as he walked, he moved into the living room, pushing a small, round ottoman toward the futon with his foot. "Well, it's warmer than it looks," he said. "The guy behind the bar said it's been hovering right around five below Celsius all month, which is way warmer than the average. The wind makes it feel much worse." Obie pushed a stack of old National Geographics from the ottoman's green, leatherette surface and sat to face the President.

"What's the average?" asked Linda.

"More like minus fifteen."

Linda laid aside her covers and sat up. "I napped a bit while you were out."

"I'm glad." Obie reached out and took Linda's stockinged left foot in both hands. "May I?" he asked.

Linda nodded, unsure of Obie's intentions but glad for his warm, sure touch. Her ankle still ached, even when she wasn't standing on it. Maybe Obie had some medical training in his past? "How's the town?" she asked, absently fingering the large bump on the crown of her head.

Obie inspected the President's foot, slowly moving it through its range of motion. "There's a post office, a little store with gas and diesel pumps, two bars, three hotels, and places to rent gear: sleds, snowmobiles, boats, ATVs and such. Throw in a bunch of houses and you've got Akkituyok. There's an RCMP post too, but it doesn't look like there's anybody there."

"Good to hear."

Obie looked up. "Apparently 'costs much' is their motto as well as their name. I tried to get you some real coffee at the store but all they had was more instant and it was fourteen dollars a jar."

"Yikes."

"I think maybe that's the price for strangers."

"That feels fair."

"I want to do some healing work with you now," said Obie, smiling gently. "Is that alright with you?"

"You mean like massage or something? Or are we talking woo-woo here?"

"Definitely woo-woo." Obie smiled. "I need your permission to touch and manipulate your body. I'll be very gentle. You okay with that?"

"Sure."

"And we can talk while I work. That might actually be better: to have your ego engaged elsewhere while your body and spirit restore themselves. That work for you?"

Linda nodded.

"So how're you doing?" asked Obie, slowly inching the sock from Linda's left foot. "Emotionally, I mean."

Linda shrugged. "Oh, you know. Just sitting around trying not to cause the extinction of humanity."

"Kind of a mind-fuck, isn't it?"

"I'm just a lil' ol' farm girl from Michigan, Obie."

"If that were the case you wouldn't be here," he said with a smirk.

"Yeah, well, that's what you say. You know something I don't know?"

Obie's eyes flashed. "I know lots of things you don't know, Mrs. President."

Linda pulled the comforter up around her shoulders as a frown clouded her face. The black hole of grief and dread that had threatened to tear her apart earlier in the day had quieted and ebbed, but it had never fully disappeared. Every now and then it shuddered and whirled as Obie's words poked at it, an angry bear roused from its slumber, or a nest of yellow jackets getting ready to swarm. Linda could feel it beginning to rise into her throat and forced it back down with a gulp. "So tell me," she said, her voice tight and controlled.

Obie placed Linda's bare foot on his lap. "Why don't you ask me some questions?" He positioned his left hand under her ankle and his right hand an inch or so above it and closed his eyes.

"Jesus. Where do I start?" Linda took a deep breath, willing her body to relax into Obie's steady hands. Only very slowly did it comply. "Okay," she said at last. "So, here's a question: if Rice and his gang got it all wrong, then what's right? What are these Strangers up to?"

"Getting right to the heart of it, eh?" he said

"Yeah, I am. You're a get-to-the-heart-of-it kinda guy, right? So get to the heart of it."

Obie shifted his weight on the footstool, straightened his back. "Okay. Let's see. The heart of it." A soft smile blossomed on his face. With eyes still closed and both hands enveloping her twisted ankle, he began to speak. "As far as I can tell, the heart of it is this: the Universe is a school, designed by the Creator for the Evolution of Consciousness. Its purpose is to know itself." Obie looked up into Linda's eyes. "God seeks companionship, Mrs. President."

Something about those words sent shivers up Linda's spine. She'd heard them before, though she could not say where or when. Though she felt silly in doing so, she had to admit that the words resonated as somehow true. "Okay," she said, her voice low. "So that's what God's up to. What about the aliens?"

Obie nodded. "Think of the Strangers as Co-Creators. They're beings who've reached a high enough level of self-realization that they can choose to consciously align with the goals and intentions of the Cosmos."

"You know you're speaking in all-capitals, don't you?" Linda smiled.

Obie laughed. "Sorry. Hard not to, you know? We're talking major players here. And there's so much I don't really understand."

Linda nodded. "So, these Strangers are like ... the good guys? Is that what you're saying? Friends of God and all that?"

Obie shook his head and closed his eyes, as if to concentrate on Linda's ankle. "I don't think that's a helpful way to think of it. First of all, you have to stop thinking of the Strangers in monolithic terms. There are lots of different beings, from various realms and levels and dimensions, from widely disparate corners of space-time. Most come from waveforms and frequencies radically different from the physical frequencies which we inhabit, and manifest into our particular realm of matter only when necessary."

"So ... what? We're talking a *Men in Black* movie here?"

"Not quite. It's not monsters and spaceships. It's more like beings from the spiritual realms, to use a general term that doesn't really mean much anymore. These are beings that have transcended their physical roots and become creatures of the Cosmos. Many of them did so long before humans appeared on this planet. Most are here to observe, I think. A few are here for purposes that many would consider exploitive, selfish, or even evil. A couple are here to actively help."

A deep and soothing warmth flowed through Obie's fingers and into Linda's bones. In the past few minutes the ache had gradually vanished. Linda blinked her eyes to rouse herself. It would be so easy to fall asleep. "Help how?" she asked.

"The focus is on the evolution of consciousness, I think. That's what the Universe is up to. So they help with that. Prodding us to mature and evolve. Sometimes pulling. Sometimes pushing. They see us as a species trapped in adolescence. Blind to our own souls. They're trying to parent us into adulthood."

"And they're doing this by putting men like Rice in charge?"

Obie opened his eyes to look at Linda. "They didn't put Rice in charge. We did."

"But they're going along with it."

"If we Imperialists truly wish to hang ourselves, they'll give us all the rope we need, yes."

"I thought you said they were here to help."

Obie was quiet for a moment. "They're here to help with the evolution of consciousness, Mrs. President. Think of this as an initiation into adulthood for the species as a whole, or at least for the culture of civilization. Initiations can be difficult and dangerous. Not everyone makes it through alive. There are dangers to be faced and overcome. Or not. There are decisions to make and challenges to meet. And there are no guarantees." He manipulated Linda's ankle through its range of motion once again, bringing his ear down low as if he were listening for pain. Satisfied by what he heard, he moved up Linda's leg, sliding his left hand forward to cradle her calf while using his right like a magic wand, waving it over her left shin and thigh as though he could somehow locate her bruises through the moleskin.

"So we're being put to the test," said Linda. "And we might not make it."

"I think both those things are true, yes. This is without a doubt the most crucial point in the history of our species. It can go either way."

Linda closed her eyes and exhaled deeply. "A great time to be President, eh?"

Obie nodded and laid his right hand on the most painful bruise on her thigh.

## 14.3

"So who are the two groups that are here to help? Sounds like one of them must be those little gray aliens like Spud, or the dead one in my underground cell. The ones that stole me from my home in the middle of the night when I was a girl. Who are the other ones?" Linda was flat on her back on the futon with her flannel shirt unbuttoned halfway up. Obie knelt on the floor beside her, his head hovering over her belly button, his ear down to listen. Linda's stomach was an atlas of Rice's insanity, a landscape of yellow and purple bruises crisscrossed by a network of main welts and secondary scratches and one scabbed, shallow incision running like a freeway through her navel. Though Linda's mind had no conscious memory of the beating, her body recalled every blow, every punch, every slash. It was all Linda could do to not push Obie's head away, so strong was her instinct for self-protection.

Obie spoke in matter-of-fact tones while he worked. "Well first, there's a great deal of variety amongst the assorted beings known collectively as 'the grays.' And second, the physical appearance into which they've mostly settled these past few decades – the tiny bodies and large almond eyes and huge heads – has resulted from a feedback loop between the Strangers and our own human expectations, especially as things have played out in our popular culture and media. Apparently, most of them have decided it best to show up looking how we expect an alien to look. That tends to obscure their diversity. They range from highly subtle and sensitive living beings to those who are little more than robots."

"Some seem to be here for what would appear to us as self-ish reasons. Others can be fairly helpful. Many seem quite perplexed by our culture's capacity for self-annihilation. The gray ones apparently have no group name for themselves. The People call them the Life, because the grays refer to each other as 'alive ones.' But the gray ones actually use that term for *all* high-frequency consciousnesses, not just themselves." Obie stopped, raised his head, brought his right hand in to hover where his ear had been. He glanced at Linda, winked, and then returned his concentration to her stomach. "The other ones you mention are called the Elders or the Angels. That's what the People call them, anyways. Personally, I've yet to meet any. These guys choose to look almost human when they dip into the physical, from all reports, though they're usually very tall and quite beautiful. The gray ones are here in great numbers. The Angels are only a few. They appear to be at odds with each other, but I tend to think they're both working for the same thing."

Linda shivered with vulnerability and closed her eyes, afraid that Obie would touch her stomach, fearful that he would not. "Kind of a good alien/bad alien thing?" she asked, forcing herself to stay in the conversation.

"From one point of view. The Angels prefer the carrot. The gray ones tend toward the stick. Parenting an adolescent can take both, I think."

Obie laid his hand gently on Linda's belly and she sighed deeply. "It's been rather more stick than carrot lately, wouldn't you say?" she murmured.

"Perhaps," answered Obie, his genial, lecturing tone at distinct odds with the intimacy of the moment. "You've got to remember that they've been at this a very long time. Most of those tales of ancient astronauts are based in real events. Various alien beings have been with humans since our very beginning, I'm pretty sure. They show up in cave paintings, religious texts, monuments and megaliths and artifacts, in fairy encounters and abduction scenarios and shamanic journeys. The fact that there are only two groups at this point who are even trying to help is a testament to how frustrated most Strangers have become with us.

Most have just given up in disgust, seeing us as hopeless addicts with no chance of survival. Some view us pretty much the same way we view cattle. At this late hour, only the gray ones and the Angels hold much hope for our evolution, as far as I know."

Linda looked at Obie. "And why are those guys sticking with us?"

"I think because they feel responsible for us. And because they believe in our potential."

"Meaning...?"

"Meaning that they were both involved in our earlier evolution, maybe even our creation, to some extent. And because they saw how great was our potential, before the cataclysms."

Linda stretched her arms overhead, almost knocking the lamp from the small table beside the futon. Obie reached out with his free hand to steady it. The afternoon sun had swung around to shine in on Linda's face through the kitchen window. She closed her eyes and let its radiance warm her battered cheeks and raw, puffy eyes. Breathing deeply, she spoke in a low tone. "I don't know what to do with all of this, Obie. It just gets more and more convoluted. You sound like some crazy website. Like some street-corner nut-job."

Obie nodded. "How did you get here?" he asked softly.

Linda smiled and opened her eyes. "Touché," she said.

Obie shared the smile. "Once you've ridden in a UFO with a homeless guy and a dead man, Linda, you've entered the domain where fundamental assumptions get challenged."

"I just didn't think I'd be challenging them all at once."

"Yeah, I know." Obie closed his eyes and cocked his head, as if listening to some distant voice. After a moment he opened his eyes and continued. "It's rough. The old, habitual ways of thinking kick back in, even for me, and I've had years to soak this stuff up. The Strangers continued my education in their own sporadic, bewildering way. And I tried for years to figure it all out. Reading. Studying. Meditating and journeying and communicating. I've seen how much crazy shit is out there. How much disinformation. How much misunderstanding." Obie got quiet again and began to move his hand in slow, small circles over the skin of Linda's stomach, as if he were stirring a pot of caramel with a wooden spoon. He lowered his head to listen for a moment, then flashed his eyebrows with excitement. "Of the few who are willing to really look at the alien evidence with an open mind, even fewer are also able to see their own mental and emotional filters, to know and understand how the culture in which they were raised has left them with a full set of insane assumptions and delusional stories."

Linda reached out and grabbed Obie's hand to call a timeout. "You're losing me here," she said. She stopped and took a deep breath and closed her eyes, as if to let a sharp pain pass through her body. Obie straightened, placing both of his hands in his lap. After a time Linda raised her head to look at him. "I mean, it's as if you're using words I know, but in ways I *don't* know. Like ... what do you mean by stories? And it sounds as though you're saying I'm insane, and my people are insane, just because we grew up in this culture. And I'm not all that keen on being called insane, to be honest." Linda stopped, her brow tight and furrowed in anticipation of words that did not come. She flopped her head back onto her pillow.

"You don't think destroying one's own ecosystem is insane?" asked Obie, his forced smile failing to hide his defensiveness. "Because that's what we're doing."

"Well ... no. Insane is like drooling on your shirt and listening to imaginary friends and stabbing kittens with knitting needles. So no, I don't think we're insane."

"And yet we're drooling pesticides on our topsoil and listening to politicians tell us we can grow forever and stabbing feedlot cattle with bolt guns, Mrs. President."

"But it's not because we're crazy!" said Linda, pointing angrily at her head. "There's no crazy in here, Obie. Okay? So don't say there is."

Obie nodded. "You're right," he said gently. "You're right." He closed his eyes and shifted his legs to sit more comfortably on the ottoman, taking a moment to cleanse the room with stillness. Even the wind calmed down a bit, as if in deference. "I've obviously got some old stuff going on here," he said, his voice tinged with regret. He sat and reflected for a full minute. Then he grinned. This smile was genuine. "In a way," he said, "we who live in this time are a walking tribute to the strength and indomitable spirit of the human animal. Even now, as wounded and confused as we are, having grown up in a culture whose fundamental assumptions stand in direct violation of reality, many of us retain the ability to claw our way out of those cultural delusions and reconnect with the Universe. Even if our egos are battered and bruised, our essential selves are intact. Which may be exactly why some of the Strangers continue to help us."

Obie opened his eyes. "Most of us are not insane, if you define the word in terms of brain dysfunction and bad chemicals. You're right about that. But if we're not mentally ill, Mrs. President, would you agree that we're certainly culturally ill? Spiritually ill? Wouldn't sanity mean being consciously connected to reality, to what's actually so? And if we start from there, how should we then regard our society? Our culture tells us that all growth is good, even though we say we know that, in physical terms, nothing can grow forever. Our culture tells us that we can fix every problem and control every outcome, even though we can see, if we just look, that most of our solutions simply lead to more problems. Our culture tells us that we will find true happiness through the things we own, that the material world is all there is, and that the rest of the planet is here merely to serve as our resource. Yet we know in our hearts that money does not, and has not, bought us true happiness and fulfillment, only comfort." As Obie spoke, his voice grew louder, and his eyes glinted, like a televangelist reaching the high point of his sermon. "In this physical plane, Mrs. President, it's the soil and water and forests and sky and plants and animals upon which our very lives ultimately depend. The structures of civilization cannot exist without those things. And yet we live inside of those structures – houses, offices, stores, factories, cars, roads, subdivisions, cities, whatever – and those structures keep most of us almost totally disconnected from the real world that serves as their foundation. So you might begin to see the benefit of just sitting for a while with the notion that not only is this culture *not* in touch with reality, but that this insanity lives inside of you."

Linda's face had grown strained and dark as Obie spoke. She held up a hand, drawing in a smooth, even breath, as if to cool her soul. She exhaled and drew another. Slowly her face relaxed. She nodded. "I guess I'm willing to sit with that for a while," she said slowly.

Obie nodded in response but did not speak.

"So these things the culture tells us, these are what you mean by our stories?"

"Yes," Obie said. "We learn these stories as children and repeat them as adults. We speak our culture into existence with these stories, Linda. So if our stories are insane, then our culture is insane, and our actions inside of that culture are insane."

Linda sat quietly, letting Obie's words sink in further. "And yet I'm still not sure it makes any sense to use that word," she said. "If I used such language, it would just put people off. They wouldn't be able to hear me."

Obie smiled with grim, tight lips. "Maybe I'm a hard-ass," he said.

"And why do you need to be such a hard-ass?" asked Linda.

"I know it's possible to wake up," said Obie, shaking his head as if it were obvious. "I know it's possible to tell new stories, to create a new culture. And the aliens are just standing there, holding out the keys to the Cosmos. If enough of us—" He stopped and took a breath. "There's no time," he said. "We need something to shock us awake...." Obie closed his eyes, pulling his shoulders forward and hunching his back, as if in self-protection. "It's nuts," he muttered at last. "And it's all so fucking unnecessary. If I could only get people—"

"So maybe that's part of the insanity, Obie," cut in Linda, her voice resonant with calm power. She reached out to take Obie's warm right hand. "Thinking we can force people to wake up and fix everything."

Obie sighed. "Maybe."

"Maybe there's something else to do with the truth besides beat people over the head with it."

Obie opened his eyes. "Maybe," he said again.

Linda gave Obie a warm smile. "Maybe that's *my* job, to help find out what that is," she said at last. She squeezed Obie's fingers. "Maybe there's more help available to us than you think."

Obie's eyes moistened, his face flushed. Slowly, as if a great weight had been lifted from his shoulders, as if he'd never dared even to wish that help might be available, he straightened his back.

Linda glanced down at her stomach and gasped. Her belly was smooth and pink. Rice's bleak, tortured landscape had almost entirely faded from view.

## 14.4

Linda sipped at her tea. "So you don't know how you do it?" she asked, pointing at her abdomen. She was sitting up on the futon. Her shirt was buttoned. Obie sat across from her on the footstool.

Obie's eyes sparked. "I don't do it," he said. "That's what makes it so fun. I get to have a front row seat at the edge of some new paradigm."

Linda laughed. "You're not like anyone else I've ever met," she said.

Obie smiled and drained his tea, placing his cup on the floor and standing. "You ready for more?" he asked. He pushed the table and lamp to the side and slid the ottoman around to the end of the futon, as if needing no answer. "Where were we?" he asked, sitting and patting the pillow.

Linda put her cup on the floor and lay back, settling into the cushions. "You were telling me how difficult it was for you, to figure out what's really going on with the aliens." She wiggled to get comfortable, pulling the blanket over her legs.

Obie smiled. "Oh, yeah. Right. It was like, I mean, you should spend some time online, surfing UFO sites. No wonder people just write the whole thing off as nonsense. Only slowly did I begin to discern the signal above the noise, and to understand that my attempts to nail down 'the truth' were only getting in the way. Once I gave up that there was one single 'Truth' that I could rationally figure out and know, I could begin to open up to a surprising notion: that the Cosmos is made of consciousness and nothing else." He placed a hand over each of the President's temples. "I think it's as Itzhak Bentov said: the universe is so wild and full and diverse that pretty much anything and everything you can say about it is true, if you look at it from a wide enough perspective. Again, it's 'all of the above,' everywhere you look."

Linda snorted sardonically. "Okay, then. The universe is made of consciousness and everything is true. Glad we got *that* one sorted out." She smiled to show she was teasing. "I think I'll just let that all sink in for a while, if you don't mind." She closed her eyes.

Obie moved his hands to hover over Linda's face. "Am I accurate in thinking that your right cheek hurts like hell?" he asked.

"Jesus, yeah," said Linda. She opened her eyes to look at Obie. "It's really tender. How did you know?"

"Well, in this case, it's because there's a faint hand-shaped bruise stretching from your jaw line to just under your eye. I see three fingers, maybe a thumb mark over your upper lip. Rice's calling card, I'm afraid."

Linda had to grip the futon to hold onto herself. "Fucker," she said.

"Swelling's down though. I don't think anything's broken."

"I guess we'll just have to thank Mr. Rice for his forbearance, then, won't we?" Linda's mood had shifted from camaraderie to loathing. She reached up and caressed her sore cheekbone.

Obie laid his right hand on top of hers, closed his eyes, and inhaled deeply. "There will be nothing of Theodore Rice left in you by the time we finish here today," he said, his voice the low rumble of a thunderhead bearing the promise of a clear, rebalanced sky. "Not if I have anything to say about it. And I do."

Linda allowed a few drops of her pain to spill from her eyes and wet their entwined fingers. After a time, she took a deep breath and lowered her hand to her side. There was nowhere to go but forward. "So tell me about this cataclysm stuff you mentioned earlier," she said huskily.

Obie nodded, letting his hands continue to explore Linda's face and scalp, letting his soft, sure voice encircle her with confidence and power. "You understand that what I'm giving you here today is just a bare-bones briefing on a body of information that would fill a library, right?"

Linda shrugged. "I guess I know it now."

"Right." Obie chuckled sympathetically. "So, I think for our purposes here, what I can say is that the Earth had been working all along just as it was designed to work, fostering the evolution of matter through ever-increasing levels or bands of consciousness, ever-higher frequencies if you will, sorting and sifting and pushing and pulling and starting over again and again, drawing the created world ever closer to the Absolute." Obie laid his hand briefly on the large lump on the top of Linda's head, leaned in to listen for a moment, then moved on. "The Earth had brought many individuals, and some small groups, to such highly refined frequencies of sensitivity and consciousness and self-reflection that they were approaching that point where they could become creatures of the Cosmos, the very co-creators God is always seeking. And I'm not talking about just humans here. There are other species on that same trajectory, some of the toothed whales being obvious examples."

"If you say so."

"Now, in a way, I'm reiterating the old notion of the *scala naturae*, the Great Chain of Being, the classical and medieval hierarchical structuring of the Universe. It's a notion that has been harshly critiqued in recent decades, as the destruction of the planetary ecosystem has become so glaringly obvious. The fear is that if we see ourselves as somehow 'higher' than the rest of creation, then we will use that as justification for the continuing exploitation, enslavement, and slaughter of the rest of the living beings on this planet, from the minerals and waters to the trees and animals and everything in between."

Obie put a hand on Linda's shoulder. "Can I get you to roll onto your left side?" he asked. Linda twisted to her left, then pushed back toward the futon's edge, her back to the room. Obie leaned over to put his right ear just above hers. "It's certainly an understandable fear, given that this has, in fact, happened," he continued in a low voice, "but one that propels these critics too far in the opposite direction, in my opinion. The problem I see lies not so much with the notion of a Great Chain, as that the chain has lost its sacred underpinnings in this era of civilization. The notion of the evolutionary nature of the Universe, hiding in such words as 'progress' and 'history,' when combined with the blindness of materialism, the dominate-and-exploit mandate of the culture of Empire, and the psychopathologies of those in power, has resulted in a major clusterfuck of a mess here on planet Earth."

Obie stopped and pulled back, as if he'd been burned. "Whoa!" he said. "I felt that."

Linda craned her head to look at him. "Felt what?" she asked. "You're on fire."

Linda stared at him without responding. Her face was beginning to redden.

"You're not really grokking this, are you?" he asked.

Linda flushed. "Screw you and your *Reader's Digest* condensed version of reality, Obie," she said angrily. "I'm not a stupid person, you know." Her eyes flashed with the power of self-knowledge.

"I've never thought you were," agreed Obie, shaking his head.

Linda turned back, her face almost buried in the futon cushion. "Just ... give me a minute, okay?"

"Okay."

Linda closed her eyes and took a series of long, deep breaths. "You really piss me off when you talk like that," she said at last. "It's like ... you're rewriting the entire history of the world and then expecting me to just get it. Like you're giving me one of those packet things you talked about. Only you're not. And I'm still reeling from having arrived here in a UFO with my dead—" Linda stopped, choking on her grief.

"I'm not trying to piss you off," answered Obie gently.

Linda wiped at her eyes. "I feel like Ebenezer Scrooge here, you know? Like I'm being dragged around the universe in my nightshirt and being shown how things really are. But I'm not sure *what* I understand at this point. And all I really want right now is a good night's sleep."

Obie tugged at his beard. "Yeah, I got that. Hopefully the spirits will manage to do it all in one night."

"I need to feel like there's some reason you're telling me all of this. Okay? I need to trust that, when we get done, I'll understand what I most need to understand, so that I can act with wisdom." She glanced up at Obie. "Can you promise me that?"

Obie nodded. "My best sense of things is that you're going to need what I'm telling you in the days and years ahead, Mrs. President," he said. "I wish we had the years I've had, but we don't. I promise you that I'm doing my best."

Linda closed her eyes and relaxed. "Thank you."

"Thank you for slowing me down," said Obie. He placed his right hand on her temple.

Linda reached up and squeezed his hand, then settled back in. "So, where were we?"

Obie took a moment to think before he spoke. "We were talking about cataclysms. I was explaining that the Earth had been functioning just as it was designed to: it was evolving consciousness. But then I took a side street, to fill in a piece of background. I was saying that, as we lost our spiritual connection to, and understanding of, the Cosmos, our understanding of evolution got twisted. Decoupled from the sacred, our inflated, collective egos used evolution as just another justification for the destruction and exploitation of the life of this planet."

"So you're saying that we're in the mess we're in because we've lost our religion."

"Well, I'd say that what we lost is our sense of the sacred nature of creation, rather than our religion. But, yeah, I think that's a huge part of it. I mean, not everybody has 'lost their religion.' There are indigenous folk and spiritual peoples, and again not just humans, who have stayed the course, so to speak. And certainly there are mystics in our midst who have managed the same. But for the most part, the people of the dominant worldwide culture, even if they worship some version of 'God in heaven,' operate in what they experience to be a mechanistic and dispirited world, a bleak landscape of so-called 'resources,' with no epic story, no truly-satisfying meaning or purpose, and no felt connection to the larger Universe."

Obie leaned forward, his voice almost a whisper. "And because we're inherently miserable without the sacred, and because we believe ourselves somehow 'at the top of the heap,' we claim the whole planet as our own, grasping sadly for the only thing we think exists: material comfort and wealth. We've forgotten that the whole of creation comprises and informs the mind of God, that it's all a part of the same amazing process. Our own unique experience, and especially our experience of our own unique-ness, does *not* give us the right to exploit or destroy anything and everything we wish. Everything is moving toward the Absolute, Linda. That's my best sense of things. Every last bit of creation is walking a sacred path towards God. Imagine that. Everything. And yet we think we know otherwise, and destroy our fellow unique members of creation without a backward glance."

"I gotta say," said Linda, clearing her throat to break the quiet atmosphere, "I'm feeling lost again." She put a hand on Obie's arm as if to steady herself. Or him. "I'm not really religious, you know? Despite what my Press Secretary would have you believe. And you're making some pretty big claims here." Linda sighed and curled back in on herself. "All this talk of God..."

"Understood. The dominant culture – call it materialist or naturalist or whatever – has relegated the sacred and spiritual to the fringes of what so-called 'thinking people' can even think about, let alone talk about, just as it has forced the indigenous and the unusable and the other to the margins and edges of the planet. Religion itself has often proven to be a powerful tool in that work of marginalizing, or even extinguishing." Obie straight-ened his back, stretched his shoulders and arms, then brought both hands to rest on Linda's velvety scalp, as if he were reading a crystal ball. His face tightened at what he saw and heard and felt. "But cultural beliefs, no matter how powerful they appear to be, cannot cancel out what's so. We can call it Reality, or the Uni-verse. We can call it the Absolute, the Ultimate, the Godhead, the Source. There're lots of words available to us. I use the word God in a provocative way, to challenge the culture, to reclaim the word, and the reality behind the word. I say we're miserable without our connection to the sacred. I could just as easily say we're miserable without our connection to the Universe. But if I say 'Universe,' the materialists will think I'm just poetically refer-ring to the same thing they're talking about. And I'm not."

"But you're not—"

"I've yet to find a human religious system that really satisfies, Linda," said Obie, interrupting and shaking his head. "I'm not even convinced there was a historical Jesus, let alone the whole 'Son of God' thing. So, no, I'm not selling a belief system. I'm just trying to see the 'what's so' of reality as clearly as I can. For me, that's what spirituality is all about, and why true spirituality and true science are, in my mind, just two aspects of the same endeavor. The Universe I perceive feels sacred to me. It feels alive and conscious and full of meaning and purpose. It feels wild beyond any imagining. And it feels worthy of my awe, my humil-ity, my deep respect and regard, worthy of my striving to manifest the vast potential inherent in my humanity, worthy of my gaining mastery and clarity and ever-more-expanded consciousness. The Strangers saw the potential in our species long ago, and have been working to encourage and guide us ever since. I feel compelled to do my part in meeting them halfway, and in helping to bridge the seeming chasm that stretches between us and them."

"Sure, religions have served as powerful tools for the culture of exploitation and control. But so has every other aspect of our existence. Sex has been distorted by this culture, but we don't say we have to give up on sex. Food and eating and agriculture have all been twisted by this culture, but we don't say we have to stop eating. So why must we give up our spiritual connection to the sacred Universe, which I would consider as fundamental to our existence as food and sex, just because of the excesses and mistakes of religion? I understand that people have been wounded by the extreme abuses of this culture, rendered unable or unwilling to do the work of teasing apart spirituality from reli-gion, or real science from the culture-bound scientific orthodoxy that too often prevails these days. I'm sorry that this is so. But I've found that it's possible to do that work, and that when I strip away the cultural filters, either path - the truly spiritual or the truly scientific – will take me to God."

Linda tensed, craning her neck to look up at Obie. "But again, I don't know how you expect people to 'get this.' It still seems like you just risk putting people off unnecessarily."

Obie shrugged. "'*If you like it or not*,' says Meister Eckhart, '*if you know it or not: secretly, from inside, the whole of nature reaches after God.*'" Obie held Linda with his fierce gaze. "If we can't come to grips with what is, Mrs. President, then maybe we shouldn't be here."

Linda sighed, closed her eyes, buried her face in her hands, unsure if it was worth it to argue the point, wondering whether she even could. A gust of wind rattled the windows and she pulled the comforter tighter. She did not want to think of such things.

"Okay," said Obie with dark determination. "Let's do this."

Linda moaned. "Do what?"

"Rice has imprinted a Specter onto you," said Obie. "Let's get that black bastard out of your soul."

Linda shuddered.

## 14.5

"So how does this relate to these cataclysms?" asked Linda, waking, dreamily plucking a lost strand from the air. The memory of Rice's "exorcism" was fading quickly, for which she was thankful. Obie had reached right inside her and yanked him out, pushing her through the hidden memories, encouraging her to relive the experience of her torture and imprisonment, calling and coaxing and holding her as she sobbed and railed and screamed. His hands had felt scalding hot on her scalp, but Linda had not resisted their power.

At last she'd collapsed. It was as if a cancer had crumbled to dust, or as if a horde of black, furious bees, swarming in her heart, had suddenly changed into butterflies and scattered to the stars. Whatever Rice had left lodged in her psyche had fled. Now she could sleep. So she had. And when she awakened, there sat Obie beside her.

Obie flashed his eyebrows and grinned, pushing a stray lock of long, sandy hair from his face. "I haven't forgotten," he said with a wink. "How are you feeling?"

Obie had stretched Linda out on her back while she'd slept, covered her with the blankets and comforter. She reached up now, ran her good hand over her head and face. Her scalp was smooth. Her eyes felt normal. "Is it gone?" she asked.

"What?"

"The hand print."

Obie nodded. "It's gone," he said. "And the Specter's gone too. That memory field might have eventually killed you, had we not forced it out. Pretty handy for long-term control of a subject: give them a psychic poison for which only you have the antidote. One of Rice's many nasty tricks. Too bad for him I have tricks of my own."

"Good. I'm glad." Linda closed her eyes and took a few deep breaths. "I feel pretty good."

"That just leaves your broken fingers," said Obie.

Linda sighed. "Just talk to me for a bit," she said. "Okay? Let me rest for a while longer."

"You got it, Mrs. President."

Linda pulled the comforter up underneath her chin. "So ... the cataclysms?"

"Right," said Obie. He took a moment to remember where they'd been. "The point to remember is that we were on track. We'd reached a place in the evolution of our consciousness where other beings, other Cosmic citizens, had become intensely interested in us. But then a rather unfortunate series of catastrophes occurred that left us confused and traumatized, from a succession of ice age freezes, superstorms, and catastrophic floods to the Toba supervolcano of 75,000 years ago that reduced humanity to maybe a couple of thousand individuals, from the rise and fall of various complex societies, some fairly intertwined with upper-dimensional races, to the interplanetary conflicts that left Mars in ruins."

Linda couldn't help but laugh. "You know, I must have slept through history class, 'cause I don't remember a bit of this."

Obie laughed as well. "Yeah, I do know. This stuff stretches so far back into our antiquity that we've largely forgotten who we are and where we came from. And, of course, very few in this culture have any interest in learning any of this, as it would give the lie to our current paradigm."

"So how come you know it?"

Obie shrugged. "The truth is out there," he said.

"Cute."

"To the extent that I know anything, we could say the Strangers helped me sort it out. There's tons of material out there. People looking at the evidence that got left behind in the rocks and the ancient texts, looking at the new evidence uncovered by more paranormal means, through channelers and travelers and such. It's largely a minefield, as various proponents tout the claims of their own interpretations. When Spud showed me that it was all-of-the-above, it resonated. That's been my working hypothesis since: there's truth in everything."

"You know Spud?" said Linda with a shiver.

"Yeah. I told you. I met him in '02. I've since encountered him dozens of times."

"I hate that little fucker."

"Understood."

"I was just a little girl—"

"*There is a field...*," said Obie.

Linda's face tensed. "Excuse me?" she said.

"Sorry. A bit of Rumi. *'Out beyond ideas of wrongdoing and rightdoing, there is a field. I'll meet you there. When the soul lies down in that grass, the world is too full to talk about. Ideas, language, even the phrase – each other – doesn't make any sense.'*"

"So, you're saying he's *not* an evil little fuck?"

"I'm saying that our acculturated ideas about good and evil, let alone reality itself, aren't particularly helpful when it comes to the Strangers. Good and evil too often shift and dance depending on one's perspective. In a living Universe designed for the evolution of consciousness, we should not be so quick to judge things by our flag-draped, beer gut standards of right and wrong."

"Ouch." Linda opened her eyes. "You know, for someone supposedly so 'conscious,' you have a fairly wide judgmental streak of your own."

"Sorry," said Obie. He sighed. "One of my standard rants."

"I understand," said Linda, smiling to show that no harm had been done. "But I'd invite you to look at that. I can see why you didn't end up in politics." She closed her eyes again. "Please. Keep going."

Obie nodded thoughtfully, apparently letting Linda's rebuke sink in. He inhaled deeply and continued. "So this period of catastrophic events left huge swaths of humanity disoriented and traumatized. And out of that trauma was born the culture in which we now live, the culture of city-building and settlement, of hierarchy and dominion and separation, of progress and competition and the accumulation of wealth, a full-on attempt to wrest control from the hands of the gods and make the world operate the way we think it should, as Daniel Quinn worked so hard to reveal in his *Ishmael* books. It started in one corner of the world and quickly spread, beguiling or shackling more and more of us to what is considered the 'holy work' of domination, exploitation and the growth imperative. Everything we were, everything we had, was eventually enslaved to serve these impulses, from our agriculture to our societal structures to our spiritual, scientific, and educational systems. Save for the few who have managed to escape the worst ravages of this culture, these ancient traumas have turned us into clutching, grasping, confused children, disconnected from the reality of the universe into which we've been born and willing to destroy the life of this planet for one last pumpkin latte."

"Wow," said the President softly. Obie's words have been delivered with a different quality from before: a quiet, powerful, articulate tone of both warning and grief. She opened her eyes and rolled onto her right side to face him. The sun had slid further across the room, highlighting Obie's flaxen hair. The wind had picked up, shaking the trailer and giving the furnace a run for its money. "That's a pretty grim view of our fellow Americans."

Obie nodded. "It's a pretty grim culture, Mrs. President. The people are merely its prisoners."

"But there are still some aliens who think we're worth saving?"

"Yeah. I think it's sort of a rescue operation, as far as they're concerned. The great irony being that just as more and more of us are beginning to claw our way out of this culture and regain our sanity, we find that we're about to kill ourselves off from our own excesses. Our sciences have brought us full circle to our lost ancient wisdoms and face to face with extinction at the same time. Not really ironic, I guess, as it's the coming catastrophe that's waking us up. But once awake, we find that we're like children holding a gun to our own heads. We're like passengers on the decks of the Titanic and the Strangers are nearby with lifeboats, calling to us to jump in and swim."

Linda shook her head. "Yeah. I don't get that. I mean, if they're so advanced and smart and capable and all that, why don't they just help us? Can't they just make machines that'll take the $CO_2$ out of the air? Don't they have sources of energy that we don't have?"

Obie sighed. "You want to give the child a bigger gun?" he asked quietly.

"I want to *help* people!"

"Of course you do. I know that. I wouldn't be here otherwise. But you've got your own insanities to face, your own acculturation inside of an insane system, your own mistaken assumptions and unquestioned beliefs. If all you've got to give is more of the same, then I don't think you'll be much help at all. We don't need more of the same. We need something so different that we can barely begin to imagine it."

"Where were you when I was choosing my cabinet?" said Linda, laughing at Obie's audacity and vision.

"Freezing my ass off on the streets of Duluth."

"Jesus. Right."

Obie waited for a moment, giving Linda time to integrate what he'd said. Then he rose and stretched his arms over his head. "You ready for a break?" he asked. "I need some water. Then we should get to those broken fingers."

Linda looked at her bandaged hand with a grimace, as if Obie's words had reminded her of the pain. She looked up at her Musketeer. "Yeah. I guess it's time."

## 14.6

Obie filled two large glasses from the tap and returned to the living room, handing one to Linda, who sat cross-legged on the futon. He took his seat on the ottoman, facing her.

"Thanks." Linda drank half her glass and placed the rest on the floor. "So tell me why they don't just help us."

Obie shrugged. "For the Strangers, or God for that matter, to just step in and somehow 'fix' everything would go against the evolutionary nature of the Universe. It would thwart the path to maturity. Remember how I said this was an initiation? You don't initiate adolescents into adulthood by making it easy for them, by doing everything for them and making sure it's all sterile and safe. That would just keep them small and immature and dependent. You get adults when adolescents have to prove their adulthood. When they grab it, take it, demand it, earn it. When they face their tests and show their worth. The universe is selecting for higher levels of consciousness. If we can't muster the awareness to not kill ourselves off, then the Universe will let us sink back into oblivion and start over."

"God, Obie. It's all so ... I don't know ... so clinical, somehow. So cold."

"You don't know the half of it," answered Obie.

"How so?"

"As far as I can make out, the major controversy right now between the alive ones, the Angels, and some of the other observer groups, is whether to let things run their course or to actually step in and kill us off before we destroy everything else. Not everybody is happy with the fact that our little human experiment in extreme disconnection is taking the majority of life-forms on the planet down with us."

"Is it really that bad?"

"Of course it's that bad. It's worse than that bad. You don't need to ask me. Check your own heart. It's the biggest shared secret of our time. Go up to any American on the street and mention how we're destroying the planet and the vast majority of them will say 'Oh, I know....' You should hear the conversations I have at the shelter."

"But I thought—"

"You thought you'd be the President who would finally come in and make everything right. Stop climate change. Get us off 'foreign oil.' Put us all in electric cars. Get the economy back in order. Put the bad guys in jail. Noble goals, perhaps, within the assumptions of the dominant worldview, but ignorant of the reality of the situation, and certainly shortsighted with respect to the evolution of consciousness."

Linda blushed with embarrassment. She *had* harbored such fantasies. And yet she'd known, in some deep and unacknowledged fold of her being, that they *were* fantasies, and that she'd not yet fully faced into the truth of the global situation. Obie had simply reached into her soul and extracted that lump of denial and was holding it out in his hand for her to examine. She squirmed at the sight of it, swallowed reflexively, and nodded her head, urging him to continue, as though he were an oncologist delivering the worst possible news.

Obie raised a hand. "It's no fault of your own. Believe me, I was in the same place once. I know the prison we're all born into. I know how hard it is to break out. But here's the thing, Mrs. President: the door's unlocked. Always has been. You ready to step through?"

Linda rubbed at her short nap of hair, a stark reminder of the changes she'd already come through. An image of Grace asleep in her bed with Minnie Mouse hugged tightly to her chest flitted across Linda's mind and her heart broke wide open. Love like mother bears growled through her veins and arteries, calling her body to fierce readiness. She remembered her dream. Walking. Always walking. With a crowd of others following, and that corner to turn. She'd hoped that Cole would be walking with her. Apparently that was not to be. But Grace remained. And Emily.

And Iain. And the hundreds of millions of people she'd promised to serve. She had no clear idea what Obie was talking about, where she'd end up after 'stepping through.' But she knew that she would take that step. She drained the rest of the water in her glass and looked at the man sitting on the stool before her. He said he was here to help her. Her eyes filled with gratitude. With Obie's help, she could go on. She cleared her throat. "Tell me what I need to hear," she said.

Obie smiled. "Ask me what you need to know."

Linda leaned back and closed her eyes for a moment to think, then looked out the window, noting the late hour and the coming dusk. She looked at Obie. "You said you're here to help me do what I have to do. I need to know what that is. Am I supposed to stop Rice? The aliens? Or something else altogether? What am I here to do?"

"Lots of questions again," said Obie with a grin.

"Start with the hardest one first."

"Okay. So make yourself comfortable and close your eyes."

Linda raised a quizzical eyebrow, then lay down on her right side. Her bandaged, splinted hand extended out over the futon's edge. She closed her eyes and Obie began to speak.

"You're walking. Walking through a city with lots of people. The streets of D.C."

Linda opened her eyes in alarm. "Jesus, are you reading my mind? This is my dream!"

"Shhh. I know. Just close your eyes and walk with me."

"Okay." Linda closed her eyes again and breathed deeply to calm her pounding heart.

Obie took Linda's fractured hand in his own and continued. "You're walking. Around the Mall. The Congress. Through the city streets. A few people join you as you walk. And then more. And more. Following. Walking with you. Quietly, with great respect. And you keep going. Through the city and then out of it. Through the countryside. Through woods and farms. More and more people following quietly. Following you. Because you're headed somewhere. Because you're looking for something. Following you because *they* want to go where *you're* going.

Because you know how to get there. You're walking. Back in the city. Traffic and noise and people everywhere. And up ahead the sidewalk turns a corner. You come to the corner and stop. The people following stop as well. They wait. They're waiting for you, Linda. So take another step. Step around that corner. Don't be afraid. All that awaits you is the truth of what is. And you're ready for that now. You can handle it. You can take it in and not be undone." He paused for a moment, and then continued. "Step around that corner, Mrs. President. Step around and tell me what you see."

Obie stopped and sat quietly. Linda had started shaking as he spoke and there were tears wetting her cheeks and dripping onto the futon. She sighed deeply, a shuddering, quaking, sobbing sigh that resonated with the deep and fundamental vibrations of the Earth beneath her. Obie stroked her bandaged fingers, as though soothing an agitated mare.

Linda's breathing calmed. "It's all going to unravel," she whispered, eyes still closed. "The world we know...."

"Yes it is," answered Obie, gravely.

"It can't keep going like it has been," she said.

"No it can't."

"There's no saving it."

"You're right. There's no saving it."

Linda opened her eyes and looked at Obie, tears spilling forth to see his gentle smile and laughing eyes. "It's going to be very hard, isn't it?"

Obie nodded. "For the survivors, yes. Very hard. But maybe you can bring some meaning to that unraveling. Maybe you can help us learn what we need to learn. Maybe you can help further the evolution of human consciousness. Maybe you should look at your hand." Obie stood abruptly and walked toward the kitchen. "You want more tea?"

It took a moment for Linda to realize what Obie had said. Ignoring his question, she rolled onto her back and pulled at her bandage, unraveling the gauze and tape to reveal the fingers Rice had shattered, probably with a length of iron pipe. The swelling was gone, as was the bruising. The sharp, throbbing pain had vanished. Holding her hand up into the sun, she slowly flexed her fingers. They'd been so damaged. The bones had been busted to pieces. Yet now her fingers looked and felt completely normal. "Jesus!" she whispered, with awe and relief. She wiped at the tears on her cheek with her sleeve.

Linda rolled back onto her side and craned her neck to look toward the kitchen. Obie stood behind the bar, watching her, a slight, crooked smile on his face. He flashed his eyebrows with amusement. "I don't know how to thank you," said the President, her voice trembling with gratitude. She remembered what Obie had said earlier and gestured to the sky with her eyes. "Or whomever," she added.

"You'll think of something," answered Obie with a twitch of his nose. He turned and started slamming through the cupboards until he found a box of tea bags, then filled the teapot and put it on the stove. "Hungry?" he asked, glancing back at Linda with a knowing smile.

Linda closed her eyes, checking in with her body. She looked back up at Obie. "I guess I could eat something."

Obie scrounged through the refrigerator. "We got some cheese here. Cheddar, it looks like. Or Colby. A bag of nasty-ass looking carrots. The rest of our stew from breakfast." He stood up and headed back to the cupboards by the sink. "And I saw some crackers in here." He pulled out a box of saltines, turned to Linda and grinned. "Cheese and crackers, Madam President?"

"That'll be fine," she said with a fragile smile.

Linda pushed herself up onto her elbow and looked about the mobile home. Though now gone, the grating pains from Rice's torture had taken a toll on her soul. The waning sunlight of approaching dusk cast a gray, hazy glow on the faded white siding of the home next door, offering no warmth at all to soothe her heart. The wind, though diminished somewhat, continued to batter their trailer, rattling Linda's nerves as it rattled the windows. The remains of her dream still pulsed through her bloodstream.

She sat up, watched as Obie sliced the cheese and arranged the saltines on a platter. The kettle sang and he poured two mugs of steaming tea. It was not *all* gray and cold. She was safe, for now. Her body was whole again. Whatever it was Rice had left inside her was gone. A Specter, Obie had called it. The black hole had receded. Linda pushed her fingers against the futon cushion to test them further, then rose and stretched her weary muscles. She'd been ready to die, down there in that cell. She'd fallen from the cliffs of hopefulness and sunk deep into the ocean of despair that lay beneath them. But instead of drowning and death, there had come rescue. Healing. Aid. Apparently her despair had been premature. She had help. Rice *could* be thwarted. Who knew what else was possible?

But Cole was still dead, and she was left to carry on without him. Even with his brother here to take Cole's place, the path before her remained unclear. She sighed, stepping into the kitchen to help Obie carry everything back to the living room. She switched on the floor lamp, to brighten the place against the gloaming. Sitting on either end of the futon with the platter between them, they sipped their tea, neither wishing to break the spell of the normal.

"It was a long, steep slope downhill," said Linda at last, looking Obie in the eye. Her voice was heavy with memory. "Like a street in San Francisco, but it went on forever. As I walked, the buildings changed. Windows were boarded over or broken. Then the walls started to crumble. The streets filled with garbage and began to buckle. There were fires and storms. Lightning. Heavy rain. The buildings collapsed and the sky turned yellow and gray. Hot. Hard and brittle and sharp. A little tree growing on a street corner shriveled and burst into flame as I passed. And as I walked I noticed that things were getting blurry, shifting and shimmering like in a desert haze. The road turned to gravel and then dust. And those people that had been following, they started down the slope with me. But as we neared the bottom I turned around and ... most of them had disappeared."

Linda stopped and stared out the window, absently picking up a cracker and cheese but not taking a bite. She looked at Obie. "I guess I've known this for a long, long time," she said.

"I think that's true for a great many of us," answered Obie.

"It's really going to happen, isn't it?"

Obie's eyes narrowed. "It's *happening*, Mrs. President. It's the 'why' behind everything you see, the reason the Strangers stepped it up back in the forties, the reason those in power created the Plan." Obie's voice grew more and more emphatic as he spoke, as if Linda's affirmation of his sense of things had ignited resentment rather than relief. "We've already pushed the climate past the point of no return; global temperatures are now on their way to levels associated with the great mass extinctions of the past, during which *most* of the species on the planet at the time died out. Our ability to extract oil is in serious decline, and fossil fuels are what powered the last few centuries' tremendous growth in population, food production, and economic growth. Surely you know this. Take away the oil and you get wars and food riots and economic meltdowns, which we've been seeing all over the planet for years."

Obie was on the futon's edge now, marking off points on his fingers like an evangelist delivering a well-practiced sermon. "The forests are dying off in huge swaths. The oceans are seriously fucked. Species are dropping like flies. And most of our attempts to 'fix' this are only making things worse. Our efforts to keep things going as they are just keep in place the very things that are killing us. Our culture has gone mad. Our leaders are mostly psychopaths. We all carry ego-structures so stiff and damaged it's a wonder most of us can get up in the morning. There's no combination of energies and technologies and resources that can maintain and support a species that insists on unending growth, and on taking more than it gives back. It's an impossibility in the physical bands. The parameters of these levels have limits that cannot be broken without consequences. We're looking at a die-off event the likes of which we cannot begin to imagine."

Linda's brow had creased as Obie ranted, as though her teacher had betrayed her by mocking her ignorance. Obie stopped sharply, inhaling deeply. He looked down at his hands. "So what am I supposed to do?" asked Linda, defiance pushing her chin forward.

Obie lifted his head and met her gaze, frown for frown and chin for chin. "You tell me, Prez."

Linda closed her eyes, breathing through her reaction to Obie's challenging tone. Her heart pounded wildly. Maybe he was *right* to challenge her: *she* was the one who had campaigned for the job of leading the nation. She searched her heart and mind for the answer that Obie seemed certain was there. She saw herself walking again, down the slope, saw the people falling away, one by one and many by many, saw the buildings turn to dust and sift away. A thin, soughing breath rose from her like smoke from a cabin chimney, taking her back through the years. She saw herself as a child playing in the front yard, saw the shiny silver disc in the sky and the strange little man at their screen door, saw Spud standing next to a large, parabolic screen, saw the Earth burn to cinders, saw the oceans boil away and her own family dying. Spud was saying something about a long, dark tunnel, and how she would help hold the torch. Linda opened her eyes to find Obie waiting for her response, one eyebrow raised in skeptical defiance. "My job is to help lead the human race through the collapse of civilization," she said, her voice softened with hesitancy, as though she were speaking a foreign tongue.

Obie nodded and pursed his lips, as though pondering her answer. "Sounds like good work for a President of the United States," he said. "A sane one, at least." He relaxed a bit back into the futon. "Anything else?"

Linda reached up to caress her scalp, as if she could not believe her wounds were healed. "I don't know," she said softly. "It's like ... these aliens ... this whole Universe ... like ... at the same time we walk down that slope, somehow we have to find some way to reach up to the stars, you know?" She smiled weakly. "I mean, there's this whole big ... something ... out there. Or in here," she put a hand over her heart, "or somewhere. All of these other dimensions. And maybe we have a place in it. But it seems we're going to have to prove that we belong there. Or here. And I have to help us do that."

Obie nodded sharply, as though she'd passed a test. "Not bad for a farm girl, Mrs. President," he said, smiling softly.

## 14.7

A knot of anxiety had taken hold deep inside Linda's soul and was mounting with every moment. The crackers and cheese sat queasily in her stomach. The growing darkness outside didn't help. Who knew what dangers the night might hide? She could feel eyes peering in from all directions, even though Obie had closed the blinds. It was all she could do to resist turning off the light, to hide herself. With a deep sigh she collected her thoughts enough to speak.

"Nothing is clear," she said. "I mean, I still don't understand why the aliens have gone along with Rice and the People. I'm not clear what they're doing here. I don't see how they're helping. I don't have a clue what to do next."

"Maybe we can tie it all together now," offered Obie.

"That'd be nice."

Obie placed the platter on the floor and crossed his legs, shifting to find the point of greatest stability and comfort. "It might help to know that the Strangers are probably as confused as we are. They have a hell of a task, as all parents and teachers do, trying to figure out how much to help, how much to hold back, when to let the child fall, when to hold her tight. I get the sense that they made what they consider some major mistakes in our deep past, mistakes that have left them feeling unsure of themselves, even guilty in some way. They're doing the best they can."

"Okay."

"The whole modern UFO experience – all the flaps, all the sightings, the absurdity, the sleight of hand – it's all had one purpose: to erode our faith in our scientific-materialist paradigm, as Jacque Vallee put it; to make plain the bankrupt nature of our culture and its assumptions. When the power elite took hold of the 'truth,' the Strangers simply played along, showing up as just who Rice and his gang imagined them to be, reflecting back our own hunger for control, our avarice, our trauma, our fear. And the psychopaths in charge, with the People sitting at the center of that web, just looked into that mirror and primped. They've taken this culture to its logical extreme, creating a vast and powerful organization that's now using mind control and remote viewing, electronic surveillance, drugs and hypnosis and genetic modification, abductions and torture and mutilations and assassinations, to solidify its sense of control and amass the power and wealth they tell themselves is the meaning of it all."

"It's as though, in our collective cultural misery, separated from the Sacred Cosmos, from the Earth, from ourselves and each other, separated from the magic and miracle of spirit, the only way out that we could see was to hit bottom so hard that we either evolve or die. The Strangers thought to go along with that, to help us use our own darkness to break free. That's the trajectory we've been on for some good long time. We're falling very quickly now. The ground is rushing up to meet us as we speak."

Linda shivered and hugged herself.

"At the same time, some of the Strangers have continued to support the original design of the planet, working with individual humans, encouraging the evolution of consciousness wherever they could. Places like the Earth are rare in the universe, Mrs. President. The mass extinction now underway represents a significant setback in that evolution. The extinction of people, human and otherwise, would be an even greater setback, as there are relatively few other places in the whole of creation now evolving consciousness at that level. With the collapse of the planetary ecosystem now underway, it's like they're working to get as many of us into the lifeboats as they can."

Linda held up a hand to stop him. She closed her eyes and took a long in-breath. Her nose and brow wrinkled, as though she were tasting something bitter. She exhaled heavily and opened her eyes, shaking her head almost imperceptibly from side to side. "But they can't push us into the lifeboats. Can they? We have to jump."

"That's exactly right, Mrs. President. This is initiation. The Strangers can only help us if we help ourselves. We've had our extended adolescence, our late nights of debauchery and rebellion and acting out. Now it's time to make a choice: to step into our adulthood, or to remain juveniles. Who do we want to be as we face into our collective situation? And here's the kicker:

adulthood, and long-term survival, requires, not rebellion, but dialogue, collaboration, even compliance. Surrender to the larger communities. And surrender is pretty much a curse word for most Americans."

"These colors don't run," said Linda with a weak smile.

"Nope. But they will fade out, and rather quickly, I think, unless we come to grips with the laws of physics, chemistry, and biology as they operate in the physical bands. Unless we surrender to the limitations of a finite planet. And unless we learn that complete control is neither possible nor desirable, that co-creation, or being in a conversation with life, as the poet David Whyte speaks of it, is the way of the Universe. The whole of reality is made of consciousness, and life is always and nothing more than a spiritual journey back to connection and conversation with the Sacred Universe. For all of our vaunted science and technology, we're pretty much just monkeys with Kalashnikovs. We've failed to notice that innovation and growth do not constitute evolution, that our ability to build skyscrapers or design new weapon systems has nothing to do with emotional, psychological or spiritual maturity. Our tools simply extend our reach. In the case of the dominant world-wide culture, we're now self-absorbed, hormonal teenagers with really long arms. And then we get angry when the Strangers treat us as such."

Linda rubbed her eyes, trying to wring out the exhaustion. "So where do you and I come in? I mean, what? Do I get on TV and try to explain all of this and ask people to, you know ... Jesus! I can't even think of what I'd ask them. Fuck. I'm still just a farmer's wife!"

"That's bullshit and you know it," said Obie harshly.

"Yeah, well, fuck you, Obie. And fuck these Inuit. I didn't ask to be the savior of humanity."

"Not consciously, perhaps. But apparently you signed up to help. A great many people have gone to great lengths to put you in a position to do that."

"Meaning the election?" asked Linda, starting to cool off.

"Much more than that," answered Obie.

"Tell me."

Obie looked away, as if the truth was too painful to face head on. "This piece will hurt," he said.

"It's a little late to worry about that, isn't it?"

"I guess." Obie turned back and looked Linda in the eyes. "You don't yet know the full extent to which the Strangers have been in your life," he said.

"Apparently not, Obiwan. Suppose you tell me."

Obie shrugged. "They've been with you from the very beginning. Even in your mother's womb, I think. Watching. Teaching. Protecting. Guiding. As you matured they introduced you to Earl, bonding you in such a way that you would be sure to partner with each other when you met years later. And to put you on the path to the presidency, they ran Earl's boat into that bridge abutment."

"Goddamn it, Obie, stop!" Linda leapt to her feet and stormed across the room to the kitchen, filling her glass with water and drinking it down before slamming it on the counter. She turned to Obie and snarled. "You can't tell me this, Obie! You cannot tell me this!"

"I said it would hurt."

"Yeah, well, fuck you and your hurt, mister. I've had enough." Linda stood fuming, her shoulders high and tight, her eyes black with anger.

Obie rose and walked to the kitchen, taking a seat at the counter opposite Linda. "You have to know this," he said quietly.

"Why? Why do I have to fucking know this!"

"Because it's what's so."

She knew that should just piss her off even more but something about the look in Obie's eyes had the opposite effect. Once more the fight drained out of her in an instant and she doubled over in tears, sobbing once again for the loss of her husband so many years ago. Obie slid around the counter and put his hand on her shoulder, walking her back to the futon. He handed her a tissue and she blew her nose.

"It seems pretty fucked up, I know," he said. He sat quietly beside her for a while, then continued in a gentle voice. "For myself, I've learned to withhold judgment. I don't see every-thing they see. I'm choosing to just trust."

"Yeah, well, you'll forgive me if it takes me a while to get there."

"I will." Obie handed Linda another tissue. "Shall I con-tinue?"

"Can it get any worse?" asked Linda.

"I don't know. You'll have to judge for yourself. I know the Strangers put your first opponent, Sims, into rehab. They were probably involved in your pregnancies and miscarriages, from that mysterious baby in your senior year to your failed attempts while married to Earl. It's the sort of thing they do. They would want you properly bonded, but they wouldn't want you encum-bered with children. I don't think they had anything to do with Governor Billings' death. That was just a lucky fluke. But I'm pretty sure the Strangers fucked with your Presidential elec-tion results. None of the human power-elite wanted you in the White House, and those bastards have been throwing elections for years. So the Strangers must've hacked in and overturned the elite's best efforts to steal your election. The Strangers burned your farmhouse, I'm pretty sure. Killed your dog. Got you in the White House, had you briefed, helped you to escape, and picked up your car and dropped it down in Vermont to make sure you were there in time to meet Cole. They were probably involved in the plane crash that resulted in Ruth's death, and watched over Cole until it was time to get him to that street corner so he could pull out in front of you. They abducted the both of you from his living room and bonded you together. Made you fall in love."

Obie's words stabbed a hole in Linda's heart and she recoiled, bringing both hands to her breast to try and staunch the horrible sensations of powerlessness and manipulation. "No!" she blurted, closing her eyes, trying to deny the impli-cations before they could sink in. But it was already too late. Her time together with Cole flushed across her entire being like one of those packets Obie described: the fantasies and feelings of attraction, coming unexpected and unbidden in the midst of danger and need; the easy bonding and mutual comfort between them; the inexplicable yet welcome sensations of love and longing that washed through her heart; the utter rightness she felt with their hands intertwined, her face in his neck, her lips touching his. It had begun that first night, after the terrible orange eyes and the bugs in the room. More had been touched than her wounded thigh. More had been manipulated than her broken bones. Linda sighed. Maybe Rice had been right to laugh.

She opened her eyes to see Obie nodding. "Jesus," she said, shaking her head. "I feel like a fucking puppet."

"Not a puppet, Mrs. President. An agent. Working under deep cover for a boss you didn't even know you had."

"A boss that burns down houses and kills dogs. A boss that killed my husband. A boss that plays with my heart like a child's toy."

"Yep. A boss that does all that."

Linda massaged her brow. "You told me all of this so I could choose, didn't you? I have to understand to freely choose."

"Yep."

"They've been engineering this for decades, you say. Some long complicated plan to put me in the White House just as the whole shootin' match burns to the fucking ground. That right?"

"That's about it, yeah."

"A back-up plan because their old friend Rice wasn't working out."

"Something like that."

"And I'm supposed to do something about all of this?"

"You signed up to help, Linda. You now have an opportunity few others have."

"Lucky me."

"You'll have help."

"They've flown the coop, Obie! The facilities are empty!"

"They've merely cleared the dance floor, Linda. It's your move. There is help available, as surely as there are those who will try to stop you. If you're working for the evolution of consciousness, the help will come to you. It has to. Ultimately, the whole of the Cosmos wants for humans to grow into their potential and evolve toward the Absolute. Lead that dance and see who follows."

Linda groaned with abandon. "This should have all happened in 2012, Obie. Like it was supposed to. In 2012, I was just a governor."

"Yeah, well, I guess the Strangers aren't using the Mayan calendar," answered Obie. He finished his water and placed the glass on the floor.

When the door burst open Linda jumped to her feet, got tangled in the covers and fell forward, landing hard on her hands and wrists. With a grunt and a moan she rolled onto her side in time to see Obie leap over her. He stopped at the open door and started to laugh. A blast of cold air swept over Linda and she pushed herself to her knees.

"Took you long enough, bro," said Obie, backing up.

Linda gasped when Cole stepped in from the cold. A tiny gray hand with three long, clawed fingers reached in and pulled the door closed behind him.

"My God!" whispered Linda.

Cole stood just inside the door, stark naked, silent, his eyes blank, his jaw slack. He looked ten years younger, his hair full on his head, his paunch replaced by a flat stomach and well-defined abs, his arms and legs smooth and well muscled.

Obie turned to Linda and smiled. "You okay?" he asked.

"I think so," she answered. Obie came over and helped her to her feet. Her wrists were sore but felt undamaged. She had no sense that she'd re-injured anything. She stared at Cole. "How?" she asked. She took a step forward. "Cole?"

Cole did not respond.

"I don't think he's in there, Linda," said Obie behind her. "But we got the body."

Linda glanced back. "How?" she asked.

"I told you you'd have to question some assumptions," he said, smiling.

Linda stepped up to Cole, reached out, took his hand. It was warm and pulsing with life. She'd held that hand before. And yet she hadn't. Because Obie was right: Cole was not there. She turned to Obie. "Did you know?" she asked. "Why didn't you tell me?"

Obie shook his head. "I guess I held it as a possibility. Would you have had me give you false hope?"

Linda turned to stare closely into Cole's face. Cole! He was ... beautiful. And he was alive! But where was he? The Cole that lived in this body? Where had he gone? Linda realized that her face was warm with tears of joy. She let them stream freely, glad to feel something other than fear or anger or pain or despair. She lifted a hand to caress his cheek. "Can we find him, Obie?" she asked.

Obie shrugged. "We'll give it a shot."

## 14.8

Ben Thomas held his gut as tightly as he could, trying to keep as much blood inside of him as he was able. He was so tired. The stars overhead mocked him with their vapid twittering, as if everything was fine as far as they were concerned. But everything was not fine. Two shots to the stomach were not fucking fine at all.

Nearby lay the bodies of the two security guards he'd hired. At least he knew where *they* were. Emily and Iain had been taken to who knows where? He'd heard Iain mouth off and looked up in time to see those bastards push the kids into ... what? A little round metal ship of some sort. A UFO, if you could believe it.

Jesus H. Fucking Christ! They'd come out of nowhere. Tossed some sort of gas canister through the front window. Jeff had bolted out the front door and they took him down in seconds. Rick headed out back and wasted one of the motherfuckers, before walking straight into their line of fire as he rounded the front corner. Whoever the fuck they were, the intruders had been dressed in black from head to toe: face masks, dark goggles, flak jackets, strange laser rifles that seared everything they touched with fierce, green beams of lightning. They looked like a swat team sent back from the future.

The gas canister had filled the house with noxious fumes. Ben had held his breath and grabbed his pistol. He was starting for the door when something crashed through the front bedroom window and the fire started. Emily screamed and Iain rushed to look. The smoke had gotten so bad so quickly that the three were forced to make for the front door, coughing and gasping, to avoid passing out. Ben had stormed out onto his front porch with his pistol raised. They'd picked him off like a fat turkey: two bolts of green fire burned into his gut. It took them less than a minute to grab the kids and shove them into that flying saucer sitting at the edge of the yard. It lifted into the sky in a flash so bright that Ben had to turn away for fear of being blinded.

Then it was just Ben and the darkness, the burning house behind him and the pain in his guts and the warm trickle of blood and the light breeze rustling the autumn leaves. Gut wounds were not good. Ben knew that much. Fuck. And those poor kids, they must be terrified. At least he'd had the sense to check Grace into the hospital the day before, after she'd fallen into that coma. He'd done that much, goddamn it. She was safe.

Something crashed behind him and Ben rolled over to see his roof cave in. His head felt strange, as if he were drunk. The smoke was filling the sky now, obscuring the stars, teaching those twinkling little motherfuckers a lesson for mocking him. The breeze rose. Ben shivered. The fire flared. Blood continued to seep.

Off in the darkness Ben could hear a crunching in the grass. Someone was approaching through the field. Those bastards must have returned to finish him off. Ben looked lazily for his pistol, thinking it had fallen right next to him. He'd get in one good shot before they did. But his gun was nowhere to be found. His head was swimming and the fire loomed over him. And then an angel appeared.

"Hello?" the angel said.

"Hi, angel," said Ben. It was hard to keep his eyes open but he forced himself. How often do you get to see an angel?

"Are you wounded?" asked the angel. "I heard shots fired." She put a hand on him, then drew it back. It was covered with blood.

"Have you come to take me to heaven?" asked Ben.

"I'm going to get you to a hospital, sir," said the angel.

"Tell the kids there's pizza in the freezer," said Ben.

"Are the kids here?" asked the angel. She looked around the yard. Her eyes were afraid. Why should an angel be afraid?

"What's your name?" asked Ben. He closed his eyes. He just couldn't hold them open any more. He was so tired.

He smiled when the angel said her name. He'd never heard of an angel named Mary.

# Chapter ⌀ Fifteen

## 15.1

"You're a fuckhead," said Emily, jutting out her chin. She picked up a french fry and dropped it to the floor with a flourish.

Rice started to answer but caught himself. He wanted so badly to slap the little bitch across the face, tell her how he'd wasted her father with a bullet to the heart. But that would only make things worse. So he would wait. For now, better to give these little shits something to hope for, like being reunited with dear old Dad. Much easier to control them. Rice picked up his cheeseburger and took a bite, not even tasting it as he swallowed. "Nice to hear the Vermont school system is teaching its students manners and respect," he said evenly.

Emily smiled slightly, noting her victory in establishing the rules of the game. She'd seen her Grandpa gunned down right before her eyes. This man was somehow responsible. And he would pay for that. She glanced over at Iain, who was hungrily devouring his meal. The clock on the cafeteria wall said eleven-fifteen: the middle of the night. Given that she hadn't eaten since her afternoon snack, she could see the sense of it. She picked up another fry and held it up in front of her as if considering where to throw it, then popped it into her mouth. It wasn't bad for a cafeteria fry, and the hot grease and salt gave her a tiny dose of energy. She needed that. She was exhausted. Bedtime had come and gone a long time ago.

They were in the Capitol. She knew that much because she'd caught a glimpse of the Washington monument as they were hustled out of the spaceship they'd been abducted in and rushed into an elevator on the roof of a nearby building. And she was pretty sure they were deep underground. She could feel it in the elevator ride, the speed and duration of it, and the oppressive atmosphere. She hadn't seen a window anywhere. There were none in the cafeteria; it was all just white cement block with the occasional picture on the wall. Their prison was carved out of rock. Escape would not be a matter of crawling out a window.

Iain finished his burger and looked up at Rice. "You promise that they're taking good care of my Grandpa?" he asked.

"He's receiving the best possible care," answered Rice smoothly. "As I said, we had no intention of hurting anybody. Had your grandfather and his goons not come out shooting, he would not have been hurt."

"I guess gassing people and starting their house on fire doesn't count as hurting people these days," said Emily.

Rice shifted in his chair. "As I said, things got out of hand."

"It was supposed to be a kinder, gentler kidnapping then, was it?" Emily's eyes glistened with loathing. She stuffed a wad of french fries into her mouth.

The smile on Rice's face teetered and collapsed. "The President of the United States has suffered a psychotic break and run away, young lady, threatening our national security. Your father has chosen to help her. Their crimes endanger this entire planet. They must be stopped. If bringing you here can put an end to this, then I'm not about to apologize for my actions."

"You really are a fuckhead," said Emily.

Iain reached out and put a hand on Emily's forearm to quiet her. He gave her a quick smile and turned to Rice. "So do you know where our father is now?" he asked.

Over near the door a radio crackled and Rice turned to see one of the soldiers take a call. He sighed and turned back to the kids. "He and the President are in Canada right now," he said, wondering why he was explaining anything at all to these fucking larvae. It was a waste of his time and talents. "We're negotiating with Canadian officials for their surrender." A ping sounded in his new implant and he smiled with relief. About fucking time.

In through the double doors came Bob and Alice. They spotted Rice immediately. Bob strode over and stood next to the table, Alice shadowing her closely. Ignoring the kids, Bob spoke to Rice. "Good news, Grand Poobah. Spud and the gang have cleared the field."

"Really?" said Rice. "Guess I got their attention. Ma Kettle still in the igloo?"

Bob shook her head. "She's on the move, boss. A fucking dogsled, no less."

Rice gave a hearty laugh. "Goddamn motherfucking son-of-a-bitch!" he said with glee. "I love it when the dice roll my way!" He stood, tossing his napkin on his plate and reaching out to drain the rest of his Coke. He looked at Bob. "You got loverboy safely behind bars, right?"

Bob nodded. "We were there waiting for him when he fell," she said, glancing briefly at Emily and Iain before turning back to Rice. "He's ours. And get this: we found his ex in a soul bank. The Life had her on ice!"

Rice nodded and pulled on his jacket. "Sweet. We've got a Specter in place and the good Lady Stardust doesn't have her pills, the poor dear." He motioned toward the door with a nod of his head. "You up for a bit of midnight hunting, Bob?" he asked.

"Thought you'd never ask, Theo," she said with a smile. "Glad to have you back."

"Any word on the body the Prez said she saw on the highway?" asked Rice, straightening his tie.

"Nothing yet, boss," said Bob.

"Guess I can't have everything."

Without so much as a fleeting look at the kids, Rice walked toward the door, stopping long enough to give the soldiers his instructions. Then he was gone. Emily and Iain could hear him whistling down the hallway.

Bob turned to Alice. "You coming?"

"Soon," answered Alice in a whispery voice.

Bob reached out and put a hand on Alice's shoulder, nodded her acceptance, then followed Rice.

Alice took a seat across from the two kids, pulling the chair far enough from the table that she could sit cross-legged. Emily and Iain stared. She was beautiful, but in such a strange, exotic way that they felt simultaneously fascinated and repelled, as if Alice were a snake drawing close enough to strike. She was so tiny, like a three-year-old, but with large, very dark, almost black eyes as old as the bedrock that surrounded them all, and just as captivating. Her hands, mostly hidden in the sleeves of her tiny red sweater, were like the hands they'd seen on little monkeys at the zoo.

"You are human children," said Alice.

Iain nodded. "Who—?" he managed to sputter.

Alice nodded slowly. "I am Alice," she said, her voice quiet and stiff, the whisper of a fawn. "I remember human children from my socialization, but that was some time ago. I had forgotten."

"I'm Emily," said Emily. She pointed at her brother. "This is Iain. They kidnapped us."

Alice frowned slightly, as though her face were a rigid, plastered mask. "You are the children of the man Rice killed?" she asked.

"What?" said Iain, rising out of his chair. "Rice just said..."

Alice cut him off with a wave of her tiny hand. "He was working against the Plan," she said evenly. "He had to be stopped. I helped put him into the Confusion."

Tears spilled down Emily's face, the outpouring of grief and fear and anger that had been building up since the attack on her grandfather's house. She pushed back from the table and leaned forward, huddling into herself as though she'd taken a blow to the gut.

Alice turned to watch her. "Do they hurt?" she asked, pointing at Emily's tears.

Emily looked up, frowned, wiped at her face.

"They killed him?" asked Iain quietly.

"He was working against the Plan," repeated Alice. She slid off her chair and stepped toward Emily, reaching up to let a tear roll onto her finger. She brought the tiny drop close to her face to examine it more closely. After a long moment she looked at Emily. "Why do you make these?"

"Because they killed my Dad!" she said harshly, hoping that anger would soothe her fear. "Because I love him!"

Alice looked again at the tear, watching it crawl like a spider along her finger. Her porcelain brow crinkled almost imperceptibly. For the briefest of moments her eyes lost their focus, as if in the space of a single heartbeat she had traveled to the ends of the Universe and back again in search of understanding. She looked from Iain to Emily, her eyes flaring. "I do not think they know of this," she said, a slight tremble in her voice, as though the realization had stirred her heart. Without another glance or word, she walked away, slipping through the double doors so deftly that they did not even seem to open.

Emily and Iain stared, unable to speak, unsure of what had just happened.

15.2

The ride was far smoother and quieter than Linda would have expected. The sled slid across the packed snow like a skater on a rink, the composite runners shushing like librarians. The dogs, a team of six harnessed in tandem, pounded the trail on soft pads, an engine of breath, bone, and muscle speeding them to the Inuit camp. It was as if the dogs knew the import of their task, and were willing to spend themselves in service. Another debt of gratitude Linda intended to one-day repay.

The night was cold and clear, the only wind that of their own passing. The heavens overhead were painted with northern light. The stars had to compete for their share of glory, peering through a gauzy, auroral curtain of cobalt, emerald and violet. Linda scanned the sky, searching for the telltale winking out of stars, searching for discs and diamonds, searching for those whom Obie called 'all of the above.' She saw no sign of them. Payok was right. They'd gone.

"Are you warm enough?" asked the man behind her. He stood on the sled's runners, the musher, he'd said, and when he leaned low it felt like he was speaking right into her ear. Linda looked around to see him. His wide grin shone out from between his fur hood and goggles, teeth sparkling in the midnight light. Linda guessed that he was in his forties, though she had to admit that it was difficult to tell.

"I'm fine," called Linda. She was. The fur parka they'd given her kept her as toasty as she could wish. And the facemask worked far better than she'd anticipated, even if it made her look like a Ninja. The only things that felt a bit cold were her toes, but they always felt cold. "What's your name again?"

"I'm called Aamai," the man said. "It means 'I don't know!'" A slowing of the sled caused him to raise his head. "On by!" he called and the dogs picked it back up.

"That's an interesting name," said Linda.

"It reminds me that I am not in control of everything," answered Aamai. "My other name is Bill. I grew up in Winnipeg. Worked as an electrician most of my life. But Sinaaq asks us all to adopt Inuktitut words as new names, as a way of shedding the sins of the past and stepping into our true selves, and our work here on Earth."

An interesting idea, thought Linda. Given all that she'd been through, and what she could foresee ahead of her, she wondered what her new name might be. What name would you give someone who has come, as Obie said, to help guide humans through the collapse of civilization? And what name would history give her? Would she be regarded as a great leader or a monster? Or both? Linda sighed. Such questions would be answered by generations hence. If there were any generations hence. For now, she had to concentrate on the matter at hand.

Payok, Aamai and an old woman whose name Linda could not remember, had burst into the trailer an hour or so after Cole's body had arrived, sent by Sina to report that the plans had all been moved up. The aliens had departed as soon as Cole had been delivered, withdrawing their protection from the sky above, leaving Cole and Linda exposed. They would all need to head over to Tuyurmiangoyok, the outlying camp that Sina and her followers had established on the eastern coast of Bathurst Island. "Right now," said Payok firmly.

Obie had sprung into action, coordinating things with the Inuit. They woke the proprietor of one of the local outfitters and acquired another snowmobile and a freight sled, onto which they loaded Cole's now-clothed body. Payok and Obie then departed as soon as Cole was secured, taking Linda's love away into the darkness, taking him from her once again. Linda and Aamai helped load an old diesel Mercedes snowcat with supplies, then found three other members of the group who were repairing snowshoes in a house on the other side of the hamlet. Those three left in the snowcat with the old woman. Then Linda and Aamai harnessed his team and followed by sled. The President was the least necessary component of whatever was about to transpire, it seemed, and now all she could do was ride and watch as Aamai drove them to their destination.

But that was bullshit, wasn't it? She could ask questions. She could seek to understand. She could do that much. Linda turned to Aamai and shouted, then checked her voice. She would not need to yell. "How far are we?" she asked.

"We're about halfway there," said Aamai. "Thirty minutes more, maybe."

Linda smiled. Though he looked as though he'd stepped out of the distant past, Aamai's manner of speech was mainstream and modern. "And I'll meet this Sina there?"

"Yes, though she may be fairly distracted with the tasks before her. Don't be insulted if she has little time for you."

"I understand. Thanks. So, what *are* her tasks, exactly? I mean, nobody's told me what this is about. This ritual thing we're going to. What's it for? And why the hurry? All Obie would say is that the aliens have gone and that we need to protect ourselves."

Aamai mumbled soothingly to his team for a moment before responding. "I think he does not want to get your hopes up," he finally said.

"My hopes for what?"

"For restoring your friend's *anirniq*, Madam President. His soul. The Tuurngait are masters of such work. As is Utterpok. But even they may fail."

Linda turned back to look out over the dog team and stare at the sky. Jesus! Can they really *do* that? Obie had said they'd try but her heart had failed to fully embrace the possibility. The thought of Cole standing before her once again, present and vital and whole, looking down into her eyes, reaching out to hold her ... that image terrified her to the core, forcing the questions that hid deep inside. Would he still know her? Would he want her? Would he love her? Would *she* love *him*? She did not know if love could survive intact through both death and resurrection; especially love as new and fragile as theirs.

Besides, what could love possibly mean when it had been manipulated by the aliens? So much had happened in so little time. One by one the underpinnings of her life had been pulled away, leaving her lost in doubt. Did the love she'd felt for the man who had helped her escape still burn in her heart? Even if it did, could she trust it?

"I think he will be glad to see you," said Aamai from behind her, as if reading her mind. Linda turned to see his grin. "I think we will succeed."

Linda raised an eyebrow. "You don't worry about getting my hopes up, I see," she said.

"Our *angakkuq* is very powerful, Madam President. We have honored the taboos and kept our word." Aamai pointed at the aurora overhead. "If we do not offend the goddess Sila this night, we may prevail."

There were too many words she did not know to follow the meaning with her mind, but Linda could feel it with her heart. "You don't sound like an electrician from Winnipeg," she said.

Aamai bowed stiffly. "Thank you, Madam President." He called out to his team and the dogs slowed to a stop. Leaping from the sled, he walked forward, kneeling amongst his dogs to speak soft words of encouragement and embrace the lead pair. After a moment he looked up at Linda. "We will rest here for a bit."

Linda pushed back the tarp and blankets and pulled herself up and out of the sled's basket, stretching her stiff legs. "Halfway there" was as remote a place as she'd ever seen. Yet this place was full beyond measure. She looked out over the landscape, noting how the sky's varied hues played across the drifts and ice patches, illuminating the terrain like a black light in a nightclub.

"We have good snowfall this year," offered Aamai. "The dogs are happy." He buried his face in the fur of a dog and sang a snatch of song: "*I temble with joy and the stars laugh along.*"

Linda ventured away from the sled, walking slowly up the side of the shallow bowl across which they'd been traveling, stretching and twisting and flexing her arms and legs and back as she made her way, feeling her way fully and gratefully into the healing Obie had brought to her. The snow was crunchy and dry underfoot, solid, as if it had melted and settled and re-frozen many times. Reaching the bowl's edge, Linda turned to scan the dome overhead, the depths of the Cosmos, the realm of great mysteries. Her heart pounded. Was Cole's spirit really "out there" somewhere, she wondered? How could such things be? The beauty of it all suddenly stuck in her throat: the sky, the stark, multicolored landscape undulating around her. This was the real world. This land, this sky, this universe of stars. This man. And these dogs. This was real. More real than the world from which she'd escaped, the world of policies and plans and backroom deals. Linda sighed, noting the silence that surrounded her. A smile played across her face as she listened. She wondered if this silence might be the voice of God.

Linda turned to Aamai, still crouching near the sled. She headed back to him. "You love these dogs," she said.

Aamai nodded. "They are my people, Madam President," he said.

"You can call me Linda."

The Inuit nodded sharply and turned back to the dogs.

"How long have you owned them?" she asked.

Aamai winced. "The *qimmiq* and I have been together for three years now, most of us," he replied. "I am building a traditional *qamutik* this winter: a sled made from wood and hides and sinew. When it is complete we will feel complete as well."

Linda stepped closer to the dogs, offering her gloved hand for one of them to sniff. "How do you choose your team?" she asked.

"I do not choose them. We choose each other. Sinaaq says that this must be the way of things now. The way of partnership. The way of co-creation." He looked pointedly at Linda. "The days of the conquerors are ending. There will be no more exploitation."

Linda flinched at his words. She was now the leader of those conquerors. And she knew that Aamai was correct. She felt her face blush at the accusation and hoped that he would not see it under the northern light. She gestured back toward the dogs. "They're beautiful beings," she said.

Aamai nodded, as if acknowledging the obvious. "All beings are beautiful."

Linda nodded in response. "Of course."

Aamai sniffed. "And yet your people misbehave like stupid children, destroying such beauty with every step, risking the extinction of all. Your gods have been as soft and lazy as you have been. They've taken far too long to punish you."

Linda sighed and looked down at the ground, unable to defend herself. The world was a mess. But she hadn't realized how much of a mess until Obie had walked her around that corner. She cringed at the memory of her dream. And standing now in the light of Aamai's judgment, she could see the full truth of it. The words "I'm sorry" spilled from her lips before she could stop them. She knew such words were far too small.

Aamai bowed. "I will accept that as a first step, Madam President. It was for this reason I was chosen to accompany you on this journey. But I must warn you that it will take every moment of the rest of your days to make those words come true." He pointed at the sky with a gloved hand. "And Sila will be with you always, to judge your actions. Do you understand?"

"I will before I leave here," promised Linda.

Aamai smiled. "Then we can proceed." With that he offered his arm and helped Linda back into the sled. Linda settled into her seat and watched, with newly-opened eyes, as the musher ran to his team and spoke to them with quiet love and respect. "Will you take us the rest of the way?" he asked calmly. The lead dogs howled at the sky in response, as though mindful of the epic poetry that would one day be written in their honor. Linda's heart hammered at the sound. It took her a moment to realize why: the dogs were calling her to greatness as well.

Aamai took his place at the back of the sled and called out. "Alright, now!" he said, and the team began to move. Lit from above by *aqsarniit*, the northern lights, they advanced across the snow and ice with sober minds and eager hearts, like youngsters on a vision quest, towards a future Linda could barely begin to discern.

## 15.3

*Cole stood at the stove, stirring the onion and garlic as they sautéed in the hot oil. Ruth stood opposite him at the counter, chopping cabbage and singing along with one of her favorite oldies as it played on the stereo in the living room. It was the best part of the day, as far as Cole was concerned: cooking together and listening to music, enjoying each other's company and anticipating a good meal and an evening of reading, or maybe a movie. And afterwards they would seal their love with their bodies. They didn't have much money, but they had enough. They were young, and smart, and they were willing to work hard. If they were patient, all of their dreams would come true.*

*"You ready for the CC, Mr. C?" asked Ruth.*

*"CC?" asked Cole.*

*Ruth turned, her hands cupped and full of long, green slivers. "Chopped cabbage," she said with a shake of her long red curls. She threw the cabbage into the wok and turned to get the rest, noting that the sliced chicken had browned just the way she liked it. She tossed in the remaining cabbage and grabbed the soy sauce from the cupboard. "Smells good," she said as Cole stirred.*

*"You wanna take over for a sec?" asked Cole.*

*Ruth stepped in and took the wooden spatula and Cole headed down the hallway toward the living room to put a new CD in the player. He chose Ziggy Stardust, swapping it out for the oldies disc that Ruth had chosen, shaking his head at her taste in music. He hit play and smiled as those lonely drums marched straight into that opening acoustic strum. Some part of him knew that he'd chosen that same disc every evening, but the thought never made it to consciousness.*

*Satisfied, he stood and walked back into the kitchen. Ruth had the stir-fry handled so he grabbed a bottle of wine from the fridge and some stemware from the cupboard above the sink, setting them next to the plates and cutlery he'd placed earlier on the dining room table. The house, their first as husband and wife, was small but cozy and clean. It served them well enough for the time being, though Ruth had made no secret of her desire for a house full of children. A larger home would one day be needed. "You want wine, I take it," asked Cole, already pouring.*

*"Just half a glass," she said.*

*Cole finished pouring and sat the bottle on the table. "How much longer?" he asked.*

*"Coupla minutes," said Ruth, picking out a piece of cabbage and testing it. It was time for the soy sauce and she added it generously.*

*Cole took the opportunity to do a quick tour of the house, checking the front and back doors and the windows, drawing the blinds. It was almost dark and he did not like the thought of people being able to watch them from outside. That was the one thing about this house he didn't like: he always felt like somebody was staring at him.*

*He stood in the living room for a minute, noting the hand-me-down furniture they'd collected from their parents. On the wall hung the paintings he and Ruth had found at a flea market on their honeymoon: a watercolor seashore with crashing waves, and a pair of wolves howling at the moon. Everything seemed in place. He started up the steps, glancing into their bedroom with the red, white and blue bear-claw quilt and Ruth's prized "velvet Elvis," a joke from her best friend from college. He stuck his head into the second bedroom - no larger than a big closet really - filled with a second-hand futon they pulled out for guests and the stacks of boxes that had never quite gotten unpacked. He flicked on the bathroom light and pushed aside the shower curtain. All was well. Looping down the rear stairway he came to the hall, inspecting the utility room before pulling on the back door to make sure it was secure. Part of him felt stupid for checking. He didn't even know what he was afraid of.*

*He stepped into the half-bath opposite the kitchen and flicked on the light to look at himself in the mirror. It wasn't just the house; it was him, too. He didn't look right. He was only twenty-three, but his hairline should be farther back, shouldn't it? His face should be heavier, his gut larger. He knew that that was stupid, but he could picture it clearly in his mind. He could see himself as older. As if he were watching himself from somewhere else.*

*Ruth's voice called him from his reverie. "Ready, sweets," she said.*

*Cole flicked off the light and walked into the dining room to find Ruth piling the stir-fry onto their plates. "Everything okay?" she asked.*

*"Do you ever get the feeling that somebody's watching us?" asked Cole.*

*Ruth turned with a quizzical look on her face. "No," she said, raising an eyebrow. "Do you?"*

*Cole sat down to his plate. "Yeah. It's weird. It's like ... all the time. Every day. Like we're living in a Barbie's Dream House and there's some little girl watching us through the windows. Like any moment the roof is going to lift off and this huge hand is going to come down and pick us up and move us around."*

*Ruth laughed and took her seat, reaching out for a sip of wine. "Sounds like you're working on another one of your stories," she said.*

*Cole shrugged. "Maybe." He forked a piece of chicken and shoved it into his mouth. "Movie tonight?" he asked.*

*"I was thinking maybe Groundhog Day," said Ruth.*

*"Good by me," said Cole. He dug into his meal. Some small part of him knew that they'd watched that movie every night since they'd moved in, but the thought never made it to consciousness.*

## 15.4

"You will sit there," said Sina to Linda, pointing at three battered metal folding chairs near the fire. Linda had assumed that they'd be inside some big tent or igloo or building but, as she and Aamai neared the site, they'd found the entire group congregated around a huge bonfire on a rocky ledge above the camp. The flames licked the sky, taller than the man who tended the fire, smoke and sparks reaching to the heavens as if longing to join the aurora. Aamai, no doubt assigned to be her keeper during the ritual, took her hand and led her to a chair.

The sight of Sina sent shivers up and down Linda's spine. She was so *young*, this Inuit prophet. She couldn't be more than twenty-one, from the looks of her, with jet-black hair hanging in long braids from her fur-lined hood. Her eyes shone like warning beacons on distant peaks. Faint blue tattoos on Sina's face, double-lined arrows pointing to her nose from four directions like a landing pad, cloaked her in mystery more effectively than any mask would have. Aamai had said her name means "the edge of the ice" and now Linda knew why. It felt as though Sina, standing here on the ice, was ready to launch herself into space, if it meant she might encounter the aliens face-to-face. No wonder these people followed her.

Linda took her seat and watched as the Inuit, maybe twenty all told, men and women ranging in age from teenagers to elders but most in their middle years, went about their business, working with quiet reverence and obvious urgency. Sina supervised with kind whispers and firm expectations as some hauled in sleds and crates to use for seating. Others piled old lumber in high, narrow stacks beyond the circle, aligning them, as far as Linda could tell based on the position of the Big Dipper, with the cardinal directions. The firewood must have come from the dismantling of the mine. That made sense; Linda had yet to see a tree on Bathurst Island. It occurred to her that traditional Inuit rituals probably hadn't centered around a bonfire, given the tree line in the far North. But these were not traditional Inuit, as Obie had pointed out. They'd been born far to the south, most of them, and raised in the mainstream Canadian culture. Of course they'd want a bonfire. Feeling the warmth on her face, Linda was glad of that.

On the far side of the fire was the snowcat she'd helped load. A few Inuit stood behind it, one unloading supplies and the others attending to something she could not see. She saw no sign of Cole or Obie and was about to ask where they were when Sina turned and strode directly to her, squatting on the snow before Linda to look her eye to eye.

"You've given your promise?" Sina asked, tossing her head back just enough to convey her mastery of the moment.

Linda glanced at Aamai, seeking guidance and receiving none. He simply awaited her response. She turned back to Sina. "I have," she said. "Though I don't know what I've promised."

Sina nodded. "It cannot be helped," she said. "Such is the time into which we've been born. Promise or no, you will succeed or fail, as will we all, according to your worthiness and the judgments of the Earth." She looked at Aamai. "Can she do this?" she asked him.

Aamai nodded. "I don't know!" he said with a grin.

Sina smiled in return. "Thank you for reminding me." She stood and walked toward the snowcat.

"I feel like a child," murmured Linda.

"That sounds like a good place to start," replied Aamai.

"Will somebody tell me what it is I'm supposed to be doing before this thing starts?"

Aamai looked her directly in the eye. "Nobody knows."

A tall, thin old man with long white hair shuffled into the firelight and made his way over to where she sat. He pulled his hood back as he neared her and Linda drew in a sharp breath. For a second he looked like a skeleton, with ghostly fire shining from his eye sockets. The old man reached out his hand and Linda took it to shake. "What a great pleasure to meet you, ma'am," said the old man, his voice thin and unsteady.

Linda stood, unsure of the protocol. "My pleasure as well," she said. "And you are...?"

"This is Utterpok," said Aamai, standing to make the introduction. "Our *angakkuq*. Our shaman."

Utterpok blew a raspberry and winked. "Don't let this young cub fool you," he said brightly. "The name's Kenny Fast. I sold Subarus in Calgary for thirty-some-odd years, until you folks decided to start collapsing the economy in '08. That and drank myself into oblivion every night. 'Fast cars, fast deals with Kenny Fast.' Just the sort of training a shaman needs, eh?" He winked again and sat down in the third chair, patting the seat next to him for Linda to join him.

Linda took an instant liking to this angakkuq and leaned against him for support. "You got any idea what the fuck's going on here, Kenny?" she said with hushed solidarity.

"Oh, no," said Utterpok wistfully. "We're just making things up as we go along, as usual." He smiled sadly and looked up to the sky. "The Tuurngait – the aliens – tell us that Cole's spirit, his *anirniq* as we say in Inuktitut, has been trapped and hidden by those fuckers who've been chasing you across the continent. Our battle plan is to upshift a level or two, find him, bring him back and put him back into his body, at which point you and he will dash back to D.C., put the bad guys in jail, and save the world. Course, you know what they say about battle plans."

"What do they say?"

Utterpok looked back at Linda and winked again. "They're only good until the battle begins."

### 15.5

*Grace was glad she'd listened when Evlyn warned her. The scary people had turned up just as the woman of light had said they would, four of them this time, harassing Linda and her friends as they traveled across the material landscape. Because they'd kept their distance, Grace, Evlyn, Jack, and Dennis had been able to escape detection.*

*The skeleton had appeared first, his wild howls piercing the sky and giving Grace and her friends enough warning to flicker away.*

*The distorted woman followed close behind, accompanied by a tall man dressed in a suit and tie, his face handsome and full of smiles, his hair a bright orange flame. They were on Linda like a colony of bats, but Linda was wide-awake and well protected. The scary ones were unable to touch her. It was a minute or so later that the strange young girl arrived. Grace noticed for the first time how much she looked like Jack.*

*"What do we do?" asked Grace as they hovered as far back as they could, floating in the blackness they'd wrapped around themselves like a cloak.*

*Evlyn beamed her confidence. "I think we just follow for now, little one," she said. "Wait until our help is needed. We do not yet know what they are up to in the physical realm."*

*Grace knelt to scratch Dennis's back and bury her face in his fur. Unlike herself, Dennis was still tied back to his body. She imagined Emily lying next to him on Cat and Jake's bed. She was glad to trust that everything was fine back home. The thought of it filled her with warmth, the thought of home and family, the thought of Dennis sleeping peacefully. She had work to do here, for now, but she would be glad to get back home.*

*Grace looked up at Jack and the old woman. "Let's not hang back too far, okay?" she said. Her father's body lay amongst these people in the dense layers below. And that was all she had of him now. Her heart ached.*

*"Okay," said Jack.*

*Evlyn beamed her understanding.*

*Dennis wagged his tail.*

## 15.6

"We've known since the beginning that to reclaim is to resist," said Utterpok circling the bonfire, his elderly voice now the voice of an elder, full and clear with maturity, power, and intention. "In the hidden depths of our hearts, we've always known that the beast of Empire would thrash and kick in its death throes. We've known that the entire Earth would shudder underfoot as this Empire died. We've known that we are called to hold this land in our hands and hearts, to walk with it as allies through the coming darkness, and toward the light that flickers beyond."

The rest of the company filled the chairs and crates that circled the fire, a ring of bright cheeks and glinting eyes, hoods thrown back from the heat of the blaze. Sina sat in the North, Obie in the East, Linda in the South and Payok in the West. Cole lay on a mat of tarps and blankets in the center, as close to the fire as they dared place him. The firelight brought a flickering life to his face, as if he was merely asleep and dreaming wildly.

Utterpok shuffled by, stopping for a moment to touch Cole's forehead with the palm of his hand before continuing. He stood straight and looked Linda in the eye. "What we did not foresee was that the economy would plummet so soon, and that the ice would melt so quickly. And we did not foresee that the battle itself would come to our doorstep." He turned to scan his audience. "And yet we might have. For we know that we cannot break the laws of the living without suffering the consequences. And we Inuit, some of the last on Earth to follow those laws, have been losing our way for some time now, turning our backs on the gods and giving ourselves to liquor and drugs, to the Christian God and the money-god. We've forgotten that '*our diet consists entirely of souls.*' We've forgotten that we are *anirniq* as well. And while some of us work now to reclaim those souls, I fear that we may be too late." Utterpok stopped and pointed at the sky. "The Tuurngait are here. They are speaking to us once again. And they do not bring good news."

Utterpok circled around to face Sina. "There is no blame in my words," he said. Sina nodded. "We lost our path long before any of us here were born, led astray by forces far beyond our ken. That is not our fault." He turned to face the circle. "But we are entirely responsible for this moment, and the next, and for who we will be from here on out, no matter from whence we came. It is time now for our testing. Can we remember ourselves?" The old man shuffled to the East and knelt before Obie as if asking forgiveness. "We must face into who we've become," he said, almost sobbing, his head hung low. "A band of electricians and postal clerks and law students and housewives, following the visions of a young school teacher from Igloolik, and listening now to the ramblings of a drunken old car salesman who hasn't got the first idea how to act like an *angakkuq*. You call me Utterpok, which means 'returns home,' but I fear I have not yet earned it. I still have so far to go." He looked up at Obie. "We have lost ourselves. And the beast has found us. As have the Tuurngait. As have you and your brother and your President. You have found us just as we are starting to find ourselves." Utterpok rose and addressed the whole circle. "So many far-flung forces, come to face each other on this frozen ground. We were right to call this place Tuyurmiangoyok, 'the place of visitors from far away.'"

He turned his face to the stars above, as if making a promise to God. "Now is the time of *piqujait*, of that which must be done. It is a time of bargaining and balance, of protection and sacrifice and the making of amends." He walked quickly to Linda's side and gestured expansively. "This great leader needs our help before she can do her work in the world." He motioned toward Cole. "This poor man must be restored so that he can join in that work." He waved his hands overhead as he spun in a circle, his face growing murky and troubled. "And the air around us is thick with dark forces." He stopped and looked once again at Sina. "Sedna and Qailertetang must be laughing heartily right now, don't you think? To hear a con-man like myself speak such pretentious words. I pray I do not overly offend them."

Sina smiled but said nothing. Linda understood why. Despite his self-denigration, Linda could see the power in this man. It flowed from him in waves so potent they almost knocked her over. He knew exactly who he was.

Utterpok grabbed his walrus-belly drum and started beating a rhythm with a thick, antler-handled drumstick. The cadence was simple, a quick, deep, throbbing beat that resonated with Linda's pounding heart. The others in the circle closed their eyes. Linda followed suit. Utterpok began to chant in a deep, resonant voice. Words she could not begin to comprehend poured across the circle like stage fog.

Aamai, sitting to Linda's left, leaned over to whisper into her ear. "Utterpok now calls on the aid of the helping spirits. It has been decided that he, Sinaaq, Payok, Immaqa and Mr. Thomas will ride the drum to the land of the dead, and from there to wherever your friend Cole will lead them." As he spoke, Aamai pointed out who was who. Payok was the tall young man with the long, flowing black hair who sat in the West. He'd come to get them after Cole's body had shown up. Immaqa was a mere girl, maybe sixteen, who sat at Sina's side. The two young women looked like sisters.

Linda leaned to whisper her response. "How will they find Cole's ... spirit?" she asked.

"We have his body," answered Aamai. "It contains the echo of his soul. They will follow that vibration."

"And what am I to do?" she asked.

"Perhaps you are to stand as guardian over his body," said Aamai.

Following an impulse, Linda stood and started forward, stepping carefully around Utterpok and kneeling on the tarps at Cole's side. She sat back and pulled her legs underneath her bottom. Removing both of her gloves and one of his, she took his hand. Sighing deeply, she closed her eyes.

Utterpok's chanting grew louder. The drumbeat quickened. Words and rhythm wove around each other like lovers, like horses pounding the prairie, like voices in a choir. The chanting sounded less like human language than the calls of seagulls and the rumbling groans of whales. The outside world faded from Linda's consideration. The present moment filled her heart. The old shaman was trying to build a bridge between flesh and spirit. The rocky ledge had become a cathedral.

Linda watched with eyes shut. At first she saw only the fire flickering on her eyelids, but after a time it was as if the drumbeat and the chanting were taking shape before her, as if words were becoming visible, as if she could reach out and touch the notes of the drum. She began to see the circle of human souls sitting around her, their hearts glowing, their faces rapt. And then suddenly she was surrounded by animals. Linda gasped with wonder and delight, squeezing Cole's hand and opening her eyes for fear of his safety. All looked as it had before: Utterpok and his drum and a circle of humans with eyes closed. Taking a deep breath she closed her eyes again.

And there they were, swirling about the circle at the edges of her vision, beings formed of firelight and song: reindeer and eagle; caribou, seal, moose, and rabbit; white wolf, mountain sheep, and fishes and birds of many varieties. A snowshoe hare hopped to Cole's side and sat near his head. A pair of caribou stood right by Linda's shoulder. Linda laughed out loud. She could feel their hot breath tickling her face. When she opened her eyes she saw humans in a circle around a bonfire. When she closed them she saw animals by the dozens flying and walking and hopping and swimming all about them, some coming to rest near individual humans. A walrus pulled up beside Sina and leaned against her leg. An eagle sat on Payok's head. A seal lay on his back at Immaqa's feet, writhing playfully. An Arctic fox tugged at Obie's sleeve.

Linda watched with eyes closed as Utterpok stood and began to stomp around the bonfire. His song grew louder, the words almost Pentecostal in feel. He pounded the drum with forceful arcs and danced a shuffling dance. "Only hearts know how to find their way in the dark!" he shouted to the sky. "Only hearts." Turning at the sound of a cough and a loud huffing of breath, Linda saw a massive polar bear enter the circle from directly behind her, felt the rasp of its fur on her face as it passed. The bear strode right inside the old man's body. Utterpok roared to the aurora above, then collapsed to the ground. The drum fell silent.

Linda opened her eyes to see all five travelers lying peacefully on the snow, their bodies tended by the remaining Inuit. Not one of them made a sound.

## 15.7

*At first she thought it was her father coming toward her. Her heart leapt and she trembled with joy. But it was not her father. She could see the difference. This was the man called Obie, whom she understood to be her uncle. Her father was still gone, absent from the Universe, even though his body still lived.*

*Obie approached quickly and shared his heart in a beam of greeting.* "*We've come to find your father, Grace,*" *he said.*

"*You know me?*" *asked Grace.*

"*Of course,*" *said Obie.* "*And I've been counting on your help.*"

"*We will help,*" *said Grace.*

"*We do not have much time,*" *said Obie.* "*Will you follow us?*"

"*We will,*" *said Grace with a firm nod.* "*Where do we go?*"

"*Your father's flesh will guide us,*" *said Obie.*

*Obie flickered out and Grace turned to speak to her companions.* "*It's time,*" *she said.*

"*Let's go, eh?*" *said Evlyn.*

*Grace gazed out over the entirety of the Cosmos and nodded. It was time.*

# Chapter ∅ Sixteen

## 16.1

"Who the hell are these people?" asked Bob, gesturing toward the fur-clad figures who had accompanied Obie into the astral realm. She and Rice were watching from inside a veil of concealment they'd crafted in the center of the Inuit's ritual circle, coterminous with the bonfire.

Rice glanced up. His former student hovered with a small group of Eskimos and a bunch of mangy animals in the sky overhead. "Carl always was real good at making new friends in strange places," he responded dryly, with a crude Southern accent. As Rice spoke, Obie and his furry friends receded further, approaching another group of souls who floated dimly in the distance above them. After a few moments, Obie and his gang flickered out, followed not long thereafter by the sparks he'd been speaking with. Was that a little girl, Rice wondered? He laughed. Carl was one twisted fuck.

Rice scanned the area around him in all directions, looking for astral stragglers, finding none. Carl's whole crew had now moved on to their final destination, totally missing the fact that he and Bob had been right there in their midst, watching them. No surprise, really. With loverboy's body as a jumping board, they'd had a clear signal to follow, and were no doubt in a hurry to make their grand *rescue. The People, of course, would be waiting for them. Easy as pie. But Rice was still pissed off. They shouldn't have to be doing this at all. Fucking bugs, giving these bastards the body like they did.*

*"Boss?" said Bob.*

*"I'm staying here," said Rice, crawling out from behind the veil.*

*"But—"*

*"You take Alice and go kick their asses, like we talked about." Rice stuck his face right into Linda's and breathed heavily. "I'm gonna dog Ma Kettle here and do her when she falters. Fuck that damned Specter shit. I've had enough of this bitch to last me two lifetimes."*

*Bob sighed. "We have no real idea who these people are," she protested.*

*Rice looked up at Bob, wincing to see her face so distorted. "Holy fuck, Roberta. Can't you keep yourself together better than that?"*

*"We don't know what we're up against," Bob replied, ignoring his jab.*

*Rice laughed. "You're up against a homeless schizophrenic and a bunch of New Age whale-munchers, Bob. What the fuck are you afraid of? Ya got Random, for chrissake. He's there right now, setting the trap."*

*"I guess you're right, boss." Bob backed off into the sky, where Alice waited in the far distance. "You take care of our girl here."*

*Rice turned back to Linda. "Oh, you bet I will, Bobby." He reached out with his tongue and licked the President's face. "You bet I will."*

## 16.2

A slight breeze had risen, pushing the flames away from Linda. She was thankful for that. Her eyes felt crushed and trampled by the smoke and the cold, and by the night without sleep. She sighed with deep fatigue. How could she sleep? She'd lost her pills. The only thing keeping Bob and Rice out of her head was the aliens. But now they'd pulled their ships back, for reasons she did not know. A test, Utterpok had said. As if she needed another test. Linda shifted on the tarp, changing positions to warm her other side. She sat at the edge, between fire and ice, and held onto herself as best she could. She imagined she could feel the hot, wet breath of the caribou, or one of their noses rubbing her cheek. The thought gave her comfort.

Aamai brought her a mug of hot, spiced tea from the huge thermos at the back of the snowcat, handing it to her with gentle consideration. The Inuit held silence and she did not intend to break it with questions or conversation. She had little idea what was happening here. She simply had to trust. And wait. She lifted the mug to her lips and let the tea console her, smiling as her throat tightened with love and loss, thankful for Aamai's attention. In such harsh times, small acts of kindness made a huge difference.

She looked down at Cole. His face flickered in the firelight as if he dreamt. Perhaps he did, somewhere. And perhaps he would come back to tell her his dreams. Obie had been right, to not get her hopes up. And Aamai had been right, to do the opposite. Linda held hope and hopelessness together in her heart, disparate and desperate twins born of this time of collapse and transformation. She looked up to the heavens, to the stars and the northern lights, to the depths of space and time. There was room enough in the world for both hope and despair.

## 16.3

*"Who could that be at this hour?"* thought Ruth, sitting up and switching on her bedside lamp. *"Cole?"* She nudged her husband's sleeping body.

*"Hmm?"* he said.

*"The doorbell. It just rang."*

*"You're kidding me,"* he said sleepily, rolling away.

*"Cole!"*

Cole rolled back and opened his eyes. *"What?"* he said.

Ruth pointed at their bedroom door, and the stairway beyond. *"The doorbell. Somebody just rang it."*

"Fuck," he muttered. Cole sighed, pulling back the covers and swinging his feet to the floor. He stood, scratched his stomach for a moment, then grabbed his robe from the back of the wooden armchair. "I'll go check it out," he said, his voice rough with sleep.

Ruth rose and followed to the top of the stairs, not bothering to put anything on. Cole clunked down the steps and stood at the door. "Who is it?" he demanded. There was no response. "I said 'who is it?'" Cole repeated, louder this time. He switched on the porch light. There was still no response. He reached into the coat closet and grabbed the baseball bat that leaned in the back corner.

"Cole?" called Ruth from upstairs.

"Just checking," answered Cole.

Raising the bat over his shoulder, he unlocked the door, swinging it inward as quickly as he could, shouting "Ha!" into the night air. There was no one there. Stepping out cautiously, bat first, he looked from side to side and out into the darkness. Not a sign of anyone.

Cole stepped back in and locked the door. "You sure you heard the doorbell?" he called, replacing the bat.

"Of course I'm sure," said Ruth, as though offended by Cole's doubt.

Cole sighed, switched off the porch light, and lumbered back upstairs to bed.

## 16.4

Obie walked back from the porch. "Nobody's home," he said. "And the door's locked." He looked around the neighborhood, a section of middle-class suburb with neatly trimmed lawns and new paint and young trees. Someone's idea of heaven. Cole's body had drawn them to what looked like a little green bungalow in the Midwest. They were not on the physical plane, but it certainly looked as though they were. Almost. The streets only extended for a couple of blocks in each direction before coming to an abrupt end. Beyond them, and filling the sky above, there was nothing but blackness, devoid of stars. Although the scene was well lit, there was no sun in the sky.

"That's my mom and dad's first house," said Grace.

*Obie turned. Before him in the street stood an odd crew, the Inuit with whom he'd traveled and these four they'd picked up. The Forces of Good, he thought with a smile. Grace, a girl of five or six dressed in sky-blue overalls and a pink blouse, took a step forward. "I saw some pictures once," she said, brushing her short dark-brown hair away from her face. "In my mom's scrapbook." She tilted her head quizzically. "How did you know me, Uncle Obie?"*

*Obie smiled. "Figured it out myself, Grace," he said. "From what the President told me. I knew I'd find you here somewhere. It's nice to finally meet you. Will you introduce us to your friends?"*

*Grace nodded, kneeling down to pet her dog. "This is Dennis. Emily says he belongs to her, but really he doesn't belong to anybody but himself." She stood up and turned toward Evlyn and Jack. "This is the woman who got me out of the glass house. She's called Evlyn. And this is the Little Prince. But really he's Jack." She turned back to Obie. "We've been keeping an eye on Linda and my Dad since they left. 'Cuz of the scary ones."*

*Obie could see that Jack was a hybrid, no doubt living amongst the alive ones, given his lack of a tether. The woman was an old soul between lives, he guessed, also untethered. Though she was fairly stable, her form flickered a bit from time to time, as if she were still integrating her many incarnations. Dennis was firmly tethered, he could see, but it appeared that Grace was not. That troubled Obie greatly. Somehow the girl had been killed. What had Rice done?*

*"I'm glad to have you here with us," said Obie. He indicated the Inuit with a sweep of his arm. "Here we have Sinaaq, our leader, and her sister Immaqa. Payok, a warrior, and Utterpok, our angakkuq." Each of the Inuit nodded in turn as he introduced them.*

*Grace considered Obie and his friends, how they had animals around them, how they seemed to be almost animals themselves. The old man stood with a polar bear at his feet, and the tall warrior had an eagle on his head. She smiled, thinking of the scary ones. Even the skeleton couldn't beat a polar bear, could he? Dennis stepped forward and came nose to nose with the white fox that sat at Obie's side. The fox growled and Dennis growled back and raised his hackles. After a moment, the fox looked away as if bored, and the little Whippet turned and took his place at Grace's feet.*

*"Do you know what's going on here?" asked Obie, kneeling before the girl. He glanced over his shoulder at the little green house. "I expect that your father is inside, but I also expect that there are some rather confused, angry people in there with him. You said you've already met some 'scary ones'?"*

*Grace nodded. "They've been chasing after my dad and Linda, ever since she came to our house," she said. "We've been protecting them." She looked with pride at Jack, Evlyn and Dennis, then back to her uncle. "There's a scary woman with a face that melts. And a strange little girl. There's a new one, a man in a suit who's got fire for hair. And a skeleton."*

*Obie looked down and rubbed at his eyes.*

*"Do you know about the skeleton?" Grace asked.*

*Obie sighed. Mr. Random. Fuck. He's still around? "Yeah, Grace," he said, "I know about the skeleton."*

## 16.5

Mary glanced at the sky as she strode back to her car. She would not have been surprised to see a wok hovering overhead, a couple of soldiers ready to take her out with their ray guns. Rice had gone mad. Who knew what he was up to now? Implants or no, he could find her if he wished. All she could do was keep moving, stopping in big, busy truck stops like this one and keeping her mind as clear as she could.

She keyed her old Toyota and started the engine, backing out under the harsh, yellow lights of the parking lot, merging onto the expressway and the relative comfort of the dark highway. She was headed south, back to D.C. She wished she knew what to expect when she got there.

Mary felt like a dog on a leash, as if forces much larger than she were leading her about the block. There was no reason she could imagine to have gone to Vermont, and yet by being there she had been able to save someone who would have otherwise died: the father of the man who was helping Linda, the grandfather of his children. Seeing those kids' bedrooms had changed her. The *Star Wars* poster. The flowered bed. The book on the floor. And that nap she took. Even though she did not know who was guiding her, she did know for whom she was now working.

She was working for those children.

## 16.6

*When Payok saw the old woman smash her fists against the front picture window, he joined in with gusto, thankful for something to do. The American, Obie, had called this whole thing a Confusion, a spell woven by sorcerers to confound them. He'd said that they might break in by refusing to believe in it, but the magic had proven too strong for that. They would be forced to play by the sorcerers' own rules. And that meant breaking into a house, which Payok knew how to do. Breaking and entering is what had put him in jail. And it was in jail that he'd found the writings of Sinaaq, and where he'd chosen his name: Payok – "he wrestles."*

*Upon his release, just six months ago, he'd walked away from his old life. He caught the Greyhound from Brandon to Lynn Lake and found a pilot there willing to trade a ride to Whale Cove in exchange for his grandfather's pocket watch. It took two more months to get to Resolute, two months of odd jobs and hitchhiking and catching a boat or plane when he could. Two months of wrestling with who he'd been and what he'd been told was true. Two months of struggling to find something that made sense. He smiled when he saw the sign: Resolute. Indeed. Payok was as unyielding as a concrete wall.*

*His wrestling had paid off. He met Aamai on his first night there. Aamai took him to Sinaaq. The prophetess had named him her warrior on the spot, and she'd taken him as her lover. And now, for reasons he did not fully comprehend, he'd been chosen to accompany her on this journey. Somehow he'd managed to follow them to this strange realm, though he'd never been here before. He decided that it did not matter that he did not understand this place. He would leave that to others. Sinaaq needed his help and protection. He did not intend to fail her. That was enough for him.*

*Payok and the old woman hammered on the glass until it splintered and then shattered in an avalanche of shards that skittered in all directions, like electric butterflies, before dissolving into nothing. An earsplitting wail broke forth from within, like the gibbering of a demon. The window began to re-form. The old woman fell back at the screaming but Payok leapt up like an eagle and slipped through the jagged opening before it resealed. Scanning the room quickly to make sure he was alone, he stepped to the front door, flipped the lock, and pulled it open. The wailing stopped. Holding the door firmly, Payok gestured for the others to enter. "I see no one here," he called out.*

*"Good work, my friend," said Obie, taking the steps up to the porch. He stuck his head in through the doorway and looked around, then turned and motioned for the others to follow. The rest of the group slipped past him into the house, save for Jack, who stood on the sidewalk shaking his head. Obie put a hand on Grace's shoulder to stop her as she entered and gestured back toward her friend. "Will he join us?" he asked.*

*Graced turned. "He wants to help," she answered. "But he cannot. His mother and father war within his heart, he says. He is not allowed."*

*Obie walked back down the stairs to speak with Jack. The young hybrid retreated a few steps, but then held his ground. "We need a lookout and witness, Jack," said Obie. "To alert us if anyone approaches from outside, and to report on our efforts, no matter how this goes. Will you do that for us?"*

*Jack nodded with relief, almost smiling. "I will watch out," he said.*

*"Thank you," said Obie. He turned and walked back into the house, closing the door behind him. The Forces of Good stood together in the neat, cozy living room. An old brown sofa lined one wall, with cheap paintings of ocean waves and wolves filling the space above it. There was an old leather recliner and a glass-topped coffee table, a bookshelf with a stereo on top, a television on a rolling cart. It did, indeed, seem that there was nobody home. Then Obie realized that they were not all present.*

*"Where's Payok and Evlyn?" he asked.*

*"Securing the second floor," said Sina, as though it were obvious.*

## 16.7

"Not a soul in sight," said Evlyn as they walked down the dark, narrow hallway.

"Then what was that screaming?" asked Payok. The eagle on his shoulder glared angrily.

The woman of light shrugged and turned to head back down to the living room to tell the others. Payok followed.

The living room was empty.

Payok strode to the front door and pulled it open. Seeing no one, he closed it and followed Evlyn into the kitchen. "Where have they gone?" he asked, feeling foolish as soon as the words spilled from his mouth. How could the old woman know? The kitchen was empty, as was the bathroom and the utility room. They started together up the back stairs, scouring the house once more. It was empty, but for them.

Back in the living room Payok again checked the front lawn. Even that weird kid had disappeared. He shut the door and turned around to call out to the empty house, "Hello?"

"I'm going to check the back yard," said Evlyn.

Payok started up the stairs. "I'll search the second floor again and meet you there," he said.

## 16.8

While Payok and Evlyn were exploring upstairs, Obie and Sina made sure that the first floor was clear. The house was tiny, and the others could watch their progress from the living room. The front of the house was one large space, the living and dining rooms sitting side-by-side and fully open to each other. The stairs, with an open banister, ran up along the far wall of the living room. A hallway that led to the back door divided the backend of the house.

On one side of the hall was the kitchen, separated from the dining room by a half-wall. Behind the kitchen, by the back door, was another stairway to the second floor. Across the hall from the kitchen was the bathroom and, behind that, there was a utility room with a washer and dryer. Obie and Sina made a quick *search, opening doors, flipping on lights, and peering into these small rooms. Clearly there was no one home. Obie called upstairs to Payok and Evlyn but received no reply. Sina started back to the living room. Obie followed, then ducked into the bathroom to check behind the shower door. He did not come back out.*

*"What the fuck?" muttered Sina, walking back to stand in the bathroom doorway. The space was tiny, crammed with a toilet, a small pedestal sink, and a shower stall, with the translucent glass door now wide open. Obie was gone. Impossible, as they could see the door the whole time and there was no other way out. But he was not there. "Obie?" said Sina, a trace of fear in her voice. Her words echoed off the ceramic surfaces and fell to her feet. The walrus shuffled back and forth beside her, as though sharing her anxiety. "Payok!" she called loudly, angling her head to the ceiling as if she could push her voice up through the joists and flooring to reach her warrior.*

*She looked at the others, who stood in the living room in a rough half-circle, watching her. "We have to find them," she said decisively. She stepped forward, grabbed Immaqa's hand, and started toward the front stairs.*

*"Wait," said Utterpok. The polar bear barked sternly. "We knew to expect this," said the shaman. "Things are not what they seem here. We must go together."*

*Sina stopped, opened her mouth as if she were going to argue, then nodded her agreement. Utterpok started for the stairs. Grace and Dennis followed.*

*Together they searched the house, the two bedrooms upstairs, the bathroom, the back stairs down to the first floor, the utility room and the kitchen and the dining room. Dennis and the Arctic fox ran ahead, sniffing the rooms as they went. There was no sign of Obie, Payok or the old woman. No sign of the "scary people" Grace had feared. No sign of a skeleton. No sign of Cole. The house was quiet. Again they searched the second floor, climbing the back stairway and checking every space. Finding no clues, they headed back down the front stairs, Utterpok in the lead, with Grace and Dennis right behind him.*

*Sina stopped for a moment to unclasp her parka, then started down the steps, with her sister right behind her. The young leader stopped halfway down the stairs and looked down at Utterpok, who stood on the landing below, looking back up at her. "How can this be?" she asked her shaman, her voice beginning to shake.*

*"Our opponents are devious," answered Utterpok, a flash of excitement in his eyes. The polar bear, scratching his neck on the newel post, chuffed in agreement.*

*The toilet flushed in the upstairs bathroom and Sina turned and started running back up the stairs, grabbing her sister's hand and pulling her along. The sisters gave no heed to Utterpok's cry of warning as they took the steps two at a time, the walrus and seal at their feet.*

*They did not return.*

### 16.9

*Ruth crawled back into bed and spooned up to Cole's back, checking the clock before closing her eyes. Only one-thirty and already she had to pee? Maybe it was the wine. She needed to stick with one glass. And what was that dream? A window breaking? And some poor animal screaming? She hugged her husband close to herself and fell back to sleep, hoping for more peaceful slumber.*

### 16.10

*Immaqa knew she should not be here. She should never have agreed to come. She didn't even believe in this shit. When Sina told her that she'd been chosen for this mission by the aliens themselves, she should have run the other way. This was too much like television. Except on television people didn't have animals tagging along everywhere they went.*

*Immaqa followed her sister down the upstairs hallway to the bath. There was nobody there. It was like a bad nightmare and Immaqa was ready to wake the fuck back up. The last thing she wanted was to run into a skeleton.*

*It was Sina's fault. What a stupid name. Why couldn't her sister just be Debbie Okalik, the schoolteacher? And why couldn't she be Agnes Okalik, instead of Immaqa? Didn't her sister realize why she'd taken the name "maybe"? As in maybe Agnes didn't believe a word of this prophet crap. As in maybe when you start seeing animals following you around it's time to check yourself into the loony bin.*

*Immaqa wasn't like Sina. She didn't want to be. They were only half-sisters, after all. Debbie could have this Inuit spirituality bullshit. Agnes was heading another direction. She'd already registered at modeling school for the fall. With her looks she could go far. She had the clear, delicate features of the Inuit, slightly softened by whichever-the-fuck white guy had nailed her mother the night she'd been conceived. Her resultant "exotic looks" drove the boys at her school crazy.*

*But then she'd had that goddamned dream: little alien guys, flying her around the planet and telling her that her sister needed her. And she'd just dropped everything and headed north. The next day! Spent her school money on plane fare! It was insane. What had she been thinking?*

*Sina stepped into a bedroom and Immaqa followed. The seal and the walrus were nosing through the closet. The bed was covered with a beautiful quilt, red and blue tulips on a white background, it looked like. But its elegance was undermined by the painting on the wall. Immaqa snorted. That velvet Elvis had to go.*

*Sina turned and smiled at her sister. "Are you okay?" she asked.*

*Immaqa shrugged and looked down at her feet. "This is all pretty strange, Deb," she answered, making sure to remind the great "Sinaaq" who she really was. She looked up at Sina. "Are we dreaming or did you guys spike the tea?"*

*Sina stared into Immaqa's eyes. "We walk the levels beyond our own, little sister," said Sina, pushing in the word "little" like a thumbtack. "The land of the dead. The realms of Sila and Sedna. Our courage and obedience here will determine the course of the world."*

*"You really believe all this crap, sis?"*

*Sina took her sister by the elbow and pulled her toward the stairs. "Your words threaten us all," she hissed.*

*Immaqa threw off her sister's grip. "Yeah, well, fuck you, Deb-*

*bie," she said angrily. She turned and stormed down the hallway toward the back stairs.*

*Sina sighed sadly as her sister walked away, took a deep breath, and then headed down to the living room. Utterpok was not there. Nor were the girl and her dog. She never saw her sister alive again.*

### 16.11

*They've built a maze from Cole's memories, thought Obie, sitting on the sofa with the Arctic fox. Like so many times before, he didn't know how he knew it; he just knew it. To test his hypothesis he grabbed a pair of CDs from the shelf under the stereo and placed them on the coffee table, leaning them against each other like an A-frame. Then he headed up the front stairs and down the back ones. Walking through the dining room he could see he'd been right. The CDs were not on the table. He checked the shelf. The titles he'd chosen were right where he'd first found them.*

*Obie laughed. As fucked up as it all was, he had to admire the twisted brilliance that had created such a place as this Confusion. The maze itself had all the marks of Mr. Random, that crazy fuck. This maze was like Random's own mind. But the style was Rice. Or Bob. Or both. Trapping Cole in his old house. Playing with his heart. Keeping him happy until they had some use for him, at which point they could rip him again from his life. The deep cruelty and sheer arrogance of these people never ceased to astound Obie. From such minds came things like 9/11 and the Miami Nuke.*

*No doubt they were watching him right now, laughing their asses off. They would split his group into ones and twos and then take them out with ease. Like shooting fish in a barrel of monkeys, as his father had often said. Obie sighed. This had to stop. When you start killing little girls it's time to go.*

*He sat in the leather recliner and pulled himself into the lotus position. The fox padded a loop between the living and dining rooms, stopping to look out the window now and then. Obie closed his eyes to interrupt the illusion. He would not stop this by wandering around a maze.*

*He would have to find a different way.*

## 16.12

A heavy snow had started to fall and the Inuit tenders had erected small tents from tarps and logs and rope to shield the travelers. The wind was increasing, flapping the tents and causing the snow to drift in tiny rivulets and gather around Linda's feet. The President hunkered down, laying her head across Cole's chest to get out of the snow. Aamai had brought her a tarp of her own, which he'd tucked around her body and legs. The fire, burned down now to half its former glory, kept her warm enough.

She could hear Cole's heart. Steady. Strong. But his emptiness still assaulted her. He was not just sleeping. He would not open his eyes and kiss her if she tickled him. He was gone from this world. Beyond the event horizon and past all knowing. "Come back, Cole," she whispered. The words clogged her throat. She knew he could not hear her.

An Inuit woman with steel gray braids pulled out a small frame drum and beat it steadily with her fingers, as if challenging the wind and snow, declaring their right to be there. Linda peeked her head up and smiled across the circle at the woman. The woman, sensing Linda's gaze, looked up and returned the smile, revealing a missing front tooth.

From somewhere in the distance came the cracking of ice. Linda looked at the sky. The snow clouds now concealed the heavens. The stars and the northern lights were nowhere in sight. She laid her head back on Cole's chest and closed her eyes.

The white rabbit was still right there, sitting next to Cole's head. And crouching beyond him, a dark figure made of shadows and static that reminded her, vaguely, of Theodore Rice.

## 16.13

*Immaqa was frantic. What the fuck was that? And where was Sina? She ran through the living room and back up the front stairs, flicking on lights as she went. She ducked into the main bedroom and slammed the door. She was alone. Goddamn motherfucking sonovabitch she was scared! That was... fuck! That hand ... all bones and sinews and shit. Reaching at her from the closet. She'd slammed the door and run like hell. And that stupid seal had stayed behind!*

*Immaqa tried to control her breathing, listening in the silence for footsteps. Nothing. She grabbed the bedside lamp, yanked the plug from the wall, and held it over her head as a weapon as she opened the door back to the hallway. It had been stupid to hide in here. She'd trapped herself. She had to get outside.*

*She looked both ways. Figuring the back door was closer, she started in that direction, still holding the lamp over her head.*

*When she was halfway down the stairs, the whole house began to shake like an earthquake.*

## 16.14

*Grace had liked Utterpok immediately. She'd watched the old man kneel down and let Dennis lick his face for as long as the little dog had wanted to. That meant he had a good heart. And the old man was strong, like the polar bear spirit that waited beside him. She could feel it.*

*But Utterpok didn't know what to do. He didn't know where everybody had gone. Grace had beamed her heart to him, and taught him to do the same back to her, hoping that then they'd be able to find each other if they got separated. But he'd never even heard of doing that. That worried her. He was good and strong, but maybe he and his people didn't know much about this realm.*

*She was glad they were sitting on the sofa when the earthquake hit. It would have knocked them to the floor otherwise. From the back hallway came the sound of a ceiling cracking, or a wall caving in. Dennis jumped into her lap, shaking so hard she wondered if he would crack too. The house stopped shaking, but Dennis didn't. She petted and kissed him until he calmed down.*

*And then she cocked her head and smiled.*

*"What is it?" said Utterpok, noticing.*

*"I think I can feel my Dad," she replied.*

## 16.15

"Fuck fuck fuck a crack fuck fuck," said Mr. Random in the darkness of the closet. "Fuck a crack a crack a crack."

"Not yet," whispered Bob, reaching out to grab his bony shoulder before he could open the closet door. "It's okay. Just a minute longer. Let them get really panicked first."

Random sighed and slumped. "Fuck fuck fuck who who who?" he chanted more quietly.

Bob remembered when she'd first found Mr. Random wandering around in the astral. He was confused, even then, but he could cobble together enough moments of lucidity that you could stand to be around him. How he'd died but stayed tethered to his decaying body nobody could ever really explain, but it didn't seem to matter. He was suggestible and eager to please, and his odd status might give them capabilities they wouldn't otherwise have. They'd brought him up to speed, located his body in a drainpipe just south of Scranton, and fetched it to the Rock and put him to work. Since he couldn't really remember who he was or what he was up to, and since he seemed to be stuck with his sorry state, he was content just to belong.

But as his body had mummified over the years, so had his mind. On the one hand he got wilder and stronger, which were certainly useful traits whilst trekking. On the other hand, he was not much fun to be around. Bob knew why Alice was creeped out by Random. Bob was creeped out as well. But mostly she was bored. "Fuck fuck fuck" did not make for stimulating conversation.

Bob listened as one of Carl's pals stumbled by, obviously terrified. Must be that tall warrior type. She heard him muttering, heard him kick the coffee table.

"Where the hell are you guys?" he shouted.

Bob reached out to steady Random, who'd started to pant like a dog when the man walked by. She smiled. Where are we? We're in every front closet in every living room in every house in every fold in this maze, asshole. And my little Alice is upstairs. And soon enough you're going to find that out.

## 16.16

*It was one thing to have visions and write about them, another thing to be in communication with an alien species, and an entirely other thing to be wandering around in the land of the dead, looking for someone she'd never met and trying to avoid these so-called "scary ones." Sina sat on the edge of the quilt-covered bed and buried her face in her hands. She understood why the tuurngait had withdrawn: this was a human mess. And it was humans who would have to make amends now, to right the wrongs, to show themselves worthy of continuing. If the aliens stepped in to fix things, humanity would be forever diminished. She understood that. But she still wished they were here.*

*She'd been hoping for a straight-on fight. Even when she was still teaching, she'd spent her summers on the front lines, monkeywrenching oilrigs and felling HAARP towers with the ICA. She wasn't cut out for these mind games, these magic tricks, this hall of mirrors. How could she fight an enemy she could not even see?*

*She collapsed back onto the bed, letting her fur parka fall open. Elvis looked down on her from his place of honor on the wall, mocking her with his unfathomable smile. As if a pretty-boy in a white jumpsuit knew anything about reality. Sina hated the culture from which such things as Elvis could grow: the fat, comfort-addled Americans that were eating up the planet; people so lost, so corrupted, that they couldn't even see the stupidity of their ways. And here she was trying to help their leader. And the President's new boyfriend. And all because the aliens told her that this President would be different. Sina scoffed. Right. She'd heard that one before.*

*Sina sat back up, leaning over to rip the velvet painting from its nail and tossing it to the floor. The walrus stood guard in the hallway, glancing at her expectantly. When this is over, Sina thought, she was going to have her say about this whole, fucked-up venture.*

*For now, she had to find Immaqa. And Payok whom, despite her best intentions, she had begun to love.*

## 16.17

*Years later, whenever Payok recounted the battle – to his children, to his tribe – he was dismayed at how quickly the tale was told. It didn't feel like it at the time, but in retrospect, all hell had broken loose, only to be quenched like a candle in the rain. It hardly seemed fair. So much loss demanded a longer story. Even the coming of the great spirit Wentshukumishiteu could not outweigh that loss.*

*He'd been running from room to room, knocking things over and breaking mirrors and plates and CDs, smashing the televisions and moving furniture and spreading trash across the floor, trying to figure out where the old woman had gone, and everyone else. Trying to figure out this madhouse. Trying to find his way back. For a moment, when the Earth had first moved, he'd thought he'd heard voices. Immaqa had screamed. He was sure of it. But he could not follow her voice, and every time he entered a room, the messes he'd made had vanished. Except once, when he returned to the kitchen to find the trash can toppled just the way he had left it. It was possible to get back. He knew that. He just didn't know the way.*

*He'd only this minute entered the living room when the ground shook again, harder and for a longer time than before. Payok fell against the bookshelf, toppling books and CDs onto the floor. The front window he'd helped smash earlier, the window that had repaired itself, shattered again, falling into shards of sharp glass. But this time, the window did not restore itself.*

*Then out of the coat closet burst a creature more hideous than he'd ever seen, a skeleton draped in dry flesh and skin, its eye sockets white with fire, shrieking like a dentist's drill. "Fuck fuck fuck fuck you you you!" it screamed. Payok backed up as the skeleton stumbled toward him. The eagle flew at the babbling monster, digging his talons into its eye sockets, blinding it with wingbeats. The skeleton slipped on the CDs and crashed to the floor, smashing its skull on the coffee table.*

*Payok knew then what the angakkuq, Aua, had meant so many years ago. Aua had told the explorer, Knud Rasmussen, "We don't believe. We fear."*

*Payok ran.*

## 16.18

Linda yelped and hunkered down over Cole. The second tremor sent a burning log rolling right toward them. Only the quick response of Aamai saved them from being burned. He stepped in and kicked away the flaming wood just moments before the log would have hit Cole's face. Linda sheltered Cole's body with her own, waiting for the quaking to stop, listening to the hurried, worried sound of cracking ice and rock as it pinged and moaned and echoed through the rocky ledge beneath her. She imagined the Earth opening up and swallowing them all, and shivered at the thought of being trapped, once again, in the fierce and torturous blackness underground. She pressed closer to Cole, her body heavy with alarm and exhaustion. It felt as if somebody were lying on top of her. Had Rice somehow followed her here, and was it he who was now trying to shake her apart?

The trembling stopped. Cautiously, Linda raised her head to look around. Despite the wind and the shaking ground, the Inuit woman across the circle continued to pound her frame drum. Linda pulled up a wobbling knee, as if she would try to stand.

Aamai squatted next to her and put a hand on her shoulder. "You okay?" he shouted into her ear.

Linda nodded, turning to face the Inuit. Snow spilled from her hood and onto Cole's tranquil face. "You?" The wind had grown so fierce that it seemed to snatch the word from her mouth and fling it into the darkness. She could barely hear herself.

"We're fine!" shouted the Inuit, grinning in the firelight. He looked up as someone called out from across the circle, then put his mouth to Linda's ear. "Stay low!" he shouted. He stood and walked away.

Linda gave him the thumbs up. She brushed the snow from Cole's eyes, then lowered her face to his, creating a tent with her hood, holding it with cold, tight fingers to keep back the storm.

Aamai and two others went about the difficult task of rebuilding the fire.

### 16.19

Alice sat in the bedroom closet, eyes closed, watching things unfold. She was glad her mother had chosen her for this mission. Someone needed to guard the sleeping humans in the bed beyond the closet door. Here, alone, she had time to think. Only one fold away, she could hear the man snoring. She wondered what was wrong with his breathing system, that it made this odd noise.

Something had shifted. When her father's people withdrew five days ago, Alice had begun to notice something in her body. It was in her chest, right above her lungs, near her throat. A tightening. A constriction. She surveyed her systems and found all to be in order. This was something new. It was as if her body was responding to the news of the alive ones' departure. When the human girl made tears, the sensation in her body had intensified.

Mr. Rice said it was a test. That resonated with her fundamental vibrations. But she thought he was mistaken about the alive ones' intentions. It was not a test for Mr. Rice and her mother, or for the organization they called the People. It was a testing for all humans. A trial. An ultimate task. A testing of this snoring man and the woman at his side. A testing of this President Linda they kept chasing. A testing of these fur-clad ones now stumbling about in the house.

Alice was no longer convinced that her father's people wished for Mr. Rice to succeed. Which meant that her own mother might be mistaken as well.

A shout came from below. Her mother's voice. Alice rose, stepping out into the empty room. Perhaps she should go discuss this before things got out of hand.

### 16.20

Utterpok shuffled back and forth across the living room floor, beating his drum and chanting a song. Grace could not make out the words. The polar bear paced the hallway between the back door and the front.

*The old shaman stopped and opened his eyes, an inner light glowing through his pupils. He winked at Grace. "Fast cars, fast deals with Kenny Fast," he said, his eyes sparkling. He closed them and began to chant again.*

*Grace smiled. She knew what he was doing. He was refusing to believe.*

### 16.21

*Obie knew he had an advantage over his enemies; he could empathize. Because he could share the feelings of others, he knew that Mr. Random, though resigned to his situation, really wanted nothing more than to be set free. He wanted to die a final death. His cries and shrieks were not the cartoonish rantings of a monster. They were the desperate, piteous pleas of a man in pain. He simply had no idea how to let go and move on. He didn't even know that he could. And so Obie could trust that this house would fall. Born of Random's mind, it wanted to die as well. For Obie, it was simply a matter of aligning with what already wanted to happen. He could help it do what it wanted to do, and in that, serve the highest good for all, including Mr. Random.*

*Obie sat in the recliner and focused his mind. His ears heard the distant sobbing of Immaqa, the harried footsteps of Payok running in the hallway upstairs, the chanting of Utterpok. But he could not let these things distract him. Dust filtered down from the ceiling above as the old woman pounded and pounded on the bathroom walls. Obie ignored it.*

*Obie did not believe in this Confusion. He did believe in earthquakes. All that mattered was that this house fall down. He knew that it would. And because he knew that it would, it did.*

### 16.22

*"Go back upstairs, Alice!" snarled Bob. She pushed her daughter aside and kicked the Inuit girl, the one they called "Immaqa," again and again. She'd have preferred just jumping inside the little bitch's brain and exploding her mind from the inside out but something*

*about these walrus-fuckers' trance kept her locked out. So be it.*
*She'd do it the old-fashioned way.*

*The girl was pathetic, really. She'd fallen down the stairs and*
*broken her ankle, poor little dear, and all she could do was pull her-*
*self away on her elbows, trying to hide under the dining room table,*
*begging like... well... a little girl. Stupid! Like she even had an ankle*
*here to break. Is this all you have for fighters, Carl? Gods, man, did*
*you really think you could beat us?*

*Bob grabbed the girl's legs, pulled her out from under the table*
*and kicked her once right in the head. The little bitch finally shut the*
*hell up. Random knelt beside her and tasted the blood that seeped*
*from her temple.*

*Remembering her father's admonition to "always use the right*
*tool for the job at hand," Bob materialized a small black cube in her*
*palm: a rubix. She knew that she couldn't actually kill somebody*
*on the astral with kicks to the head. That was just for fun. To get*
*rid of someone in this realm, the quick and easy answer was to toss*
*them down a black hole. Then the techs could mop up the bodies*
*matter-side at their leisure. Bob twisted the rubix and tossed it at*
*the Inuit chick. Random scooted back. The girl was sucked inside*
*the cube as it disappeared through the floorboards.*

*One down, seven to go, thought Bob. She wiped her boot on the*
*rug and walked into the kitchen for a glass of water, smiling at how*
*powerful the Confusion was. Like she really had boots to have blood*
*on! She thought for a moment of her parents back in Cleveland, long*
*since dead in prison. She smiled. They'd have been so proud.*

*Bob failed to notice the look on Alice's face, the slight, almost*
*imperceptible grimaces that had flashed across her tiny face as Bob*
*had delivered her kicks. Alice was not proud.*

### 16.23

*Evlyn hooted as she pounded the bathroom walls. The shower tiles*
*had cracked and broken away and the pipes had burst, spraying the*
*floor with a mist of hot water. And already there were fractures around*
*the room's edges, as if her pounding, and the earthquakes, would*
*splinter this place to brick and timber. It felt good, the pounding, the*

*destruction of this house. She'd lived so many lives. She'd been stabbed, beaten, raped and murdered too many times to count. She was tired of it. The human race had gone to shit. If they couldn't muster the moral resolve to pull themselves out of the slime into which they'd fallen, then they deserved to be sent back to "Go."*

*A large piece of the ceiling fell onto the sink behind her, not just wallboard but joists and insulation. She could see straight through to the roof, where a beam of darkness shone through a crack in the sheathing. She smiled and went back to her pounding.*

*The old woman was furious. She'd been helping and they killed her! And that poor little girl! She'd sacrificed her own life for her father. Evlyn beat the wall with her fists and the whole house shuddered underfoot. She could do no less than that little girl.*

### 16.24

*When the house shook again Ruth screamed.*

*Cole pounded back up the stairs and burst into their room. "You okay?"*

*"What's going on?" asked Ruth, sitting up on the bed. The sounds of distant pounding and a girl sobbing had awakened them both. Now the whole house was shaking, as if they were having an earthquake. Ruth grabbed her robe and stepped into her slippers. A loud scraping sound came from above and she looked up, expecting to see the little girl Cole had spoken of, lifting off their Barbie's Dream House roof. The scraping stopped. She looked at her husband with panic in her eyes. "Did you see anything downstairs?"*

*Cole shook his head. "There's CDs all over the floor. Otherwise, nothing."*

*"What's happening?" asked Ruth, stepping into Cole's arms.*

*"I don't know," he sighed into her hair.*

*The velvet Elvis fell to the floor.*

### 16.25

*The roof of the house rose up and tumbled away as if a tornado had taken it. At once they were all together again, left confused* and shaken in rooms all over the same little house, as though scattered like cornhusks by the twister. Their opponents were there as well, and were already attacking. Random made for Obie as the latter rose out of the recliner. Obie tried to dodge the skeleton as he approached but Random was impossibly fast, putting Obie into a chokehold from behind before Obie could complete his move. The fox nipped at Random's legs. The living room wall behind the recliner fell outward into the blackness.

Utterpok and the polar bear, now standing side by side, started toward Bob in the dining room. Bob launched herself at them feet first, kicking them both in the chest with such force that they tumbled away like bowling pins. The bear landed on Grace, pinning her against the sofa. Dennis managed to squirm away. The polar bear righted himself and tried again.

Alice slipped out the front door.

Sina sped down the hallway from the back and slammed into Bob just as she regained her footing. They fell to the floor; the Inuit woman's hands clutched at the distorted woman's neck. The walrus huffed up and pinned Bob's legs. The polar bear caught her foot in his jaws. The floor underneath them buckled.

Payok rushed into the room from upstairs, his eagle landing on Bob's face and digging in with its talons. Evlyn followed and began pounding on Bob's stomach. Payok turned to help Utterpok to his feet. Obie and Random held fast in their embrace; Obie pulled desperately at the skeleton's sharp fingers as they sought to close his windpipe.

Bob exploded. That's how it looked to Payok. A detonation of radiance and power filled the dining room, tossing back Sina and the polar bear and old woman like test dummies, like paper dolls, like leaves in the wind. Dennis barked a furious warning. When the explosion dimmed they saw Bob, standing calmly with a slight smile on her face. In her hand was a small, black cube. "You guys are a joke," she said. She twisted the rubix and threw it at Obie.

"No!" shouted Utterpok and Grace at the same time. Utterpok tried to deflect the cube with his hands. The cube drew him in as it passed and he was gone. The polar bear flickered out. The cube was not deflected.

*Obie saw her throw. He wrapped a leg around the skeleton, twisted and let himself fall, bringing Mr. Random into the path of the approaching rubix. Random was sucked away as the cube passed over Obie, sparing him a similar fate. The air was filled for just a moment with Mr. Random's final words: "Thank thank thank thank thank!" he shouted. The rubix disappeared through the wall. It was over in seconds.*

*"Goddamn you, Carl!" shouted Bob.*

*The Confusion buckled and quaked again. The floor beneath Bob fell away, taking her with it. Through the gaping hole in the floorboards, all they could see was starless black.*

*Grace walked to where Utterpok had disappeared, her face lined with tears. She picked up his drumstick where he'd dropped it. His drum was nowhere to be found.*

## 16.26

Linda pushed herself to her feet when Cole's tarp was ripped away by the gale. The cold wind tore through her body like shrapnel, leaving her joints so stiff that it hurt to move. She looked around for Aamai, hoping to wave him down and get his help. Her Inuit musher was over by the woman with the drum, dancing with two other Inuit men and another woman. The four of them were pounding a slow, steady rhythm on the ice with their feet, as if calling on the Earth itself for help and protection.

Linda looked down at Cole. Snow was drifting quickly around his body. Though she was loath to interrupt the dancers, Linda needed some help to find another tarp. She took a quick step forward and then stopped. A dreaded voice had started laughing in her ear. Rice! It felt as if that bastard hovered right beside her, breathing down her neck. Linda quivered with revulsion at the thought of his hands on her. She heard Rice shout "Now!" Then the shooting started.

Rising over the lip of the rock ledge was a ship, a larger version of the "wok" she'd ridden in, glowing blue-hot against the dark sky, hovering in place as if the wind could not touch it.

Out of the top popped two men in black uniforms with rifles. They aimed and fired down on the circle.

Linda screamed as bright beams of yellow power pulsed and spattered across the circle. The Inuit screamed and scattered. Linda fell down onto Cole, shielding him with her body. She looked up to see a beam of light cut across the old shaman's chest.

## 16.27

*Evlyn knew that a fall through a floor would not spell the end of the distorted woman. She was right. Bob flew up out of the hole and hovered in the air above the dining room table. "Alice!" she screamed in a rage.*

*Alice was nowhere to be seen.*

*"She left," said Grace, stepping forward, her head held high.*

*Bob looked down on the girl. "You're the little shit that got in the way before," she said with disgust.*

*"She didn't like what she saw," said Grace, ignoring Bob's words.*

*"Who?" said Bob.*

*"Alice," said Grace, stepping closer. "She sees what you've become. She sees how sick you are." Dennis stepped quietly to Grace's side.*

*Bob held out her hand. "You're next sweetie," she said with a grotesque, melted smile.*

*While Grace spoke with her, Payok, Sina and the old woman surrounded Bob from behind. Before she could materialize another cube they were on her, pulling her to the tabletop and engulfing her in arms and legs and bodies. Bob exploded again but this time her opponents were not thrown off. Their interwoven arms and legs and fingers and hearts and intentions held them tightly together. Grace's words had shifted things. This woman was sick. She needed help. And they knew that, to help her, they first had to contain her.*

*Bob struggled, biting and kicking like a lunatic, trying to rise into the air above and then falling back down under the weight of her adversaries. She let loose a bloodcurdling scream that split the walls around her. The kitchen fell away into splinters and dust. The neighborhood beyond the walls bowed and buckled and broke into pieces. Bob screamed again and again and again, heaving with unspent rage. Sina and Payok held fast. As she hummed an old French children's song, Evlyn engulfed them all with her light.*

*After a while Bob's screaming turned to sobs.*

## 16.28

*"My God," whispered Cole. The stairs had been ripped away from the wall, leaving huge gaps where the cold night air seeped in. He stepped forward, holding onto Ruth's hand as she followed. The noise had abated. All they could hear now was a woman's quiet weeping. They had to go see what was happening.*

*"Cole?" said Ruth, her voice urging caution.*

*"The house is falling apart, sweetie," he said, turning to whisper in her ear. "It's not safe. We have to get out of here."*

*Cole tested the top step with his right foot. It shifted a bit, but felt strong enough to hold his weight. He took another step and turned to Ruth. "It's okay," he said. Together they crept down the stairs.*

*Ruth gasped. The house was half gone. What remained was a shambles. At the bottom of the stairs stood a strange man in a long, red robe. He looked like something out of the French Renaissance. He nodded as she and Cole neared him and passed by. In the dining room a pair of what looked like Eskimos, and an old, old woman made, it seemed, from light, held a young woman in their arms. The young woman's face was buried in the old woman's neck. She was the one who'd been crying. Next to them stood a cute little girl in overalls, and her skinny little dog. And everywhere there were animals. A little fox stood on the sofa, watching them. An eagle perched on top of the stereo. And a huge walrus filled the floor in front of the Eskimos, scratching its belly with both flippers.*

*"What—?" said Ruth, awe and confusion in her voice. It was all she could think to say.*

*The little girl brightened. "Hi Mom. Hi Dad," she said. The little dog thumped his tail against the floor.*

*An aftershock rumbled and the rest of the house fell away, and the neighborhood with it, leaving them all suspended in the heart of a bright, blue nebula, a buckled wood floor beneath them and the old brown sofa sitting crookedly at the edge. Ruth and Cole looked at each other. They both knew exactly where they were.*

*One of the Eskimos screamed in pain and disappeared.*

## 16.29

The ground shook again and Linda shouted, coughing as the icy wind filled her throat. A beam of yellow sliced an Inuit man in half right in front of her, then swept across the circle, slicing across Payok's arm as it moved. She and Cole would be next.

Suddenly, the rock beneath the wok exploded upward in a torrent of stone and dust. Linda watched in confusion and disbelief as huge, monstrous jaws pushed up from the Earth and swallowed the flying ship, the men, and their rifles, in a single, crushing mouthful. The beast fell back into the Earth like a breaching whale falls back into the sea, leaving a pile of boulders where none had been before. The ground stopped shaking. The wind fell to silence. The snow diminished to a few stray flakes and the clouds broke apart, revealing the first light of dawn.

Aamai and the others stopped dancing. The woman who'd been beating the drum stood and stared at the pile of boulders. "Wentshukumishiteu!" she said. She fell on her knees with arms overhead and bowed in awed thanksgiving.

Linda, overwhelmed by the impossibility of what had just happened, remembered to breathe, and grounded herself in the physical: she brushed the snow from Cole's face and bent to listen to his heart. It was still beating.

## 16.30

*"What the fuck!" shouted Rice as his soldiers disappeared. He stormed up onto the ledge and kicked at a boulder. "You assholes get back here!" he screamed.*

*The boulder was unimpressed.*

16.31

Cole turned at the touch of a hand on his shoulder.

"We have to go, little brother," said Obie.

Cole turned back to Ruth, sitting on the sofa with Grace snuggled in her arms. He needed to say something but he didn't know what.

Ruth smiled. "I know, Cole," she said softly. "You have work to do. So go do it."

Cole looked down at his feet, and then back at Ruth. Tears clogged his throat. He nodded once, smiled with thanks and love, then turned to Obie. "What about Grace?" he asked.

"They've got some catching up to do, bro. Leave 'em be. They'll figure things out."

Cole leaned over and put a hand on Grace's head. "I'll see you back home, girl," he said. The words cut at his heart. He did not know if he could make them come true.

Grace opened her eyes and smiled. "Take care of Cornfed, Daddy," she said. She closed her eyes and buried her face against her mother's neck.

Cole reached out and took Ruth's hand and squeezed. "I'll see you," he said.

"Yeah," answered Ruth. She buried her face in Grace's hair and closed her eyes.

Cole turned. There stood Obie, with the Eskimo woman standing behind him, her face pained with worry. The crying young woman had slipped quietly out the front door when her captors released her. The old woman of light had followed close behind. The animals had apparently all wandered away. "So how do we do this?" asked Cole.

"Click your heels and repeat these words: there's no place like home." Obie grinned.

"Forgot my ruby slippers, Obie," said Cole. "You got another way?"

Obie shrugged, turning to include Sina, now traveling without her angakkuq and her warrior. "Getting home's the easy part," he said to them all. "You're already there. Your bodies eagerly await you, ready to reconnect. Just open your eyes."

*"My eyes are already open, Obie," said Cole.*
*Obie shook his head. "Your other eyes, little bro," he said.*
*Cole opened his other eyes.*

## 16.32

Linda gasped. "Cole!" she cried, bursting into tears. She threw herself down onto him, burying her face in his neck and squeezing him tight.

Cole reached out and patted her back with fumbling, mittened hands. "Hello, Linda," he said softly.

All of Linda's doubt and worry melted away at the sound of his voice. It just didn't fucking matter anymore. Whether the aliens had manipulated her or not, her heart still longed for this man. For now, she could let it be. She raised her head and kissed him gently on the lips, afraid to scare him away again. Cole's eyes welled with joyful tears.

The sound of boots crunching on snow interrupted their reunion. They both looked up. There stood Obie, his face grim.

"We could use your help," he said, gesturing around him.

Cole and Linda looked out across the circle.

The ground was littered with bodies.

# Chapter ⦰ Seventeen

17.1

Alice nodded at the two privates at the door, who stood with rifles drawn and comms in hand. Alice understood. The entire operation was on alert this morning, since Mr. Rice's return. Sick to death from trekking and furious at his defeat, he'd lashed out at anybody and everybody he could. These soldiers understood that the children behind this door were key to the future of this organization. The General's surprise visit an hour ago had made that very clear. The soldiers were not about to let Mr. Rice down. They had seen him angry before.

Rice had tried to flick over to the Confusion, Alice eventually learned, just after some huge creature had swallowed his shooters. But the signal was lost by then. He'd immediately popped back to the physical to learn that Bob had not yet returned. "Get the fuck back here!" Alice had heard him screaming to her mother's body in the room next door. She'd risen at the sound of a crashing lamp and stepped out into the hallway to find Mr. Rice on his hands and knees, vomiting on the tile.

"What the fuck happened?" he'd demanded, seeing Alice out of the corner of his eye.

"We were defeated," replied Alice, evenly.

"Defeated?" laughed Rice through his vomit. "We don't get defeated, baby-cakes. We don't—" Rice had moaned in pain, wretched and heaved, and then recovered enough to speak. "How could we be defeated?"

Alice had watched curiously. Mr. Rice had been too long between treks. The effects on his body were worse than ever. She'd stepped back quickly as Rice hit the floor, fainting face-first into his undigested cheeseburger.

Alice looked up to the soldiers at the door. "I need to speak with the human children," she said. She did not expect to be challenged. As part of the Trekking Team, and as a fully functional Earthside human-alien hybrid, she far outranked these soldiers, even in her tiny body. The privates stepped aside. One of them punched the lockpad and the door slid open.

It was darker in the little room. Alice adjusted her eyes, then turned to the soldiers. "You may close the door," she said. They looked at her blankly, then the closer of the two shrugged and touched the pad. The door slid shut.

The female, Emily, was lying on her cot, her face red and raw from a night of tears. The male was sitting at the table. His face was tight with what Alice knew to be anger. They were watching her closely.

"Your father has been restored," said Alice, having calculated that this would be the best way to begin.

"What?" said Emily, sitting up.

"Your father's soul has been reconnected to his body," Alice explained. "He now lives as you do."

"Why should we believe you?" asked the male, Iain.

"It is what is so," explained Alice.

Emily stood and stepped quickly toward the tiny hybrid. "Are you here to help us?" she asked, her voice shaking. She reached out and touched Alice's upper arm, hesitantly, as though petting a wild animal. "Can you get us out of here? Can you take us—?" Emily stopped, choking on a sob.

Alice nodded. "The alive ones have withdrawn from Mr. Rice and the Plan. I will now follow their lead. We must leave this place before Mr. Rice acts to prohibit us." Alice headed to the door, then turned. "I will return as soon as I can."

"You're leaving?" asked Emily.

"I must make sure my mother cannot follow us," said Alice.

Iain was now standing as well. "How do we get out of here, Alice?"

Alice looked up at him, noting the expression on his face. Her mother would have called that look "hope" and laughed at it with scorn. But Alice noticed the curious, warming sensation in her chest and found that she enjoyed it. She sensed she was sharing in the sensations of these two human children. It was almost as if she were one of them. "The soldiers will stop me if I try to escort you through the facility," she said. "We will attempt another way. Though I do not know if it will work."

"What way?" asked Emily.

Alice stepped over to the wall and pushed her hand and forearm into it as if it were nothing but illusion. She pulled her hand back out of solid rock and turned to face the human children. "This way," she said.

Iain's eyes went wide. Emily took a step back in surprise, then smiled and nodded. Alice imagined sitting one day with these two and speaking to them of their lives, and of her own. There would be so much to learn. The thought of that brought forth again the warming sensation in her chest.

"My father's people could escort you this way with ease," said Alice. "For myself, I am unsure of my abilities. I am a new type of being and my limitations and talents are not yet fully understood. But we have help on the other side."

"Help?" asked Emily.

"Yes," nodded Alice. "Another like myself, though very unlike. I met him only recently. His name is Jack."

## 17.2

The plane smacked into the ground and Ruth screamed and the sky flashed like lightning and Cole awoke from his dream to hear a soft knock at the door. "Yeah?" he said, groggily.

"We need to get going," said Obie through the door. His voice was thick with regret.

Cole sighed. "Just a sec," he said. He rubbed at his eyes. The light through the bedroom shades was gray and lifeless. The sky must have clouded over, he thought. It had been sunny before. But it was still the same day. They'd only slept a few hours. He breathed deeply, letting the cool air rouse his lungs and stir his blood. It was time to get moving again. There would be no real rest until this was finished. Sina had already arranged their flight.

Linda stirred beside him, rolling over to trap him with her right arm. Her fingers rested on his bare stomach. "You can't go," she whispered.

Cole smiled. Going was the last thing he wanted to do. Yet Obie's request could not be ignored. He hugged her to him, rubbing her shoulder and head with his hand. He still hadn't gotten used to his own body, let alone hers. The aliens had changed it. It felt stronger, smoother, calmer, younger. As if the aliens, having taken him into the shop for a blown head gasket, had thrown in a full tune-up and detailing for free. There was an energy coursing through him now that he'd never known before. And he could feel it in Linda as well. They were both ... awake.

"We gotta get up, sweetie," he said gently. Linda groaned and Cole hugged her tighter. He understood. The day had almost destroyed them all. The injured were given first aid and transported quickly by snowcat back to Akkituyok. The bodies of Utterpok, Immaqa and the others, sliced to pieces by the killers Rice had summoned, were an assault on everyone; their blood, spilled out on the snow and ice, created stains that would never wash clean. Some of the survivors stayed behind to prepare the dead for burial, wrapping the bodies in caribou hides. They took them by dogsled and snowmobile out onto the snow-covered tundra, where they would be left face up, protected by traditional cairns of stones. The morning's work was accompanied by loud weeping and the shedding of many tears. The Inuit did not speak much, though more than one commented on the aptness of their hamlet's name: "costs much."

The funerary ritual would take place late in the night. Cole and Linda asked to attend but were refused; they would not be allowed to stay that long. "We will risk our tribe no further," said Sina, her grief and anger palpable. Feeling both guilt and regret, neither Cole nor Linda were inclined to argue. Cole's resurrection, and what assistance the Inuit had given Linda, had come at the price of great and personal loss to Sina's group.

As if to add to the confusion, the Strangers returned at dawn, filling the sky with ships of all shapes and sizes. They passed overhead in slow, somber sweeps like mourners in a funeral parlor, keeping their distance and yet claiming their right to be there. Most of the Inuit noted the aliens' appearance and then ignored them. Sina scowled at the sky for a full minute before turning her back. It seemed she had anger enough for the Tuurngait as well.

Being so far out of their element, there was little Cole and Linda could do to really help the Inuit grieve. So they carried and gathered and packed and hauled when an extra hand was needed, eyes low, heads bowed in deep thanks and deeper sorrow. Both sighed with relief when Aamai told them it was time for them to leave.

He took them back on his sled, saying little to Cole and Linda the entire hour. He sang softly to his dogs instead, a quiet dirge that rose above the shushing of the sled runners and evaporated in the silence of the clear, blue sky. At one point he stopped the sled and went to sit amongst his team, sobbing loudly. The dogs whined cheerlessly, in communion with their musher. After a while Aamai returned to the sled and took his position. The dogs understood, and pulled them quietly across the snow without a word.

"You take my bedroom in the back," Aamai told them, when they stepped into the trailer. It was ten o'clock in the morning. Cole was about to protest but Linda stopped him with a touch to his arm. She took his hand and they walked down the hall, closing the door behind them. With a finger to her lips to silence him, she pulled back the covers, sat on the bed, and began to remove her clothes, motioning for Cole to do the same. They undressed quickly, eyes furtive and shy, and crawled into each other's arms. There Linda wept deeply, releasing her grief and joy. Soon they were both asleep.

Cole snapped out of his reverie when his brother knocked again. "Cole?" Obie said, his voice sharp with impatience.

"Coming," said Cole. He pushed back the comforter and stood to pull on his clothes. "Gotta get up, Linda," he said again, leaning over to rub her legs. Linda opened her eyes and got up, struggling to keep herself somewhat covered with the blanket, but then giving up the struggle. She stepped into the bathroom to pee, then pulled on her long johns, jeans and flannel shirt. Cole stood watching as she came back out. Linda reached up to rub her head. "You like it?" she said with an uncertain smile.

Cole nodded. "Love it," he said. "You ready?"

Linda took a deep breath, glancing nervously at the door, then back to Cole. She smiled bravely. "I guess."

Cole opened the door and they headed back to the living room. Obie was sitting cross-legged in the recliner. Payok sat on the futon, his eyes dark, his left arm and hand bandaged where the energy beam had hit him while he lay in trance. Sina sat next to him, her face taut and drained.

The young visionary stood as they entered the room. "Thirteen," she said, lifting her chin in defiance.

"Thirteen?" said Cole.

"Thirteen dead," said Sina. Her hands made their way to her hips. Her eyes held Cole's like the talons of an eagle. "You'd better be worth it, you son-of-a-bitch."


## 17.3

Cole and Linda sat side-by-side in ladder-back wooden chairs pulled from the table. Linda glared. It felt like they were on trial and she didn't like it. She opened her mouth to speak but Obie stopped her with a gesture.

He looked at Cole. "I just got back from Clare's," he said, gesturing with a nod toward the hotel in the town center. "She's got a phone. I spoke with an Officer Fairly in Hindrance." Obie stopped, glancing nervously toward the two Inuit. He uncrossed his legs and leaned forward a bit. "Both your daughter, Grace, and our father are in the hospital, Cole," he said. "And Emily and Iain are missing."

"What?" said Cole, rising from his chair. He stared down at his brother. His hands were shaking. "Is Grace OK?" he demanded. "What did Ken say? When did all this happen?" He took a deep breath, looking from face to face, then sat back down heavily. He rubbed his eyes with his fingertips, then looked at his older brother.

"Fairly says he spoke with Dad yesterday afternoon, just before Dad drove Grace up to the medical center in Waitsfield. Says that Grace had fallen into a coma the night before. Wouldn't wake up in the morning. Last night Fairly got a call. Sometime between seven and eight. An anonymous tip reporting a shooting and a house fire. Fairly notified the fire department and raced up to find Dad on the front yard, shot in the gut. Both of Dad's security guards were dead. No sign of Iain or Emily. By the time the fire squad arrived the house was almost gone."

A dark cloud passed across Cole's face. "Were there—?" His voice was choked and wobbly.

Obie shook his head. "I asked. Fire inspectors went through the remains late this morning. No sign of Emily or Iain inside. But you need to know something, Cole. I don't know if you noticed this when we found you in that house, but Grace's cord has been severed. She's untethered now, just as you were."

"What cord?" said Cole, shaking his head in confusion.

"The astral cord, bro. Some call it the silver cord. It's a visual representation of the strong connection that exists between one's spirit, as it travels the astral realms, and their body, that waits back in the physical. Grace's cord has gone missing."

"Oh, Christ," moaned Cole. Tears squeezed from his eyes and flowed down his face.

"Yeah," said Obie. He took a deep breath, as if making space for Cole's fear and grief. "I'm not sure we can know exactly what that means," he went on. "Her body's in a hospital in Vermont, apparently. Her spirit ... well, we both saw her in the house. But we do know, now, that the two can be rejoined." He smiled gently.

Cole exhaled heavily and looked down at his lap.

"Fairly said that Dad's in bad shape, but he's stable. The cops have no idea who did it, and Dad's not talking. But we, of course, can guess what happened."

"Fucking Rice," murmured Linda.

Obie nodded. "I should have known this was a possibility," he said, looking directly at his brother. "Rice always takes out an insurance policy when he can."

"We have to get down there," said Cole, rising, panic in his eyes. He looked around the room, as if he would grab his wallet and keys and rush out the door.

"So the white man's just gonna jump into the trap," offered Payok gruffly. "Looks like this Rice knows what he's doing."

Cole whirled angrily to face the Inuit warrior. Then he stopped. Payok's eyes were tired, tight with grief and pain. Cole took a long breath, then turned back to Obie. "So what do we do now?" he asked. He sat back down.

Obie put his hands up as if in denial of his brother's assumption. He shook his head. "Wish I could help, little bro, but I'm not leading the dance now. You tell me."

Cole leaned back but made no reply.

Linda reached over and took Cole's hand, then looked at Sina with one raised eyebrow. "What do you need from us?" she said.

"Redemption," said Sina without hesitation.

"Redemption," repeated Linda, nodding, as if Sina had given the answer she'd expected. "For the loss of your sister, Immaqa. And your shaman, Utterpok. And the eleven others of your group who died today."

Sina sat without expression, giving Linda nothing.

The President continued. "Redemption for the costs you've borne to help us." She looked back and forth between the two Inuit. "You want justice. You want this all to make sense. You want this loss to be honored. You want it to count for something. You want my promise to be fulfilled."

Slowly, almost against her will, Sina nodded.

Linda frowned, irritated at Sina's failure to see who she really was. "I want the same, Sina," she said, tossing back her head. Her breathing had become hard and quick and she inhaled deeply and held it, in an attempt to calm herself. Her eyes had grown fierce. "I too want redemption. I want justice. I want it all to count for something." She glanced over at Cole. His eyes were red. His face was wet. She turned back to Sina. "Cole and I bear the cost as well," she said, "as you've just heard." She gestured toward Obie with a nod of her head. "My chief of staff was murdered. And my friend Pooch—" Linda stopped. Her throat had clogged with grief. She swallowed her pain and continued, her voice suddenly quiet and ragged. "My mother has been taken. Just like Cole's kids. We don't know..." She looked down at her lap, then back up at Sina, letting silence say the rest as she held the young woman's gaze. The room was still. There was no wind. In the kitchen a clock ticked.

"And Ruth," said Cole, breaking the stillness, his voice low.

Linda turned to face him. She squeezed his fingers. "What about Ruth?" she asked.

Cole's face was white with confusion. His eyes were closed. "I ... I remember it now. A dream I woke up with. Just before Obie knocked. I was in an airplane. A jet. There was a UFO dogging us, just past the left wingtip. The pilots said something about turning back. And then this bright flash." Cole sighed softly, his eyes moving rapidly under their lids as if he were watching a movie. More tears spilled out over his cheeks. He exhaled deeply, then opened his eyes and looked at Linda. "They ... they shot down Ruth's plane," he said. "They showed me. They let me experience the whole thing."

Linda nodded gently. "Yeah. We saw. That's where we found your body. In the wreckage."

Cole frowned. "Why would they show me?" he asked. "How could those bastards...?"

Sina rose from the futon and knelt at Cole's feet, taking both of his hands in her own. "You must hear me," she said. Cole's eyes focused on hers. "The Tuurngait – the aliens – they exact a heavy price. And they demand that we meet them as they are, not as who we would wish them to be. This is who they are, Cole Thomas. You must understand this. They are beings – spirits, gods, demons, angels, aliens, whatever – willing to interfere with events in this realm so that you could one day meet the woman who would be President of the United States, so that you could partner with her, and help her do what she must now do. Just as they were willing to spend the life of my sister to bring you back. Perhaps it is ours to judge them. Perhaps not. I do not know. I know that I am sometimes furious at the prices they demand. But judge them or no, we must first work to move beyond our emotional reactions, so that we may see them as clearly as we can, and see the true reality they reveal to us. Only then can we make our choice freely, to either align with them or resist them."

Sina glanced for a moment at Linda before returning to Cole. "Your people have strayed far from the mark, with your culture of exploitation and consumption and growth. With your addiction to comfort and material wealth. You have offended the Universe deeply. You have broken the rules that govern all of life on this planet. Were the consequences of your actions contained within your own borders I would leave you to your fate. But that is not the case. Your sins threaten us all. That is why I agreed to help. You can complain neither of exploitation nor disregard at the hands of the aliens. They simply treat you as you have treated all life on this planet." A scowl came to Sina's face as she spoke, tightening the tattoos on her face, bringing harsh focus to the glare in her eyes. Her grip on Cole's hands tightened. "The spirits will be satisfied," she said huskily, "just as the god Wentshukumishiteu demanded payment this morning. Do not sneer at the bargains they offer you. After the destruction your way of life has caused, you'll be lucky to get anything at all."

Sina rose, breathing deeply. Her face fell to peaceful calm as though, having expressed her anger, she could now make room in her heart for compassion and empathy. She leaned forward to kiss both Cole and Linda on their foreheads, like a blessing. She stood back and glanced at Payok, who rose to stand beside her, cradling his arm and hand against his stomach. "My people need me," she said with a slight smile. "I must go. Transportation has been arranged. May the spirits be with you on your journey."

Sina strode to the trailer door with Payok in tow, then turned and spoke to Cole. "This is not about your children," she said, "though I shall pray for them." She looked at Linda. "This is not about avenging your mother." She glanced back and forth between them. "This is about the whole of life on this planet. You need but listen. The whales are singing to you even now. The eagles cry. The polar bears chuff and growl. The Arctic bumblebees fly and buzz. Even your own people are tossing and groaning in the nightmares of their lives. When you understand this, you will begin to understand the Tuurngait a little bit."

The Inuit prophet turned her gaze to Obie and her eyes softened further. A smile crept onto her face and sat there for a moment, happy to come in from the cold. "Goodbye, my friend," she said at last. "Remember that a hunt that fails to show proper respect will give the offended spirits cause to avenge themselves. And remember that the age of separation has ended, as we spoke of that first night. Your Mr. Rumi was correct. There *is* a field. Perhaps one day we'll meet there."

"I'd like that," said Obie.

Sina nodded once. Then she and Payok were gone.

### 17.4

Mary had stuck with the busiest Interstates. Though traffic was not nearly as heavy as it had been even a few years ago, and though the road surfaces were suffering greatly from a lack of maintenance, the Interstates gave Mary the sense of comfort she sorely needed. In the summer of Mary's thirteenth year, her Aunt Allison had taken her on a road trip across the country, giving the shy, lanky teenager a two-week reprieve from her father's insanity. It was her first taste of the larger world, and her first awakening to the notion that there were other ways, besides her father's way, for human beings to be. Ever since, the Interstates had meant freedom to Mary. Freedom and safety. She rolled down her window to let the cool autumn air soothe her fatigue. Her stomach was sour and heavy. She did not know what awaited her in D.C., but she suspected that, at some point, she would come once again face-to-face with the unpredictability of Theodore Rice.

Mary exhaled loudly, trying to dispel her anxiety. Where was Rice now? And Bob? Where were Linda and her friend Cole? Mary had no way to know. It had been almost three days since she'd fled the People. Three days since she'd extracted her implants. Three days since she'd unplugged from the web of information on which she'd grown to depend. She was flying blind. And she was scared. Rice must have taken Cole's kids, thinking he could use them to control the President. Maybe they were down in the Rock, right now. The thought made her heart pound. She knew she could not let him get away with such things.

But she also knew she was not really flying blind. It was more like she was operating on instinct, following promptings and whispers she might previously have ignored. It was as if she had a shard of lodestone buried in her heart, leading her towards, always towards. Where she would end up she could not say, for certain, but there were signs and portents along the way.

Mary got onto the inner Beltway just as the sun was nearing the western horizon. She took 295 to New York Avenue NE, a straight shot to the heart of the nation's capitol. She caught a glimpse of the Washington monument. The sun, distended and gleaming in the day's final glory, sat behind the monument's base. The huge orange disc stretched beyond both sides of the national phallus like a pair of glowing testicles. Mary laughed. Even with no real idea of what would come next, she knew that she was in the right place.

Because those testicles were shrinking.

## 17.5

The wok that had brought them all to the far north would not be taking them back south. Linda understood why. It was time to leave their mother's arms and take a few steps on their own. It was time to grow up. Though she had no idea how they'd do that, she knew that they would try. There was no other path to redemption.

She looked through the window to the twilight beyond, wondering what awaited them back home. Cole snored peacefully at her side. Obie had disappeared into the cockpit. This little CJ3 was quieter than the Piper Comanche single-prop that had hopped them from Akkituyok to Resolute Bay. A wealthy supporter of Sina had been waiting for them there on the dirt and snow airstrip. He'd raised an eyebrow as the President boarded, but said nothing. Linda had been impressed. Sina's reach extended farther than she would have guessed. She leaned back and closed her eyes, thankful for the gentle ride. Now she could reflect and make plans.

Once again she was forced to think ahead before the past had even begun to sink in. What had happened back there? Where in the Universe had Cole been? What were these aliens up to? What did it all mean? What she needed was a week of rest and conversation. She needed information and understanding, insight and opinion. Instead, they were wading right back into the fray. There would be little time for rational analysis. Linda smiled to herself at the thought. She wasn't sure the aliens would submit to rational analysis.

Obie came back from the cockpit and smiled as he caught Linda's eye. With a nod of his head he invited her to a conversation at the back of the plane. Kissing Cole gently on the forehead, Linda rose and joined his brother in the last row of seats.

"We're coming up to Baffin right now. We'll follow it south," said Obie in hushed tones. "Beck figures we've got maybe seven hours in the air. Plus a stop in northern Quebec to refuel. Some little place he knows where they won't ask any questions. Don't know how long that'll take, given it's a Sunday night. He won't fly anywhere near D.C., but he's got a friend with a strip on Delmarva. Add another four or five hours to get a car and make the drive."

"Beck is our pilot, I take it," said Linda.

"Yeah. Not his real name, he says. He'd rather not know anything."

Linda laughed quietly. "I don't blame him."

"Yeah." Obie twisted in his seat to face Linda more directly. "So how you feeling, Mrs. President?" he asked. "We haven't had much time to talk."

Linda rubbed at her fuzzy scalp. "Not bad. Tired, mostly. My toes are still frozen from our time out on the ice, but otherwise I'm fine."

Obie nodded toward Cole. "How's my little brother?"

Linda shrugged. "He's okay. Worried about his kids. Distracted. He seems ... different."

"He *is* different. He's been killed and resurrected. It's gonna take him a while to understand what that means." Obie peered over the chair's back to make sure Cole was not listening. "This morning, while we were carrying one of the bodies to the dog-sled, I asked him how long he'd been living in that house with Ruth. He told me that he couldn't be sure, but that it felt like about a year."

"Jesus," said Linda.

Obie nodded. "Yeah. A couple of days for us, a year for Cole, living again as a young man with his wife."

"You saw them there, in his house? And you met Grace? It's all true?" asked Linda.

Obie nodded.

"Did he seem ... I mean, when he realized what was going on. Before you brought him back. Was he—?"

"It's a mind fuck, isn't it?" answered Obie, his eyes soft with compassion. "You fall in love with the guy, then he gets killed, then he comes back, and you learn he's just spent a year with his dead wife? And here he is, back in your life, loving you, and you him, and it turns out your tea was spiked with some alien love potion to begin with, and you don't know what to trust anymore, do you? You don't know what to hold onto."

A few tears had pooled in Linda's eyes as Obie spoke. The first one jumped and the others quickly followed. She hung her head in acknowledgment. "That's about it, Obie," she said thickly.

"You learn that the dead aren't really dead. That we're all here to evolve toward the Absolute. That the universe is teeming with life and consciousness and that it's almost impossible to know what's really going on. Words like death and reality and right and wrong start to lose their meaning. We're standing buck naked in that field Rumi talked about." Obie continued in a more gentle tone. "And here you are, living a life in the physical realm, and now you learn that the world as you've known it is unraveling under your feet. And strangers like Sina and me come along with our Jedi robes and fur parkas and tell you that you, Linda Travis, the President of the United States, that you are the one who's been called to do something about it all." Obie reached out and took Linda's hand. "It's enough to send a girl back to the farm, isn't it?"

Linda smiled and wiped her eyes. "Do you know what to do next, Obie?" she asked.

Obie grinned. "Nope. If I did they'd have made *me* president." He laughed softly at the thought.

"I mean, what the fuck, Obie? Rice is still there. The General's still in charge. They must own Singer by this point, if they didn't before. They own my cabinet. They own the fucking military. I can't just show up at the gate and order people to arrest them. They'll laugh in my face."

"That's probably right."

"And I can't just go get on TV and talk to the whole world, like I'd thought I could." Linda's voice was getting louder and Obie gestured for her to speak more quietly. "Sorry," she said in a loud whisper. "But, Jesus, Obie! What the hell would I say? Tell the world the aliens are here? Tell them the U.S. government has been taken over by a secret group of psychopaths? Tell them that global-industrial civilization is going the way of the dodo? They'll put me away, Obie. The House and the Senate will eat me for lunch. Rice has the power to deflect anything I say or do. Anything."

Obie sighed. "I guess this is why you earn the big bucks, Linda," he said. His eyes flashed. "You do have one thing going for you though."

"What's that?"

"All those things you just said are true."

## 17.6

The bizarre, tingling sensation that flooded Emily's body, when she passed through a solid rock wall, made her want to laugh and scream at the same time. She gave a slight yelp as she stepped into what felt like open air, shaking her arms and shoulders as if she were covered with ants. She stopped abruptly. She'd expected the room to be lit. Her brother had already passed through. But the room was completely black. Had she somehow become trapped in the stone? Her heart started pounding. "Iain?" she said, her voice wavering.

"I'm here."

Emily exhaled in relief. "Is there a light?"

"I can't find a switch."

Alice slid into the room behind Emily. "I apologize," she said into the darkness. Emily could feel the air stir as Alice passed by her. "I should have turned on the light when I brought Iain through. I assumed he would find it." The overhead fluorescents flickered on. There was Alice, behind some shelving on the far wall by the door, her hand on the switch. Iain had been looking in the wrong place.

"That's okay," said Emily. "We made it." She looked around the room. They were in a supply closet. Metal shelves were stacked with cleaning products and office supplies. The shelves also contained cases of snack foods and soft drinks. "Cheese Noogies!" said Emily. She stepped forward and started opening a box.

"You should not consume such things," said Alice. "The pharmaceuticals they contain are meant for the sleepers."

"Sleepers?" asked Iain, struggling to open a Mylar bag.

"Sleepers are the humans who are kept in a docile, childlike state, in order to more easily control them. Control is part of the Plan."

Emily stepped forward to face the strange, tiny girl. "How many of us humans are sleepers, Alice?" she asked.

"Almost all of you," she replied.

Iain put down his snack. He shivered. The room was cold and

they had no extra clothes. "Do you know where we are now?" he asked.

Alice nodded. "I believe we have two more walls to transverse before the freight elevator."

"Good," said Emily, sitting on a stack of boxes. She was exhausted. And she could see the weariness in Alice's face as well. Alice had not returned until later in the afternoon. She'd proven unable to escort Iain and Emily through the hundreds of feet of solid rock above them in one movement, even with Jack's help. They'd been forced to make their way through the facility wall after wall and room after room, with Alice taking them through one at a time. And Alice had left them repeatedly, to return to her normal activities and maintain the illusion that all was in order. Rice was so sick he believed her reports without question.

It had taken them hours. They got lost twice, as Alice was unsure of the way, and could find no diagrams or blueprints for the maze of tunnels and chambers and laboratories that riddled the ground beneath the National Mall. Each time they got lost they had to backtrack. Once, just as Iain slipped into a bathroom, two soldiers entered through the door. Alice and Jack managed to pull him back without discovery, but the close call had caused them to sit tight until the soldiers departed.

Halfway through each "transverse," as Alice called them, half-way through the strange grayness that seemed to go on forever, they'd meet a shadowy figure, Jack, who would reach out and pull them along. Jack was taller than Alice, and older it seemed, but he had the same small stature, the same exotic features, the same strange, black eyes the shape of large almonds. He never said a word.

Iain looked at his watch, then at his sister. "Jeez, Em. It's almost eight." He turned to Alice. "You still think this elevator's the way to do it?"

"I am not skilled enough to escort human flesh through that much stone," answered Alice, nodding to the immensity of rock overhead. "Apparently my own human vibrations distort my ability to shift frequencies. I believe the elevators are our only choice."

"And the freight elevator might receive less regular use," mused Iain with a nod.

"You don't think this Rice guy is standing there waiting for us?" asked Emily. She grabbed a packet of peanuts and opened them up. Sleeper or not, she was starving. And surely peanuts are okay? She shoved a handful into her mouth.

Alice thought about this for a moment. "Mr. Rice has no doubt been alerted to our absence at this point," she said. "I have not checked in with him for three hours. He will likely have posted extra guards, looking for us only in the physical bands. I do not believe he will try to follow us in the astral."

"Great," said Iain. "So, what? Do we just step out and say 'boo!' to the guards?"

Alice shook her head as she had so often seen humans do. "No. We will have to move diagonally through the rock at that point, to enter the elevator unseen."

"And how far is that?" asked Emily. Alice looked so tired.

"I'm not certain," said Alice. "I remember using the freight elevator only once, when I was just an infant. It's about eight feet, I think, depending on the angle we take," said Alice.

"And how wide are these walls we've been walking through?" asked Iain.

"About six inches," said Alice.

## 17.7

Eventually, Linda had just given up and gone to sleep. Leaning her head on Cole's shoulder, she'd stumbled into a fitful doze filled with sharp dreams and aching joints. Obie had dimmed the cabin lights and stretched out on the floor in the back. The aircraft hurtled southward.

When Linda awoke the plane was on the ground and Cole and Obie were laughing together on the tarmac. She'd slept through the landing, and somehow Cole had slipped past without waking her. She must have been dead to the world. Linda rose and limped to the open cabin doorway on sore, stiff legs. Obie was sitting on the bottom step. Cole was standing nearby, stomping his feet in the cold night air. They both wore the parkas the Inuit had given them.

"You boys having a good time?" asked Linda, playfully.

Cole looked up and smiled. Obie turned and grinned. "Cole here scored us some weed off a polar bear," said the older brother, laughing at his own joke.

"Sina said we had to blow this joint!" added Cole. He stepped forward and helped Linda down the steps.

"We're refueling, I take it?" she asked.

"Yep. Got a full tank now. Obie got the windows and I emptied the litterbag. Beck's gone in to swipe his card and pee in a real toilet." He gestured to a small shack on the edge of the paved airstrip. She could see their pilot inside, speaking with a very short man in a snowmobile suit.

"Any problems?"

Cole gave her a warm smile. "Everything's fine, sweetie. We were just talking about the stupid things Dad used to say." Cole puffed up his chest and walked about with stiff legs. "You kids quit hittin' each other or I'm gonna knock heads!" he huffed. Both brothers doubled over in laughter. Linda smiled, glad to see the two men connecting.

The shack door slammed and the pilot approached the plane. "All set?" he asked. The four of them boarded. In just a few minutes they were in the air again.

Obie reached into the overhead compartment and pulled down a duffel. "I've been meaning to give you guys something," he said as he unzipped the bag. "Wanted to wait until you were both awake." He pulled out an oddly-shaped object wrapped in soft brown sealskin and handed it to Cole.

Cole undid the wrapping. "What's this?" he asked.

"Utterpok's drumstick," answered Obie. "The Inuit shaman who died. Payok gave it to me before he and Sina headed back to the camp." He looked at Linda. "He'd seen Grace pick up Utterpok's beater in the astral level, after the old man fell. He thought maybe..." he looked nervously to Cole, "you know. When you see Grace again. You could.... He thought she'd like to have the physical beater. Here in this world."

Cole smiled sadly. He had no idea how it would turn out for Grace. He handed the stick to Linda and she looked at it carefully. It was a thick length of polished wood with a curved handle of reindeer antler. Eighteen inches long, at least. The handle was carved with a delicate pattern of animal figures. On one side was an oval with a symbol inside. "Jesus," whispered Linda.

She pointed out the symbol to Cole and Obie. "Fuck me," said Cole.

"What?" said Obie, looking from one to the other. He examined the symbol. It was a circle bisected by an inverted capital L.

"That's the symbol Rice drew on Cole's car," explained Linda.

"Is it?" asked Obie.

"No, it's not," said Cole firmly.

Linda was confused. She looked at Cole, whose expression had gone weirdly slack. "Cole?" she said.

"It wasn't Rice," he said. "Not if Rice is the motherfucker who shot me in Ottawa. He wasn't the guy who drew on my windshield. And he wasn't the guy that shot Pooch."

"So that's what you meant," murmured Linda, recalling. She took Cole's hand. "I remember. Your last words before Rice shot you. Rice said to me 'you look different' and then you said to him 'so do you.' I remembered those words. Down in that alien's cell Rice put me in. I couldn't figure out what you'd meant."

"You're saying there's somebody else out there fucking with you guys?" asked Obie, incredulous.

Cole nodded. "Same build. Tall and skinny. A pretty boy with red hair. But not the same guy that shot me. I'm sure of it."

Linda pointed to the symbol on the handle. "You got any idea what this means, Obie? We saw it on the train, too."

Obie pulled at his Van Dyke. "Not a clue, guys," he said.

The intercom crackled and the pilot's voice came through the speakers. "Uh, you folks may want to come up here," he said nervously. "We've got company."

Obie hurried up the aisle, with Linda and Cole close behind. He opened the cockpit door and one by one they looked through the front windshield.

Linda laughed. "Don't worry, Mr. Beck," she said. "We've been through this before. I think it means we're on the right track."

In the sky just ahead was a circle of glowing UFOs.

## 17.8

It was an eleven-block walk from her hotel room to the White House, but Mary couldn't afford anything closer. As it was she'd had to use most of her cash. She wanted to avoid using her plastic for as long as she could. Techs were no doubt tracking such things as a matter of routine.

Mary swung south through the Mall, trying to look like a tourist. Difficult to pull off on a Sunday night in October after 10 PM, especially in this economy; the place was dead. Mary pretended that she lived nearby, and that she was merely headed home after the theater. She knew that the silence was deceptive, that this entire area was watched and patrolled at all hours by unseen eyes and ears. She knew some of those eyes and ears would belong to the People. So she kept her collar high and her hat low and tried to look decisive.

That, too, was difficult, as she still did not know where she was going or what she was supposed to do. She'd thought about just walking through the regular checkpoints, like she'd done hundreds of times, as if she'd never left. She even considered just going straight to Rice, telling him what a mistake she'd made, and asking to be forgiven. She wouldn't mean it, of course, and therein would lay the problem: Rice would know. And then she'd be in his hands. Better to just watch for now, she thought. Watch and trust. Whoever or whatever it was that had prompted her to return would issue her marching orders soon enough.

For now, she needed a place to hang out until those orders came. She noticed the National Sylvan Theater coming up on her left. Lots of eyes and ears on that, given last summer's series of protest rallies, but surely far fewer this time of year, this late at night. And surely far fewer in the trees that surrounded it. What surveillance there was would no doubt be automated. It would take a while for red flags to reach an analyst. She had time. And if she stumbled around a bit and then hid against the wall, wouldn't they just think her a homeless person? It was her only idea, and she needed to get off the street. Mary acted as destitute as she could and headed for the trees.

## 17.9

"Alice you goddamned fucking little traitor!" screamed Rice as he stumbled down the hallway. "Goddamned motherfucking monster!" He slammed his way into the cafeteria and knocked a pile of trays to the floor. As it was late, there were only a few others in the room. They found something else to look at. "Any of you guys seen Alice?" he bellowed. Some of the diners shook their heads. None of them spoke up. Rice turned and pushed his way back through the doors.

"Fuck, fuck, fuck!" he cried to the ceiling. Alice was gone. And loverboy's fucking larvae. And when Rice found their snotty little asses he was going to kill them all. He'd just fucking had it. Mary'd bugged out, that bitch. Now Bob was gone. Who knew about Random? Not like you could tell with a fucking mummy! And now Alice? Jesus H. Fucking Christ, he'd given his life for that little morph. This is the thanks he gets?

Rice marched down the barracks hall and checked Alice's room again. Nothing out of order. As if she'd just evaporated. The guards hadn't seen a thing. He'd personally interrogated those fuckers at every checkpoint. No, sir, haven't seen a thing, sir, nyah nyah nyah. Motherfuckers. Like three little kids can just walk out of the place. The General would have his balls for breakfast.

He opened the next door down and shook his head in disbelief. She was one clever little shit, he had to give her that. Alice had built a strange, alien cage around her mother's body. It looked as though a team of robot spiders had woven a coffin-shaped web from bits of wire and foil and flexible conduit, creating some sort of Faraday shield or RF anechoic chamber that surrounded both Bob and her bed. Alice must've spent hours, scabbing parts and materials from labs and supply closets all over the facility.

The techs had never seen anything like it, but said it was clearly designed to keep Bob's soul from reconstituting in her body.

But Alice hadn't stopped there. Under the bed was what looked to be an explosive device. The design was bizarre, as if the little hybrid had downloaded plans from the Life's own version of *The Anarchist Cookbook*. She'd housed the bomb in a clear plastic food container she must have stolen from the cafeteria, and attached it to the cage with what looked like insulated cat 5 cable. Inside was a complicated network of circuit boards, chips, modules and wires. At the heart of it sat what appeared to be a spinning rubix. The whole thing buzzed with warning. Rice sighed. The techs wouldn't touch it. He'd have to get some ordnance disposal goons down here to disarm that fucker.

Rice slammed the door and turned back toward his own room. The puking was mostly over now but he could feel the headache coming on. It always went this way. Fuck. He never should have gone on the trek. Should've just trusted Bob and Random to handle things. Only they hadn't, had they? And he still didn't know what had happened.

Rice opened his own door. The facility was crawling with soldiers now. Army ants, and he'd stirred them up with a stick. They'd find those goddamned kids. It was just a matter of time.

In the meantime, a couple of oxycodone and a hot shower. He still smelled like fucking puke.

17.10

"We did it!" said Emily to Alice, kneeling and extending her hand for a high five.

Alice reached up and took Emily's fingers in her tiny hand, as if to steady herself. "Yes," she said, nodding. It almost appeared as if she had a smile on her face.

Emily looked around. She could hardly believe it. They'd stepped through one last wall and were met with cold night air. It was just after midnight, and they were behind the stone column of a small white building that sat near the base of the Washington monument.

Alice sat down on a cement bench at the column's base and hung her head. She was exhausted. They'd made it through the rock to the elevator, but it had taken three tries, and it had cost her in ways Iain and Emily could not begin to understand. They'd had to transverse two more floors and at least a dozen rooms before they reached the surface. Had it not been for Jack, they'd have been lost forever in the rock.

Iain stepped out under the sky and surveyed the area. "We got a bunch of trees this way," he said, pointing. "Can we make it that far before we rest?" Alice had told them what she knew of the surveillance capabilities of their pursuers. Iain was scared.

Emily rose and pulled Alice to her feet. "I'll help you," she said. Alice did not reply.

The three of them started walking along the sidewalk, cringing as the occasional car passed them by. There were no streetlights on this side of the road, for which they were thankful. They came to a point opposite the trees and started to cross the street. A taxi sped into view as they stepped over the center line, blaring its horn. Emily pulled Alice back as it zipped by.

### 17.11

Mary peered across the street at the sound of a horn to see three children approaching her. Oh, my God! "Alice?" she squeaked. Ignoring her cold, sore joints, she pushed herself up to hands and knees, then scrambled to her feet. She stepped out in front of the theater. "Alice?"

The children stopped.

Mary stumbled toward them and they stepped back. "Alice?" she said again.

The smallest child raised her head. "Greetings, Mary," she said.

Alice collapsed to the ground.

### 17.12

"What time you got?" asked Obie.

Linda checked her watch. "Just after two."

Obie nodded. "Pretty good," he said.

The plane had just come to a stop on the little airstrip on Delmarva. "Not far from Assateague," Beck had said. They'd come in from the ocean side, avoiding the city. But they'd seen the lights of D.C., glowing in the distance. Somewhere in that glow were Cole's children, they hoped. Somewhere was Linda's mother. Somewhere was Theodore Rice. Linda exhaled her apprehension in a loud, long sigh. How would they ever find them all?

Obie looked from Cole to Linda. "You guys okay?" he asked.

Linda looked up and chuckled once, a short, gentle sniff of surrender. What was there to say? The situation was determined to drag them along, whether they were okay or not. "How long of a drive we looking at?" Linda asked.

"Beck says maybe three hours, this time of night. He called and got us a rental. Should be by the hangar."

The three of them rose and pulled their bags from the overhead compartments. As they'd arrived in the far north with almost nothing on them, the Inuit had given them what clothes they could spare, and some food and a little cash. Obie still had the pistol he'd carried when he rescued Linda. And Cole had Utterpok's drumstick. Linda laughed again to herself. Not much of an army, she thought, to take down the most powerful secret organization in the world. She squeezed Cole's hand and they started forward to the door.

Cole turned and kissed her on the lips. Linda pulled back to study his face. The tics were gone. The goofiness. The odd misalignment of self and body. It was as if the aliens, the alive ones, the Tuurngait, in fashioning his new body, had tailored one that fit who he was, and thrown away that old thing he'd grabbed off the rack. Cole Thomas now fully inhabited the body in which he stood. His eyes connected directly to his soul in a way they hadn't before. He belonged here now. He was finally himself.

Linda buried her face in Cole's chest and neck and sighed deeply. Not much of an army, she thought again. That was true. But enough now, maybe. Maybe they would be enough.

They stepped down to the tarmac and scanned the clear sky. Not a UFO in sight. They were on their own. They would have to be enough. They were all they had.

They got into the rented car and drove off into the night.

## 17.13

*Grace watched from above as her father and Linda stepped out of the plane. When they reached the ground they both stopped and looked up into the sky, as if they were gazing right back at her. She wished she could just call out and let them know she was there. But the universe did not seem to work that way.*

*It had been a time of good-byes for Grace. After her father and her Uncle Obie had left the Confusion, Grace and her mother had sat together on that old, brown sofa for what had felt like days, catching up with each other as the bright, blue nebula pulsed and glowed all about them. Ruth was filled with joy to hear of Grace's life. Grace demonstrated how she'd looked as she'd grown up after her mother had passed on, morphing smoothly from the three-year-old she'd been to the five-year-old she was now. Her mother had delighted at that. She was happy to hear about Emily's growing mastery of the violin, and of Iain's newfound knack for writing stories. She was even happy to know that Grace's father had found a new love.*

*But Ruth remembered very little of her own experience. She recalled dying in the plane crash. She remembered the time she'd just spent with Cole in their first house. But those memories were dwindling quickly, like dreams fading in the morning sun. The years since she'd last seen Grace were mostly a blank. It felt to Ruth as if she'd just died. This realm was all new to her, and she was anxious to explore it. Ruth and her daughter wept in each other's arms. They laughed and hugged and cuddled. But in the end, Ruth had to go. That life was done. She could not hang onto it.*

*After Grace bid farewell to her mother, she'd gone to find Evlyn, whom she had seen leave the house to follow that woman with the twisted face, apparently not trusting one so broken to stay out of mischief. Grace found her old ally in the astral levels of deep space, talking with an Elder who looked strangely familiar. The melting woman floated between them, silent and dim and curled up in a ball. The Elder turned and noted Grace's approach with a raised eyebrow, then laid his hands on the twisted woman's head. They flickered away together just as Grace drew near.*

"Greetings, little one," said Evlyn.

"Hello," said Grace. "Who was that?"

"He's the one who shot me at the border," Evlyn said, gesturing toward the spot where the Elder had hovered. For a moment, Evlyn morphed into the big French Canadian she had been before, complete with a large, bloody wound in his chest.

"Ah," said Grace. *That's where she'd seen him before; he was the Elder she'd seen crawling out of a dead body just before her father and Linda had boarded the helicopter.* "Did he say why he did that?" *Grace asked the woman of light.*

"He would only say that it was necessary," answered Evlyn, settling back into her dominant form. *She knelt to scratch under Dennis's chin, then looked up at Grace.* "He is taking that twisted one to a place of healing. She may be gone for a very long time."

Grace nodded. "And you?" she asked. "I'm going to go help my father now. Will you come with me?"

*Evlyn spun and rolled and beamed her heart, radiating both great sadness and great joy.* "I cannot, little one," she said. "It is time for me to move on."

"Move on?" asked Grace.

"I have finished my work on this plane," she said, her glowing light both glad and full. "The Elder just informed me. It is time for me to spiral onward and continue my journey."

"I didn't realize that's how it worked," said Grace. "I shall miss you."

"I will miss you too," said Evlyn. "Can you please take a message to the one who was my wife back in your world, and tell her that I am happy and well?"

"I will do that," said Grace.

*Evlyn shared her full being, enveloping them both in her light. Then she pulled away.* "We shall be entangled forever," she said. *With a final, bright flash, she was gone.*

*Grace shook off her memories and watched as her Uncle Obie descended the steps and joined his brother and the President on the tarmac. After Evlyn had departed, Grace had followed her father's vibration, finding him in flight with Linda and his brother, the three of them heading back to Washington D.C. to confront those from whom the President had been running. Grace knew that they were still in danger. While the skeleton had disappeared into the void, and the Elder had taken the twisted woman away, that tall guy with the flaming hair had not been in the house. He was still around. And he did not look like a nice man. Grace doubted they'd seen the last of him.*

*The three humans below her began to walk across the airstrip, toward a car that sat glinting in the starlight near a large, metal building. Grace followed. Save for Dennis, who still dogged her heels, Grace was now alone in this strange, astral realm. She'd hoped to have more help, but apparently that was not to be. Jack had already disappeared by the time the house had fallen apart. The old shaman, Utterpok, had vanished into the void with the skeleton. Evlyn had had to go. Grace whirled about, sending her perceptions outward in all directions, wondering how a Universe so vast and full could feel so lonely. She felt, in that moment, like the little girl she still was. She wanted to go home.*

*Dennis nosed in and licked her hand. Dennis, who had faced off with an Arctic fox. Dennis, who had helped search the Confusion, and stood beside her as she'd opposed that scary, twisted woman. Dennis, who had been with her from the beginning. Grace pulled her little dog up into her arms and buried her face in his furry neck. Even though she had no real idea what to expect next, she still had Dennis. They would just have to trust that help would come if it were needed, as help had come before. In the meantime, she and Dennis would do their best. That's all anybody could ever do, wasn't it?*

*Obie opened the driver's door and got behind the wheel. Cole and Linda climbed into the back seat. Grace moved in, to better view the two as they settled into each other's arms. She could feel their hearts, glowing like bonfires, beating together as one. They were tired and scared, but they were also very happy. She was glad that her father had found such joy. The engine started and the car begardan to move.*

*"You ready to see the capitol, Dennis?" Grace asked.*

*Dennis thunked his tail against her leg.*

*Together, they headed for the distant glow.*

# Chapter Eighteen

## 18.1

*I wonder what Albert Singer's balls feel like* thought Rice as he rode the elevator back down into the Rock. He pictured himself just reaching out and grabbing them, squeezing so hard that Singer's eyes rolled back in his head. He could imagine the "Acting President's" testicles popping in his hands, their juices wetting his fingers and staining the Veep's tailored Italian slacks as he dropped to his knees. It would be delicious.

The stupid fuck deserved no less. Imagine, him actually shouting at Theodore Rice. The man didn't have a fucking clue. He thought Rice was just the bureaucrat in charge of some special black ops unit the General had put together. Wrong answer! Rice was really going to enjoy Singer's first real briefing, once Ma Kettle was out of the way. And the General! Not only had he stood there and let Singer rant, but he'd gotten angry with Rice as well! As if he'd been any help with this situation, the fucking drunk. Perhaps it was time for "Fearless Leader" to go. Maybe it was even time to get rid of the General's position altogether and make *himself* the director. After all, he'd been at this since before these guys were even born.

The door slid open and Rice stepped out of the elevator. He turned right and started down the main corridor, trying not to think about where he was headed. Rice put his fingers to his eyes and pressed hard against them, hoping to push the headache back out of the way. The worst was over, yes, but this motherfucker was hanging onto his frontal lobes like a pit bull with tetanus.

It wasn't like Singer and the General didn't have a point. Sure. It had been a cock-up from the beginning. Mary should never have let the Prez out of her sight. Bob had blown her best chance to take Ma Kettle out early on. Even Rice had made mistakes. Wasting those troopers at the border was just plain stupid. They were still making a stink about it up in Vermont. And that fucking Mexican food: his asshole was *still* burning. It was as if the Universe itself was against him. Testing a guy was one thing, but this was just fucking nuts.

Rice came up to the sealed doubled doors to the Lodge. The two soldiers on duty snapped to attention. "Can we help you, sir?" asked the short one.

"Just thought I'd dummy check the Lodge, guys," said Rice, knowing that his casual tone would make them all the more nervous. "Anything to report?"

"No, sir," said the short one. "Nobody's been through this entrance since you gave the alert, sir. Nobody except for security forces, that is. Sir." The tall one nodded in agreement. The short one punched the lockpad and the door slid open.

"Would you like one of us to accompany you, sir?" asked the tall one.

"No, thank you, private," answered Rice. "I can find my way. I was here when they built the place, you know."

Both soldiers stepped aside to let Rice pass. "Very good, sir," said the short one.

Rice stepped into the Lodge. The door slid closed behind him.

The D.C. Lodge. He hadn't been down here since before he'd left for Vermont, when he'd stopped in to check on Mork. She'd just sat in her stupid little box, dormant, like a fucking gargoyle.

The dim light in the hallway unnerved him. Rice found the lightpad and brought the glowstrips up as high as he could. That helped. He started down the long curving hallway, bending forward a bit so as not to hit his head on the tunnel ceiling.

So the whole country was in an uproar. He understood. Misplacing your President is not like losing your keys. House and Senate members were passing resolutions left and right, jockeying for camera time to see who could look the most worried. The media had already chewed through one Press Secretary and was busily flaying another. Military and police were industriously searching the entire fucking planet, building by building. Foreign governments were doing everything they could to help, even though Rice knew that every last one of them hated the U.S. and couldn't wait for the day it went belly-up. But fuck, what did they expect him to do? The bugs were actually helping the President. Had been since the beginning. They were probably the ones who spiked his enchilada! How for fuck's sake was he supposed to counter that?

Rice came into the first of three central chambers, the circular hubs in a network of spidery tunnels that stretched westward from the White House toward the Potomac. With the Life gone, most of the techs and scientists had filtered back to their own labs on the human side. Only a couple remained behind, monitoring one experiment or another, waiting for their alien colleagues to return. One of them was Gellow, who'd attended the first briefing with Linda Travis.

Gellow looked up at the sound of Rice's approach. "Mr. Rice?" he asked warily. He pushed his glasses into place.

"Just stretching my legs, Tony," said Rice. "Thought I'd nose around. See if there's anything astray." He wouldn't say anything more. He couldn't take the risk of even thinking about it. He didn't know who was monitoring him.

"Your security forces scoured the place yesterday, Mr. Rice. Twice. And there have been–"

Rice held up a hand to stop the scientist. "I won't get in your way, Gellow," he said.

Gellow shrugged and turned back to his console.

Rice circled the chamber halfway, stopping at the entrance to another small tunnel. He ducked into an office on the corner and snatched something from a drawer without even looking at it, letting his hands find what he needed without his brain getting involved. He started down the smaller tunnel, which took him to another hub. Rice noted there the wok he'd stashed for his own personal use. He smiled and took the second tunnel on the right, sighing out loud. He didn't understand. Why had the Life departed? Why? They'd been working so well together. The Plan was proceeding ahead of schedule. It had taken them decades to get to this point. And they just walk away? He'd given his whole life to this project. Rice stopped for a second to lean against the wall as the migraine pain knifed through his head, plunging into his eye and scraping his skull. "Fuck!" he hissed, wincing to hear his voice bounce so loudly off the rock walls. The last thing he needed was for Gellow to hear him.

It wasn't right. He'd been abandoned. Once again. It was just not right.

Rice completed his journey, stepping into a small room on the left. He punched the light. There was Mork, just as he'd left her, sitting in her gray, metal box, her knees up to her chin, her arms wrapped around her shins. She'd gone dormant just after the President skipped town. As had a bug or two in every human-alien facility around the world. He'd never seen anything like it. Just another betrayal. It was as if they were mocking him.

"Hello, love," said Rice.

Mork stared forward with wide-open, black almond eyes.

"Service alright, Mork? They changing your sheets often enough?"

Mork did not respond.

Rice stepped close in front of the alien and pulled the letter opener from his jacket pocket. He smiled. His fingers had found just what he'd wanted. With a practiced hand he plunged the letter opener into Mork's left eye. Then he stepped back, leaving the blade to hang. A black, gooey liquid dripped slowly down Mork's leathery face. Rice looked up toward the sky and spoke through the rock. "Come and get me, buggy-boys," he said.

Rice turned and walked back the way he'd come. He failed to notice that, this time, Mork responded.

## 18.2

Alice opened her eyes. Something was wrong. She scanned the room. The wrongness was not here. Gray dawn light filtered in through the hotel blinds. Mary and the human children still slept. She could hear their undisturbed breathing.

Alice uncrossed her legs and slid down from the armchair in which she'd spent the night. Her energy was still low, but better than it had been. The salad Mary had procured for her had helped. So had the hours of quiet retreat. She stepped quietly past the two beds and stopped at the door. Opening it might awaken the humans, which she wanted to avoid, so Alice shifted her frequency and slipped silently through the dark, heavy wood. The hallway was empty.

She closed her eyes. The wrongness was underground, ticking and grating like a broken clock. Alice sent her awareness across the city and through the rock, expanding out into time and space as her mother had taught her. She flinched. There was so much wrongness in this city that it hurt to let it all in. Her mother had shown her how to build the inner walls she would need, in order to survive amongst these humans. But some new wrong had broken through those walls. Some great pain. Something deep underground. She followed the wrongness back to its source.

It was the alive one they called Mork.

Alice started down the hall.

## 18.3

Heads would roll. Or maybe they'd just splatter. Whichever hurt more. Rice would see to it himself. When soldiers started abandoning their posts in the middle of an alert it was time to shake shit up. Things were getting way too sloppy. Maybe that's why the aliens had abandoned him. They would only return when he got his own house in order. So be it. That was the sort of work he most enjoyed anyways.

Rice stalked the halls, glad to be back in the human half of the facility. He said nothing to the other soldiers he passed at their posts. He didn't want to show his hand. He'd find those AWOL motherfuckers swigging lattes in a break room one day soon and put a couple of bullets into their heads. If the bugs wanted action they'd get action.

He turned down the hallway that led to his office. The General's call had interrupted his breakfast and he still hadn't had his second cup of coffee. Maybe the bomb squad had arrived by now. They said they'd be here first thing. Rice felt a tickle on his head and reached up to smooth his hair. He sneered. Maybe that tickle was Bob, dogging his every step, trying to get through, screaming at him to get the Faraday shield off her body so she could reconstitute. Fuck her. Let her simmer. She'd failed him once again. Got her ass whupped by a gang of arctic Ewoks. He'd let her come back when he was damned well good and ready.

He punched the lockpad and his office door slid open. There stood Crazy Carl with a pistol pointed at his face. Fuck.

"Hello, Ted," said Obie.

"Carl," said Rice with a slight nod. "How 'bout them Cubs?" He noticed the President, seated at his conference table, and her loverboy standing off to the left. Rice smiled. Something inside of him relaxed. If nothing else, this would be really, really fun.

"Just lost to Houston, I heard. Finished two games out. No pennant, once again. Sorta like you, Ted."

"Ooh, nice metaphor," trilled Rice. "I love it when you go all Harry Caray. You missed your calling."

Obie stepped back and gestured with his head. "Sit down, Ted."

Rice shrugged. "I was hoping we could dance longer," he whined with mock sadness. He moved into the room after Obie, nodding at the President before taking the seat nearest the door, opposite Linda. "Good to see you looking so well, Ma'am," he said with a smile. "The new 'do suits you. Kind of a Sinead O'Connor thing, isn't it? Very sexy. *Vogue* will be calling for your cover shoot."

Linda looked directly into his eyes but did not respond.

The door slid closed. Obie took a position to Rice's right, standing with his back to the wall. He did not lower his gun. Cole took a seat on Rice's left, next to Linda. He reached out and took the President's hand.

Rice smiled, looking back and forth between Linda and Cole. "So, you guys are honeymooning in D.C. You been to the Folger yet? I hear their new *Othello* is marvelous."

"Cut the crap," said Cole.

"Ah, loverboy's a 'cut the crap' man, is he? That should certainly make things easier." Rice sat back and stretched his arms, cupping his head in his hands. As though the gods had smiled upon him, his headache had disappeared entirely.

Linda nodded slightly, as if in agreement with his assessment. "I'm glad we finally have a chance to talk, Mr. Rice," she said evenly. "We have some catching up to do."

"Indeed," said Rice, raising an eyebrow. He'd been expecting something coarse and insulting. "I'm afraid I've let the place run down a bit since you left, Mrs. President. My apologies." He noticed the remains of his breakfast on the table and leaned forward to grab his cup. "Do you mind?" he said, pointing at the thermal carafe.

"You don't seem surprised to see us, Ted," said Obie, ignoring Rice's request.

Rice turned to his former protégé. "You forget that I command the world's largest and most advanced surveillance organization, Carl, utilizing alien technologies undreamt of by the cattle. And you forget our operatives in the astral realm. I am a very difficult man to surprise."

Obie waited for Rice to continue. Rice looked around the room, then back at Obie.

"Nevertheless, you are incorrect. It hadn't occurred to me that I'd find you here this morning. I figured you all halfway to Tierra del Fuego by now. I take it you entered through the Watergate conduit and came up through the Lodge? No doubt you can tell me the whereabouts of a couple of missing soldiers."

Obie smiled. "You'll find them nicely wrapped in a storage closet near their post, Ted. They looked almost relieved to see us."

"Did they?" said Rice. "I must not be paying them enough."

Obie shrugged. "You're pretty much running blind at this point, aren't you Ted?"

Rice smirked. "Blind, my boy?"

"Blind arrogance," said Cole with disgust.

Rice looked at Linda. "Is he just here for color commentary or should I consider him a player in this game?" he asked, gesturing toward Cole with his head.

Cole just stared and said nothing.

"Blind as in you didn't see us coming because you've been taken out of the game, Ted," said Obie. "And Cole's right. Only arrogance would forget to close down the Watergate conduit. Only arrogance would assume we had no choice but to keep on running forever. And only arrogance would find it impossible to believe that the alive ones have decided to back another horse."

Rice started to laugh, pointing at Cole and Linda. "You mean these two?" he said. "Please. I've been with the Life from the beginning. They're not about to hand the operation over to some farmer's wife and her new boy-toy. You've spent too many winters on the street, man. The rotgut has ruined your mind."

"You don't know what happened, do you?" asked Obie.

"What happened where?" said Rice.

It was Obie's turn to smile. "You weren't at Cole's house, Ted. Another bit of arrogance on your part. You thought we'd be a piece of cake. And nobody's returned yet, have they?" He started to laugh. "And you've been puking your guts out."

"I think you'll find that I still have all the guts I need, Carl."

"Bravado," said Carl dismissively. "Your same old song and dance. Seems like you'd be tired of it by now." Obie took a seat, two chairs separating him from Rice. He laid his handgun on the table. "So let me give you a quick update, Ted. Random's gone. Caught himself a rubix. Lucky break for him. Bob ran away. As did Alice. My guess is that neither have reconstituted. And I haven't seen Mary yet. Did she run too?"

Rice opened his mouth for a smart retort and then clamped it shut. Carl did not need to know what Rice did and did not know. He looked at the President, who regarded him with gentle eyes.

Right. They probably worked it out ahead of time. Linda would be the good cop. Keep her little hands clean. He turned back to the bad cop. "So what is it you kids want?" he said.

It was the good cop who responded. "First, I want to apologize, Mr. Rice. And then I want to talk about you and I working together."

Obie and Cole looked at Linda in shocked disbelief.

## 18.4

Mary ran down the hotel stairway and through the lobby to the street. What she saw in the morning light surprised her. When had this neighborhood become so run down? Sure, she didn't get out of the Rock or the White House all that much, but she wasn't a total recluse. Hadn't it only been a month ago that she'd had a kebab at Cyrus's? Now it was closed. And had that pile of trash been sitting across the street then? It looked as though it had. Mary glanced up and down the street. To her eye, the so-called "great recession" was a slow-motion avalanche moving steadily toward the great city's political center, cracking and taping windows, closing businesses, scouring out potholes, and leaving overflowing dumpsters and empty parking spaces in its wake. It wouldn't be long now before it engulfed the National Gallery and lapped against the steps of both the White House and the U.S. Capitol. Would anybody notice, even then? Or would they, like she, be so intent on scoring a quick lunch that they wouldn't even see the garbage underfoot? Mary squinted up at the sun as it peeked through the thick, autumn haze, pulled her coat tighter around her, and headed toward the White House.

She'd dreamt of Alice. The tiny thing had fallen down a well and broken her leg, and the well had begun to cave in. Alice had screamed and Mary had gasped herself awake. She'd scanned the room, seeing only Cole's two children sleeping in the other bed. Rising quietly, she checked the bathroom. Alice was not there. An image of the White House popped into her mind. Mary knew where Alice had gone.

Pulling on her jeans and sweater, Mary had awakened Iain and Emily to tell them she had to go. She'd made them promise to stay right where they were, then grabbed her coat and ran.

She hurried west on H Street and angled southward on New York NW. As she walked her urgency grew tattered with doubt. What was she doing? Was she going to walk right back into Rice's hands? Based on a dream? And yet, Alice was gone. That dark well was going to collapse. The dream had been a warning. Mary kept walking.

She cut across 15th Street at the light and hurried along the east side of the Treasury Building, taking the first set of steps and ducking through the door. She flashed her ScanIdent at the waiting uniform and checked her watch with an irritated sigh, a gesture intended to intimidate. Seeing her department holo, the guard let her through without a moment's hesitation. A stylized Earth inside a red oval was pretty much a free pass anywhere in the city, no questions asked. None of these goons knew what her department did. They just knew that that symbol meant power.

Mary headed to the first set of elevators on the left. Now she had to pass through Rock Security. It was almost seven-thirty. Hopefully Al would be on. He would remember her. She didn't use this entrance much, but she didn't want to chance the main White House guards.

The elevator came to a stop and she stepped out into a quiet, empty corridor. She headed right and followed the hallway as it veered to the left. She sighed with relief. There was Al, sitting behind the guard station. He sat with his back to her, reading the Post. His bushy white hair shone slightly green under the overhead fluorescents. Mary approached as nonchalantly as she could. Her heart was pounding.

"Any news, Al?" she said.

Al turned and smiled, then checked it. "Hi, Mary," he said. "Haven't seen you in a while."

Mary rummaged in her pocket for her ScanIdent. "Got called out on assignment," she explained. "Had a lead on the President." Mary quivered inside. She hadn't had any idea what she would say. The words just came, as if written by an unseen hand. She found her Ident and handed it to Al, who looked at it warily.

"Got a comm here says I'm not supposed to let you in, Mary." Al looked genuinely apologetic. "Says, in fact, that I'm supposed to call security if I see you."

Mary started to laugh. "Oh my God," she said, "What a baby!"

Al frowned. "Who you talking about, Mary?"

"Rice," she said, still chuckling. "I steal his parking space one time and he's gotta pull stupid shit like this." She shook her head as if to say *what a goofball.*

Al smiled hesitantly. "Be that as it may...," he began.

"Oh I know, Al. I won't put you in the middle of it. Just let me talk to the General and he'll pass me through. They're probably watching on the cams right now, laughing their asses off."

Al frowned again but did as she suggested. He got on the phone and punched through to the General's secretary. He handed her the phone.

"Wanda? Hi, it's Mary. The General there?"

Mary listened for a moment.

"Okay. Listen, I'm here at Treasury 4 with Al. He's got some comm from Rice saying to arrest me, the bastard. Any chance you can clear me in?" Mary listened again. "Okay. I'll wait here for you then." She hung up the phone.

She turned to Al. "The General's out. Wanda's gonna come up."

Al smiled, relieved to have the pressure off his shoulders. "So no success with your lead, then?" he asked.

Mary frowned. "My lead? Oh, the President. Nope. Another wild goose. But we gotta chase 'em all, don't we, Al?"

"Yep," said Al. He sighed. "I don't know how you intelligence people keep going. Not in this crazy world." He smiled, as if to offer his understanding and gratitude to a front-line hero.

The double doors behind Al slid open. Out stepped two soldiers, guns already drawn.

## 18.5

"You have my attention," said Rice.

Linda nodded. "I thought I might. But we need a couple of things from you first."

Rice shrugged. "Coffee? Danish? A lumbar cushion, maybe?"

"I want to know where my kids are," said Cole. His voice was stark and low.

Rice turned to Cole with a sigh. "Couldn't tell you, Mister President," he said.

"You bastard!" said Cole, rising. Linda stopped him with a hand on his arm. Cole sat back down.

"Was that not right?" asked Rice, turning to Linda. "Will you not be getting married then? Just keep him on as the official State Rentboy?" Rice started to laugh.

"Please tell us where they are, Rice," said Linda, calmly.

Rice sighed and looked at Cole like he might regard some rich woman's poodle. "Well, despite the powerful prognosticatory powers of your big brother here, Alice did reconstitute. You'll be happy to learn that the little shit has absconded with your two larvae. We have yet to figure out how they got out of here or where they've gone."

Cole's eyes widened. A slight smile flashed across his face, but he was too angry to sustain it. "And my youngest, Grace? What did you do to her, you sick fuck?"

Rice looked at Linda with exasperation. "Is this how we shall become friends and partners, Linda? With names and accusations?" He turned back to Cole with an expression of loathing. "I have no idea what happened to your third child, Mr. Thomas. Didn't even know you *had* a third child. Perhaps when you ran away with our Mrs. President here, the girl shriveled up and blew away. That happens, you know. Abandoned children have a way of ... surprising us."

Cole flinched at Rice's words but held his gaze. "She's in the hospital, Rice."

"Ah. I'm sorry to hear that. At least you must find comfort in the knowledge that the hospital staff won't leave her like you did."

Cole started to rise again.

"Leave it, Cole," said Linda, as gently as she could. She flashed Rice a piercing look. "Where's my mother, Rice?"

Rice leaned forward and rubbed his head. "You know," he said with an air of boredom, "maybe you guys should go talk to the milk carton folk. Put up some posters or something. Come back when you've got your people all accounted for. I'm busy here." He picked at a fingernail.

"Is she here?" asked Linda.

Rice looked up. "You mean the Queen Mother?"

Linda nodded.

Rice sighed. "No. She isn't," he said.

"Where is she?"

Rice waved the question away. "I don't know. Dead, maybe. Some topside asylum, most likely. The General set it up. You know the drill: three square salines a day and all the TV she can sleep through. Probably happy as a lark."

"You speak so casually of death," said Cole.

Rice smirked. "You, of all people, should realize how ridiculous that is to say."

"I want her back," said Linda evenly.

"Well, I suppose that'll depend on whether you can sell me on this new, improved Linda Travis," said Rice.

A knock sounded at the door. Rice smiled.

"Who's that?" whispered Obie.

"How's about I call out and we'll see, Carl?"

Linda nodded.

"Yes?" said Rice loudly.

"It's Sergeant Gordon, Mr. Rice."

Rice looked at Obie. "Shall I?" he said in a low tone.

Obie pointed at the gun. "Get rid of him. Or you get a bullet in your head."

Rice smiled. "Oh, don't worry, Carl," he said in a mock whisper. "I'll get rid of him. This is way too much fun to have it be interrupted now." Rice rose and stepped to the door, making sure to slide it open only slightly so that the sergeant could not see in. "Yes, sergeant? Oh! My goodness, it's Mary! Please, sergeant, I'll take her from here. Yes, leave the cuffs." Rice stepped back and Mary came in.

Rice closed the door and rubbed his hands together in anticipation. He looked around the room. Mary stood to one side, looking at the others in shock. "It's like Old Home Week!" he said, cheerily.

## 18.6

Alice slumped against a concrete pillar. Across a small paved drive was a strange red building. She had no idea what a German Evangelical Lutheran Church was. She simply knew that Mork was directly beneath her.

She was exhausted. She'd never been topside on her own before. She'd had no idea it was so noisy. Or that there were this many humans living here. She understood better Mr. Rice's disdain. Most of these people felt barely conscious.

Alice had known that a tiny alien-human hybrid female could not simply walk across the city without drawing unwanted attention. She'd been forced to use the skills of her father's people to the best of her abilities. When she could, she walked through walls, traveling unseen in dark hallways and empty rooms. Though it took concentration and energy, it was much easier going than when she'd had to escort the human children. When circumstances forced her to cross open space, she boosted her vibrations and slipped a band, walking unseen a half step above the physical. This was more difficult, and she was not sure she had been entirely successful. More than one dog, out for its morning walk, had noticed her and barked. And one woman ran from her, as if she'd seen a ghost. Alice regretted such things, but accepted what was so. It was the best she could do.

Now here she was, more weary than she had anticipated and facing the most difficult part of her journey. It could not be helped. The wrongness from below was increasing. Mork was calling. She did not know why. Alice looked around to make sure she had not been seen. Satisfied, she closed her eyes and sank down through the concrete walkway.

18.7

"It's nice to see you again, Mary," said Linda. "Please, sit down."

Mary glanced at Rice, who'd already taken his seat closest to the door, then at Obie, who greeted her with a cautious nod. She stepped to the left and sat next to Cole, smiling at him warmly, as if she already knew him. She had so much to say, but didn't know where to start. What was going on? And where was Alice? Mary placed her cuffed hands on the table. The nylon restraints had rubbed her wrists red. "It's good to see you too, Mrs. President," said Mary, with a smile that looked more like a grimace. Her heart pounded, to see Linda again.

"Not what you expected, I take it?"

Mary shook her head, trying to clear her growing anxiety. The air in the room was filled with a pressure, a scream, a pain she could not comprehend. "I ... no. I didn't know what to expect. I haven't been here..."

"Mary released herself on her own recognizance," Rice explained to Linda. He turned to Mary. "Had a change of heart, dear?" he asked. "Seen the error of your ways and all that?"

"No," said Mary, shaking her head in confusion. "I was look-ing—" She turned to Linda. "They had decided to kill you," she said, pleading. "I couldn't stay." She looked quickly to Cole. "I've got your kids," she said. "They're in my hotel room. The Blankenship, on 5$^{th}$."

Linda gave Mary a warm smile. "Thank you," she said.

Mary looked at her hands and blushed.

Cole hung his head in thanksgiving.

"We were just pondering the whereabouts of the good Presi-dent's mislaid mother, Mary," said Rice. "You have any idea where she got shelved?"

Mary looked up at Linda. "I'm sorry. No. The General—"

"Yes, that's what I told them," cut in Rice. He turned to the President. "Pity. If I knew, I could give her to you as a sign of good faith. We'll have to query the General later and track her down. For now, shall we proceed?"

Linda sat and scowled for a moment, clearly unhappy with the situation. Cole squeezed her hand. She flashed him a quick smile but kept her attention on Rice, who was sitting smugly across the table from her. He was the key here. Sina had said that the age of separation was over. The words had gone into her and stuck, filling her with some new vision she'd never before seen. Though she barely knew what they meant, she knew that those words must guide her now.

"You said something about an apology," prompted Rice.

Linda nodded. "You were right, Mr. Rice. There was way too much that I did not understand. I panicked and ran, and that has helped to create the mess we now find ourselves in. I made judgments based on assumptions that have proven to be false." The President stopped. She would only give so much.

Rice grinned. "This is fun," he said brightly. He looked around the room. Cole and Obie scowled the same scowl. Mary looked confused. Rice winked at Linda. "Keep going, girlfriend," he said.

Linda sighed. "Here's the situation as I see it. Right now, you continue to wield a great deal of power, even though that won't last for long. Your inner circle has been decimated. The alive ones have withdrawn their support. On your own, your organization becomes irrelevant."

"Oh, I don't know, Linda," laughed Rice. "The United States Government has been irrelevant for decades now and it seems to be doing fine. Besides, we're hardly powerless. We hold key positions in every department, from governance to intelligence to the military, the press, and the corporations. One word from me could get you committed to an asylum for the rest of your life. I could set you up as a figurehead. I could bury you in scandal. Or I could have you murdered. Accidents happen all of the time, Mrs. P. Surely you know this?"

Linda nodded. "This is all true. It's why Obie didn't put a bullet in your brains as soon as you walked in the door. It's why we're here, negotiating a deal. Your death would create a power vacuum I'd really rather avoid right now. Much better to forge a working relationship while you turn the organization over to me."

Rice smiled. "To you?"

"Yes. As of right now, I am the new Director of Operations for the People."

"Farm-girl goes to the big city and makes good, eh?" Rice laughed. "You forget I have friends in high places, Prez. We've managed to get along without you so far, though only the good Lord knows how. Why should I hand you the keys?"

Linda pointed toward the sky. "They're not coming back, Rice," she said, shaking her head.

"Really?" said Rice, a tinge of uncertainty in his voice. "I didn't get that memo."

"You got it, fucko, you just didn't read it," said Cole.

Rice picked up his coffee cup and hurled it at Cole, barely missing his head. The cup hit the cement block wall behind Cole and shattered. One shard hit Mary on the face and she pulled back with a cry. The cup's handle bounced back onto the table, coming to rest in front of Linda.

The President picked the handle up and examined it thoughtfully, then looked at Rice. "Cole is very angry with you," she said. She turned to Cole. "I need you to trust me," she said gently. She looked at Mary. "Are you okay?" Mary nodded, rubbing at her face.

Rice laughed. "Well, they say that coffee's bad for you. Maybe you should send Ziggy here out for some cuff cutters. Give him something useful to do." He nodded toward Cole. "Then Mary will be able to defend herself."

Nobody responded. Rice's smile eventually faded away. "So what makes you so sure, Prez?" he said, clearing his throat. "Been sleeping with the Spud-meister? They say once you try gray you never go gay." He turned and winked theatrically at Mary. Mary glowered, glanced nervously at Linda, then looked down at her lap.

Linda tossed the broken handle on the floor. "They're not coming back because I will not allow them to," she said, her voice low and full of power.

"Really? So you'll be taking over a human-alien organization with no aliens. That should prove interesting." He squirmed a bit in his chair. "You got plans after that, Linda? Repealing the law of gravity, perhaps? A guest gig on *Dancing With the Heads of State*? Relocating the White House to the far side of the moon?"

"I know why you've done what you've done, Rice," said Linda. "The aliens showed themselves and you didn't have any way to think about them except for the beliefs and expectations of your time. They were a threat to the American project, it seemed. A threat to the whole planet. How could you know? But there was a part of you that knew that you needed them. The atomic bomb scared the hell out of you. You knew you were out of control, even then. You knew you needed help."

"'You're preparing your crew psychology report, aren't you Prez?'" Rice grinned. He loved it when he could work in a good movie quote. He frowned, looking around the room. Nobody else seemed to get it.

"As time went on," continued Linda, "you found that these aliens could be worked with. They had magical technologies that would allow you to remain in the delusion of control. All it would cost you was some sharing of our planet one day, and the promise of secrecy, which seemed to align with your own purposes in any event. What you failed to notice was that it was all a lie, a ruse. You could not understand that your conception of the alive ones was simply a projection of your own mind, as shaped by the world in which you'd been born and raised. The world was spiraling ever more out of control. The climate was warming, even then. The ecosphere degrading. The oil would run out one day, and with it the economy. You've known this for decades, though you are barely able to admit it to yourself. You needed a magical fix and the aliens promised you one. No wonder you could not see the lie. No wonder you could not feel their disgust for you and your organization. Ironic, since you share that disgust with them."

Linda looked over at Obie to see him smiling at her. "You're doing fine, Mrs. President," said Obie. "Keep going."

"So you're right, Mr. Rice," said Linda, turning back to him. She smiled. His grin was gone. She allowed herself to hope that maybe she could get through to him. "The world *is* in trouble. The climate, the oil, the environment, the economy, it's all going to unravel. You thought that if you stayed in control you could forge some better way. You thought your Plan was the answer. In your own way, you love these people whom you call cattle."

"You're bringing tears to my eyes, Prez," said Rice. But there was no smile on his face.

"You wanted to help, didn't you Mr. Rice?"

Rice looked around the room with suspicion, as if he was being set up. He returned his gaze to Linda and nodded, almost imperceptibly. "They have the technology to save us," he said.

"Perhaps they do," replied Linda. "Perhaps one day they'll use it. But I think we will all be surprised by how things play out. I think their goals stretch far beyond saving our human world. We have forgotten, at our own peril, that we are not the only ones here. In any event, we cannot control them. What we can do is find, on our own, a sane and more grown-up response to this situation of our own making. The ball is now in our court, Mr. Rice. You wanted the alive ones to be the wise parents you wish you'd had, the parents who will step in and fix things for us. Instead they are proving to be the wise parents we most need, allowing us to stumble and fall and learn what we need to learn. We are going through our initiation into adulthood, Mr. Rice. We may not make it. And the alive ones may one day intervene, to stop us before we destroy everything. But it's possible we may prove ourselves worthy of survival, after all. If we do, it will come from our own efforts. The alive ones have withdrawn support from your strategy. Now it's time to find another."

Linda stopped. She'd said what she could.

Rice sighed deeply, running his fingers through his hair. He closed his eyes tightly, as if shutting off the outside world. For the longest time he just sat, silent. Then he opened his eyes and smiled at Linda. "So what do you propose, Mrs. President?"

## 18.8

Alice floated down from the ceiling, perplexed by what had just happened and thankful to be alive. Halfway down, at the moment of her greatest exhaustion, the small human girl she'd seen briefly in the Confusion had appeared at her side and wrapped her arms around Alice's heart, giving her strength and comfort and adding to her power. "Don't worry," she had said, "We can help you." The girl had glanced below them and smiled. Alice looked down to see a skinny little dog leading the way. She focused on her vibrations and continued her descent until she slid into the safety of air.

The girl and her dog departed without a word. Alice sent them her deepest gratitude. She might otherwise have been trapped in the rock forever, her own molecules fused with those of the granite, quartz and sandstone through which she'd transversed.

Alice knelt in the lightless cell. Before her sat the alive one the humans called Mork. The whole Lodge was filled with this alive one's silent alarm. Now able to perceive it clearly, Alice understood what it meant.

YOU IMPERIL YOURSELF, said Mork.

I CAME TO YOUR CALL, answered Alice.

MY CALL WAS ONE OF WARNING, LITTLE SOUL. YOU ENDANGER THE NEW PLAN.

I UNDERSTAND THAT NOW, said Alice. MUST YOU PROCEED?

I MUST, answered Mork.

MAY I WARN THE OTHERS?

EACH MUST DO AS THEY ARE CALLED TO DO, said Mork.

Alice rose and stepped forward, reaching out to pull the knife from Mork's eye.

YOU MUST HURRY, said the alive one.

YOU WILL BE LOST, said Alice.

IT CANNOT BE HELPED.

Alice nodded, accepting the reasoning but vowing to herself to return if she could. She hurried out the door and down the corridor, making her way through the dark stone tunnels, thankful for the highly sensitive eyes her father had given her. She stopped every now and then to catch her breath. Her body was nearing its limit.

She stumbled into the central hub and circled the two scientists. "You must flee, Mr. Gellow," she called as she hurried by. Gellow raised an eyebrow and then turned back to his console.

Alice ran up the tunnel to the human side of the facility and came to the double doors. She attempted to transverse the door but her exhaustion, and the door's thick lead cladding, prevented success. She reached up and touched the buzzer, then slumped to the floor.

The door slid open. There stood two soldiers, stunners drawn. They looked at each other and smiled. "Here's the little traitor," said the soldier on the left.

"You must warn Mr. Rice," said Alice, struggling back to her feet. Her voice was thin. "The facility will soon be extinguished."

The soldier who had spoken grabbed Alice by the wrist. "I think first we'll just lock your little ass up for safe keeping," he said.

Alice called on energy she did not think she had. She passed through the soldier's legs and was gone.

## 18.9

"So, you get my cooperation. What do I get?" asked Rice.

"You get to see your work mean something, Mr. Rice," answered Linda. "The People can turn their skills and power to finding some other way through the mess we've created here. Power and control don't seem to be working. There must be some way for us to live more peaceably on this planet. And I think the people will follow us down that path, if only we will lead them. The universe that the alive ones promised you is still available to us, I think. The wonder. The magic. The whole cosmic story. It's ours, if we can grow up and take our rightful place in it. But we can't do that if we kill ourselves off. And they won't let us, if we do not prove ourselves capable of playing well with others. I think we can do it, Mr. Rice. You have skills and knowledge that will be useful for that. And right now you have the authority of command within this organization. I need your help."

"I get to keep my Scooby-Doo lunchbox and my secret decoder ring?" he asked.

"You get to keep your life," said Obie.

Rice nodded to his former protégé. "Is he gonna be involved in this new gig, Linda? Cuz if he is, I'm not sure I wanna play. He's so serious."

Linda nodded. "My guess is he'll be playing a part, yes," she said. She smiled at Obie. "He's a good man."

Rice sighed, bringing his hands together in front of him and resting his chin, as if deep in thought. He closed his eyes for a few moments, then smiled broadly and opened them again. "Okay," he said. "I'm in. When do I get my company car?"

Linda took a long, slow inhale. "There's just one more thing," she said.

"Oh? What's that?"

"Well... you're a psychopath, Mr. Rice. I'm sure you must know that."

Rice grinned. "Oh, that." He clicked his tongue. "Yeah, it has tended to pop up on my performance reviews."

"So you'll understand that I will never be able to fully trust you."

Rice nodded. "I wouldn't have it any other way," he said.

Linda nodded once. "Good. So you won't be offended, then, if I have Obie keep that gun on you while we clean this all up."

Rice glanced at Obie, then back at Linda. "Like you say, Linda: Carl's a good man." He started to laugh but then noticed Linda's eyes go wide. He turned to see what she was staring at. There stood Alice, just inside the door.

"Alice!" cried Mary, rising.

"We must evacuate the facility," said the tiny child, wobbling on her weary legs. "It will soon discorporate."

Mary was able to catch her before she hit the floor.

18.10

Cole had to admit it: Rice surprised him. The man was an organizational dynamo. Linda had been right; his authority and reach were astounding. As soon as they'd ascertained the meaning of Alice's warning, he'd gotten on the phone. Almost instantly there were helicopters on the roof and buses on the ground. There were almost two hundred souls in the Rock. They had to get moving.

The primary problem was that nobody really understood what was going on. The facility would discorporate? What did that mean? Was Mork some sort of bomb? How could that be? When would she detonate? And what would that mean for the city above? Alice could not say. The techs could measure the astounding energy flux around Mork's body. Mary could sense the building pressure. Rice knew instinctively that the little neomorph was right to advise evacuation. But none of them really knew what to expect. Whatever was happening, it was unprecedented.

So they worked as quickly as they could and hoped it would be enough. Rice sounded a general alarm, gave the order to evacuate, and advised all personnel to assist the President and her companions in any way possible. With that machinery set in motion, Rice headed out into the facility, stalking it like a madman, rushing from office to office and lab to lab, encouraging his colleagues to hurry, making sure there were no holdouts. He scoured the cafeteria and kitchens, thinking some confused workers might try to hide there as the alarms blared. He procured some cuff cutters and freed Mary's hands. It was as if he truly loved his people, just as the President had said. But Obie still followed him everywhere, his old Smith & Wesson hidden in the folds of his jacket.

Cole and Linda, though anxious to reunite with Emily and Iain, spent as much time as they dared looking for her mother, fueled by the faint hope that, despite Rice's assurances, she'd been locked away somewhere in the labyrinthine underground facility that sprawled beneath the nation's capital. A soldier escorted them to the medical wing on the human side, but none of the doctors or nurses there would admit to knowing a thing, even face to face with their President. Linda believed them, but she and Cole kept looking anyways. She knew now how thoroughly information could be compartmentalized, how completely something could be hidden right under one's nose. The doctors' denials were not enough to extinguish her hope.

Mary stayed in Rice's office with Alice, doing what she could to soothe the tiny being now curled in her arms. A quick breakfast had restored some of Alice's energy, but the constant pain and pressure of Mork's psychic alarm assaulted them both, driving them to distraction. Linda had encouraged them to head topside right away but Alice had refused, insisting without explanation that her presence was still required. Mary would not leave without the child. And a part of her would not have traded this moment for anything; it was the first time Alice had ever let Mary hold her.

Within fifteen minutes the facility was almost deserted. It was then that Rice remembered Bob, her body still lying on her bed, surrounded by Alice's homemade, lacework Faraday shield and its menacing protective device. "We have to get her out of here," said Rice, when he and Obie stepped into Bob's room. He looked frantic with concern. "But she's rigged to blow."

They phoned Mary and asked her to bring Alice. The two arrived at Bob's door, just as Cole and Linda came running up, to find Obie squatting next to Bob's bed, tracing the device's multicolored wires with a careful finger. Alice cut to the chase. "It is a deception, sir," she said. "Intended to thwart Mr. Rice." Understanding immediately, Obie reached out with a laugh, knocking the cage away with a flick of his wrist as Rice shouted a warning. The cage fell to pieces. Alice's "explosive device" twinkled its tiny lights, but did not go off.

Rice sighed and joined in Obie's laughter, shaking his head in admiration and wonder. "Ya got me, kid," he said to Alice with a wink, reaching out to tousle the child's hair. Then he knelt by Bob's bed and took her hand gently in his own. "Wakey, wakey, Bob," he said softly. "It's time to blow this joint, darlin'. Before it blows us."

The six of them watched and waited for a full minute, but Bob did not immediately reconstitute, as Rice had predicted. She remained in her comatose state. Rice sighed sadly and squeezed Bob's hand.

A terrified soldier ran past the open door, then returned, incredulous. "Mr. Rice! You folks gotta move! Techs say she's about to detonate! We may have only minutes!" His forehead was glistening with drops of fear.

Rice looked up at Obie and Linda, an expression of pleading in his eyes. "I've got a twelve-footer stashed in the back, Carl," he said. "Should fit through these halls. We can use that to fly her out of here."

Carl agreed and Rice spoke to the soldier. "Tell the techs monitoring Mork to fly that wok back here, private. And then get your ass out of here." Slouching with relief from being told what to do, the soldier took off down the hall.

Linda didn't like it. "Bob's as much a psychopath as Rice," she explained. "I'm not keen on having her running loose. She could come back at any time."

"The wok can restrain her, can it not?" asked Rice. "If we ask it to?"

Obie agreed that the wok could probably hold Bob, body and soul, were she to reconstitute. But Linda remained wary. She had little idea what the woks actually were, how they worked, or why they were still even there. And she was determined to solve her problems without the help of the Strangers. But then Alice spoke up.

"We do not have much time," she said in a quavering voice, looking up at the adults who towered over her. "Mork is scream-ing! Can you not hear her?"

Linda sighed her frustration and gave her assent.

Rice helped Cole carry Bob to the wok, now hovering just out-side her cell door. The hatch melted open as they approached. Obie stood with his gun at the ready. Rice and Cole slid Bob's body into the low-ceilinged compartment. Cole stepped back to Linda's side as Rice bent to straighten Bob's legs. Mary retrieved Bob's knitting basket and placed it beside Bob's feet.

It was then that Rice whirled about, punching Mary in the nose with an upward swipe of the heel of his hand. He turned to confront the others. On his face was a smile. In his hand was a small black cube.

Mary fell without a sound.

Linda gasped.

Alice disappeared.

Obie fired his gun.

## 18.11

Alice knelt in the utter blackness of Mork's cell. WILL YOU TELL ME WHAT YOU HAVE LEARNED? she asked.

WE HAVE NO TIME FOR THIS, answered Mork. The rock underneath was beginning to pulse.

WE HAVE TIME, said Alice.

AS YOU CHOOSE.

MAY YOU LEAVE WITH OUR THANKS AND BLESS-INGS, said Alice, according to the old way.

MY LIFE HAS HAD MEANING, answered Mork in the traditional response.

YOU MUST SHARE IT WITH YOUR TRIBE, said Alice.

I HAVE LEARNED THAT LIFE IS A VESSEL FOR THE POSSIBLE, said Mork. I HAVE LEARNED THAT THE TRUE PLAN CANNOT BE THWARTED, THOUGH IT CAN BE DIVERTED FOR A TIME. I HAVE LEARNED THAT THE ONLY EXPECTATION WE SHOULD HOLD IS THE EXPEC-TATION TO BE SURPRISED.

I WILL TELL THE TRIBE, said Alice.

AND I SHALL GO TELL GOD, said Mork.

Alice rose. MAY YOU LEAVE WITH OUR THANKS AND BLESSINGS, she repeated.

NOW YOU MUST RUN, said Mork.

Alice ran.

The little human girl helped her along.

## 18.12

"You're wearing a Sentry," said Obie. He'd emptied his gun. The bullets had vanished. Rice's hidden shield had swallowed them whole.

"You don't think that little popgun of yours has been running the show here, do you Carl?" said Rice with a smirk.

"Why?" asked Linda. She gestured at Mary on the floor. Mary was not moving.

Rice glanced down for a second. "Why what, girlfriend?" he said. "Why did I kill Mary or why did I go along with you or why am I betraying you now?"

Linda nodded. "All of it," she said.

"Because I could," said Rice. "Because she pissed me off. Because it was fun. Because there's no way in hell I want to live in this nature-boy tree-hugging world you seem bent on." Rice twisted the black cube in his hand. "But mostly because I just can't see myself playing Sonny to a Cher who's stupid enough to think she can control me."

Linda shrugged. "I had to try," she said.

Rice smiled. "Of course you did, sweetheart. And that's why I'm going to live to fight another day, and you're going to die. Just like your mother."

"What?" said Linda.

"I lied," said Rice with a grin.

Cole stepped forward to stand in front of Linda. Rice laughed. "Twofer Tuesday," he said. He drew his hand back to throw the cube.

A black ball the size of a grapefruit popped into existence near the wall opposite the wok and hovered motionless in the air. Its shiny blue-black surface cast a pallor that dimmed the air itself, dwarfing the menace of Rice's rubix. Rice stamped a foot. "Godfuckit, Zach, it was *your* body on the highway, wasn't it? This is none of your goddamned business!" he snarled.

The black ball upheld its perfect stillness as the universe revolved around it, a pushpin pressed into the drawing board of reality by God's own thumb. All around them the carved rock began to quiver and quake. Rice glanced at the ceiling, then looked at the black ball and smiled. "Too late, dickhead," he said. He threw the cube.

In that instant, Obie fully understood the dream that had first brought him to Linda in the Ottawa Lodge: a huge, square drain in the floor, like a black hole, and Linda was being sucked into it. And he remembered Sina's parting words: the age of separation is ended. *There is a field....* With a deep breath, Obie launched himself at Rice, catching the rubix with his chest. His momentum carried him forward as the cube drew him in. He crashed into Rice with one final embrace, drawing his former teacher into the cube with him. In an instant both men were gone, lost in a black spiraling gasp. The cube maintained its trajectory toward Linda and Cole. The black ball flickered into place right in front of them, consuming the cube like the ocean consumes a raindrop. Then it, too, flickered out, vanishing too swiftly even for memories to follow it.

The rock underfoot began to shudder and crack. Whatever it was Mork had unleashed, it was almost upon them.

## 18.13

Linda would never have believed that the wok could hold them all, but it did. They dragged Mary's body in next to Bob's, then crawled in themselves. The rock underfoot heaved and shook. The walls and ceilings were cracking, filling the air with dust. Small shards had begun to fall. At the last moment Alice appeared, her eyes hazy and harried, her face streaked with dust and fatigue. In the corridor behind her, a wall of nothingness rushed toward them like a colony of bats. Linda leapt out to help the child aboard, then ducked back inside as the nothingness struck, jerking in her legs as the hatch melted shut. The wok began to glow around them.

"You have any idea how to fly this thing?" asked Cole.

Linda reached out and grabbed his hand, then donned the metal helmet she found near Bob's head. She took a deep breath and asked the ship to take them to the nearest hospital.

The ship did not seem to move. But of course it did just as she asked.

# Chapter ⊘ Nineteen

## 19.1

The wok landed on the helicopter pad on the roof of Truxton University Medical Center in Falls Church, Virginia. Mary was still alive. The door opened and Linda and Cole looked out to see a confused and very frightened looking orderly sneaking a cigarette.

"We need a stretcher!" shouted Linda. The young man scooted inside.

In less than a minute an emergency team with a gurney burst through the doors and approached the wok. Though obviously bewildered by the sight of their lost President emerging from some sort of strange spacecraft, they snapped into action when Linda shouted again. "We've got a severely injured woman in here!" she cried. "Get your asses in gear!"

They did. In short order Mary was transferred to the gurney and wheeled inside. One young resident, a tiny Indian woman with stunning eyes, lingered behind, unsure as to whether or not they should just leave this strange crew on their roof.

Linda smiled. "I must ask you a favor," she said.

The woman nodded her head.

"I need for your people to not talk about this for a while. Until I can come back and speak with you. Can you make that happen for me?"

The woman nodded again. A slight smile came to her dazed face. "Glad to have you back, ma'am," she said.

Linda took her hand. "Thank you." She crawled back into the wok and the door re-formed behind her. The wok vanished into thin air.

### 19.2

The wok reappeared just inches above the small lawn next to the National Building Museum on 5th and G Streets. The door melted open and Cole climbed out to see Emily and Iain standing on the street corner nearby, staring off to the south and west. The National Academies building had collapsed entirely.

"Emily!" shouted Cole. "Iain!" The kids could not hear him over the blaring of sirens and the rumbling murmuring crying shouting gasping of the city and its people. He ran forward and came up behind them, grabbing them both in his arms. After a short and tearful reunion the three of them climbed back into the wok. It vanished once again.

### 19.3

The wok made one last appearance on the face of the planet that morning; it drifted slowly out of the sky over the paddock next to Cole's home in Vermont. The family's black Welsh pony, Fanny, snorted as the craft dropped into view, but did not retreat as it landed less than ten feet away. The door melted open. Out climbed Emily and Iain, with Cole and Linda right behind. Emily flung herself at the pony, burying her face in the horse's soft mane. Iain walked up to pat Fanny's nose.

Cole and Linda turned to see Alice kneeling beside her mother's body. "May you leave with our thanks and blessings," whispered the strange, tiny being. Then she stood and joined the others in the grass.

The wok rose into the air and tipped slightly toward the onlookers, as if to say goodbye. Then it lifted toward the sky as though grabbed by an unseen hand and was gone in an instant.

The weary travelers made their way back home.

## 19.4

Cole and his two older children left almost immediately to check on Grace and her grandfather. Linda stayed at the house, passing on the thirty-minute drive to the hospital in Waitsfield. It was way too early to show herself to the world. She had no idea whom to trust or what to say. She did not know if it was safe to reveal her whereabouts. And she was exhausted beyond all description. She gave the three her love and sent them on their way, then flopped back onto the sofa and turned on the television, which still sat on the end table where they'd left it. Alice crawled up beside her and Linda wrapped an arm around the girl's tiny shoulders. Linda yawned deeply and Alice echoed her. They both desperately needed sleep. But first, they needed information.

The news from Washington D.C. was shocking. Vast areas of the city had fallen in on themselves, as if enormous quantities of sand, silt, gravel, clay, and rock had simply vanished, creating a giant sinkhole that had tried to swallow the nation's capitol in a single gulp. Major damage extended from the Potomac on the west to 8th St NW on the east, from the Tidal Basin on the south to K St NW on the north.

The National Mall was now laced with a network of canyons, as were major portions of George Washington University. The Lincoln Memorial had mostly disappeared into the Earth, save for Honest Abe's head, which had rolled out like a bocce ball onto a small section of untouched lawn. The Washington Monument had fallen and shattered, it's tip pointing accusingly at the White House. The White House, with no means of evasion, had collapsed in on itself like an apprehended felon, leaving a pile of jumbled excuses. The Capitol Building, sited outside the primary zone of destruction, had been swallowed up as well, its dome sitting lopsidedly on a pile of rubble like a scoop of ice cream spilled from a cone. The Statue of Freedom pointed toward the sky at an awkward angle, trying to shift the blame. It was as if someone had planned a controlled demolition of Washington D.C. that would take out the heart of the U.S. government while leaving the rest of the city as untouched as they could. It was stunning.

Linda and Alice stared at the images. One aerial shot struck them in particular, as the harsh morning sun, having burned through the haze, put the damage into stark relief. They looked at each other with wide eyes. Both knew what that spidery network of sinkholes and chasms and gullies indicated. They knew what had been hidden directly underneath. They knew what those images meant: the human-alien facility, "the Rock," had been taken completely away.

There were surprisingly few casualties given the extent of the damage: many injuries but only a dozen or so dead. As the story unfolded through the morning, it got stranger and stranger. There had been hundreds of reports of UFO activity in the skies over D.C. before and during the "event." There were reports of people being lifted up out of their chairs or their cars, of people being "magically protected" from harm as buildings fell all around them. There were reports of an exceedingly high degree of absenteeism, as people called in sick or otherwise just didn't show up to their jobs. And it turned out that there had been multiple-car pile-ups on virtually every major artery into the city, backing up traffic for miles and preventing huge numbers of people from making it to work. Reporters told lurid tales of miraculous coincidences and amazing escapes. The public ate it up.

Yet there *had* been casualties: deaths and injuries, traumas and loss. And there were many people now being reported as missing. It would be a long time before they would know the full extent of it. Linda frowned, thinking again of the high costs the aliens could demand. The aliens. The gods. God. The Universe. There was simply too much that lay beyond her comprehension. She sighed deeply, vowing to simply witness without judgment. At least for now.

Equally stunning was the news from around the globe. What had happened in D.C. had happened elsewhere. There was similar, extensive damage reported in Ottawa, Riyadh, Moscow, Tokyo, Reykjavik, Canberra, and Berlin, with less widespread damage to Brussels, Santiago, Beijing, Khartoum, Oslo, Baghdad, Port-au-Prince, Capetown and the Vatican. In each location the pattern repeated: government-related buildings, monuments, and structures had fallen into sinkholes and chasms. Apparently the People and their Plan had extended far beyond the United States and Canada.

As the morning wore on, reports filtered in from other areas. From the deserts of New Mexico and Australia to the base of Mt. Shasta in California, from the Antarctic icecap to the hot tropical forests of the Amazon basin, new canyons and chasms and rifts had opened up around the planet, just as they had in D.C. Some of them were small, the size of a single car or house; others were almost as vast and complex in structure as what was becoming known as "the Washington sinkhole." There was even a report from the observatory on Mauna Kea of a new crater on the moon. Everywhere the same pattern seemed to prevail: few casualties and a great many UFO reports. The Internet went wild. When a local station ran an interview with an older woman who claimed to have seen the missing President in a UFO on the ground in D.C. shortly after the chaos began, all hell broke loose in the blogosphere.

No one in the mainstream media could explain what had happened. There was no radiation. No traces of chemical explosion. No falling missiles. No mushroom clouds. There had been no associated earthquakes of any significance. The ground underneath had simply vanished, and whatever was above it had filled in the void. It didn't make any sense. It was a mystery. But of course many people thought they knew exactly what had happened.

As she watched the news, Linda came to understand that, though she'd been there, even she didn't really know. It was too big. And she was too tired to try to wrap her head around it now. She realized she'd been hoping for word of her mother. None had come. Part of her knew that she should be there, in the fray, acting like the President she'd been elected to be, overseeing and commanding and making decisions, encouraging and cajoling and empathizing and reassuring. But she couldn't do it. She just couldn't.

It wasn't just because she didn't know whom to trust, or whether it was safe for her now. It was something far deeper than that. Something fundamental had shifted, as though the hand of God had reached inside her and flipped a switch at the base of her spine. The rules she thought she'd been playing by had been revealed as illusions. Progress, the future, the "American way," even such primary notions as physical reality and life and death, every bit of solid ground she'd thought she was standing on had fallen away beneath her in the past week, threatening to swallow her up as surely as the sinkholes threatened the capitol city. President Linda Travis was no longer sure what mattered. She was no longer sure if anything mattered. And that realization pinned her to the sofa: sore, exhausted, and filled with frozen grief and paralyzing doubt. She did not know if she would ever get up again.

As the news droned on, Linda remained on the sofa, hugging Alice to her like a life preserver. The velvety nap of the President's shaved head cushioned her scattered thoughts. The Vice-President would have to handle things, she thought as she drifted into sleep. That's what he was for, wasn't it? He would have to make do.

Finally she slipped into that further realm, to seek the answers she could not find in this one. She did not notice when Alice moved over to the recliner, crossed her legs, and closed her eyes as well.

### 19.5

"Grandpa!" said Emily happily, running toward his bed.

"Careful, Em," cautioned Cole. He followed his daughter into the room, his hand on Iain's shoulder. Emily stopped short and approached more slowly.

All three stood and looked down at Ben Thomas. His face was the color of dirty sheets, his hair was matted, his eyelids veined and pale and moist. Emily ran a finger along the IV line that ran into his arm.

Cole's father opened his eyes. "Hi, kids," he said, his voice a rasping whisper. He glanced up at Cole. "Grace okay?" he asked.

Cole nodded. "She's one floor up, Dad. Still in a coma."

Ben nodded, an almost imperceptible gesture. "I'm sorry," he said. There were tears in the corners of his dull, drained eyes. He fumbled for Emily's hand and grasped it firmly when he found it. "I'm glad... to see you guys," he said, looking from Emily to Iain. Iain moved around to the other side of his bed and took his grandfather's other hand. Ben sighed and closed his eyes.

"Nothing to be sorry for, Dad," murmured Cole. He stayed a couple of steps back.

Ben smiled and spoke, with eyes still closed. "You never were much of a liar, Cole," he said.

After a while, Cole excused himself to go sit with Grace, leaving Emily and Iain to stay with their grandfather, who'd fallen back to sleep. He nodded at the nurse he'd spoken to earlier as he walked past their station. His father would be fine, the man had said, though it would take a good, long while for him to get there. One bullet had destroyed a section of Ben Thomas's colon, though no bullet had been found, and there was no exit wound. The other had grazed a kidney. And it had been well past "the golden hour" before he'd arrived at the hospital. But an unknown somebody had fashioned a field dressing even before Officer Fairly had arrived. That dressing had probably saved his life. Cole thought he knew who that somebody was, and prayed for Mary's recovery.

Cole sighed as he walked down the hallway. His father would be "fine." Cole wondered what that meant. Perhaps "I'm sorry" was the beginning of it. He'd wait and see. But he knew now that such things were possible. He knew now, in fact, that much more was possible than he'd ever imagined. Cole, himself, was no longer who he'd been. The whole world had shifted on its axis. That's how it felt.

He caught the elevator just as the doors were closing and squeezed in with an apologetic smile. Stepping out onto the next floor, he made his way down the hallway. Grace was in the room at the end on the right, with two large corner windows looking out across the valley. Cole was thankful that there was nobody in the other bed.

A young nurse with short, straight, orange-red hair popped out as he reached for the door. "Are you the father?" she asked. The look in her dark green eyes almost destroyed his composure. It was as though she could see right into his heart and share his deepest feelings.

Cole nodded.

The nurse pulled Cole into the room and closed the door behind her, as though to speak in private. She gestured toward Grace with a nod of her head. "She'll be back," she said.

Cole frowned. "How do you know?" he said, his voice low and demanding.

"I'm not supposed to say things like this," the nurse said, glancing back at the door. She looked Cole in the eyes. "You understand?"

Cole nodded. He gestured toward Grace. "Tell me."

The nurse paused, regarding him with soft, sure eyes. "I just know. I always know. They ... the patients ... the one's who're, you know, gone... they tell me. Whether they're finished here and are passing on. Or if they're coming back." She stepped toward the hospital bed, then turned back to Cole. "Grace told me. Last night. She's coming back." Her eyes welled up as she spoke. She reached out and put a hand squarely on Cole's chest. "So you just hang on, Dad. Okay?" she said. "Just hang on. She's coming back."

Cole nodded. The nurse returned his nod and left without another word, closing the door. Cole walked to Grace's bed and took the seat beside her and watched her as she slept. After a while he said the same thing his father had said. "I'm sorry."

## 19.6

*"Nothing to be sorry for, Daddy," said Grace as she watched her father. She knew she would not be heard. Reaching out to her body, she tried again to feel her way back. Again, she failed. Her body was right there. She could reach out and touch it. But she could not get back inside. And she did not understand why that was.*

## 19.7

Linda looked around the room. Alice sat cross-legged and silent in the recliner, her eyes closed, her breath faint. The afternoon sun had brought a warm glow to the room. Thankful for that, Linda closed her eyes and tried to recall her dream. Only ... it hadn't been a dream, had it? There, sleeping on Cole's living room sofa, Linda had been given the gift of remembering.

It was the day of her escape. She was at Long Fall, Earl's old family farm in West Virginia, what the press called "the Ranch." The sun was setting behind the mountains and she'd headed off into the woods, to take a short, brisk walk before dinner. Mary was with her. And two Secret Service agents. Some of the trees were in their full autumn colors. Others were just beginning to turn.

Linda stomped down the trail, furious. They'd taken her again. In the night. Spud. A few others. But no other humans. Nobody from the People. They'd taken her right from her room, stolen her away from under the noses of her security detail, floated her right through the glass of her second-story bedroom window and up along a beam of blue stardust to their ship waiting overhead. It was huge and terrifying and glorious.

Inside the ship, it seemed, she'd found herself standing at the edge of a huge inland lake, surrounded by a vast desert plain. To the west were distant hills, brown and dusty, rising up toward the sky. It reminded her of a scene from some Biblical movie. The sun burned hot and white directly overhead through a gauzy haze. She could feel the heat through the soles of her shoes, the flinty sand on her face. She could smell the sea, and smoke in the breeze.

People everywhere were running and screaming, streaming toward her and past and beyond, clinging to children and clothing and their treasured belongings. Their eyes were wide with terror. There was fire coming down from the sky. Fire like balls of lava. Like falling missiles. Fire like flaming arrows. Linda could see to the north that a city was burning.

"*Those who cannot remember the past are condemned to repeat it,*" said Spud over her shoulder. Linda whirled to confront him, but there was no one there.

"What is this?" she'd shouted.

"*There are none so blind as those who will not see.*"

Linda had picked up a rock and thrown it. "Come talk to me, you fuck!" she'd screamed. "If I need quotes I'll look in my *Bartlett's*!"

The fire rained down on the fleeing crowds. A woman with a child in her arms burst into flame right in front of her. "How can you do this?" she cried to the heavens.

This time there was no response. Around her the destruction continued.

Linda had looked up just in time to see the fireball that hit her. Her whole body turned to flames, burning away everything that she was and would be and ever had been. The sky turned black and then she was back in her bed. She'd fallen to sleep in an instant.

Linda had taken the path down to the river and headed toward the base of the falls. Mary followed close behind. The memory of her abduction rattled in the President's skull as she stepped carefully over the rocks and roots. She looked up and smiled. The rhododendrons were beginning to crowd the path. Linda imagined them slapping the faces and arms of Mary and the Secret Service goons who followed her, two young men whom she'd never met before, both of whom she was certain were members of the People. She pushed through and hurried on.

The path curved away from the river and up over a small ridge. Linda increased her speed, noting the river as it flowed below her. It was beautiful this time of year. The autumn leaves played in the eddies and painted the rocks at the foot of the falls. This was where, on a weekend visit to his parents, Earl had told her of his desire to run for the state senate. Together, they had decided to give it a try, and that one decision had changed the course of their lives in ways they could never have imagined.

Mary was huffing behind her, trying to keep up. "You okay, Mrs. President?" she called out. The agents had fallen behind.

Linda ignored her and kept on. The path wound its way back down to the river and opened up before her. There were the falls, towering above, majestic and cold in the twilight. Linda plunged without hesitation into the pool of water at the fall's base.

"Mrs. President!" called Mary.

Linda turned to see her warden, doubled over and struggling for breath at the river's edge. The Secret Service agents crashed around the bend to join her.

"I'm just taking a swim, Mary!" Linda said with scorn. "You guys are such wimps!" She pushed at the pill container in her front pocket, hoping its presence would not be revealed by her wet clothing.

Mary frowned, hands on her hips. The agents puffed themselves up, as if to say this was no big deal.

Linda strode further into the pooling water. It was up to her waist now, deliciously cold, and she kept moving forward. The memory of fire from above had clung to her body all day long. She needed those falling waters, to wash the flames away.

"Please be careful!" shouted Mary from the shore. The agents had taken positions on either side of her, watching the woods and the ridge behind as if every tree were a potential assassin.

Linda just waved Mary off and plunged into the falls, almost dropping to her knees but catching herself and pushing against the water's weight to regain her feet. She turned slowly as the water pounded her shoulders and head and face. She let her head fall back and screamed into the twilight, delighting in the sound of her voice as it echoed off the stone wall behind the falls. Spent and tired, she fell back against that cold, rocky face, smooth and wet and dark. She could barely make out Mary and the agents through the sheet of falling water.

And then the tiny gray hands had grabbed her from behind and pulled her into the rock and sent her on her way.

The President opened her eyes with a gasp. There stood Alice, her fingers on Linda's forearm. "I require food now, Mrs. Linda," she said. Linda rose to get Alice something to eat, smiling at the touch of the strange, tiny hands that pulled her into the kitchen.

## 19.8

"You give up?" asked Iain. There was victory in his eyes.

Linda looked out over the board. Iain now controlled the entire world, save for her little corner of South America, and the few armies he hadn't even bothered with that sat, lonely and impotent, on Eastern Australia. He'd just taken the last of her armies on Brazil, attacking from North Africa, destroying the integrity of her only continent. He pushed his pile of pieces across the ocean and picked up the dice.

Linda scrunched her nose. Emily and Alice had long since given up and gone upstairs. It was down to the two of them. There was no way she could win. "You're a little shit, you know that?" she said, smiling.

"Yes!" Iain pumped his fist and grinned broadly. He stood and raised both arms over his head. "I beat the President of the United States at Risk!" he crowed. He sat back down and started to pick up his pieces.

"No, no," said Linda. "I play the game, you make the popcorn. That was the deal. I'll clean up and you get started."

Iain shrugged a "whatever" and headed toward the kitchen. Linda scooped the brightly colored armies back into their containers and put away the cards and dice and packed it all in the box.

Somewhere along the way it had turned to night. Linda peered into the darkness, remembering the spotlights in the trees and the glowing eyes. Was that really only a week ago? How could that be? The woods tonight were dark and still, the sky overcast and starless. The forces that had driven the week's events had rebalanced, like a hurricane now spent, an avalanche now settled. Or maybe those forces had been appeased, as Sina had demanded. Whatever it was, this was a very different night. The urgency that had filled that evening was gone, displaced by a welcome sense of safety and calm. This was a day for a fire in the woodstove, an early dinner of frozen pizza, and a game at the dining-room table, with a movie and popcorn still to come. This was a day for the normal they had all once known. Linda doubted that normal would ever fully return.

None of it was normal for Alice, of course. The girl was an unknown. A riddle wrapped inside a mystery wrapped inside a flour tortilla, as Earl used to joke. Linda smiled to hear the girls upstairs, whispering. Emily was showing Alice her violin, from the sounds of it. Linda took a long, slow breath. Perhaps, to Emily, Alice was no mystery at all.

Cole had come back mid-afternoon, Emily and Iain right at his heels. He'd charged through the door, wrapped Linda in his arms and kissed her deeply, letting his two older children know exactly how things now were. Emily and Iain simply smiled and fell onto the sofa, exhausted and glad to be home. Cole and the kids spoke of their grandfather and Grace. Linda told them what she'd learned from the news, and they watched the television for a while together, to learn of anything new.

But Cole had been distracted. As much as he wanted to stay, he had to get back to Grace. He'd made a quick phone call to Cat and Jake, his closest neighbors, telling them that they'd returned and that he would explain it all as soon as was possible, and asking, in the meantime, that they pass the word to the rest of the community: for now they just needed to be left alone. Then he turned to his family, kissed them all, even Alice, and headed back to the hospital. Emily and Iain had both taken naps in their rooms. Alice and Linda had watched the news and dozed on the sofa.

"Popcorn!" called Iain as he poured on the melted butter. The four of them sat side-by-side on the sofa in the family room and watched some action-comedy thing Iain had said was great. It was okay. Alice had never watched a movie before and said she felt "seriously assaulted" by the rush of images and noise. It was not long before she'd wandered back upstairs. Emily followed. Linda stayed until the end, mostly in support of Iain, who so clearly needed her to love it as much as he did. But she was glad when it was finished. Iain headed upstairs to chat with his Google-Land friends, with strict instructions not to mention that the U.S. President was staying at his house. Linda washed the dishes and stared out the window. She waited for Cole to call.

Eventually Linda strolled upstairs to check on the girls. She smiled to see them lying together on Emily's bed. Emily was reading *The Little Prince* out loud and Alice was entranced. "I've never traveled with birds," said Alice.

Emily looked up at Linda, her eyes wide with wonder at her new friend. "Any word from Dad?" she asked. Linda shook her head. Emily hesitated, then asked another question. "Will Grace be okay?"

"I hope so," said Linda, turning away to hide the tears that welled in her eyes.

"Grace is the third child of your father," said Alice, pushing herself up onto her elbows.

"Yes," said Emily.

"Why is she not here?"

"She's been ... sick," said Emily. She got up and pulled a scrapbook from her shelf. "Would you like to see her?"

Alice sat up. "Yes."

Emily sat down and flipped through the pages, finding a recent snapshot of her sister. "This is her at her last birthday party," she said.

"This is Grace?" asked Alice, the skin of her forehead wrinkling slightly, as if she were experimenting with how to make a frown.

Emily nodded.

Alice smiled slightly. "I have met her," she said with a nod.

The phone rang and Linda went down to answer it.

Alice came face to face with Emily, seizing her with her huge black eyes. "I have met her," she repeated slowly.

### 19.9

Cole woke with a start. It was after midnight and the room was darkened. Something was wrong. The beeping had stopped.

The beeping.... He launched himself toward the call button but the nurse appeared before he could punch it.

"What is it?" she asked, making her way to Grace's bed. She was an older woman, stick-thin and full of energy. Her eyes were kind. She quickly checked Grace's pulse as Cole looked on. "We're gonna need some help," she said as she punched a button on the intercom system. At once an automated voiced announced a code blue in Grace's room.

The cardiac monitor started beeping again. "Grace," whispered Cole. He stood at her bedside, watching as her eyes moved rapidly behind their lids. "She's dreaming," he said as the nurse hurried about. The door opened and the room was soon filled with doctors and residents and nurses.

The thin nurse reported what had happened. "But she's normal now," she said. As if to prove her wrong Grace flat-lined again. The doctors and nurses crowded around. Cole stepped out of the way.

And then Grace disappeared. She was there, and then she wasn't. The resident who'd been holding the stethoscope to her chest almost fell forward as his hands dropped to the bed. "What the—?" he said. He pulled back immediately. One nurse turned and ran out of the room. A young, male resident gasped. Grace's bed was empty.

Then Grace reappeared, looking as whole and real as she had a moment before. The medical staff stepped back. Cole moved forward and put his hands on the railing. "C'mon, Grace," he said, his voice soft but intense. Grace disappeared again. A nurse behind him began to weep. The rest stood transfixed. After a minute Grace reappeared briefly, then flickered out again. Cole held on.

And then the Universe itself disappeared. All that remained was Cole and Grace, two hearts, two sparks, two souls alone in the void. Cole reached out and took Grace's hand and asked whoever was listening for help. The Universe flickered back into existence and Grace, once more on her bed, opened her eyes and smiled.

"Hi, Daddy," she said.

One of the residents fainted.

## 19.10

Cole and Grace drove up to the house just before 9:00 the next morning and Linda and the kids ran out to meet them. Moments later Dennis appeared, running across the pasture, barking his fool head off. Cat followed behind, trying to keep up. "Sorry!" she called out. "He woke up in the middle of the night and I kept him in as long as I could but he's been barking all morning and then he escaped out the cat door—" Cat stopped short and her jaw fell slack, to see the missing President walking out to meet her. Dennis did not stop short.

Hugs and kisses and welcome-homes filled the morning air. Dennis's tail would not stop wagging. Fanny ran the paddock's perimeter, kicking up her feet. Even the goats joined in the party, bumping heads and nibbling fingers, which delighted Alice to no end.

Alice met Grace in the flesh and Grace told them all how Alice had appeared in the night and shown her how to realign with the frequency of her own flesh. Alice told how Grace had helped her to transverse the solid rock over Mork's cell. Cat frowned in confusion, to see this strange, tiny child, and to hear such things from children so young. After a while she just shook her head in surrender, said goodbye, and headed back home. The rest of them went back into the house. They were finally all together again.

Nobody knew where to start. There were too many stories needing to be told. Cole had died and come back to life. Emily and Iain had seen their grandfather shot before their eyes. They'd flown in a UFO and walked through walls to escape a psychopath. Grace had traveled across the Universe and battled scary people. Linda had been chased and threatened and beaten and abused. She'd fallen in love and then had that love taken away, and then restored once again. Alice had seen the alive ones leave and the Plan disintegrate, and had watched her mother disappear into the sky. Grace had seen her dead mother take off on her own next adventure. They tried to speak of these things but found themselves strangely tongue-tied. As if to speak of them would dishonor them. As if to speak of them would bring them into the world of the mundane, where they could never be fully understood.

After an uncomfortable silence, Alice slid down from the sofa, where she'd been sitting with Grace, and addressed them like the ambassador she was, looking each in the eye as she spoke. "It is time for us to say goodbye to our dead," she said. "We must honor their lives and release them, so that they may freely take the next steps on their journeys." When nobody spoke she cocked her head quizzically. "Do you not know this?"

Linda laughed with delight at Alice's wisdom and reached out to hug the girl. "You're right, Alice," she said, her face buried in the tiny hybrid's long, straight, milk-and-honey hair. "That's exactly what we need to do." Her throat caught as she spoke and she started to weep. And that was the beginning of it.

They cried. For Linda's mother, whose whereabouts remained unknown. For Obie, the amazing uncle the kids had never known, and the friend and advisor that Linda would sorely miss in the days and months ahead. For Ruth, the kids' mother, whom they still missed every day. They cried and laughed and told stories and cried some more. They cried for Grandpa Ben still in the hospital. They cried for Pooch and for Keeley, for Utterpok and Immaqa and the dead Inuit whose names they had never even heard. They cried for the guards Ben had hired to protect his grandchildren. They cried for Mary, who might still live, and for Jack, who was trapped between worlds. They cried for the world, for the forests and oceans that were groaning under the weight of the human assault, for the animals and plants that cried out for their aid, for the polar bear and the walrus, the caribou and eagle, the rabbit and the seal and the fox, who had come to their aid.

Alice insisted they go even further, including Mork and the other alive ones who'd stayed behind to help, who had perished in the destruction of the human-alien facilities. Including Bob, Alice's mother, gone now on some healing journey of her own. Including Mr. Random. And including Mr. Rice. Though Cole recoiled at the idea, Linda understood. "The hunt that fails to show proper respect will give the offended spirits cause to avenge themselves," she said, repeating the last words they'd heard from Sina. "The age of separation has ended." So they said what they could, to honor Theodore Rice.

At last they cried for themselves, for Cole and Linda, for Iain and Emily and Grace, for Alice, even for Dennis. They cried for their pain, their fear, their exhaustion, their love, and their loss. They cried until their tears were no more. They cried until they were finished. They cried until the new light dawned in their souls. Though Alice did not join them in the tears, she was present in every way she could be, with soft words and gentle touches and her deep, dark eyes.

"May you leave with our thanks and blessings," she said at last, her face to the heavens. And that was the end of it.

19.11

Cole made lunch, heating some soup he'd found in the freezer and making a salad from the greens an unknown neighbor had left on their porch. They sat together at the table, eating peacefully, sharing kindnesses and passing the salt. Emily and Grace competed for Alice's attention. Alice chose to sit between them, watching them both intently, even smiling her stiff, slight smile as Grace goofed around. Iain sat quietly, slurping his soup and staring out the window. Cole smiled and sighed. Linda smiled in return.

It was Iain who broke the spell. "I don't want to go back," he said, wading into a patch of silence.

"Go back where?" asked Linda, after a moment.

Iain shrugged. "I don't know," he said, looking around the house. "I just don't want to go back."

"I don't want to go back to school," said Emily.

"I don't want to go back to Washington," said Linda at the same time. She and Emily looked at each other and broke out laughing.

"I'm not sure I even want to be here," said Cole, admitting something he hadn't even known he was feeling.

"How can a person go back anywhere?" asked Alice, innocently. The whole family cracked up.

It was Iain, again, who finally put it into words. "I mean, how can we go back to our old life after all that's happened?" he asked, looking around the table.

Nobody had an answer for him. As sad, tired, and beat up as the past week had left them, it seemed that none of them were all that glad to be back in "the real world." They'd tried it: the movie, the pizza, the popcorn, the games. It was fine for an evening, as a reprieve from the intensity, but, ultimately, it just didn't satisfy. For all its pain and loss, the past week had meant something very real, for themselves and for the world. Their regular life felt pale and bland in comparison.

After lunch the kids headed upstairs. They were going to witness as Dennis told his story. Alice would translate. Linda and Cole settled down on the sofa and turned on the news.

The world was in turmoil. That was the phrase that kept bouncing around in Linda's head. Due in large measure to the more than ten-year-long "great recession" that had circled the globe, rescue and cleanup resources were stressed beyond their limits in places all over the planet. Reports continued to filter in, of strange events and unexplained destruction. Albert Singer was clearly in way over his head. The world was demanding answers and he had none to give. And he was really awful at making things up.

"We can't just hide here," said Linda after a while.

Cole nodded but said nothing. He knew she was right, but he did not want to admit it. He reached out and took Linda's hand and squeezed. For now, they were safe. His children. His love. He would cherish this moment for as long as he could.

Upstairs Dennis barked and the kids laughed.


19.12


It was two more days before Linda made her whereabouts known to anyone else in the government. It took that long for her to find and put together a small group she felt she could trust.

Alice's help was instrumental in that regard. Her knowledge of the worldwide organization known informally as "the People" was extensive. She knew which members of Linda's cabinet, which Senators and Congressmen, and which military leaders, had not been a part of that operation and its "Plan." Linda had been greatly dismayed to learn how few there were whom the People had not in some way compromised.

Linda turned first to the Undersecretary of the Navy, an amiable older man named Stan Walsh whom she'd met earlier in the year at a White House reception. Initially suspicious of her phone call, he finally agreed to bring together the nine others Linda named for a meeting, all of whom had been cleared by Alice.

Many in the group were quite irritated by the time Linda, Cole and Alice walked into the vacant ski-club Cole had found and rented in nearby Granville. Walsh had told the group only that an answer awaited them, and had relied on his reputation, and in some cases his personal relationships, to compel the others to make the trip to rural Vermont.

They sat shivering and grumbling in the cold empty space, then rose in surprise as the President walked through the rear door. "We have work to do, folks," Linda said with a smile. She shook hands and gave a couple of hugs and then the ten of them sat for a meeting that lasted the rest of the day. Eyebrows were raised as she told her tale, but the presence of a tiny human-alien hybrid brought Linda the credibility she needed, and the fire Cole started in the woodstove warmed their bodies and soothed their concerns. Two military leaders, two cabinet members, two senators, two congressmen, one Supreme Court justice and the Deputy Director of Central Intelligence: this group would serve as her core, her starting point. From here, she would take back her government.

"But it may not look like you think it should," said Linda, toward the end of their meeting. "This hidden government, this network of powers that has been controlling things behind the scenes, will not be taken down with a frontal assault. Not right now. Even with the aliens having withdrawn their support, the shadow government still has a great deal of power and wealth at its disposal. If we try to take them out with accusations and arrests and trials, I fear it would tear us apart. These people are used to being in control. It's possible that many of them are psychopaths. They will not give up easily. And I, for one, have no wish to meet with the same sort of accident Ed Bickle encountered."

Helen Hurt, the Secretary of the Interior, shifted in her chair. Her expression was pained. "So, what is it you're proposing, Mrs. President? And what do you need from us?"

Linda smiled. "I need you to trust me, Helen," she said. "All of you." She looked around the room. "I need you to be here for me. I need you to hold me and support me and encourage me when it seems hopeless. I need you to be my council of elders." Linda stopped for a moment, letting her words sink in. She knew the work ahead of them might feel huge and daunting to these people. She leaned forward a bit, to decrease the distance between them. *The age of separation has ended.* "I don't really have a clue what to do next, Helen. Everything has changed. Everything. And I'm afraid that I shall have to lead us all down a path that many will not wish to travel. I will look ... crazy, I think. Sometimes I will look as if I've lost my mind. And I don't think I'll be able to do this if I don't have you all behind me."

Linda looked at her council members. There was much that they did not understand, but these were good people. They could learn the truth of things, just as she had. They would have to. "Are you up for this?" she asked, moving from face to face. None of them looked away. Every one of them eventually nodded. Linda let her tears of gratitude slip down her face, in honor of their courage.

### 19.13

"Good afternoon, General," said Linda as she stepped through the wall, hand in hand with Alice.

The General looked up, surprised, glancing for a moment at the tiny child before settling his gaze on the President. "Interesting," he said, regrouping a smile.

Linda looked around his office. It was rich and well appointed, with huge windows looking out over a small pond. She returned his smile. The General was just a small, tired old man who thought his medals meant something. "You got out while the getting was good, I see," she said.

The General nodded. "It's always nice to have a place to... retire to. When things start to get out of hand." His eyes flicked nervously back to Alice for a moment, before returning to the President. "You doing okay?" he asked.

Linda nodded. "Nietzsche was right."

"Really? How's that?"

"You didn't kill me, General. You made me stronger."

The General said nothing.

"Do you know where my mother is, General?" asked Linda.

"I'm afraid I have no idea, Mrs. President," he said. "That sort of thing fell to Mr. Rice."

"He said you took care of it," said Linda with cold tension in her voice.

The General smiled. "I'm certain by now you've learned not to believe Mr. Rice," he said. He settled back in his executive chair and put his hands behind his neck in a display of confidence. "Our little morph can walk through walls now, I see," he said, not looking at Alice. "I'm glad you've returned her to me. That little trick will come in handy."

"You can't be that stupid," said Linda. "The whole game's changed. Certainly you're not going to keep playing the old one?"

The General leaned forward, bringing his elbows to his desk and resting his chin on his hands. "You got a better offer, I suppose," he said.

Linda smiled. "Let's just say I have a different game. One we should have started playing a long time ago."

"A different game, you say?" mused the General. "And obviously a game you think so compelling that I shall fall over myself with eagerness to join."

"There's a seat at the table for you, General. If you agree to follow the rules."

"I see." The General sighed. "And what do we call this new game?" he asked.

"How about we call it 'Avoiding Extinction,' General? Or maybe 'Growing Up as a People'? You interested in a game like that?"

The General frowned. He swung his chair around, to stare for a moment at the ducks in the pond. "I might be," he said without turning back. "As you say, the old game seems to be over. Our friends in high places have taken their ball and gone back home. And then there's Rice and his gang..." His words trailed off. He turned back to face them, glancing over at Alice and smiling. He looked back to Linda. "There's a place for me at the table, you say?"

"If you follow the rules," answered Linda.

"And who's making the rules?" asked the General.

"The planet and her creatures are making the rules, General. The laws of physics and biology and chemistry are making the rules. The Universe is making the rules."

The General raised his eyebrows. "Quite a game you're proposing," he said.

"The only game worth playing, General. Should be interesting. Are you in?"

The General smiled.

## 19.14

Two days later Stendahl Banks got the highest ratings of his career. At four thirty-seven in the afternoon, an ACN Special Report broke into their regular programming, interrupting an episode of their hit game show, *Yes We Can!* There sat Stendahl Banks in what looked like a large, open lounge area. Across from him, next to a woodstove with a fire blazing brightly, sat Linda Travis, her head now shaved. As the two of them spoke, word spread like wildfire around the planet. Soon, tens and hundreds of millions of viewers were watching. ACN's feed, made freely available to anyone and everyone, saturated the airwaves.

"So, I don't know where to begin, Mrs. President," said Banks nervously, obviously bewildered by the whole thing. "I suppose the first question is, what happened? Where have you been? What's going on? And how did you end up coming to me?"

Linda smiled. "Times are so urgent we have to ask our questions four at a time, don't we, Mr. Banks?"

"Excuse me?" said Banks.

Linda waved him off. "Just a joke for an absent friend," she said wistfully. She shifted in her chair and held her hands out to warm them in the fire. She turned back to Banks. "You need to understand that I don't know what to say to you, Mr. Banks. There's much that I don't yet understand. I'm not sure what will help. And much of what I have to say will profoundly challenge the belief systems out of which we've been operating, and which most people regard as reality itself. Learning to question such fundamental assumptions is not easy, Mr. Banks. So I need you to go slowly with me. I need you to ask really good questions. I need you to hang in there with me, even when I sound insane. And I need you to agree to just suspend judgment for a while, and let this play out. It will take some time to unravel this past week's events, Mr. Banks. I need your help with that. Today, and in the weeks and months and years to come. I need your help. Can you do that for me?"

Stendahl Banks thought for a moment, then nodded his head. "I can help," he said. He was completely disarmed.

"Thank you," said Linda. There were tears welling in her eyes.

"You'll tell me where to stick it if I get out of line, right?" joked Banks.

Linda laughed. "You know I will."

The interview proceeded from there. The President spoke of that first briefing, so many months ago, of the conspiracy to hide the presence of alien beings on this planet, of the secret government that had slowly taken control of the world. She spoke of her escape and of the chase that ensued, of her capture and her torture and of how she escaped once again. She spoke vaguely of those who helped her along the way, some of whom had given their lives so that the truth might be told. She described how the aliens have now withdrawn their support from this shadow government and explained how the recent disruptions and destructions around the planet were a manifestation of that withdrawal. She told of what she had come to understand about the planetary crises they now face, from the decline of fossil fuels to the chaotic climate and the destruction of soils, oceans, forests and entire ecosystems. "We're on our own now, and it's time for us to prove that we are worthy of survival," Linda said to the camera. "We have been terribly, terribly off." The world sighed.

She said nothing of Cole and his children, of Keeley and Pooch, of Obie or the Inuit. She named few names. She insisted that she be allowed to take the time she needed, the time the country needed, to uncover and resolve the situation in a way that would help the planet and her many living creatures, rather than simply serve the interests of politicians, bankers, or the media outlets. And she insisted that there would be no witch-hunt, to seek out and punish those who have stood in the way of the truth. "We will find some other way through this, Mr. Banks," she said. "Those who need to be contained will be contained. The rest of us will find some way to come together again, as we face into our new situation. The withdrawal of the Strangers is punishment enough."

There was anger and disbelief and ridicule aplenty. Some called for impeachment proceedings. Others called for commitment papers. But there was gratitude and relief as well. There was something about this President that seemed more real than any politician most folks could remember, even as crazy as her story might sound. She was telling the truth as she saw it, just like she said she would. She said hard things. She said them straight out. And in these bleak economic times, there was something strangely comforting about that. As tough as these times were, it actually felt good to at least know and speak the truth of it. People had had enough of the lies.

They ended the interview and turned off the cameras. Banks sat still and calm in his chair, looking at Linda as Cole came up behind her and massaged her back. "Thank you, Mrs. President," said Banks.

Linda knew what he meant. She hadn't outed his own involvement with the People. She hadn't mentioned those fake videos of her death that he'd made for Rice. She arched an eyebrow. "You're going to make it up to me, Mr. Banks," she said. She stood and walked away.

Stendahl Banks nodded. He had to admit that she was probably right. He unclipped his body mic and stood to stretch his legs. Around him his crew wrapped equipment and loaded the truck. If they hurried, he could be back in his own bed in Alexandria tonight. He stepped out onto the ski club's front porch and looked up at the sky. It was after seven and the stars were out. He hugged himself against the cold October air and sighed.

He did not know if he would like Vermont.

## 19.15

Linda had known she was speaking off the cuff, but she just couldn't help herself. When Banks had asked about rebuilding Washington D.C., she knew that it would never happen. And she knew that she could not go back there. "I'm afraid it's way too early to talk of such things, Mr. Banks," she had said. "It may be that the systems in which we've been operating have been built on some fundamental mistakes. And if we are truly at the breaking points of energy and economy and the environment, I'm not sure it serves any of us to spend the time, money and resources it would take to rebuild the massive structures that housed those systems."

Linda shifted in her chair, leaning forward eagerly as if she'd finally found her life's work. "I don't know what will happen in the coming months and years and decades, Sten, as we dig to the bottom of this mess we've created and find our way through it. I just don't know. We'll have to figure that out together, won't we? Not just the government and corporations and banks, but the American people as a whole, each and every one of us. We'll have to figure out who we're going to be in these challenging times. And we'll have to maintain the peace here at home, as we end the war our entire culture is now waging all around the globe: the war against the land and the seas and the atmosphere; the war against the poor and powerless; the war against reality itself." Linda settled back in her chair and smiled. "I'm not sure most of us really have a clue about what's going on here on planet Earth, Mr. Banks," she said.

Stendahl Banks sat back and smiled in return.

"In any event," continued Linda, "I intend to remain in Vermont for now. I will discharge my duties from here, with only a skeleton staff. The rest of it will have to wait for another day."

"Will the American people accept such changes?" asked Banks, visibly surprised by Linda's declaration.

Linda nodded, thanking Banks for getting right to the heart of it. "I think that's my job in all of this, Mr. Banks," she said. "To help the American people understand that, by learning to live within the laws of this world, we will find a life far more satisfying than anything we've achieved by breaking those laws. The journey together will entail a great deal of change, and we may find that facing into that change with eyes wide open will be the greatest and most fulfilling thing we've ever done. We've been acting like petulant children, Mr. Banks, demanding our own way at every turn and throwing a fit when we don't get it. I, for one, think it will feel really good to grow up and start acting like an adult."

Stendahl Banks could not keep his head from nodding in agreement. "Why Vermont?" he asked.

"Personal reasons," said Linda with a wink. She left it at that, and Banks didn't pry.

"You were great!" said Emily through the screen door as Linda and Cole walked past the security agents now guarding the house and up the steps to their home.

"You guys see the whole thing?" asked Linda.

"Yeah," said Iain. "Even your hair looked okay."

Linda rubbed her head. "Thanks, kiddo. High praise."

"So are you moving in here?" asked Emily. She helped Linda with her coat, holding it as the President pulled her arms from the sleeves.

Linda hesitated. She and Cole had talked about this on the way home. But she was still nervous. It was all moving so quickly. And she did not know what she would do if the answer were "no." At last she asked her question. "Would you like me to?"

"Duh," said Iain, rolling his eyes.

"Sure," agreed Emily.

Linda sighed and smiled. "Then I guess we can work something out," she said. Emily and Iain went upstairs to tell Grace and Alice.

"We can't stay here," said Linda, turning to Cole.

"I know," he said gently.

"It's going to be hugely disruptive, wherever we go. You know that, right?"

"I do know that."

"It's going to change your lives completely, if you hook up with me."

"It already has, Mrs. President." Cole pulled Linda to him and kissed her gently on the forehead. He pulled away to look her eye to eye. "Like Iain said, we can't go back."

"They'll be ripped out of their schools," said Linda.

"I think maybe we'll home-school now," said Cole.

"They'll lose touch with their friends."

Cole smiled. "You trying to get rid of me?" he asked.

"I'm trying to make sure you really want this," she replied.

"A lot of people went to a great deal of trouble to get us to this point, Linda. It would be a shame to chicken out now."

Linda stared into Cole's eyes for the longest time. She still hadn't gotten used to those eyes: so calm, so certain, and as deep and vast as the night sky. His body was so new now, strong and clean and sure. It fit him now, this body. He walked more surely in the world with it, confident that he should be here, not doubting for a moment that he belonged at her side. Linda noticed that her heart was pounding like an unbalanced washing machine, as if it were about to fly off its axis, head straight for the sun, and burst overhead, filling the sky with fireworks. Then an uncertainty darkened her face and she looked away, as if she could relieve her doubts by denying them.

"Can we trust this?" she asked at last. She brought her eyes back to the man before her.

"Trust what?" said Cole.

Linda inhaled deeply. "Can we trust a love that was created by aliens?"

Cole grinned, searching the room around him and the ceiling overhead, then returning to meet her gaze. "I don't see any aliens around here, Linda," he said. His eyes sparkled.

"C'mon, Cole," said Linda, shaking him gently by the shoulders. "I'm serious."

Cole pulled Linda closer so that they were touching heart to heart. "Feel me, my love," he whispered into her ear. "There are no aliens in here. The heart that wants to embrace you is my own. The mind that wants you and respects you and adores you and needs you, the skin that craves your touch, the blood that rushes toward you, it's all mine, Linda. It's all me. If the aliens pushed us, it was over a cliff from which we might have fallen in any case. But they're not pushing me now. And I'm still falling, Linda. I'm still falling..."

Linda buried her face even deeper into Cole's neck and sighed deeply. She flashed on her dream of Earl, tossing a tennis ball to a big, black dog. Earl, too, had come to her with the aliens' assistance. He'd swept her off her feet, set her on her way, and then fallen by the wayside, as if his work were finished. And now they'd brought her Cole...

It hit Linda then that her fear was not that the aliens had given them their love, but that they would take it away. She didn't think she could withstand that. And she knew from experience that there were no guarantees.

Linda let the fear wash over and through her and beyond. She came back to the present moment and squeezed the beautiful creature in her arms, then pulled away and crinkled her nose. "Don't say I didn't warn you," she said.

"I won't."

"I'm thinking maybe Montpelier," she added.

"We'll make it work."

Linda listened to the kids as they broke out laughing overhead. She thought of her other dream, of that last corner, of that long walk down the slope. She shuddered, to think what future these kids might see. "I hope we can," she said, her voice almost a whisper. "I hope we can."

## 19.16

The phone woke them from sleep and Cole answered. "Who?" he said groggily. "What?" He listened for a bit. "How did you get this number?"

Linda sat up and turned on the light. Cole's face was dark with anger. He looked at her, the receiver held away from his head, then covered the mouthpiece with his hand. "Got a guy here says he needs to speak with you," he said. "Are you—?"

Linda nodded and took the phone. "Hello?"

"That was well done," said the voice, an older man from the sound of it, with an elegant British accent. "Brilliant. Love the hair."

"Who is this?" asked Linda.

The older man laughed. "One of the people you could not name today," he said. "A good friend whom you've not yet met. Perhaps you should just call me the Fisherman."

Something about the man's voice shook Linda with alarm, as if electric ice were pouring from the receiver. She caught hold of her pounding heart and asked the only question she could think to ask. "Why 'the Fisherman'?"

"Because I'm the one who's got a line on you, Linda," the man said coolly. "I'm the one who will reel you in if you try to break away."

The man's arrogance pissed her off; the jolt of anger restored a bit of her self-assurance. "I guess the fact that your alien buddies have taken a powder has you folks all a-flutter."

The man laughed. "It's an interesting time, Mrs. President, I'll give you that. You should know that their departure is the reason you're still alive."

"And suppose I just tell you to go fuck yourself and hang up?" asked Linda.

"I would expect nothing else, Mrs. President. It'll be interesting to watch when you figure out just where Mr. Thomas got it all wrong. Glad to hear you're doing so well. Forgive me for disturbing your sleep. I just wanted to let you know I'm here."

"How did Obie get it wrong?" blurted Linda. But it was too late. The man had hung up.

"Who was that?" asked Cole.

Linda exhaled noisily to forestall a scream. Her body trembled. She tried to smile but found she could not. Cole took her in his arms.

They packed and moved the next morning.

### 19.17

The six of them spent long days together in the hidden mountain home they'd rented, as far removed from the world as they could make it. To the extent that Linda had to interact with people face to face, she let them come to her, meeting them at secret rendezvous points around the state. Stan Walsh guarded them all with grace and dedication, and with what felt like half the armed forces some days. Linda had no idea who this "Fisherman" was, or what the dangers to them really were, but she would err on the side of great caution and damn the rest of the world. She knew that soon enough she'd have to dive back in. There'd be meetings with the Congress and the Senate, the Joint-Chiefs, the Supreme Court. There'd be speeches at the United Nations, television interviews, and personal appearances. She'd promised leadership. She would have to deliver on that.

But not today. The beliefs and assumptions of politics and economics were not the only stories that would have to change; Linda was committed to changing her personal stories as well. With the future feeling so uncertain, Linda vowed to find more and more meaning in each moment of her life. She honored that she was caught in the carelessness of new love and the dictates of grief and healing, so she let the days take care of themselves. And she didn't give a damn what anybody thought about that.

There were happy things, and sad, in those quiet days. They called and checked on Mary. Rice's blow to her nose had thrust a few tiny shards of bone right up into her brain, but it seemed she would pull through. The doctors were cautiously optimistic for a full recovery. The thorough search of all D.C. area hospitals had yielded nothing; Linda's mother was not to be found. Slowly Linda came to accept that Rice had at last told the truth, and that her mother had been lost in the blackness as surely as Obie had been. They learned in an email from their pilot, Beck, that Sina's group had gone missing. "Out onto the ice," he wrote. Nobody seemed to know why, and Beck's email could not be returned.

Linda tracked down Keeley's sister's number, and she spoke with her old friend on the phone. "Hi, Cornfed," said Keeley, fumbling with the handset. Her voice was faint and shaky.

"Oh, Keeley." It was all Linda could say before bursting into tears. The two women cried together over the telephone lines for a full five minutes before either was able to speak again. Linda told Keeley what she knew of Grace's encounters with Pooch and Jack in the astral realm, relaying the message Pooch had given Grace: to tell Keeley he was happy and well. The message seemed to bring Keeley some measure of relief, but failed to assuage her grief.

"He's still gone," explained Keeley.

"Yes he is," answered Linda.

Linda filled Keeley in on the past days' events, and invited her friend to come join them in Vermont. The President could use all the trusted advisors she could get right now, and Keeley's experiences with the aliens would make her viewpoint invaluable. "I just can't," said Keeley, after considering the offer for a moment. "Not yet. Give me time." Linda agreed to give her all the time she needed.

It was a staggering blow when Alice disappeared. Grace ran into Cole and Linda's room at dawn to wake them. Alice's sleeping chair was empty, save for a short note written in her perfect script. *My father has come for me,* she wrote. *I must go. There are things I need to learn elsewhere, before I can complete my work. You must continue without me. And there is news of my mother.*

There was nothing else. No signature. No loving farewell. No girlish hearts or flowers drawn in the margins. Just simple block lettering in black ink on a white sheet of college ruled. And yet the strange little child's love was all over it. They knew. And they cried for her loss. A search of the home and the grounds proved fruitless, as they knew it would. She was gone. All they could do was hope that her "work" would bring her, one day, back into their lives. Until then, they could look to the stars and smile, knowing that she was out there somewhere, and beaming her their hearts, just as Grace had described.

Linda and Cole spent long hours talking every evening, sharing their experiences and pondering what it all meant. So much of what had happened now felt like a dream. This was more true for Grace than for any of them. Her own experiences in the astral realm could barely hold their own against the stark reality of the physical. She was becoming a five-year-old girl, once again. When Cole found Utterpok's drumstick in his bag and gave it to Grace, it took Cole's prompting for her to remember who the old shaman was.

Neither Cole nor Linda felt like they knew very much. Who were the alive ones? Who were the Angels, and the rest of those whom Obie had termed "all of the above"? What were they up to? Why did they leave? And what had they been doing with Rice and the People in the first place? Were they truly "good," as Obie seemed to think? Linda remembered her own childhood fury and terror at the aliens' hands, and wondered if "good" people could do such things. Hadn't Obie said that some aliens were "here for purposes that many would consider exploitive, selfish, or even evil?" What was *their* role in all of this? Cole and Linda kept coming back to these same questions. They had few answers, and what answers they had felt provisional, at best.

"I miss Obie," said Linda. "He seemed to know what was going on."

Cole sighed. "I guess now it's we who will have to figure things out," he said.

"You telling me I have to act like an adult?" she asked, playfully.

"Not a bad trait in a President," he answered.

Linda remembered her promise to Aamai, that night on the ice. He'd told her it would take her every moment of the rest of her days to make up for the sins of her people. Unexpectedly, the thought buoyed her. It was good work. Worthy work. Work that meant something. She would do her best to keep that promise. The present world was collapsing. A new world waited to be born. Perhaps she could help find some better way from here to there.

Linda stared at the dark ceiling as Cole snored beside her. Her dreams these days often jolted her to wakefulness, filling her with an urgency to get back to work. Perhaps she was being prodded. And perhaps whoever was prodding her was right to do so. She rolled over to snuggle up to Cole, only to stop short. His hands were both raised in the air, just an inch or so above his stomach, and his fingers were dancing and stretching, as if he were typing in his sleep. The sight of it stirred an ember of fear in Linda's heart. She reached over and pushed his hands gently back down and held them in place. Cole sighed and rolled over and Linda spooned up against his back and concentrated on her breath, hoping to get back to sleep.

She failed.

Cole, she realized, was Mr. Thomas too.

## 19.18

The next morning they found another note, this one inscribed in the marble countertop in the kitchen. It was beautifully etched, expertly beveled, a perfect circle about a foot across, bisected by an inverted capital L. Nobody had seen a thing, of course. The security guards had reported no intruders. The video cameras showed no shadowy figures lurking in the corners. None of the children had heard a sound. Stan Walsh was livid when he heard of it. Such a thing should not have been possible.

And yet, there it was.

Cole ran his fingers along its edge. It was a quarter of an inch deep, at least, and very smooth. "I get the impression somebody up there is trying to tell us something," he joked. Nobody else felt like laughing.

When Cole found out just what it was they'd been trying to tell them, he didn't laugh either.

# Postscript

Here ends Book One of the *None So Blind* series. Book Two, *Rumi's Field*, is now downloading from the Universe. Book Three, *Imbolc*, will follow after that. There may be a fourth volume that pushes its way into the mix somewhere, but don't hold me to that.

# About the Author

The being now known as "Timothy Scott Bennett" landed on this planet in rural "Michigan," one of the so-called "United States" currently occupying a large portion of the landmass known to some as "North America." Astonished by what he saw around him, he set about to learn all he could of art and science, religion and spirituality, writing and filmmaking, in order to better understand the society into which he'd been born, and the strange behaviors of the human beings he encountered. He believes that if he can help to make clear and conscious the assumptions, beliefs, taboos, denials, and orthodoxies of the dominant global industrial culture, some humans will be able to break free of the confines and limitations of that paradigm. He trusts that this will be a good thing. To that end, he and his wife, Sally Erickson, created the feature-length documentary *What a Way to Go: Life at the End of Empire,* a film which journeys through the present predicament on Planet Earth, looking at climate chaos, mass extinction, oil depletion, overpopulation, and the global culture of domination and disconnection that now appears to be unraveling. He currently lives with Sally in coastal "Maine," which is another of those "United States." He rides his bicycle, watches for whales, soaks up the sun, wind, and fog, and remains utterly astonished.

www.ingramcontent.com/pod-product-compliance
Lightning Source LLC
Chambersburg PA
CBHW051508250626
47156CB00001B/4